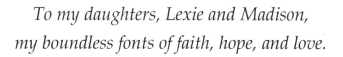

To my daughters, Lexie and Madison,
my boundless fonts of faith, hope, and love.

TABLE OF CONTENTS

ACKNOWLEDGEMENTS

First, I must thank my daughter Madison for inspiring this novel. I'll admit, I was a little worried when she told me she wanted a book about fairies. I thought... "*Fairies? She's in sixth grade. She's too old for fairies.*" Of course, I was picturing Tinkerbell inside my head. But then, I realized I could introduce her to real *faeries*... to the very grown up, beautiful, and sometimes terrifying *faeries*, better known as the *Tuatha Dé Danann*, the Celtic deities born in Irish Mythology. Now, that was a topic I could get excited about. I've always been intrigued by the *Sidhe*. There is Irish blood coursing through my veins after all. And so... this novel was born.

Madison forced me outside my comfort zone. Romantic suspense is my genre. I've never written a fantasy novel, let alone one steeped in Irish Mythology. I spent a little over a year immersing myself in Celtic Mythology, learning about the *Tuatha Dé Danann*, and searching for the perfect setting in Ireland. Of course, this took time away from my family, so I must thank them for putting up with the neglect. I swear I spent the last year with one foot in this world and another foot firmly entrenched in *Otherworld*. My husband Tobin and my daughters, Lexie and Madison, inspired three of the characters in this book. They also served as my sounding boards. They weighed in on each scene and plot twist while the story unraveled inside my head. Their advice proved invaluable.

I'd like to thank Ray T. Christian II and Evonne Christian for designing a stunning book cover the old-fashioned way... by hand! I'd also like to thank Aaron Bertoglio for digitizing their artwork. A huge thanks to my insanely talented friend Kari Kunkel Anderson for working her magic in graphic design for the final book cover and Brian Garabrant for designing the perfect maps. These amazing artists helped bring this story to life.

I am extremely grateful for my beta readers; Lilli Arrington, Kathryn Ehrhardt, Emma Pearson, Michael Delancy, Faddwa Brubaker, Rita Gibson, Heidi Lieu, Valerie Norman Dannels, Devon Yorkshire, and Gail Neeves. Their feedback and advice proved incredibly useful. I'd also like to acknowledge one of my most cherished friends, Heidi Lieu, for serving as my editor. Thank you for your help!

Finally, I would like to thank my parents for encouraging me to pursue my dreams, for believing in me, and for never once questioning my ability to achieve all the dreams I've hung my hopes on over the years. I love you with all my heart.

BEFORE YOU BEGIN YOUR JOURNEY

There are several Celtic names, words, and phrases in this book that you may find difficult to pronounce. I've included a glossary and pronunciation guide at the end of this book to serve as your guide. I hope you enjoy learning this beautiful language as much as I have.

Go n-éirí an bóthar leat.
--Kimberly

MAP OF KILLARNEY

Devil's Punch Bowl

L. Looscaunagh

Molls Gap

Portal

Mangerton Mountain

Black Valley

Ladies View upper lake

Purple Mountain

Torc mountain

Torc Waterfall

Shehy Mountain

Tomies Mountain

McGillycuddy Reeks Mountains

Muckross Lake

Dinis Cottage

Tomies Wood

Muckross House

Castlelough

Muckross Abbey

Dunloe Castle

River Flesk

Ross Castle

Inisfallen Island

Loch Lein Lough Leane

Killarney Town Center

St Marry's Cathedral

killarney
county kerry, ireland

MAP OF OTHERWORLD

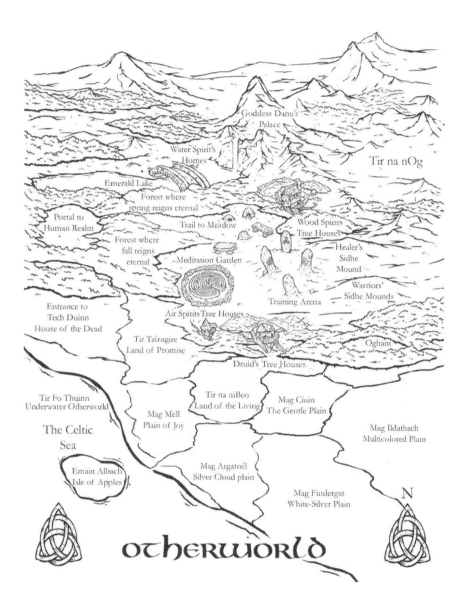

PROLOGUE

The handsome, fair-haired *Sidhe* bowed deeply while extending his palm. His hand shook a little when he did. His eyes remained glued to the floor. He couldn't bear to gaze upon the Goddess Danu. Tears fell from his eyes every time he tried. Her flawless skin literally glowed, although her beauty flowed from within. Her hair fell to her waist in a dazzling display of copper and gold. He'd heard her eyes were a burnished gold, but he'd never been able to look closely enough to determine their true color.

Goddess Danu stepped closer. Her bare toes flashed briefly beneath the gold and ivory gown.

Bevyn diverted his gaze. Her beauty shone so brightly, it made his heart ache. She was truly that beautiful, and Bevyn knew beauty. His people, the *Tuatha Dé Danann*, were a regal, god-like people with unearthly beauty and unfathomable grace... but even their beauty paled in the presence of the Goddess Danu, for she was their mother, the great goddess of the *Tuatha Dé Danann*. Most *Tuath*, also known as the *Sidhe*, were good and kind, like the Goddess Danu. A few were not. Still each served a purpose. The good and the bad balanced one another. Most days.

Bevyn's eyes slid toward the bassinet. He was hoping to catch a glimpse of the babies, the three newest members of the *Tuatha Dé*. Warmth spread from his fingers all the way down to his toes when the goddess accepted the scroll. He forced his eyes from the bassinet and cleared his throat. "Tis a message from the druids."

Goddess Danu unraveled the scroll. The druids often communicated with her telepathically, but she had erected barriers around her mind earlier that morning. Truly, she didn't mind hearing her people's thoughts, but there were so many *Sidhe* and so many random thoughts. Sometimes she longed to hear other things... like birds chirping, babies cooing, or silence. She read the scroll and sighed. Loudly. "Fetch Perth."

Bevyn's breath rushed out all at once. "Perth?" What could the Goddess Danu possibly want with the *Far Darrig*? The *Far Darrig* were small and wily like *Leprechauns* but even more mischievous. They stole bright, pretty babies and left odd, fretful children in their place. They tortured *Sidhe* and human children with nightmares, and they were totally enamored with the color red. He hadn't a clue why. Bevyn couldn't stand the color red.

"Tell no one," the goddess implored. The scroll disappeared into thin air. Goddess Danu reached inside the bassinet. The soft glow surrounding her pulsed when she lifted one of the babies from the bassinet. Softly, she began to sing a lullaby in the old language.

Bevyn stumbled from the room. He was momentarily blinded but certain he'd never seen a more beautiful sight. Of course, he'd never seen the Goddess Danu sing to a new-born baby before.

Gently, the goddess removed the blanket swaddling her child. She placed a kiss on her forehead and heart. She wrapped her daughter snuggly inside the blanket and re-turned her to the bassinet. She kissed each baby the exact same way, on her forehead and heart.

The goddess had known this day would come, but she hadn't realized it would arrive so quickly. Regrettably, time bowed to no one. He was his own master; tricky and impos-sible to predict. Goddess Danu had hoped to have a few days at least with the babies, but the druids' message im-plied she should act quickly. The warning replayed in her head.

> *Violence, evil, and darkness are threatening the bal-ance between the realms. If they reign, they will de-stroy the realms. Love, faith, and light can restore the balance, but your daughters must accept this task willingly. Their lives are in danger, for the Goddess Carman knows they exist. Secret them away until they reach the age of reason. They must be able to distinguish between right and wrong be-fore they confront the Goddess Carman's sons. Pro-tect the border and the Chosen Ones at all costs... or all will be lost.*

She shook her head. The universe demanded balance, and so the Goddess Carman held the darkness that countered the Goddess Danu's light. Carman was the Goddess of Dark Magick. She'd been banished to the human realm over one hundred years ago, when she began casting spells that increased violence and war. She'd grown relentless in her efforts to invade *Otherworld*. Goddess Danu wasn't sure whether she wanted to rule or destroy all the realms. Carman enjoyed destroying things. Once she destroyed all the fruit in Ireland, simply because she could.

Goddess Danu was working toward a solution, but she'd have to build a prison strong enough to hold Carman first. She wasn't entirely sure what to do with Carman's sons; Dain, Dother, and Dub. All three were mentioned in the prophecy. Dain was violence, Dother was evil, and Dub was darkness. The Goddess Danu's daughters were the counterweights to the Goddess Carman's sons. Grania was love, Maolisa was faith, and Niamh was pure radiance.

She gazed at her daughters' angelic faces. The Goddess Carman would presume the *Chosen Ones* were living in *Otherworld*. She knew the Goddess Danu preferred to keep her children close. Carman would never suspect she might secret them inside the human realm. The Goddess Danu could barely comprehend that possibility herself. Time worked differently in the human realm. Still, most children reached the age of reason by the time they were twelve. Her daughters could join her in *Tír na nÓg*, awaken their powers in *Ogham*, and fulfill the prophecy then.

Bevyn burst through the palace doors. He was dragging the *Far Darrig* by the collar of his coat. Perth's feet barely touched the floor. Three *Sidhe* guardians followed in their wake. The goddess had called them telepathically. She waited for them to draw closer. The guardians curtseyed while Bevyn and Perth bowed. They held those positions while awaiting the goddess's instructions.

Goddess Danu shared the prophecy through an unspoken thought. She instructed the guardians and the *Far Darrig* on their responsibilities. They knew instinctively that the safety and security of all the realms hinged on their ability to fulfill the responsibilities imparted by the goddess.

The *Sidhe* guardians bundled each baby in a special cloak, known as the cloak of concealment. They lifted the babies from the bassinet.

The air in front of them twisted, forming a portal between the realms.

The *Far Darrig* and the guardians stepped forward.

The portal closed.

The bassinet flickered, then faded.

Bevyn hesitated. When the goddess said nothing, he left.

She stood there rigidly, then sank to her knees and wept.

CHAPTER 1 - ÉIRE

Twelve years later…

I dropped my backpack on the floor. "Mom! I'm home!" I stopped abruptly when I saw the suitcases by the door.

My older sister, Lexie, squeezed past me. "Madison, stop blocking the door!"

My godmother, Channa, rounded the corner. "Hey, girls. Welcome home." She pulled us together for a group hug.

I relaxed into her arms. My godmother and I were very close. She took care of me whenever my parents had to rush Lexie to the hospital. Lexie had a kidney transplant shortly after I was born. The medicine she was on weakened her immune system, so she was sick a lot. My godmother was always there for us, taking care of me… of our entire family, really. Still, a midweek visit, when everyone was feeling well, was a little out of the ordinary. "Hi, Cha Cha." I'd been calling her "Cha Cha" since I was a toddler, and the name had stuck. "What are the suitcases for?"

"You'll see." She patted my arm reassuringly.

A door whisked open upstairs. "Was the bus early?" Mom walked dazedly down the stairs.

Our dog Miko tore past her. I scooped him up and ruffled his hair.

Lexie eyed Mom incredulously. "You forgot us."

Her face sheeted white. "I'm so sorry." While most of our friends walked home from the bus stop unescorted by a grown-up, Mom would not allow it. We were old enough, I was twelve and Lexie was thirteen, but Mom had a protective streak ten miles long. Thankfully, she was discreet about it. She would just happen to be out walking Miko when the bus rolled around.

I could tell she was worried about something. That pinched look on her face gave her away. "Mom? Is everything okay?"

Cha Cha steered us toward the living room. "I think we should sit down."

My heart skipped a couple of beats. I forced myself to breathe. Conversations that required sitting seldom turned out well for me.

Miko jumped down when I perched on the edge of the couch.

"What's wrong?" Lexie wrung her hands as she settled beside me.

Mom squished in between us, took a deep breath, and gently clasped our hands. "Remember when we were talking last night... about how odd it is that your father hasn't called?"

Lexie nodded. "He always calls to say goodnight." Dad was working in Ireland this week. He was helping their government improve security. He manages border security for the United States, but a lot of different countries were soliciting his help these days.

"Did he call?" I studied her face.

Mom stared at our entwined hands. "No. I called the bed and breakfast where he's staying. They haven't seen him for days. He was supposed to check out of the hotel this morning, but he didn't. His suitcase and clothes are still in the room."

My stomach twisted nervously. "So, Dad's not coming home tonight?"

She shook her head. "His suitcase is at the bed and breakfast, and his flight departed this morning. I'm pretty sure he's missed that flight."

Panic surged inside of me. Dad wouldn't leave his luggage behind. He would have called if he'd missed his flight. He should have called last night... and the night before that.

"Sounds like a great excuse to travel to Ireland," Cha Cha added brightly. "Who wants to solve the mystery of the missing dad?"

My thoughts tangled in her words. *How could she sound so...* My eyes searched hers. Suddenly, I understood. She was putting a positive spin on this so we wouldn't feel scared. I fought to ignore my racing heart so I could put a brave face on for Lexie and Mom.

Miko dropped his stuffed poo emoji on my foot.

I eyed him worriedly. "What about Miko?"

"He's going to stay with Ms. Heidi. She'll take good care of him," Mom promised.

Lexie grabbed the poo and threw it across the room. "What about school?"

Cha Cha's eyes widened. "If you had to choose between Ireland and school…"

"School," Lexie insisted. "It's spirit week. Tomorrow is pajama day, and Friday is crazy hair day. We're having a dance party in the hallway, and the principal is dying her hair blue."

Everyone gaped at her.

Finally, Mom spoke. "I'm sure someone will take pictures. I've already e-mailed your teachers and asked for your school work. We'll swing by the school and pick it up on our way to the airport."

"You can wear your pajamas on the airplane," Cha Cha promised. "We'll stop by Party City and purchase a can of blue hairspray so you can make your hair crazy too."

"My daughters will not be traipsing around Ireland with blue hair," Mom protested.

"We could do green instead." Cha Cha winked at me. "Green would blend right in in Ireland… and if we dye our hair green, the *Leprechauns* won't pinch us."

Mom shook her head. "Leprechauns only pinch people on Saint Patrick's Day. Besides, we're Irish. They can't pinch us because we have Irish blood just like them."

She folded her arms across her chest. "How many *Leprechauns* have you met?"

A smile teased at my lips. Saint Patrick's Day was second

only to Christmas in our house. We built elaborate *Leprechaun* traps. Those pesky little men would steal the coins, leave some sort of riddle or note taunting us, sprinkle gold dust all through the house, pee green pee, and leave tiny green footprints on all the toilets. Still, no one ever got pinched. Mom claimed they couldn't pinch us because we're Irish.

She rose from the couch. "I'm sorry to spring this trip on you at the last minute, but I'm worried about your father. I'm sure there is some reasonable explanation. Maybe the rental car broke down. He may have lost his phone, or he could be traveling in a remote area without cell phone service."

Cha Cha draped an arm around her. "Tobin is smart and incredibly resourceful. He ate tree bark, grasshoppers, and ants when he was in the military. So, wherever he's at, I'm sure he's fine."

I prayed she was right. There was so much violence in the world these days. I'd seen the news... well, snippets of news. Mom hurriedly changed the channel every time we entered the room. Still, with all those countries asking my dad to improve their security, I wondered if there was any place where people remained truly safe.

* * *

"Look at those airplanes," Lexie exclaimed.

I peered out the window. The Aer Lingus airplanes proudly displayed three leaf clovers on their tails. "Can we fly on one of those when we go home?"

"I don't know if they fly into Virginia." Mom stood. We gathered our luggage and followed her off the plane.

The Dublin airport looked just like the airport we'd flown out of in Virginia, with lots of glass, metal columns, and polished floors. We followed the other passengers through customs before stopping at the car rental counter.

A goofy grin tugged at Lexie's cheeks every time she heard someone speak with an Irish accent. I loved the melodic lilt that Cha Cha called a brogue, but some of their words were difficult to understand.

We walked through a glass tube, which looked like something you might see at the International Space Station. I buttoned my coat when we entered the parking garage. The air was surprisingly crisp in Dublin.

Mom stopped short of the silver rental car. "Oh, no. I totally forgot."

"The steering wheel is on the wrong side of the car," Lexie marveled.

Cha Cha laughed. "They drive on the opposite side of the road in Ireland."

"This should be fun," Mom grumbled. Her tone suggested it was anything but. We crammed our luggage into the trunk and climbed into the car.

Our drive into the city was markedly uneventful. The landscape was flat, although there were several trees. The city center reminded me of Washington D.C., with a blend of modern and historic buildings dotting the streets.

Mom turned down a street lined with brick townhomes.

She parked in front of a pale brick brownstone with black wrought iron balconies, stark white columns, and white framed windows. Lush flowers spilled from the window boxes. The dark sign hanging near the door read "Amberley House Guests."

I shot upright. "This is the bed and breakfast where Dad is staying!" I'd seen the sign in one of the pictures he'd been contemplating when he made the reservations for his trip.

We tugged our luggage from the trunk and hurried up the stairs. A little bell sounded when Mom opened the door. We piled into the foyer.

"Why don't we check out the dining room and courtyard while your mom checks in," Cha Cha suggested.

Mom nodded her head. "Good idea."

We discovered two dining rooms inside the bed and breakfast. The first dining room was casual with square wood tables scattered across a red and white tiled floor. This dining room overlooked a courtyard with round mosaic tables and chairs. A larger dining room was tucked just around the corner. That dining room boasted foil wallpaper, plush carpet, thickly padded chairs, and granite table tops.

My stomach growled when the smoky scent of bacon wafted through the air. We followed the scent back into the casual dining room.

"We're a little late for breakfast, but I'll ask if they serve brunch." Cha Cha turned when a round, rosy-cheeked woman stepped from the kitchen.

"Oh! I'm sorry. I didn't hear you come in." She wiped her hands on a surprisingly clean apron.

Cha Cha smiled apologetically. "I know we're a little late for breakfast, but we've just arrived from the United States. Would it be possible for us to order a late breakfast or an early lunch?"

"Why, certainly," she replied. "Will fried eggs, fried tomatoes, pork sausages, bacon rashers, and toast suffice?"

"That sounds wonderful." Cha Cha looped her purse over the back of a chair. "Four plates please. Their mother is in desperate need of coffee. I would like some tea, and the girls will drink orange juice if that's available." She motioned for Lexie and me to join her at the table.

The rosy-cheeked woman set four rolls of napkins stuffed with silverware on the table. "I'm certain we have orange juice, fresh coffee, and tea on hand." She bustled back inside the kitchen.

Mom collapsed into the empty chair. "Tobin's luggage is still here, but he hasn't returned. The staff is moving his things into our room. They're also carrying our suitcases upstairs." She handed Cha Cha a key to the room.

She tucked it in her purse. "Will you be going to the embassy or the police department first?"

"The embassy." Mom breathed a small sigh of relief when the woman returned with our drinks. "I want to look through his belongings before I leave so I can see if there are any names or phone numbers for the people he was supposed to meet."

Lexie guzzled her orange juice. Her cup hit the table with a loud thunk. "That was the best orange juice. Ever."

Cha Cha smiled at her enthusiasm.

Mom nursed her coffee. "I think you girls should stay here with Cha Cha. You can help me look for Dad tomorrow, once you're all rested."

A baby on our flight cried all night, making it impossible to sleep. I was exhausted, but I didn't want Mom facing this alone. "I don't think you should go by yourself."

She leaned over and gave me a hug. "I'm sure these meetings will be boring, honey. I just want to ask them to help find your dad. I promise, you can help just as soon as we generate some ideas on where he might be."

Tears welled in my eyes. I didn't want to make her feel any worse, so I blinked them back and kissed her cheek. "I love you, Mom. We'll find Dad. You'll see."

The door to the kitchen burst open. The cook backed out with all four plates balanced in her arms. She slid the plates in front of us while noting the empty cups. "I'll return shortly to refill your drinks."

"Thank you." Cha Cha waited for her to leave and then leaned forward conspiratorially. "I forgot to ask her to skip the meat for me." She divided her sausage and bacon between Lexie and me.

We ate quickly, knowing Mom needed to leave. She made sure we were locked safely inside the suite before leaving for the embassy. She hadn't found anything useful inside Dad's suitcase.

I changed into my pajamas while Lexie took her medications. We brushed our teeth and climbed into bed.

Cha Cha perched on the edge of the double bed, which was really just two single beds pushed together. "I know it can be difficult to sleep during the day, but please try. You didn't get any sleep last night, and we have several long days ahead of us." She brushed our hair back before kissing each of us on the forehead.

I turned to face Lexie when Cha Cha stepped away. "Hey, sissy, are you okay?" She'd been on the verge of tears ever since Mom had left for the em-bassy.

Her eyes glistened. She swiped at her tears, trying to be brave.

I wrapped my fingers around her hand. "Maybe we should pray."

She sniffled softly. "Okay."

I closed my eyes. "Please, God, keep Mommy and Daddy safe."

"Help us find Dad, guide us, and keep us safe," Lexie added softly.

"Amen." We stared at one another, neither wanting to abandon the other, even if only to sleep.

My lashes grew heavier each time they brushed against my cheeks. "I love you, sissy."

"I love you more," she mumbled sleepily.

"Not even possible," I countered.

She smiled at my canned response. This debate over who loved the other more was part of our nightly routine.

Our hands remained clasped long after we fell asleep.

* * *

"Why is it so cold?" Lexie snuggled deeper inside her quilted coat.

"Ireland is chilly this time of year." Cha Cha cinched the belt on her coat. We were walking along a cobblestone street in a touristy area near the River Liffey.

"You've been here before?" I cupped my hands together, blew warm air between my fingers, and shoved them back inside my pockets.

She nodded. "Yes, but it's been twelve years at least."

"Do you know anything about their border?" Mom stopped to show a pub owner Dad's picture. We'd been sifting through the tourist areas all afternoon, sharing Dad's picture from Mom's cell phone, but no one recognized him.

Cha Cha looked thoughtful. "The only land border is the border between Northern Ireland and the Republic of Ireland. The rest of Ireland is surrounded by water. Are you sure he wasn't helping the government with port or maritime security?"

Mom looked worried. "I just assumed it was their land border." Her cellphone rang. She tensed as she walked away.

A small, deeply wrinkled man stumbled from the pub on the corner. He climbed on the back of a dog, who then trotted around the corner.

"Did you see that?" I gasped.

Cha Cha's head spun the direction I was pointing. "What?"

"That man riding the dog!" I frowned when I realized how ridiculous that sounded. "Maybe it was a miniature horse. They disappeared around that corner." I sprinted toward the end of the block. Cha Cha and Lexie ran after me. I stopped short when we got to the corner. "He's gone."

Lexie braced her hands against her knees while she tried to catch her breath. "You're just tricking us." I could tell she wanted to wring my neck.

"You may have just spotted your first *Cluricaun.* They're always pranking people, and they've been known to ride dogs." Cha Cha scoured the crowded sidewalk.

"What was that all about?" Mom tucked her phone back inside her purse after catching up with us.

"Nothing." I frowned, questioning what I'd seen. "I think I was imagining things. Any news on Dad?"

She shook her head. "The embassy staff has called every government agency involved in Ireland's national security. No one recalls meeting your dad. It is possible he met with a government contractor, so they're generating another list of people."

"That's odd." Cha Cha frowned. "Why wouldn't he meet with government officials? They're the ones managing national security."

Lexie tugged on Mom's hand. "I'm starving."

"I'm sorry, honey. We've been walking around for hours. I'm sure you're all hungry." She nodded toward the pub across the street. "Let's grab a bite to eat."

We hurried across the busy intersection. Music spilled out onto the sidewalk when the door to the pub swung open. The men who were leaving held the door for us. Mom ushered Lexie and me inside. A lively band played the fiddle, a flute, and uilleann pipes. We wound through the crowded restaurant until we found a table.

Cha Cha peeled her coat off. "I'll brave the bar so we can place our order." She peered at the menu scratched across the chalkboard. "I think you'd enjoy the MiWadi and toasties."

Lexie and I exchanged glances. "What?"

She hung her coat on the back of her chair. "MiWadi is an Irish soda. You can't get it in the United States. There's orange, apple, blackcurrant, or orange with pineapple."

Lexie perked up. "I'll try the orange MiWadi."

I wiggled out of my coat. "Blackcurrant sounds good."

"I could use a cup of coffee," Mom answered tiredly.

I peered at the menu. "What's a toastie?"

"It's like a grilled cheese sandwich, only better. They have cheese or ham and cheese." Cha Cha eyed a plate on the table next to ours. "Looks like they serve them with sweet chili jam."

"Sounds good," Mom agreed. "Ham and cheese for Lexie and me. Cheese for Madi."

Cha Cha did a little jig on her way to the bar, which made me laugh. "This music makes me want to dance."

"Me too." A smile tugged at Lexie's cheeks.

Cha Cha returned with our drinks. "Here you go. I'm off to get the toasties and chips."

Mom's eyes collided with mine. "Wow. That was fast."

Cha Cha plopped our plates onto the table.

I dug into the warm, gooey sandwich. I was a lot hungrier than I'd realized.

We didn't speak for some time. We were too busy eating, and the music proved a welcome distraction... for a short time at least.

"Where do you want to look next?" Cha Cha inquired softly. Her head was tucked close to Mom's.

I listened in on their conversation while watching the band. I knew it was rude to listen in, but I was worried about Dad. I'd been so certain there was some misunderstanding or confusion about his departure date. After searching the entire day and the phone call from the embassy, I knew that was just wishful thinking. My father was truly missing.

"I don't know," she answered in a hushed tone. "Honestly, I thought someone in the government would have recognized his name or recalled meeting with him. This isn't like Tobin to just up and disappear."

Cha Cha released a worried breath. "Maybe we should drive up to Northern Ireland to see if the *garda* patrolling the northern border have seen him. The border is only two and a half hours away."

Mom shrugged. "That's as good an idea as any. We'll leave in the morning."

My eyes snagged on something red. My breath caught when I realized it was another *Leprechaun* or *Cluricaun* or whatever it was Cha Cha had labeled them. The rest of the room fell away while I watched him. He wove seamlessly through the crowd. Clearly, this wasn't the same man. He was a little taller, he looked steadier on his feet, and he was wearing red. The other man was dressed in black. "Look!" I urged in a loud whisper. "There! Tell me you see him. He's wearing a red hat."

Cha Cha's eyes widened. "Who? Where?" She leapt from her chair.

"Dad?" Lexie cried excitedly. "You found Dad?"

"No. A... uh *Leprechaun*." I peered through the sea of blue, tan, and black pants. My shoulders fell. "He's gone."

Mom tugged me back into my seat. "Please, don't do that to me. I thought you saw your father."

Lexie burst into tears. "I miss Dad."

I blinked my own tears back as best I could. "I'm so sorry, Lexie. I wish it had been Dad."

Mom stood. "I'm going to walk Lexie back to the bed and breakfast. Will you stop at the market across the street? We could use some snacks and bottled water for our trip tomorrow." She helped Lexie into her coat.

"Sure. We'll stop at the market and meet you back at the hotel. Fifteen minutes tops," Cha Cha promised.

She planted a kiss on my forehead. "Stay close to Cha Cha. No chasing little men in red hats."

I forced a smile.

Mom snuggled close to Lexie as they shuffled out of the restaurant.

Cha Cha reached for my hand. "Did you really see a man with a red hat?"

I stared remorsefully at our hands. "I shouldn't have said anything. I didn't mean to make Lexie sad."

She pulled me close. "I know you didn't mean to make Lexie sad. Lexie just got her hopes up for a minute there. She misses your dad."

"Me too," I admitted tearfully. "I thought we'd find him by now. I assumed this was all a big misunderstanding, that we'd have a good laugh, and enjoy a vacation together in Ireland."

"We'll find him. Don't you worry." She patted my back. "Now, about that little man... how tall would you say he was?"

"He was taller than the man on the dog but shorter than me." I shrugged. "Three feet maybe? He was deeply wrinkled, like the other man. He had red hair, a red beard, coat, and hat."

She scanned the room. "That sounds like the *Far Darrig*." She stood, pulling her purse over her shoulder. "You're going to see a lot of strange things in Ireland. You should know, not everyone can see the things you see. There's magick here, but you have to believe."

I zipped my coat. "Believe? In what?"

She chuckled. "In the unbelievable. What else?" She linked her arm in mine as we left the restaurant. We ducked into the corner market and purchased biscuits, Chipsticks, Crisps, bottled water, fresh fruit, and juice before walking back to the bed and breakfast.

I hadn't realized how tired my legs were until we climbed the stairs. They felt leaden by the time we reached the third floor.

Cha Cha stuffed her key into the lock and nudged the door open.

My heart stalled.

My godmother dropped the bag she'd been carrying. Our groceries rolled across the floor.

I swallowed the massive lump in my throat while staring slack-jawed at the room. I closed my eyes and forced myself to breathe while a full-blown panic attack struggled to burst free.

Mom and Lexie were missing.

Chapter 2 - The Fear Gorta

"It's okay. We're okay," Cha Cha said.

I stepped forward to pick up an orange, stumbled, and fell to my knees. "They should be here." I stared up at her helplessly. "Why aren't they here? They left before we did. They were walking straight back. Why didn't we see them on our way here?"

Her mouth opened and closed without a single explanation spilling forth. She gave me that look, the one that suggested I might break if she answered truthfully.

Pain ripped through me. I knew. The empty room, my panicked thoughts, and the fear clawing at my chest were proof enough. My entire family was missing.

Cha Cha toed the groceries across the threshold. She closed the door, sidestepped an orange, and knelt beside me. "Please, Madison, I know this is scary. Stay strong. Have faith. Trust in God."

"First Dad, then Lexie, and Mom. How... how can this be?" A sob escaped my lips... then another... and another, until I collapsed beneath the weight of them all.

My godmother gathered me in her arms. She rocked back and forth, whispered soothingly, and prayed. After a while she fell silent, lost in her own thoughts. When my tears subsided, she eased me back onto my knees. "Remember, at the restaurant, when we were discussing magick and how important it is to keep an open mind when you see unusual things?"

I brushed at my tear-streaked cheeks. "Yes." An image of that man with the red hat formed inside my mind.

She smiled, somewhat hesitantly. "Do you remember the story about how your parents and I met?"

I nodded. "You met in the waiting room outside the NICU the day I was born. One of your friends had a child in the NICU, and you were there for her. You spent time with Mom and Dad when they weren't allowed inside the NICU, during the nurse shift changes, and you've been friends ever since." I'd heard that story a million times.

Her eyes softened while those memories played inside her head. "That's right. I had a friend whose child was in the NICU. What I've never revealed until now is that child was you."

I frowned. That didn't make any sense. "Why would you have been there for me? You didn't meet Mom or Dad until the day I was born."

She rubbed her forehead. "I knew we'd have to have this conversation eventually. I just didn't realize it would be so difficult." Finally, she looked at me. "I think the most important thing you need to know is how much I love you. I would never hurt you, and I've never lied to you. You've known me your entire life. You can trust in that. Right?"

I searched her eyes. I could tell this conversation and my response was important to her, but I couldn't grasp why we were having this conversation now, when my family was missing. Still, I knew Cha Cha well enough to trust there was a reason and she'd connect the two events for me eventually. "Yes. I trust you. I know you love me and you would never hurt me."

She released the breath she'd been holding. "Good. I want you to hold onto that knowledge while I try to explain. I'm not like most people. Just like that *Cluricaun* and the *Far Darrig* you saw earlier, there's a little magick inside of me."

A smile tugged at my cheeks. I suspected that was a little wishful thinking, but I was willing to play along. "Okay."

She looked surprised by how easily I'd accepted her claim. Her eyes narrowed, and then she looked nervous again. "I... uh... I have some friends with some special powers who I think can help. I need to speak with them. I think I know why your family is missing. If my suspicions are correct, then my friends can help us find them."

My heart leapt. I didn't care who her friends were as long as they could help find my family. I dug through her purse, grabbed her cell phone, and shoved it at her. "Call. Please call."

She shook her head gently. "I don't need the phone to speak with them. That is part of the magick I was referring to. I can communicate with them telepathically." She eyed me cautiously. "I'm going to close my eyes while I speak

with them. Promise me you won't freak out if anything...
unusual... happens."

"Unusual?" I was so overcome with disappointment, I
wasn't sure I'd heard that last sentence correctly. I didn't believe for one minute my godmother could speak telepathically. Was this some elaborate ruse to make me feel better or
distract me? I swallowed. Hard.

"There's a slight possibility... I mean... It's been a while,
so I'm not sure, but... I might glow. A little." Her brow furrowed. She seemed frustrated by her inability to explain
things.

I was still contemplating that word... *glow*.

She squeezed my hand. "I promise I'll explain everything
just as soon as I speak with them." She pushed up off the
floor, took a few steps, and sank onto the nearest bed.
"Just... don't scream and don't leave the room. Trust me.
You're safe. This is perfectly normal." She mumbled then,
under her breath. "Whatever normal is."

I didn't move. I couldn't move, respond, or even breathe.
I was worried about her... and me. I thought she might be
losing it, which didn't bode well for me. She was the only
grown up I had left in a foreign country. Still, I could sense
something monumental was about to happen. I don't know
how or why, but the air felt heavy. It was as if I were dangling over the edge of something, like my life was about to
change in a very big way.

Cha Cha closed her eyes. Her expression smoothed, ac-
quiring a serene look, like she wasn't thinking at all. She
didn't speak or move.

I blinked a couple of times. Was her skin brightening or was that thought just planted inside my mind?

The soft golden haze pulsed into a bright, nearly blinding light.

I gasped and scrambled back onto my feet. Still, I couldn't take my eyes off her. She looked stunning, and she was quite literally glowing.

With a deep intake of breath, her eyes flew open. The bright light fell away. "Your father is safe. He's in *Otherworld* with the *Sidhe*, trying to restore the border between the realms."

I edged closer to the door. "She? Who is she?"

Her eyes captured and held mine. "He is with the '*Sidhe*,' which is spelled S – I – D – H – E, not 'she' like you are thinking."

The two words sounded the same. I feigned interest so she wouldn't notice I was trying to escape. "What's a '*Sidhe*?'"

Her head tilted, as if she were contemplating how best to explain. "The *Sidhe* are a unique race of people, gifted with special powers. They are the descendants of the Goddess Danu, also known as the *Tuatha Dé Danann* or tribe of Danu." Frustration rode her next breath. "Humans seldom acknowledge us by these names. They refer to us as faeries instead."

I pictured Tinkerbell in my head. "Wait." Every muscle in my body froze. "Us?"

She nodded. "I am *Sidhe*, as are you."

I shook my head. My parents were missing, and my

godmother no longer appeared sane. I fumbled for the door.

She captured my hand and guided me onto the bed. "I know this sounds crazy, but it's true. I'm not just your godmother. I'm your *Sidhe* guardian too." She propped her knee on the bed as she turned to face me. "You are one of three *Chosen Ones* who are destined to fulfill a prophecy. Your lives were in danger because of this prophecy, so the Goddess Danu ordered the *Far Darrig* to hide you in the human realm. He exchanged you for a NICU baby, a little girl who was very ill." She studied my expression. When I didn't freak out, she continued. "You know how your parents refer to you as a miracle baby?"

I nodded. My baby book was filled with pictures of me in the NICU on machines that monitored my heart and helped me breathe. I nearly died, but my parents refused to give up on me. The doctors were shocked by some miraculous improvement. Everyone claimed it was divine intervention. That was the only possible explanation for my sudden recovery, unless…

"The *Far Darrig* traded you for the NICU baby when no one was looking," Cha Cha repeated.

My heart skipped a couple of beats. "The *Far Darrig*? Isn't that what you called the man I saw at the restaurant, the one with the red hat?"

She nodded. "The *Far Darrig* have special powers like we do, but they can be mischievous and mean. They cause children, both human and *Sidhe*, to have nightmares. Apparently, they find that entertaining. They're notorious for stealing babies and leaving *changelings* in their place."

I sighed. Every explanation she offered raised more questions for me. *"Changelings?"*

"The *Far Darrig* replace the human babies they steal with faerie or *Sidhe* babies. When these babies are exchanged they are called *changelings*."

"Why would anyone do that?" I exclaimed.

Her shoulders lifted in a delicate shrug. "For a lot of reasons. In this case, the *Far Darrig* hid you to keep you safe."

I tugged my hand loose, stood, and paced across the room. A million questions raced through my head. I tried to focus on the most important one. "Does this mean my parents aren't my true parents?" The thought made me feel nauseous.

"No," she answered firmly. "Your parents raised you. They are your parents in every sense of the word. The Goddess Danu created you, so she is your mother too. Basically, you have two moms, a *Sidhe* mother and a human one."

I stilled. *Were two moms better or worse than one?* "Do I have two fathers?"

She shot me a look that suggested that was the most ridiculous question I'd ever asked.

My eyes widened with understanding. "I have a father in Heaven and a father on Earth." I resumed pacing. "How does the goddess tie into all that?" She wasn't mentioned in the Bible.

"The Goddess Danu is just one of many living things God has created," Cha Cha said. "God is her father. She answers to him, the same as you and I."

I turned that thought in my head. God is all powerful, so he could create anything he wanted. Arguably, he could create the *Sidhe*, the *Far Darrig*, and the Goddess Danu if he wanted to. I'd held fast to my belief that *Leprechauns*, faeries, and unicorns existed, even when my friends made fun of me. They called me a baby for believing in these things. I didn't let that stop me. I knew that believing required a certain amount of faith. There were kids at my school who claimed that God didn't exist. I still believed in him. I didn't have to see him to believe he existed. I had faith in a lot of things. Still, I wondered. Should I extend it to this?

"Would you like to see your dad?" Cha Cha asked.

My fears came rushing back. "What about Lexie and Mom? Do your friends know where they're at?"

"No." She pushed off the bed. "They are going to help us find them, though."

My eyes narrowed. "If Dad is safe, then why hasn't he called?"

"His cell phone won't work in *Otherworld*." She rolled her eyes. "I'm guessing the *Sidhe* who lured him there didn't bother telling him that."

Other... *world?* I shook my head, afraid to even ask. "Why were you glowing?" I knew the glowing was real. I'd seen it with my own eyes.

She shrugged it off. "The *Sidhe* glow when they communicate telepathically with the Goddess Danu. She's filled with so much energy... some of that energy escapes when she's speaking with us."

I stared at her. This time, I spoke really slow. "So, this

friend you were speaking with was the Goddess Danu?"

She nodded.

I felt guilty for doubting her. She was my godmother after all. There had to be some way for me to test this story without insulting her. "Can I speak with the Goddess Danu?"

She shook her head. "We have to journey to *Otherworld* so you can cross over into *Ogham*. *Ogham* is a realm of trees that lends knowledge and wisdom to the *Sidhe*. You must eat the berries from the Rowan Tree, which is your birth tree. This will awaken your powers, which helps ensure you are strong enough to communicate telepathically with the Goddess Danu."

I scrubbed my face with both hands.

She crossed the room and opened the door. "I want to speak with the innkeeper. She'll know if your mom and Lexie returned to the bed and breakfast. If they didn't, we can retrace our steps back to the restaurant. Maybe they stopped somewhere unexpectedly."

I stepped out into the hallway, relieved we were finally doing something. "Does Mom know about this whole *Sidhe* thing?"

She locked the door. "No. We'll have to explain that and a whole lot more when we find her. The goddess has requested our presence in *Otherworld*. We're going to continue searching for your mom and Lexie in the meantime, and we need to pick up some supplies before the *Chosen Ones* and their guardians arrive. We'll travel together through the Tomies Wood."

"Why do we have to go through the woods?" I loathed hiking, mostly because of the bugs.

She started down the stairs. "The portal to *Otherworld* is hidden there, and the journey itself is important. This journey will help you prepare."

"Prepare? For what?" I was still questioning whether this *Sidhe* world was real. How could any of this be true? Maybe Cha Cha ate something at dinner that was causing these delusions. Maybe she had a fever or was just freaking out because Mom was gone. Still, she did glow. I'd never seen anyone glow before.

"There is a prophecy you must fulfill... an important one." She stopped briefly, waiting for me to catch up. "I'll explain more later. For now, let's focus on finding Lexie and your mom."

I nodded eagerly. I forced all thoughts of *Sidhe*, of prophecies, and goddesses from my mind so I could focus on finding my family.

* * *

The early morning sun reached through the window, stretched across the floor, and warmed my nose. My eyes fluttered open.

"You're awake." Cha Cha tightened the belt on her robe before perching on the edge of my bed. "How are you feeling?"

I pushed up off the pillows. "Tired, worried, and sore."

She patted my leg gently. "Well, that's certainly understandable." We'd scoured the streets of Dublin until everything closed. Then, we called every hospital listed in the phone directory, thinking they might have been involved in an accident. We hadn't found Mom or Lexie or a single soul who'd seen them.

I shoved the covers aside, anxious to begin searching again. "Did you speak with your friends?"

"Yes." Her eyes drifted toward the window. "The *Sidhe* are still searching for them. Your father is helping them."

My thoughts circled back to the conversation we had last night. "What do they look like?"

"The *Sidhe*?" She glanced at me, surprised.

I nodded. I'd tossed and turned all night, thinking of all the things my godmother had revealed. After some serious soul searching, I'd discovered I believed her. Now, with all those uncertainties resolved, I was anxious to learn more about the people who were searching for my family.

"Honey, you're *Sidhe*." She chuckled softly. "They look just like you and me."

I contemplated the curl dangling in front of my face. There were countless shades of brown with gold highlights streaked throughout. I tucked the curl behind my ear. "So, they all have brown hair?"

Her smile widened. "Not exactly. Our hair color varies, but we all have these metallic highlights, naturally… bronze, copper, silver, or gold. Our skin tones have gold or silver undertones as well. And our eyes look like precious metals or gemstones."

I held my arm next to hers. We both had caramel colored skin with gold undertones. Cha Cha's eyes were topaz while mine were an impossible shade of gold.

"The *Sidhe* tend to look brighter and more striking over-all," Cha Cha revealed. "People are drawn to that, so we often mask or mute our appearance while we're in the human realm."

I could understand why. Complete strangers frequently remarked on my hair and my eyes. They couldn't believe they were real. This annoyed my mom to no end, especially when those people started touching my hair. "I wouldn't mind learning how to do that."

She laughed. "Madison, you're already muted."

I frowned. That muting didn't appear to be working very well.

Cha Cha hopped off the bed. "Come on. We've got a ton of things to do today."

We took turns in the bathroom, showering and getting dressed. Cha Cha finished long before I did. I was still working through all the tangles I'd acquired while tossing in bed.

"Here, let me help." She sat next to me on the bed.

"Thanks." I handed her the comb.

She sectioned off my hair. "There are so many things I want you to know before we arrive in *Otherworld*, I don't know where to begin." She was quiet, and then, "Would you like to know your *Sidhe* name?"

I turned to look at her. I hadn't stopped to think I might have another name. "I… ah… yes. Please."

She nodded and waited for me to turn back around. Gently, she worked through the knots. "Your *Sidhe* name is Grania. Across all the Celtic languages, Grania means love."

"Grania," I murmured. The name sounded foreign but felt oddly familiar. "Mom told me that Madison means gift from God."

She hummed her agreement. "I can think of no greater gift than the gift of love."

That coaxed a smile out of me. "Do you have a *Sidhe* name?" I couldn't imagine calling her by any other name. I couldn't even bring myself to call her Channa instead of Cha Cha.

She nodded. "My *Sidhe* name is Fianna, which means warrior." The comb stalled. "In many ways, these names reveal who we are, just like our birthmarks."

I rubbed the odd shaped mark over my heart.

She sifted her fingers through my hair, searching for any remaining knots. "The glamour the Goddess Danu created for you distorts your birthmark. That glamour will fade when we cross into *Otherworld* so you can see the image, which is a Celtic love knot."

I turned back around. "What about the others?"

She set the comb on the dresser. "There are three *Chosen Ones* in all. All girls, born at the exact same time… Grania, Maolisa, and Niamh. Your names stand for love, faith, and light. I've heard Maolisa's birthmark looks like a Celtic cross, and Niamh's birthmark looks like a Celtic spiral."

"Do we look alike?" I slipped the scrunchy from my wrist and pulled my hair back, twisting the elastic twice.

Her mouth opened and snapped shut. "You know… I don't know. I guess we'll find out tonight." She stood and reached for her coat.

I tugged my shoes on. "What if their parents don't allow them to come?"

"They'll allow it." She handed me my coat. "If they don't, their *Sidhe* guardians will compel them to do so."

Compel? I stilled. "Can you compel people?"

"Absolutely." She held the door for me. "All *Sidhe* guardians have that power."

"Will I have that power?" My stomach fluttered excitedly. "Just think, I could compel all those bullies at school to do the right thing."

"We won't know until you visit your birth tree." She checked the lock on the door. "Our powers vary based on who we are. Because you represent love, I suspect your powers will be tied to that attribute."

I followed her down the stairs. "I really hope you're talking about love in general… like a love for animals or mankind… and not the mushy stuff." I couldn't stomach the mushy stuff. Besides, boys were goofy… and annoying.

Cha Cha laughed. "I'm pretty sure it's the former and not the latter, Madison."

We snagged a couple of scones from the breakfast bar, stepped outside, and hustled down the front steps. My breath formed little clouds in the crisp morning air. "Where are we going first?"

She peered up at the darkening sky. "The police department."

I stumbled over a pair of spindly legs. "Oh, I'm so sorry!"

The frail man steadied me. Twinkling eyes softened his gaunt face. "I'm the one who should be apologizing."

My heart clenched when I realized he was homeless and likely starving. I extended my hand, revealing the scone I'd nearly squished. "Would you like a scone?"

He smiled up at me. A few of his teeth were missing. "Thank you, miss." When he took the scone, he dropped a gold coin in my hand.

"You don't have to pay me. I'm happy to share." My breath caught when I realized he was no longer there.

Cha Cha spun wildly. When she realized we were the only people remaining on the street, she turned and stared at me.

I turned the coin in my hand. The word *"Éire"* was stamped beside a harp on one side. A horse stood proudly on the other.

She stepped closer. "That's a twenty-pence from 1985." She steered me toward the car. "You should keep that with you at all times."

"Why? 1985 isn't that old. I mean… I'm pretty sure my parents were alive back then." I slid into the passenger seat when she opened the door.

She didn't breathe another word until we were both locked inside. "That extremely rare coin was a gift from the *Fear Gorta*."

"The *Fear Gorta*?" I turned around, half expecting him to be in the car with us.

"A supernatural being who begs for food as a test of sorts. He brings good fortune to those who help him." She eyed the coin when I opened my hand. "I have a feeling you're going to need that coin. Please, keep it safe." She typed an address into the GPS before easing away from the curb.

I zipped the coin inside my pocket. My mind was reeling. So many strange events had transpired over the past few days. I was certain my godmother was telling the truth, as unbelievable as it seemed, but all these revelations were causing me to question who I was and what was expected of me. "Can you explain this prophecy? Why did the Goddess Danu feel she needed to hide me?"

"You must visit your birth tree before we discuss the prophecy," she answered apologetically.

I sighed. This was yet another response that didn't fit with my understanding of how the world worked. "When are we leaving for *Otherworld*?"

She turned down a tree lined street. "Tomorrow morning. We need to buy backpacks, rain slickers, and hiking boots before we leave. We'll do that just as soon as we finish speaking with the police."

Fear surged within me, bringing tears to my eyes. I wanted to see my dad, but we had to find Mom and Lexie first. Lexie needed her medication. The longer she went without it, the more likely she would die. I prayed the people with her knew that... that they would find some way to keep her alive.

* * *

Cha Cha grabbed the *Far Darrig* by the front of his little red coat before slamming him up against the brick building. "Why are you here?"

I gasped. My godmother was far stronger than she appeared.

"Last I checked, Ireland was a free country," he sputtered indignantly.

"First the restaurant and now the hotel?" she growled. "Are you spying on us or cursing my charge with nightmares?"

His eyes slid toward me. "I was merely curious. I can feel her power simmering just beneath the surface. Besides, she's very pretty."

My eyes widened. How could he feel my power? I didn't think I had any power until I ate the berries from the Rowan Tree.

She frowned at his remark. "Her mother and sister have disappeared. I don't suppose you know anything about that?"

"I know nothing about them." He looked completely offended. "Maybe you should ask the *Fomorians*, the *Fir Bolgs*, or the Goddess Carman's sons. They are your enemies, not I."

She grudgingly released him. "Have you shared your observations with any of them?"

He brushed the wrinkles from his coat. "No. I avoid those vile creatures at all costs."

"I apologize for the rough handling then." Cha Cha looked a little chagrined. "I may have overreacted a bit."

"You cannot deny your true nature any more than I," he offered politely.

"Why do you cause children to have nightmares?" I blurted. This *Far Darrig* seemed nice. His personality didn't jive with the mean-spirited creature Cha Cha had described.

He looked genuinely surprised. "I have very little power over such things. Sometimes an innocuous thought, an observation, or some question in my head causes others to experience nightmares. Often I find there is a lesson or some value to be gained from the experience."

"How so?" Curious, I stepped a little closer.

"Nightmares warn children, they help them make better choices, and they prepare them for the harsher side of life. Nightmares build empathy, understanding, and they help us cherish those people and experiences that make us feel happy," he answered rather stoically.

Cha Cha looked stunned.

He stood a little taller. "And while the *Far Darrig* may exchange human and faerie babies, there is always some compelling reason why. Every exchange contributes to the greater good."

"The greater good according to who?" she scoffed.

"Why, the Goddess Danu, of course." He winked at me before strolling confidently down the street.

Cha Cha gaped at him. This was the first time I'd ever seen her truly speechless.

"Cha Cha, you really should be nicer to him." I tugged on her arm until she followed me up the steps leading into the bed and breakfast. We were greeted by the aroma of freshly baked bread. "Oh, wow. That smells amazing. Can we eat now, before we head upstairs?"

She shook her head, trying to clear her thoughts. "Sure… um… yes, that sounds good." We crossed through the foyer and joined the other patrons in the casual dining room.

I dropped my shopping bags on the floor and slid onto a chair at the only available table. I was so accustomed to searching, I instinctively scoured the room. A lump formed in my throat. All the families sitting around me were talking and laughing. They were happy… together… safe.

I choked on a mangled sob. Being here felt wrong. It felt like giving up. I raked through my thoughts, trying to identify something… anything more we could have done. We'd filed a report with the police department and the embassy. We'd called all the hospitals, and we'd asked countless strangers if they'd seen Lexie or Mom while sharing pictures from Cha Cha's cell phone. The people and places varied, but the answer was always the same. *"No. I'm sorry. I haven't seen them."* We'd run out of time, and now? We were forced to leave without them.

Cha Cha lifted my chin, then folded me in her arms. "Oh, honey. Please don't cry. We're not giving up. There are plenty of people who are still searching for them."

The tears I'd been holding back pushed through my lashes, dampening my cheeks. "I don't want to leave without them."

Her hand ran soothingly down my hair. She spoke with the waitress in hushed tones, gathered our bags, and guided me toward the stairs. "They're going to deliver our food to the room. Come. Let's go upstairs."

"I'm sorry," I replied miserably. "I didn't mean to cry."

"Don't apologize." She leaned forward conspiratorially. "I'll let you in on a little secret. I feel like crying too. Unfortunately, I'm not a pretty crier like you. That's why we're going up to our room. I'm going to indulge in a big ol' ugly cry, and I don't want to worry about what those folks..." she lifted the bags while motioning down the stairs, "think about all the snot that will be pouring from my nose."

I tripped over the next step. I turned to look at her, and then suddenly, we were both laughing.

She smiled wryly as we continued up the stairs. "Or we could just laugh. Laughing works too."

I felt much better by the time we arrived at the room. Now, with all those toxic emotions out of the way, I could think a little more clearly. "The *Far Darrig* mentioned some people he thought we should question about Mom and Lexie's disappearance. Do you think we should question them?"

She set our shopping bags on the floor, turned, and locked the door. "Perhaps... although, that could prove difficult."

"Why?" I unzipped the backpack Cha Cha had purchased for me, stashed Lexie's medications inside, and settled on the floor beside my suitcase.

She set the new hiking boots beside me. "Well, the *Fomorians* aren't like us. They're demons who live beneath the sea. They battled the *Tuatha Dé Danann* for control over Ireland centuries ago. They ruled over us for a time. We fought for our freedom and eventually regained control. There's a lot of animosity between us. We barely speak now."

I stopped and stared at her. "Demons?"

She nodded. "They manipulate the harsher elements, the more destructive side of nature, to achieve their objectives."

I searched her face, seeking some evidence that she might be joking. "What... like evil spirits?"

She shook her head. "No. They exist in solid form."

I shuddered. "What are their objectives?"

"They're trying to displace humans and destabilize Ireland so they can regain control over this island." She unzipped her suitcase. "Sadly, humans don't even know they exist. They dismiss the *Fomorians'* attacks as freak accidents. Violent storms provide the perfect cover. Would you believe lightning strikes, fallen trees, hurricanes, flooding, and mudslides were being caused by demons?"

I shook my head. "No. I'd just blame the weather." I chewed my bottom lip while contemplating how my family might fit into all this. "What could they possibly want with Mom and Lexie?"

"I don't think the *Fomorians* have your family." She shoved some clothes in her backpack. "The weather was clear. There weren't any storms the night they disappeared."

"What about the *Fear Bogs*?" I couldn't recall exactly how that word was pronounced, but that was how it sounded.

"The *Fir Bolgs* are intimidating, physically, but they're not as violent as the *Fomorians*. They fought for Ireland once and lost. Most live on the western side of Ireland now, in an area known as Connacht. I'm sure they'd like to rule over the entire island, but I can't imagine them kidnapping humans to achieve that objective." She zipped her suitcase.

"Why would the *Far Darrig* considered them to be vile?" I persisted.

She pushed up off the floor. "I haven't a clue why the *Far Darrig* would lump the *Fir Bolgs* in with the *Fomorians* and the Goddess Carman's sons. Perhaps there is some conflict or animosity between them that I am unaware of."

"What about the Goddess Carman and her sons?" I knew I was grasping at straws, but we'd ruled nearly everything else out.

She sank into the chair by the desk. "The Goddess Carman has been imprisoned in *Tech Duinn* for years. Her sons are another story. I think they are the most likely culprits, but we must wait to explore that possibility until we arrive in *Otherworld*. Her sons are connected to the prophecy."

I busied myself with the backpack. This prophecy was beginning to scare me. How awful must it be if I can't even hear it before crossing over into *Ogham*? What sort of understanding and strength could be gained from eating berries, anyway? Each day seemed to bring more questions than answers. Still, there was only one question I really wanted answered.

Were Mom and Lexie safe?

CHAPTER 3 - TÍR NA NÓG

I studied the *Chosen Ones* while they studied me. Skylar, whose *Sidhe* name was Niamh, had pale blond hair and sky-blue eyes. Everything about her radiated hope and light. Zoey, whose *Sidhe* name was Maolisa, had strawberry blond hair and bright green eyes. Courage sparked in her eyes. We looked nothing alike, and yet... I sensed we were very much connected.

Our guardians completed the introductions before venturing into their own conversation. I stepped closer to the girls, eager to discover what they knew about the prophecy and how they felt about traveling to *Otherworld*. Like me, they were traveling without their families. I knew how difficult that could be. "Thank you for coming."

Skylar hurried forward and gave me a hug. "Brigitte told me about your family. We'll do everything we can to help you find them. I promise."

I nodded, my throat suddenly clogged with tears.

Zoey rubbed my arm soothingly. "Ciara and I have been praying for them."

"Thank you." I was worried I might cry, so I pursued a safer topic. "Where are you from?" Both girls spoke English, but their accents suggested they might be from different countries.

Skylar shrugged the backpack off her shoulders and dropped it by the door, the same way I did at home. "I live in Paris."

Zoey eased out of her coat. "I'm from Helsinki, Finland. Where do you live?"

"I live in Virginia, near Washington D.C." I freed a couple of hangers from the closet so I could hang their coats.

"I can't believe we're here," Zoey whispered. "You should have seen what Ciara did to my parents. They wouldn't let me leave until she planted this idea in their heads."

"An idea?" I hung their coats inside the closet while they removed their boots.

Zoey nodded. "Ciara offered to take me on this 'educational trip.'" She threw air quotes around the word "educational." "When my parents said 'no,' Ciara just stared at them, and then suddenly, they were insisting we take this trip."

Skylar giggled. "Brigitte did the exact same thing."

I thought back on my conversation with Cha Cha. "They can compel people to do things." I walked toward the bed. "Did they say anything about the prophecy?"

Zoey eyed her guardian thoughtfully. "Ciara mentioned it briefly. She explained we are traveling to *Otherworld* so we can fulfill a prophecy. She wouldn't say what the prophecy involves, only that there is one that affects the three of us."

"Our lives were threatened because of that prophecy. That's why we were hidden in the human realm." Skylar sat next to me on the bed. "I'm not sure I want to know what a prophecy like that entails. Let's talk about something else."

My gaze shifted between the two of them. "It's kind of weird discovering you have sisters you never knew existed."

"Not just sisters but triplets," Zoey corrected. "The prophecy doesn't seem nearly as important as learning you exist. I mean… we're family. Family is everything."

I nodded. While our relationship was new and unexpected, I agreed. Completely. Families stand by one another no matter what.

Brigitte turned down the bed she was sharing with Skylar. "We really should get some sleep. We have a three-and-a-half-hour drive and an extensive hike through the Tomies Wood tomorrow."

"We're going to have to leave early if we want to reach *Tír na nÓg* before nightfall," Ciara agreed. She set her backpack on the bed she was sharing with Zoey.

"*Tír na nÓg*?" I frowned. "I thought we were going to *Otherworld*."

"*Tír na nÓg* is just one of many realms located in *Otherworld*," Cha Cha explained. "That is where the *Tuatha Dé Danann* live. Your father is there with them."

"What's it like?" Skylar turned to face them.

Brigitte glanced at the other guardians. "Where to begin?" She sat on the edge of the bed. "*Tír na nÓg* is not like any place you've ever been. There's no electricity, no cell phones, vehicles, sidewalks, or streets. Aside from the Goddess Danu's palace and our homes, there are no buildings. We spend a lot of time outdoors."

"No cell phones?" Zoey repeated.

I was more concerned about the lack of electricity.

Cha Cha shrugged. "We don't need cell phones. We communicate telepathically." She rose from the desk. "Our lives are simpler but more advanced in a lot of ways. You will understand once you've experienced it for yourselves."

"*Tír na nÓg* is beautiful," Ciara added fervently. "The air and water are cleaner, the soil is richer, and the food is more nutritious because we cherish our environment. We live longer and are much healthier as a result."

Brigitte nodded. "*Tír na nÓg* is quite literally the Land of Youth. There is no illness or disease. We are nearly immortal once we eat the berries from our birth tree. That is just one of the many powers we are gifted – the ability to heal quickly. We stop aging in our mid-twenties because our bodies heal the damage that typically results from aging. The healthier environment in *Tír na nÓg* helps a lot. Our bodies age while we are in the human realm, just not to the same extent as everyone else."

Skylar, Zoey, and I exchanged glances. As usual, our guardians' claims evoked more questions than answers.

"We can talk more about this tomorrow," Cha Cha chided. "Now, let's get ready for bed."

We took turns in the bathroom; showering, changing into our pajamas, and brushing our teeth. Each girl shared a bed with her guardian. Thankfully, there were three double beds in our suite. We prayed before surrendering to sleep.

I slept fitfully, thrashing about until the blankets tangled around my legs. I woke a few hours later, plagued by a dream involving the *Fir Bolgs* of all things. The primitive warriors appeared out of nowhere. They were racing toward my dad while throwing spears at me. The anger in their eyes was chilling.

I stared at the ceiling. I couldn't shake the feeling that the *Far Darrig* had inspired this dream. I kicked the covers aside, padded across the hardwood floor, and peeked between the filmy white curtains shimmering in front of the moon drenched window.

The *Far Darrig* stood on the sidewalk below, leaning against the lamp post. He tipped his little red hat.

My breath caught. Clearly, there was something about the *Fir Bolgs* we should be concerned about. I pressed my hand to the cold glass.

He smiled, but his eyes remained sad.

Tears welled in my eyes. I wasn't sure how I knew, but I did. He'd been shunned, and he was terribly misunderstood. Silently, I vowed to treat him with respect. I whispered my thanks and quietly returned to bed.

* * *

I forced my leaden eyes open. The soft hum from the windshield wipers kept lulling me back to sleep, but Brigitte had just mentioned something I could scarcely believe. "What was that?"

Her eyes met mine in the rearview mirror. "We don't need indoor plumbing in *Tír na nÓg*. The *Sidhe* use all the energy they acquire from food, so there is no need for bathrooms."

No bathrooms? I straightened, my interest piqued. "Why don't you use electricity?" I was going to ask earlier, but I'd fallen asleep.

Cha Cha peered between the seats. "The *Sidhe* can harness power from air, water, and wood. We use this power to complete tasks that would normally require electricity."

I tried to imagine how that might work.

Zoey tore her gaze from the rain splattered window. "Are there many humans in *Tír na nÓg*?"

"Very few," Ciara answered. "Those who are permitted to cross over are given two options. They can choose to forget *Tír na nÓg* the moment they leave, or they will be rendered completely incapable of discussing it with other people."

I wondered which option my father would choose. "Will our memories be erased?"

She shook her head. "No. You are *Sidhe*. Once you eat the berries from your birth tree, you will feel a connection to that place and seek to protect it."

Skylar looked relieved. She leaned between the seats. "What kind of things do you do for fun?"

"We listen to music, dance, play games, and compete in different activities." Brigitte's smile hinted at fond memories. "We eat together as a community. We're always celebrating something, so dinner can be quite festive."

Skylar nodded, obviously pleased. "What kind of activities are you involved in back home?" Her gaze shifted between Zoey and me.

"I compete in swimming," Zoey answered. "I love any activity involving water. My parents own a boat, so we spend a lot of time sailing around the archipelago."

"The archipelago?" The word sounded familiar, but I couldn't recall what it meant. I was picturing an archaeological site in my head.

"Islands," she said. "The Helsinki archipelago includes three hundred and thirty islands."

"Wow." I made myself a promise. When I found my family, we were going to see those islands.

"What about you?" Both girls looked at me.

I bit my lip nervously. I'd tried a bunch of sports, but none of those activities clicked for me. My mom claimed I was drawn to more cerebral things. I suspected most people would consider me a nerd, so I was a little hesitant to admit the activities I gravitated toward. "I like competing... in a lot of things."

Zoey smiled encouragingly. "Like what?"

"Well... um... I'm in the chess club. I like playing board games." I chuckled under my breath. "Actually, I like *winning* board games. I like competing in math tournaments, science competitions, and Odyssey of the Mind. I also enjoy performing in talent shows and musical theater. I'm an anchor for our school's morning news show. I serve on our student council, and I'm a peer buddy. I like helping students who are struggling."

Skylar's eyes widened. "That's a lot of activities."

My cheeks flushed pink. I felt both embarrassed and relieved. "What about you?"

"I like school," she admitted, "but I love football. I've played football since I was four."

"Football?" I couldn't picture her strapping on those shoulder pads and tackling people. "My dad played football."

Zoey's gaze bounced between the two of us. "I think Americans call it soccer."

"Oh," Skylar gasped. "Of course."

I laughed. "Now that I can picture."

The SUV slowed. We abandoned the conversation while admiring the boldly painted storefronts that marked Killarney Town. Bright red, yellow, pink, and green buildings framed the busy streets. I wanted to explore the bustling town, but I knew we had a long hike ahead of us. I didn't want to get stuck in the woods after dark.

Brigitte wound through the streets, stopping for several pedestrians along the way. We traded the two and three-story buildings for a winding road, sprawling farmland, and a glittering lake. A swell of mountains framed it all, like a picture-perfect postcard. Heavy clouds, lush trees, and endless shades of green. I barely registered the window as I soaked it all in. This was the Ireland I'd envisioned when my father first announced his trip.

Brigitte turned into a parking lot and eased into a space between two faded lines. "The rental company will retrieve the vehicle if we leave it here. I just need to drop the keys inside the house."

I followed her gaze. A Tudor style mansion emerged beyond the trees at the far end of the lane.

"House?" Skylar sputtered. "Surely, that's a palace."

"It looks like something you'd see in a fairy tale," Zoey agreed.

"That is Muckross House," Ciara explained. "The Tomies Wood are located on the opposite side of the lake."

"There is a castle, Ross Castle, a little further around the lake," Cha Cha offered while gathering her things.

I added Ross Castle to the list of places I wanted to explore once Mom and Lexie were safe. I crammed my rain slicker inside my backpack and jumped out of the SUV. The air was damp and cool, but the rain had stopped. The sun peeked through the clouds. I inhaled deeply, savoring the smell of rain drenched soil, warm pine, and soapy smelling flowers.

Brigitte led us past a wide expanse of lawn with perfectly manicured gardens. "The mansion has been converted into a museum. Feel free to use the facilities while I deliver the keys. We can grab some pastries from the restaurant before we leave."

We followed her up the stone steps leading into the museum. After a quick bathroom break and a few furtive glances into several Victorian style rooms, we walked over to the garden restaurant, purchased several pastries, and met back outside. We stopped briefly to admire the gardens and the view.

Cha Cha pointed toward the mountains on the far side of the lake. "That's where we're heading. That swath of trees filling the saddle between those mountains is the Tomies Wood."

Ciara led us down the trail leading out onto the peninsula. "There's a bridge at the end of the peninsula, where the two lakes meet. We can cross over there."

I read the park sign identifying the two lakes. "What does *Lough Leane* mean?"

"Lake of Learning," Brigitte replied. "That's the lake on your right." A horse drawn carriage jostled along the trail in front of the lake.

Ciara pointed toward the lake on our left. "That's Muckross Lake, also known as Middle Lake." An elderly couple sat on a bench near the shore, tossing breadcrumbs to the swans.

"There don't appear to be many bugs," I observed with some relief.

"I'm afraid that will change by the time we reach the other side." Cha Cha eyed me worriedly. She knew I struggled with anxieties. I refused to go outside for an entire summer once, when my sister was stung by a bee. Bugs, of all shapes and sizes, topped my list of anxieties.

"How long of a hike are we looking at?" Zoey asked as she caught up with me.

Ciara glanced at the sun instead of her watch. "Ten hours at least."

My stomach twisted nervously. "So, we'll be hiking in the dark."

"Don't worry. We each carry a light." Cha Cha linked her arm in mine. "Are you excited to see your dad?"

I took a deep breath, trying to ease the tension in my chest. "I am. I'm thankful he's okay. I just wish I could say the same for Lexie and Mom."

She nudged my shoulder with her arm. "Do you think the *Sidhe* are feeding him tree bark or ants?"

My face scrunched. "Ugh! How can you even suggest that?"

"What kind of food do you eat in *Tír na nÓg*?" Skylar, who appeared unfazed by this talk of eating ants, nibbled a freshly griddled Farl with jam.

Cha Cha consulted a list inside her head. "Fruits and vegetables... eggs, yogurt, and cheese... nuts, seeds... truffles and mushrooms... oatmeal, potatoes, and bread."

"No meat?" Zoey glanced worriedly at Skylar and me.

"We can make mushrooms taste like any meat; pork chops, bacon, steak... Trust me, it's all in the seasoning." Brigitte laughed, clearly noting our skeptical expressions.

"What's your favorite food?" I asked Zoey. I wasn't sure if people from Finland ate the same foods as me.

"Grillimakkara with mustard," she answered without hesitation.

Skylar folded the farl into her mouth. "Grilly what?"

"Grilled sausage," Ciara clarified.

"Ah." Skylar brushed the crumbs from her hands. "Croque-Monsieur is mine."

"That's a hot ham and cheese sandwich," Brigitte explained. "They're my favorite too."

I thought about the toasties I'd eaten with Cha Cha. "I wonder if every country has their own version of a ham and cheese sandwich."

"We eat ham and cheese on rye bread for breakfast," Zoey confirmed. "I dip mine in cloudberry jam."

I glanced at her, surprised. "I've never heard of a cloudberry before. What do they taste like?"

She stopped to think about it. "Cloudberries taste like raspberries and sour apples only better. I'll send you a jar if you'd like."

Skylar nodded excitedly. "I would love that. I've never met a jam I didn't like."

Zoey grinned. "What's your favorite food, Madison?"

Cha Cha snickered under her breath.

"Broccoli," I admitted.

My godmother's eyes glinted with mischief. "She likes broccoli so much she owns a broccoli skirt and a broccoli pillow."

The girls gaped at me.

"I like pizza too," I added, "but not with broccoli. Broccoli stands alone, and cheese pizza is the only kind that will ever enter my mouth."

Everyone burst out laughing.

"I like pizza." Skylar admitted happily.

"Me too," Zoey agreed.

I smiled. Maybe we weren't so different after all.

We stepped onto the stone bridge connecting the peninsula to the other side of the lake. Mountains loomed before us. Muckross Lake glistened on our left, and *Lough Leane* shimmered on the right.

"What's that?" Zoey pointed toward an island in *Lough Leane*. There were several islands, but this was the largest one.

"That's Innisfallen Island," Ciara replied. She peered out over the slate blue water. "The stone structure you see peeking through the trees is an old monastery that dates back to the 7th century. The High King of Ireland Brian Boru studied there, among the saints and scholars of Innisfallen Island."

"The story behind that monastery is quite magical." Cha Cha motioned us toward the side of the bridge. "Apparently, Saint Finian dropped a book in the water while reading near the lake. He searched as best he could but couldn't find the book. He prayed he might find some remnant of the book, which was quite precious to him. Imagine his surprise when he ventured onto Innisfallen Island and discovered the book lying there in pristine condition. There was no water damage whatsoever. He was so grateful, he decided to build a monastery dedicated to research and scholarship on the very spot where he discovered the book. People came from far and wide to study there."

I smiled, intrigued by the story. "So that's why it's called *Lough Leane*."

She nodded. "The Lake of Learning."

"What's the story behind that building?" Skylar pointed toward the tower guarding a stone fortress on the edge of the lake, halfway between Muckross House and Innisfallen Island.

"That's Ross Castle." Brigitte braced her forearms against the stone wall while studying the tower. "There's a legend surrounding that building too. Ross Castle was built by the O'Donoghue clan. Rumor has it that O'Donoghue, who dabbled in black magick, was sucked out of a window in the grand chamber, near the top of the tower. He disappeared into the lake, along with his horse, his books, and a table. The legend claims he built a great palace at the bottom of the lake, where he resides still today. He rides out of the lake on his trusty white steed once a year on the first of May, the anniversary of the day he first disappeared. Those who have been lucky enough to see him have been blessed with great fortune."

Skylar, Zoey, and I peered into the water, hoping to catch a glimpse of O'Donoghue and his horse.

Cha Cha chuckled. "You're not likely to see him in October." She pushed off the stone wall. "There's a restaurant up ahead. Who's hungry?"

"I am!" Skylar grabbed Zoey's hand, ducked under her arm, and then skipped across the bridge. She didn't stop until we reached Dinis Cottage, a weathered tea house overlooking Muckross Lake.

Zoey set her backpack on the bench. "Can we eat outside?"

Ciara gazed up at the sky. "Sure. We should enjoy the sun while it lasts." Thick white clouds crested the mountain tops, but the sun was shining directly above us.

Brigitte nodded. "I'll see what's on the menu." She walked up the trail leading toward the restaurant.

We settled in at the picnic table closest to the lake. A fishing boat bobbed next to the dock. Insects skipped along the surface of the lake, tempting fate. Fish lunged and sank, forming a small dollop of water that rippled across the water while they ate. Birds circled overhead, watching and waiting with keen eyes. The insects weren't the only ones tempting fate today.

Skylar rested her chin in her hand while she watched the birds circling overhead.

I glanced at Cha Cha. She was sitting directly across from me, watching the woods instead of the lake. "Have you eaten here before?"

She nodded. "A few times. The menu is limited, but the food is great."

Brigitte strolled down the trail. "Will vegetable stew, bread, and MiWadi suffice?"

Skylar turned to look at her. "What's MiWadi?"

"A fruit flavored soft drink." She glanced at Zoey and me.

"That sounds good," Zoey answered.

Skylar nodded. "I agree."

"Me too." I noticed she didn't include anything with meat, which was fine with me. I'd been toying with the idea of becoming a vegetarian for some time now. I didn't like the thought that an animal had to suffer because of me.

Ciara stood. "I'll help you carry it back. Zoey, will you carry the drinks?"

"Sure." She untangled her legs from the bench so she could join them. She returned with the MiWadi a few minutes later. "I wasn't sure what flavor you would like, so I got a variety."

"Thanks." I chose the bottle marked "summer fruits." The blackcurrant MiWadi I'd tried a few days ago was really good, but this bottle had a picture of a strawberry. Strawberries were my favorite fruit.

Ciara and Brigitte appeared, balancing trays loaded with food. Ciara set her tray on the table. "We grabbed a little something for dessert."

Skylar's eyes brightened. "Oh! I love pie."

Ciara set the bread in the center of the table while Brigitte plunked a bowl of stew in front of each of us. "Bon appétit."

I smiled. That was one of the few words I knew in French. "Bon appétit." Little tendrils of steam drifted up from the stew. "This smells delicious."

Zoey dipped a chunk of bread in the broth and popped it in her mouth. "Oh. Wow. This broth is amazing."

I nodded in full agreement. When there wasn't another drop of stew or bread to be had, we dove into the lemon meringue pie.

"We're about to get wet." Brigitte nodded toward the darkening sky. "The sooner we get to the forest, the better."

Cha Cha and I returned the dirty dishes. We gathered our backpacks and walked briskly down the trail. We paused briefly when the trail branched in two different directions. One trail disappeared into the trees, the other veered toward the lake. "We'll stick close to the lake until we reach the Tomies Wood," Cha Cha explained. "We can duck into the forest and climb Tomies Mountain from there."

"You might want to get your rain slickers out." Ciara caught a raindrop in the palm of her hand.

We pulled the rain slickers from our backpacks, tugged them on, and continued down the trail. Ross Castle and Muckross House were still visible on the other side of the lake. The canoes and kayaks were gone. Most of the hikers were walking the other way.

Brigitte frowned at the lake. The water appeared black beneath the sunless sky. Everything else looked gray. Fat, filled to bursting rain drops speckled the water, forming ripples that overlapped one another.

Zoey eased closer to Ciara. "When we were in the car, you said something about harnessing power. How does that work?"

She glanced at the other guardians before answering. "I'm a water spirit so I draw power from water. I can draw water from the ground or a lake and shoot it into the air like a geyser. I can coax the clouds to rain, hail, or snow. Like all *Sidhe*, I can shapeshift and fly. Because I'm a *Sidhe* guardian, I can plant ideas, create illusions, erase memories, and compel people to do things they wouldn't normally do."

Zoey's feet ground to a stop. "You can shapeshift?"

"And fly?" Skylar grabbed Brigitte's arm. "What about you?"

She draped her arm around Skylar's waist so she'd continue walking. "I'm an air spirit, so I draw power from wind. I can move and deflect objects with a simple flick of my wrist. I can shapeshift and fly, and I possess all of the powers bestowed on guardians, which Ciara noted."

My heart beat erratically. "Ciara, you said all *Sidhe* can shapeshift and fly. Does that mean…"

Skylar jumped up and down excitedly. "We can fly!"

Ciara burst out laughing. "Yes. Once you visit your birth tree, you'll be able to fly."

"But your powers vary based on your purpose," I persisted, recalling my conversation with Cha Cha.

"And your spirit," Cha Cha clarified. "I'm a wood spirit, so I draw my power from plants and trees. I can grow things… quickly. I can also shapeshift and fly, plant ideas, create illusions, erase memories, and compel people, like other guardians do. You will draw your power from one of those three things; air, water, or wood. You'll be able to shapeshift and fly, but we don't know what sort of power you will have beyond that… not until you visit your birth tree."

"We're not supposed to use our power in front of humans unless we're protecting others or concealing our identity," Brigitte warned. "Occasionally, the goddess makes exceptions. Planting that idea inside your parents' minds so you could join us in *Tír na nÓg* was one such exception."

"The *Sidhe* were once enslaved," Ciara explained. "The *Fomorians* forced us to use our power for their gain. We don't want to repeat that part of our history, and we don't want to be imprisoned in a science lab while humans torture us with their experiments."

"We use our power discretely because it helps ensure our security." Cha Cha's voice grew solemn. "This power must only be used for good. We coax rain when there's a drought, stop the rain when there's a flood, or draw the excess water into the ground. We calm the winds when there's a forest fire, increase the winds to hurry a storm along, and lure humans and animals to safety when their lives are in danger."

I was relieved to hear they were using their power to help others.

"What sort of shape…" Skylar yelped as a magnificent white horse came crashing through the trees.

I was so startled, I nearly fell into the lake.

"Woah!" Cha Cha caught me.

The horse skidded to a stop directly in front of me. He lowered his head, nudged my shoulder, and sniffed me.

There was a sharp intake of breath.

I tried to steady my breathing while admiring the beautiful beast. He had the longest tail and mane I'd ever seen. His coat was so shockingly white, he glowed against the dreary landscape. My hand rose. My fingers inched toward his glistening coat.

"Don't touch him," Cha Cha breathed.

I gazed into his obsidian eyes. I sensed no malice… just loneliness mixed with excitement and a hefty dose of curiosity.

He snorted softly. His breath formed a cloud in the cool, damp air. He nudged my shoulder again.

"That's not a horse, Madison. It's a Kelpie," Cha Cha warned through gritted teeth. "If he senses any bad intentions, his coat will turn adhesive and he'll drag you into the lake."

I frowned at the warning.

He shook his head, watched, and waited for me to respond.

He looked so angelic, standing there in the mist. My fingers ached to touch him. I loved horses, although he was no ordinary horse. He was the closest thing I'd ever seen to a unicorn. The only thing missing was the horn. My fingers drifted closer.

His eyes closed. Gently, with the tiniest puff of breath, he pressed his nose to my palm.

Everyone froze.

My eyes slid closed.

His voice whispered inside my head. "Welcome home, Grania."

I smiled. His voice sounded gentle and kind. "Thank you." My fingers slid over his velvety soft nose. "Thank you for welcoming us."

He sighed softly. "For twelve years we have waited for the *Chosen Ones* to arrive… to restore the balance between the realms."

My eyes flew open. I searched his eyes, trying to decide. Did he know about the prophecy?

He peered deep into my eyes. "You need only speak my name should you require my help."

"Your name?" I inquired breathlessly.

"Elgin." He spoke aloud this time.

"Elgin," I repeated. He was offering his help. "Can I kiss you?" I wanted to throw my arms around him and never let him go.

He nodded.

I pressed a kiss to his nose. Then, unable to resist any longer, I flung my arms around his neck and buried my face in his mane. "Thank you, Elgin. I will remember you, always."

He acknowledged Zoey and Skylar, nodded respectfully toward our guardians, and walked gingerly into the lake. He swam briefly before disappearing beneath the waves.

Our guardians released a collective sigh of relief.

I tore my eyes from the lake.

Ciara stared at me. "You touched a Kelpie."

"His mane felt like silk." My fingers rubbed together, remembering exactly how he felt. "His coat wasn't sticky."

"Well, at least it wasn't a Selkie," Brigitte noted with some relief. She started walking down the trail.

"What's a Selkie?" Zoey eyed the forest and the lake.

"Selkie's are seals that shed their skin. They turn into beautiful women or men and dance naked along the shore." Ciara chuckled.

Skylar gasped. "Why would they do that?"

She shrugged. "Nobody knows."

My eyes narrowed. "The *Sidhe* don't dance around naked in *Tír na nÓg*, do they?"

Cha Cha laughed. "No. We wear clothes that help us blend into the environment. Of course, we dress like humans when we're in the human realm."

I studied their attire. Our guardians were wearing hiking boots, blue jeans, and rain slickers. Skylar, Zoey, and I were wearing the same attire. "Now I know why you insisted on green when we were shopping for the rain slickers."

Cha Cha smiled. "That yellow slicker was fun, but sometimes it's better to go unnoticed."

"We were talking about shapeshifting before we ran into that... uh... Kelpin?" Zoey guessed.

"Elgin," I interjected. "His name is Elgin."

"Before we ran into Elgin," she corrected. "What kind of shapes do you shift into?"

"I'm a water spirit," Ciara answered, "so I can shapeshift into any creature that lives in water; a dolphin, fish, frog, turtle, crab, or waterfowl. I can also transform into aquatic plants."

"What's your preferred shape?" Zoey asked.

She stopped to think about it. "Probably the dragonfly because no one pays it any mind. Dragonflies make the best spies."

"What about you?" I glanced at Cha Cha.

"I can shapeshift into any plant or tree, although I try to avoid that. Trees are very confining." She frowned at the thought. "I can transform into any woodland creature; fox, deer, mouse, bear, snakes, insects, you name it; but I prefer birds. The Peregrine Falcon is my favorite because he can fly two hundred forty miles per hour."

I couldn't imagine driving let alone flying two hundred forty miles an hour.

"What about you?" Skylar asked Brigitte. "Since you're an air spirit, does that mean you shapeshift into things that fly?"

A smile danced in her eyes. "Yes. I can shapeshift into anything that flies."

Zoey stopped short, nearly causing a pile up as we rounded the bend. "Look at all those flowers." She gazed in awe at the purple mountainside.

"The Rhododendron Forest." Ciara studied the terrain. "We can cut through there into the Tomies Wood if you would like."

We nodded excitedly. I'd never seen so many flowers blanketing the ground, and they smelled amazing; sweet, like honey, and surprisingly spicy.

"Okay," she agreed. "That may actually save us some time."

Initially, the Rhododendron Forest was easy to navigate. The bushes were knee high, and they were scattered enough so we could see the ground. Gradually, that changed. Before long, those spicy smelling flowers were tickling our waists. We were bobbing in a purple sea, only there wasn't any water, only flowers as far as the eye could see.

"I didn't anticipate this," Ciara finally conceded. Flowers pressed in on us from all sides. We were forced to walk single file while we climbed the hillside.

"The rhododendrons didn't look this tall when we were standing by the lake," Brigitte grumbled. The bushes swelled above our heads, forming a wall of flowers in every direction.

Cha Cha squeezed past Ciara so she could take the lead. "Follow me."

We walked behind her, single file. Daylight was fading. The air was cool; the clouds misting more than sprinkling. Suddenly, I noticed something odd. The plants were leaning away from us. "Cha Cha?"

"Yes?" She kept walking, without even sparing a glance.

I tried poking one of the flowers, but it shrank even further away. "Are you moving the plants?"

She chuckled. "I'm coaxing them out of the way."

"Are you manipulating anything else?" Zoey queried behind me.

"I'm thinning the rain." Ciara peered up at the darkening sky. "I've forced half the moisture back into those clouds. I can't hold that precipitation back forever, though, just long enough for us to reach the Tomies Wood. The foliage on those trees will help keep us dry when those clouds finally burst."

"Anything else?" Skylar asked.

"I'm warming the air around us." Brigitte smiled when we turned to gape at her. "I didn't want you to feel chilled."

"Wow." Zoey glanced at her hands. "I'd love to be able to warm the air like that. Imagine never having to feel cold again."

The flowers tapered off as we crested the hill, allowing us to walk alongside one another. We hiked across the softly rounded hilltop and peered at the other side. The valley cradled between the mountains was heavily treed, but this side of the hill was bare, as were the mountains on our left. The lake, with all its historic sites, beckoned on the right.

Ciara's hair fluttered softly in the breeze while she studied the trees. "The Tomies Wood." She nodded at the other guardians and started down the hillside.

Cha Cha pointed at the mountain guarding the other side. "That's the Tomies Mountain. The portal is on the other side, behind the Gap of Dunloe."

I followed her down the hillside. "The portal to *Otherworld*?"

She nodded. "This portal serves as the border between the human realm and *Tír na nÓg*. This is the border your father was working on."

"So, we have to climb that mountain after we cross through the woods?" Zoey's gaze shifted between the shadowy forest, the mountain, and the darkening sky.

"Yes." Cha Cha grimaced. "I'm afraid we've still got a fair amount of hiking even after we climb the Tomies Mountain."

"I wish we could fly." Skylar sighed. "Flying would take a lot less time."

Brigitte nodded in full agreement. "That it would."

She perked up, her interest piqued. "Is flying difficult?"

"Not really," Brigitte shrugged, "but it does require some practice. You may earn a few bumps and bruises along the way."

"How does it work?" Zoey's brow furrowed while she contemplated that very thing.

"You'll acquire wings when your birth tree awakens your powers in *Ogham*," Ciara explained. She laughed at the stunned expression on Zoey's face.

"Don't worry," Cha Cha offered consolingly. "Your wings will retract between your shoulder blades when you're not using them. Look how long you've known Ciara, and you didn't once suspect she had them."

"How can a tree give us these powers?" Skylar wondered aloud.

"The trees in *Ogham* don't give us these powers," Brigitte corrected. "We are born with them. They're just dormant until you visit your birth tree. Trust me, that is as it should be. Imagine a two-year-old *Sidhe*, who can generate a massive storm, throwing a temper tantrum because he lost his favorite toy."

"He? "My eyes widened with surprise. "Are there boy *Sidhe*?"

Cha Cha burst out laughing. "Of course, there are boy *Sidhe*. What made you think they were all girls?"

I forced my eyes from the forest. I'd been obsessing over the dangers that might lurk in those trees ever since I first laid eyes on them. "Well, every *Sidhe* I've heard about has been a girl... the *Chosen Ones*, our guardians, and the Goddess Danu."

"I can see why she would think that." Brigitte gazed uncertainly at the trees. "Do you girls need to rest before we enter the woods?"

Zoey slowed. "How are we supposed to see when we're walking through those trees?" The sun had slipped behind the mountains while rain clouds doused the moon and stars, so the forest was eerily dark.

Our guardians looked around to ensure we weren't being watched. We hadn't seen any hikers on the trail for hours. Finally, they stretched their hands in front of them. A pinprick of light danced above their fingertips before growing bigger and brighter. Cha Cha's light was gold, Brigitte's was blue, and Ciara's was green. Within seconds, each guardian had a lantern of sorts hovering in front of her.

I shook my head. I was too scared to enter the woods, even with the additional light. My heart beat wildly, making it difficult to breathe. "What sort of animals live in those trees?"

My godmother straightened to her full height. "There is nothing in that forest more powerful than me."

My jaw dropped, just a little. I eyed the light pulsing in front of her and wondered if that might be true. Still, it was difficult to believe.

She closed the distance between us. "We can do this," she whispered. "Your father is waiting for you in *Tír na nÓg*. You'll be in his arms before the night is through."

Grudgingly, my feet agreed to move. "What about Lexie and Mom?" Every step closer to my dad felt like a step further away from them. I could feel it, like two giant rubber bands pulling me in different directions.

She linked her fingers in mine. "Our *Sidhe* warriors are looking for them, in addition to the *garda* and the embassy staff."

I released a shaky breath. "Lexie needs her medication. Without it, she could reject her kidney."

"I know, honey." She wrapped her arm around me. "The people searching for them are really good at what they do. I'm certain we'll find them soon."

Silence descended as we stepped into the trees. We weren't the only ones who had quieted. The entire forest seemed to be holding its breath.

"Wow," Skylar whispered reverently.

I marveled at the lime-green moss blanketing the boulders and trees. "This place is really pretty." A kaleidoscope of green, gold, and blue light bobbed invitingly on the trail in front of us. I continued forward, my fears and anxieties abandoned at the edge of the forest.

With a loud "whoosh," the clouds released a torrent of rain.

Ciara shrugged. She was walking on the trail ahead of us. "Sorry, girls. I couldn't hold that rain off any longer."

"I can hear it, but I can't feel it," Skylar mused. She extended her hand, determined to catch a rain drop.

I peered up at the thick canopy of trees. "The trees are protecting us."

"Yes," Cha Cha winked, "they are."

"I love the sound of rain," Zoey confessed.

"Me too," Ciara agreed. "I sleep better when it's raining."

"I like the way the soil smells after a good rain." I took a deep breath. The soil in the forest had that same fresh but musky scent.

A smile played on Cha Cha's lips. "Do you remember how afraid you used to be to walk on the sidewalk after it rained? You were so scared of the worms that washed up. Then, when your mom told you those worms were going to die, that they'd never make it across that sidewalk before they dried out, you forgot all about being afraid. You started saving those worms instead." She chuckled softly. "You looked so cute scooping up worms with those tiny scraps of paper so you could place them in the grass."

Zoey grinned. "Madison, that is so sweet."

Skylar shortened her stride so she could walk beside me. "How old were you when you did that?"

I shrugged. "I don't know. Three, maybe?"

Cha Cha shook her head. "You were just a baby, only one and a half years old." Her smile widened. She leaned forward as she answered Skylar. "She kept saving worms all through elementary school."

Zoey slowed, waiting for us to catch up. "I saved a seal that was caught in a fishing net, once. That felt really good, better than getting high marks at school."

"Wow." I rubbed the goose bumps on my arms. "I would love to do that."

"I raised a baby bird that lost its mother," Skylar offered. "I was so sad when we had to let her go. She still visits our bird feeder, though."

Brigitte turned so we could hear her. "That's the *Sidhe* in you. The *Sidhe* feel a deep connection to animals and the environment. Animals sense that connection, so they're more likely to trust us, especially when they're hurt."

A rustling sound drew our attention to the forest. Skylar grabbed my arm, bringing me to an abrupt stop. I sucked in a breath while craning to hear the sound again. My heart beat hard and fast. I held perfectly still while mentally preparing to run.

"Deer," Cha Cha finally said. "A doe and two fawns."

I released the breath I'd been holding. Skylar and Zoey did the same.

"We'll be out of the woods soon," Cha Cha promised as we resumed walking. A smile tugged at her lips when Brigitte began to sing. She joined in, as did Ciara, their voices merging in perfect harmony.

I listened intently, trying to decipher the lyrics. They were singing about a red rose, a bonny Irish lad, and Killarney's green woods.

"It's a love song," Skylar whispered, "based in Killarney."

Zoey nodded. "It's pretty but sad. I think she loses him in the end."

They sang the song again and again, until we'd memorized the lyrics and could no longer resist joining in.

We were so immersed in the song, we didn't notice the branches hurtling toward us. Skylar squeaked when a thin branch landed between us. A massive, winged beast came barreling through the trees. Leaves fluttered all around him, landing softly on the ground.

Brigitte backed us against a tree. The trunk shifted, softening and then hardening all around us while the branches kept us from fleeing. It wasn't until we were hidden safely inside the yawning trunk that I realized Cha Cha was the tree. She sealed the bark around Zoey, Skylar, and me.

"Wh... what is that?" Skylar stammered.

"Shh," Cha Cha whispered. "Don't say anything."

I stopped wriggling. I could see through the textured bark but just barely.

Ciara and Brigitte doused their lights. They flung their backpacks on the ground. Ciara widened her stance, her hands thrust up and out. Water dripped from her fingertips, trickling down her arms. A pool of water formed on the ground. Brigitte was standing in the exact same pose. Blue sparks arced between her fingertips like tiny streaks of lightening. Wings sprung from their backs. Both looked ready to attack.

My eyes followed theirs. The clouds shifted, unveiling the moon. Light streamed through the battered trees. A massive beast towered over our guardians, picking at the branches that littered his wings.

I leaned closer, not quite believing what I was seeing. He looked like a dragon, but he had three heads anchored atop three long necks. The rest of him looked like you would expect... a broad chest, four legs, and a long, pointy tail. His purple, green, and blue scales glittered even in the dark forest.

My gaze traveled back up his necks. Each head sported horns, razor-sharp teeth, and a pair of eyes that glowed like liquid gold. He was still plucking away at those branches with his teeth like he didn't have a care in the world.

I wondered how something could be so terrifying but beautiful at the same time.

"The *Ellen Trechend*," Cha Cha whispered.

His voice sounded deep and warm. "The Goddess Danu sent me." He appeared unconcerned with the electricity and water dripping from our guardians. His necks stretched toward the tree. All six eyes peered at Skylar, Zoey, and me.

"Why would the Goddess Danu send you?" The water beneath Ciara's feet widened until it touched the dragon's feet. He had long, skinny toes and talons, like you'd find on an eagle or hawk.

"This area is crawling with *Fomorians*." He eyed the water with distrust.

My eyes widened. The *Fomorians* were demons who lived beneath the sea.

"That's not possible," Brigitte scoffed. "The *Fomorians* can't fly, they can't survive outside of water for more than a few hours, and the ocean is seven hours away."

He shook all three heads. "The *Fomorians* have found a way to adapt so they can live in fresh water. They have seized Black Valley and Upper Lake."

The color drained from Brigitte's face.

"We were planning to hike through Black Valley," Cha Cha explained.

"The *Fomorians* have aligned with the Goddess Carman's sons. The Goddess Danu is concerned they may be searching the Tomies Wood for the *Chosen Ones*. She asked that I retrieve you and deliver you safely to the border between the realms."

"Surely, the goddess would have told us if that were her intention," Ciara argued.

"We were singing," Brigitte reminded her.

Ciara folded her arms. "We're guardians. We can get them there safely."

Tiny puffs of smoke escaped his nostrils when he snorted. "You cannot carry them. Your wings aren't strong enough. My wings are stronger than the wings of a hundred *Sidhe*." He shook his feathers out as he began to preen. "I can carry all six of you and deliver you to the portal within ten minutes time."

"Ten minutes?" Skylar sounded awestruck. "We still have four hours of hiking ahead of us."

Brigitte remained oddly silent. Ciara stepped in front of her when she began to glow. The light dimmed, and Brigitte stepped forward again. "The *Ellen Trechend* speaks the truth. The goddess asked him to retrieve us."

"I have a name," he complained.

Cha Cha lifted her arms. The tree faded from the top down, disappearing into the ground.

Brigitte and Ciara remained standing in front of us.

Zoey poked her head between the guardians so she could see the *Ellen Trechend*. "What's your name?"

His smile revealed the sharpest teeth I'd ever seen. "I am called Naois."

She squeezed between the guardians. "I'm Zoey. This is Skylar and Madison."

Naois frowned. "Why do you not use your *Sidhe* names?"

I stepped out from behind Ciara. "Our *Sidhe* names were just recently revealed to us. We are still getting used to them."

All three heads swung toward me. "Grania. You do not fear me?"

I gazed into his eyes. There were no irises or pupils, only a swirling mass of light. I pondered how I felt while gazing at my reflection in his eyes. I didn't look scared, only intrigued. I sensed no threat, only a strong desire to protect. His presence felt like a gift. He was magical, a beast you would only expect to find in dreams. A smile tugged on my cheeks. "No. I think you're beautiful, and I would love to fly with you."

Naios's deep, hearty laugh shook the ground and tickled my bones.

Skylar stepped closer. "Can I touch your horns?"

His eyes widened, as big as saucers. "I can't say that I've ever been asked that before." He lowered his heads toward each of us.

A deep rumbling escaped his chest when we touched his horns, like a cat with a thunderous purr.

Our guardians looked puzzled by the sound.

My hand drifted across his blue, purple, and green scales. How many people treated him like a threat when he was only there to help? I frowned. Had anyone touched him lovingly before?

"I don't think I can hike another four hours," Zoey admitted. She pressed her palm to Naios's cheek. "Are you sure you don't mind carrying us?"

He blinked then. Just once. He glanced at our guardians and then back at us. "I wish to ensure your safety."

"The goddess must think very highly of you," Cha Cha mused. She shared some unspoken thought with the other guardians.

Brigitte offered a curt nod. "Thank you, Naois. It is very kind of you to help."

"Ready?" Cha Cha asked.

I stepped back, trying to glimpse the wings shimmering behind her back.

A small puff of smoke escaped Naois's nostrils. He nodded.

Cha Cha pushed off the ground, shot skyward, and landed on his back. She reached down, as if offering her hand, but she was too far away for us to clasp hands. Her arm narrowed into a thin, leafy vine that wrapped around my waist. I'd barely squeaked out my surprise, when she pulled me up onto Naois's back. She lifted Skylar and Zoey while Brigitte and Ciara flew up and settled in between us.

"Protect their heads from the trees," Naois warned. His front legs curled under his chest. The muscles in his back rippled, and his wings unfurled. He crouched low to the ground, then leapt straight through the trees.

My breath caught. I clung to Naois's neck as he burst through the trees. His necks strained and stretched until he finally leveled off. He soared smoothly beneath the clouds, his massive wings rising and falling on either side of me.

Ciara's hand rose, and the rain suddenly stopped.

The clouds thinned into delicate wisps of smoke. The moon emerged, bathing the terrain in a soft, silver light. Trees and rocks and rivers stretched beneath us. I could see Muckross Lake and *Lough Leane*. I blinked back tears from the wind so I could peer in the opposite direction. Several rivers fed the lake on our left. "Is that…"

"Upper Lake," Cha Cha said, pointing.

A shiver bit at me. Upper Lake was the lake the *Fomorians* had seized. I leaned closer to Naois. The heat radiating from his back made me feel safe and warm.

He circled a small clearing before touching down. He crouched low, resting his belly against the ground. Skylar, Zoey, and I slid off his back and landed like a sack of potatoes by his pointy toes. Our guardians' landing was a bit more graceful. Of course, they flew down.

Skylar jumped back onto her feet. "I can't believe we were flying… like really flying… in the sky… on a dragon!"

Zoey swept the tousled hair from her smiling face. "That was the most amazing thing I've ever done." She pushed up off the ground. "Thank you, Naois."

I stood and gave him a hug. Like Elgin, there was something about him that tugged at my heart. "Will we see you again?"

He grinned. "I certainly hope so."

"We should get moving," Brigitte warned. "Be safe, Naois."

He nodded all three heads.

We backed away as he spread his wings and catapulted into the night sky.

Our guardians summoned their lights. "The border is on-ly a short distance away." They led us back into the trees.

Zoey studied our surroundings. "We're not in *Tír na nÓg*?"

I shared her surprise. The moss was an impossible shade of green... the trees grew taller... the flowers were larger... the place felt magical.

Ciara shook her head. "No. We must enter *Tír na nÓg* by foot. That's just one of many security precautions we have implemented. Only those with good intentions can enter *Tír na nÓg*, so we are assessed first."

I hadn't realized there was a test. I frowned, my anxieties getting the best of me. "Are there people standing guard? Is someone going to question us? What if we have no inten-tions? What if someone lies?"

"You are about to find out." Brigitte shoved a thick cur-tain of vines aside.

I joined Zoey as she ducked beneath the vines. Thin wisps of steam curled above a hot spring. I ventured closer, unable to resist the pull of the entrancing scene, while Zoey sank onto the moss carpeted rocks framing the pond.

"This is the entrance to *Tír na nÓg*." Cha Cha spoke soft-ly, directly behind me.

I tried to acknowledge her but could not. The air felt misty and warm. My fingers rubbed together, marveling at the moisture, which wasn't like any moisture I'd felt before. This moisture held expectations. It conveyed a deep sense of responsibility while promising peace and belonging. I peered through the mist, sensing... *more*. A silent song hung in the air. The water was calling to us, inviting us home.

Ciara spoke loud enough to break the spell. "In order to cross over into *Tír na nÓg*, you must step into the hot spring, speak five words in the old language, and then open your heart and mind. The enchanted waters will weigh your intentions. Anyone harboring bad intentions toward the *Sidhe*, the Goddess Danu, or *Tír na nÓg* is sucked through a portal and deposited into *Lough Leane*, the Lake of Learning. For those with good intentions, a portal opens into *Tír na nÓg*. You may find yourselves momentarily blinded by the light, but your eyes will adjust. When the portal opens, you simply take a step forward."

"The gravitational pull is different in *Otherworld*," Brigitte warned. "You will move with very little effort, glide more than walk."

"This portal will only assess one person at a time," Ciara added. "This helps ensure each person is evaluated on his own merits."

"I'll enter first so you can see what happens." Cha Cha sat on a boulder near the edge of the pond. Her eyes locked on mine. "I'll be waiting for you on the other side." She tugged her hiking boots off, shoved her socks inside the boots, and tucked them beneath her arm.

My heart stalled. "What about the words? What if I forget them or say them wrong?"

Her eyes sparked with amusement. "No *Sidhe* could ever forget these words."

Skylar looked equally concerned. "What if the spring doesn't like me? I may have bad intentions I know nothing about."

Brigitte laughed. "I am certain the enchanted waters will accept you. You don't harbor any ill will toward the *Sidhe* or the Goddess Danu. You radiate light, Skylar. Everyone senses this about you."

Cha Cha stepped into the water. The steam gathered around her. She waded a little further. "Don't delay. I'll be waiting on the other side." She closed her eyes. "*Tír na nÓg, Draíocht Dúchas, Taisce Baile.*" A piercing light flashed in front of her. She stepped forward and promptly vanished. There was nothing, not a ripple in the water or in the air to suggest she'd ever been there.

The portal snapped closed so abruptly, I felt unsteady in the sudden darkness. "Woah."

Ciara steadied me. "You're next." She helped me onto the boulder where Cha Cha had removed her boots.

Zoey joined me. "What do those words mean?"

"Land of Youth, magick birthright, treasured home," Ciara gritted before doubling over with a groan.

Brigitte scanned the trees. "Hurry. Something's coming."

"I feel nauseous." Ciara fell to her knees.

I reached for her, wanting to help, but Brigitte intercepted me. "Madison, quickly!" She ripped my boots and socks off before shoving Skylar on the rock beside me.

I splashed out into the water, frightened by whatever *thing* was coming. The steam enveloped me.

"Do you remember the words Channa spoke?" Ciara urged.

Brigitte was tearing through the laces on Skylar and Zoey's boots.

I nodded. *"Tír na nÓg, Draíocht Dúchas, Taisce Baile."* I stumbled back when the light exploded in front of me.

"Step forward!" Brigitte screamed.

My heart seized. I scrambled forward, tripped on a rock, and landed on… *grass?*

"Madison!" Dad crushed me to his chest.

"Dad! You're okay?" I flung my arms around his neck.

"I am." Tears clogged his throat.

All the courage I'd been clinging to disintegrated in my father's arms; that sudden rush of relief replaced by the fears I'd fought so hard to squash. "Mom and Lexie… they're gone. We tried to find them…"

Zoey snapped into existence right beside me. Another burst of light, a high-pitched shrieking sound, and Skylar appeared on her hands and knees. She clawed at my arm. "Brigitte and Ciara were attacked."

"Attacked? By who?" A quiver filled with arrows appeared on Cha Cha's back. A bow dangled from her hand.

"Ravens," Skylar sobbed. "Hundreds of them."

"The *Sidhe Sluagh*," Cha Cha growled. A light flashed, erasing her from sight.

CHAPTER 4- OGHAM

Light pulsed so rapidly, I couldn't see the *Sidhe* jumping into the portal to help. Finally, the flashing subsided. I blinked a few times, trying to clear my eyes. Slowly, I registered my surroundings. We were kneeling in a grassy meadow surrounded by trees. My father stood and helped us to our feet.

With widening eyes, I registered the *Sidhe* warriors who had been standing just outside my periphery with their swords drawn. Metal armor, that looked to be a mix of platinum and gold, framed their broad shoulders. That same armor protected their hands, arms, chests, and legs. Short swords, knives, and star shaped weapons dangled from the wide metal belts adorning their narrow waists. The elaborate floral pattern stamped into their armor was so unexpected, it made my heart ache. A soft platinum hood hid most of their hair but revealed strong, masculine faces. Their skin was pale but radiant, with just a hint of frost. Massive, snow-white wings worthy of angels jutted out at least a foot on either side of them, even though their wings were folded be-hind their backs.

One of the warriors approached Dad. "We shouldn't lin-ger near the portal. It's not stable."

Dad grabbed my hand.

I broke from his grasp. "What about Cha Cha and the others? I'm not leaving them."

"Me either." Zoey's hands fisted against her hips.

Skylar swiped at her tear-stained cheeks. "We have to go back and help them."

Admiration shone in the warrior's eyes. "The *Sidhe Sluagh* don't stand a chance against your guardians. Besides, I sent six of my fiercest warriors. They'll return shortly."

My mouth opened and snapped shut. The warrior's ex-pression left little room for argument.

Dad coaxed us onto a wide trail. "Come, you must be ex-hausted."

The warriors moved seamlessly, positioning themselves in some tactical formation that ensured our protection.

I peered back over my shoulder, determinedly avoiding the warriors' gaze. "Where are they? Shouldn't they be back by now?"

"They'll be back any minute," Dad promised.

My thoughts were hijacked by the trees. I turned a full circle, trying to reconcile what I was seeing. The trees that lined the left side of the trail had emerald green leaves, while the trees on the right sported deep gold leaves. It was as if spring reigned on one side of the forest while fall ruled the other.

Skylar stepped into the pale blue light streaming through an opening in the trees. "Where is this light coming from?"

The warrior who had insisted we leave sheathed his sword. "From the moons."

She held her hand out while admiring the light. "But it's blue."

He stared as if confounded by her.

Her eyes flew to his. "Wait. Moons… as in plural… more than one moon?"

His expression remained stoic, his posture stiff. "Yes. We have three blue moons in *Tír na nÓg*."

Zoey stepped behind him while studying his wings. "Are you an angel?" His wings were thick and fully feathered, while our guardians' wings were sheer and looked far more fragile.

Finally, he cracked a smile. "I am not an angel. I am Cathal, a *Sidhe* warrior."

He looked a little more relaxed, so I sat and pulled my socks and boots back on. Skylar and Zoey did the same. "There are no footprints behind us, and I feel lighter. A lot lighter. Are we even touching the ground?"

"Barely." Dad chuckled. "There's less gravity here, which does take some getting used to."

He'd been here so long, he was probably used to it by now. I frowned, suddenly recalling all the questions I wanted to ask. "Why are you here?" I pushed back onto my feet. I didn't want to have this conversation in public, but the questions tumbled out anyway. "Why didn't you call? Do you have any idea how upset Mom and Lexie were? We were so worried about you. How could you do that to us?"

He stepped in front of me, blocking everyone else out. "I'm sorry, Madison. I didn't mean to worry you. I thought I was meeting with government officials when I flew to Ireland. When they asked me to help strengthen their border, I didn't know it was the border between two realms. Cathal didn't reveal that until we arrived at the hot spring. Of course, Cathal didn't look like he does now. He looked human. My cell phone stopped working when we entered the Tomies Wood, so I couldn't call. And time... well, time works differently here. I lost track of how much time had passed in the human realm."

"What's a *Sidhe Sluagh*?" Zoey was staring in the direction we had walked.

I abandoned the conversation with Dad so I could hear Cathal's response.

"The *Sidhe Sluagh* are rogue spirits who are not welcome in either Heaven or Hell, in the human realm or in *Tír na nÓg*. They often appear as an unkindness or a conspiracy of ravens. They seek out the souls of the dying and those who have lost hope. I have never heard of them attacking the *Sidhe* before."

"Those who have lost hope?" My stomach plummeted.

Our guardians appeared at the end of the trail. Several warriors walked beside them. Thankfully, no ravens followed.

A warrior strode forward, his long strides obliterating the distance between our guardians and Cathal. "The *Sidhe Sluagh* fled."

Cathal nodded, acknowledging the report. "Were they trying to enter the portal?"

A sound, like a growl, escaped the warrior's chest. "They were trying to steal the guardians' souls."

Cathal frowned. "Everything is out of balance. There is too much evil in the human realm."

Skylar dove into Brigitte's arms. "Thank God, you're okay."

She held her close. "Thanks for sending help."

Cha Cha studied the expression on my face. "Are you okay?"

"No." My voice broke. "What if the *Sidhe Sluagh* attacked Lexie and Mom?" I swallowed against the nausea roiling in my stomach. "They were feeling hopeless when they left the restaurant."

"Oh, honey. I don't think your mom or Lexie lost hope." She grasped my hands, then gave me a hug. "They were just missing your dad."

"Those are two very different things," Ciara agreed, her arm anchored around Zoey.

"We will find them," Cathal promised.

The warriors nodded.

Dad coaxed me from Cha Cha's arms. "You're exhausted." He brushed my tears away with his thumbs. "Let's get you to bed."

We continued down the trail in silence, although I suspected the *Sidhe* were speaking telepathically again. I studied our guardians while we walked. There were some subtle differences in their appearances. Their eyes shone more like gemstones, their skin looked radiant, and their hair fell in glossy waves. They looked flawless, not frazzled like you'd expect after battling crazed birds and hiking all day. I wasn't sure if it was the moonlight, if they were just energized after fighting the *Sidhe Sluagh*, or if they'd been masking their appearance in the human realm. I suspected this was how they truly looked.

I stopped short when we reached the clearing. One of the three moons Cathal had mentioned appeared to be touching the Earth. The other moons were further away, but they lined up neatly with the first moon. All three moons shone in an impossible shade of blue.

My gaze fell on the emerald green lake. The water glowed from within, like the sun had slipped beneath it. A stunning waterfall sang at the far end, marking the closest mountain. Mossy boulders and trees skipped around the opposite bank while a meadow hugged the shore in front of us. Sessile oak trees held elaborate tree houses that kissed wispy, low lying clouds along the edge of the meadow. Additional homes lie nestled within *Sidhe* mounds. Fireflies danced in the meadow while the heavily treed mountains stood guard.

"It's so beautiful," Zoey murmured.

"Breathtaking," Skylar agreed.

I nodded, unable to speak. Gradually, my thoughts organized themselves into one achingly simple wish. "I wish Mom could see this."

"Me too." Dad's arm tightened around me.

Tears warmed my surprisingly cold cheeks. "Where are the other *Sidhe*?"

"You will meet them in the morning," Cathal assured me. He issued some unspoken command to the warriors. Some sauntered toward the mounds. Others faded into the trees.

"The goddess didn't want you feeling overwhelmed," Dad explained.

Skylar turned, excitement brightening her face. "Is the goddess here?"

Cathal nodded but only once. "The goddess is there, behind the waterfall."

"You'll meet her after you visit *Ogham*," Brigitte reminded us.

A stone bridge, covered in moss, emerged from the luminous lake. The arch formed a perfect half circle when the bridge locked into place. With the reflection in the water, there appeared to be a full circle, half in and half out of the water. My breath caught. The bridge formed a looking glass, displaying the world as it should be... connected, balanced, and at peace.

"We should get some sleep." There wasn't an ounce of surprise on Ciara's face, like bridges magically appeared out of nowhere every day. She nudged Zoey, who was still staring at the lake. "Shall we?"

She pointed at the bridge. "That bridge... it just magically appeared."

"Yes." Ciara chuckled. "The sooner you say 'goodnight' to your friends, the sooner we can walk across it."

Zoey yanked Skylar and me together for the world's fastest hug. "Goodnight."

Skylar's laughter brightened the surprisingly quiet night. "Goodnight."

A smile tugged at my lips. "Goodnight, Zoey."

A warrior followed them as they strode toward the lake.

Cha Cha glanced questioningly at Dad. "Where are you staying?"

"With Cathal and the other warriors." Some unspoken message passed between them.

She nodded. "I think Madison should sleep with me, then."

"I agree." He kissed the top of my head. "You'll be more comfortable with Channa. I know you have a lot of questions but, please, try to get some rest. I promise, we'll talk in the morning."

I nodded, too tired to object. "I love you, Dad." I burrowed into his chest. I was thankful we'd found him, but my greedy heart wanted more. I wanted my entire family safe, together, and unharmed. I forced my arms to release him before I started crying again.

"We'll see you in the morning." Brigitte rubbed my arm.

Skylar smiled and gave me a hug. "Sleep well."

Cha Cha twined her fingers with mine. "Are you hungry?" She swung my arm as we crossed the meadow.

"Yes." I knew it was late. I didn't know how late, but my stomach assured me it was well past dinner time.

"Me too." She continued walking toward the trees. "We'll eat and get settled in to sleep."

I peered back at my dad. He was still standing there, talking to Cathal. "Where do the warriors sleep?" I glanced at the warrior walking behind us and turned back around.

Cha Cha pointed toward a small hill with a stone entrance at the far end of the meadow. "Over there." She stopped in front of a tree. "This is it… my humble abode."

My head fell back as I followed her gaze. "Oh!" We were sleeping in one of the treehouses.

She held out her palm. "Up you go." A ladder formed rung by rung between the ground and the deck above. "I hope it's not too dusty. I haven't been here since the day you were born." She flew up to the treehouse while I tested the ladder she'd just willed into existence.

The warrior held the ladder when I began to climb. "Only sweet dreams tonight."

"Thanks, Diarmuid," Cha Cha called from above. She held the ladder at the top. "Careful. We're a long way from the ground." She helped me scrabble up onto the deck.

I turned and peered over the edge. We were at least twenty feet off the ground. I hadn't realized the ladder was that long. Diarmuid appeared to be standing guard. I waved to Dad before following Cha Cha inside the house.

She brushed aside the sheer netting that served as her door. Light sparked in the palm of her hand. She dropped it inside the lantern.

My hand trailed over the furniture while I explored the house. Everything was made of wood; the furniture, the floor, the walls, and the ceiling. I peeked at my fingers. The place wasn't dusty at all. "It's spotless."

She smiled. "An air spirit cleaned the house for us."

I set my backpack on the bench near the door.

She pulled plates, cups, a pitcher, basin, and bowl from the cupboard. "I'm going to the garden. I'll be right back." She strode out the door and leapt from the porch.

It took me a minute to process what I was seeing. I still couldn't believe she had wings. I tugged my boots off and tucked them under the bench. I hung my rain slicker and coat on the hooks next to the door and then stood there, uncertain how I might help.

Cha Cha breezed past me. She set a pitcher of water and a bowl filled with fruits and vegetables on the counter. "I've got mushrooms, lettuce, and tomatoes for dinner and berries for dessert." She grabbed another bowl from the cupboard, tore the lettuce, and sliced the tomatoes.

I poured our drinks, gathered the silverware, and set the table.

She sliced the mushrooms, sprinkled a pinch of seasoning on top, rubbed her hands together, and held them over the plate. Warm basil, rosemary, and thyme scented the air.

I stepped closer. "Are you cooking... with your hands?"

She grinned. "Best superpower ever." She set the steaming mushrooms on the table.

I transferred the berries into a small bowl, carried them to the table, and sat down next to her. "Thanks for making dinner."

She smiled. "Piece of cake."

I took a sip of water. I'd never really cared for mushrooms, but this one smelled delicious. I set my cup down, determined to at least try it. I cut a small piece, captured it between my teeth, and bit down. "Oh. Wow."

She laughed. "See? I told you. Just like a pork chop."

I ate half the mushroom before speaking again. "I know there's a goddess, the guardians, and warriors, but what kinds of things do the other *Sidhe* do?"

She stopped to think. "Well, there are artisans. They make a lot of different things… these dishes, our furniture, jewelry, and clothes. The bards; they're our storytellers and musicians. They help keep our history alive. We have a healer. He helps care for people, animals, and plants. We also have ambassadors, guardians, warriors, and druids."

I dug into the salad. The lettuce was crisp, the tomatoes sweet and juicy. I shoved another forkful in my mouth. "What's a druid?"

She leaned back, folding her arms across her chest. "The druids are a lot of things. They serve as our historians, our advisors, prophets, and teachers. They teach us how to control our power and ensure we use it wisely."

I set my fork down. "So, you still attend school in *Tír na nÓg*?"

She laughed. "There's no dodging school, Madison. You will have to study and train under a druid once you return from *Ogham*."

"What about my school back home?" I had a week's worth of schoolwork in my backpack that I hadn't even touched yet.

"I wouldn't worry about that schoolwork or an extended absence. Time works differently in *Tír na nÓg*. You could train here for months, and those in the human realm would hardly notice you were gone. There are a lot of advantages to living here. Time is just one of them." She plucked a berry from the bowl.

I yawned, suddenly more tired than I'd ever been.

Her eyes softened. "You must be exhausted."

I carried our dishes into the kitchen. "I am."

"Me too." She used water from the pitcher to wash the dishes. The matching basin served as a makeshift sink. I grabbed the dish towel, but she waved me off. "Go... get ready for bed."

"Are you sure?" I felt guilty leaving the work for her.

She nodded. "I'll be done in a matter of seconds."

"Okay. Thanks." I retrieved my toothbrush and pajamas from the backpack, turned back around, and froze. Several vines whispered across the floor. I stepped back, sucking in enough air to scream, but then I noticed the vines were weaving an intricate pattern of loops and knots. Cha Cha was checking their progress and flicking her wrist every so often. I stepped closer, intrigued. "What are you doing?"

She tugged blankets and pillows out from beneath the window seat. "I'm making our beds."

I pointed at the self-weaving vines. "That is not how we make beds back home."

She laughed. "Trust me. You're going to love sleeping in this hammock."

I studied her furniture a little more closely. Her tree-house didn't contain any beds. Why didn't I notice that before? "I've never slept in a hammock before."

She smiled. "You're in for a real treat then."

The lantern dimmed when I tugged my sweater off. I shimmied out of my jeans and bent down to remove my socks. I straightened when I caught sight of my birthmark. There, just above my camisole, were two clearly defined hearts intertwined within a slightly larger one. I touched the mark. "This looks like a tattoo."

Cha Cha stepped closer. "That's because the image is so clear. I assure you that is not a tattoo. That Celtic heart is part of you."

I hopped on one foot while wrestling with my pajama bottoms. "You're going to have to explain all this to Dad. I don't want him thinking I got a tattoo."

Cha Cha gathered the vines. "I'm pretty sure your father will understand." She suspended the makeshift bed on hooks anchored in the tree and the exterior wall while weaving a second hammock for herself.

I stuffed my jeans and sweater inside my backpack and climbed onto the hammock. The bed swung wildly. I clutched the vines until we reached an understanding. The hammock gentled, and I relaxed, easing into the pillow and blankets. The vines felt surprisingly soft. I fingered one of the knots. "What kind of knot is this?"

"That is a trinity knot." She hung her bed a short distance from mine. "There are Celtic knots for all sorts of things, but I find this one soothing, especially when I sleep." She snuffed out the light and climbed into bed.

Moonlight painted the room blue. I remembered then, there were no windows or door, only the sheer netting protecting us from bugs. "I'm glad Diarmuid is standing guard."

Cha Cha fluffed her pillow. "No one with bad intentions can enter *Tír na nÓg*. The border may be crumbling, but it is still secure." She whispered under her breath. "For now."

I fought against my anxieties. "Why do we have a guard, then?"

She turned so she was facing me. "The warriors are extremely protective. That attack by the *Sidhe Sluagh* made them nervous, and... well... the *Chosen Ones* are important. Every *Sidhe* here would sacrifice his life to keep you safe."

I was about to ask another question when the goddess began to sing. I'm not sure how I knew it was the Goddess Danu singing, but I felt her presence in the song. There was something vaguely familiar, some elusive memory, tied to that song, but I couldn't pinpoint what it was. My lashes grew heavy. My anxieties eased. "Only sweet dreams," I whispered and drifted off to sleep.

* * *

A high-pitched chirp pierced my dreams. I bolted upright. The hammock tipped, dumping me onto the floor. "Ugh!"

My godmother leapt from her hammock with all the grace you'd expect from a faerie. "Madison! Are you okay?"

I checked my knees. "I'm fine." I sank back onto my bottom and stared at the bright purple bird perched on the edge of my hammock. He was eying me with interest. "Is that your idea of an alarm clock?"

Cha Cha laughed. "That's a violet-backed starling. He must have squeezed through the netting." She pressed a couple of berries into my hand. "They're very friendly. Watch. He'll eat from your hand."

The bird hopped down from the hammock. He plucked a blackberry from my hand, fluffed his wings, and settled in to eat. The contrast between those bright purple wings and his snow-white chest was rather startling. He was, hands down, the prettiest bird I'd ever seen.

Brigitte rapped on the wood framing the doorway. "I brought some clothes for Madison." She set the neatly folded garments and a pair of boots on the bench near the door. "We're meeting in the meadow for breakfast."

Cha Cha retrieved the clothes. "We'll be down shortly."

Brigitte's wings fluttered as she leapt from the deck. A fiddle, a flute, and a uilleann pipe sprang to life outside.

I set the remaining berries next to the bird, washed my hands and face in the basin, and changed into the new clothes. The green, bronze, and gold tunic fell in velvety soft folds over the comfortable leggings. A sleeveless duster added a layer of warmth. Brown knee length boots completed the ensemble, with laces crisscrossing down the front.

Cha Cha strapped two leather cuffs over my forearms. "These are bracers. They help protect your arms." She retrieved a wooden box from her dresser. "You should carry a knife with you at all times." She pulled a small dagger from the box and slid it into the bracer.

The Celtic design on the handle drew my fingers like a magnet. Raised, interlocking lines formed a pattern like the trinity knot Cha Cha used to tie the hammock, only this design had four sides, shaped like a shield. "What do we need knives for?"

She shrugged. "You never know."

My heart stuttered. "I don't know how to use a knife."

"Cathal or one of the other warriors will teach you." She slid a knife into her bracer before leading me out onto the deck. She peered over the edge. "*Maidin Mhaith.*"

"*Maidin Mhaith,*" Diarmuid greeted cheerily.

I'd heard that greeting enough in Dublin to know what it meant. I peeked over the edge. "Good morning, Diarmuid."

He grinned. "*Maidin Mhaith,* Grania. I trust you slept well."

I nodded, noticing he'd greeted me by my *Sidhe* name. "Yes, thank you."

Wings sprung from Cha Cha's back. "Why don't you go ahead and climb down? Diarmuid will hold the ladder at the bottom." She helped me scoot off the deck and turn around.

I felt my way down the ladder, rung by rung. Diarmuid backed away when I reached the lower rung. I turned and gaped at the meadow. Hundreds of *Sidhe* were milling about. Some were lounging on benches; others were eating at tables carved from fallen trees. My eyes widened. I hadn't realized the boulders I'd seen last night were stone ovens. A familiar scent beckoned me. "Is that… cinnamon?"

Diarmuid grinned. "Yes. They put cinnamon in the sweet potato bread."

Cha Cha dropped lightly onto the ground. She linked her arm in mine. "Are you ready to meet everyone?" She noted the panicked expression on my face. "Not *everyone*," she corrected, "just the *Sidhe* who live near the lake and the ones who traveled here to meet you."

"Um… that doesn't really narrow it down for me." I eyed the meadow nervously. "Why would they travel to meet me?"

"Because you're one of the *Chosen Ones*." She walked with all the confidence one would expect from a *Sidhe* guardian, who was totally in her element.

Dad and Cathal walked toward us. Dad was dressed like Cathal this morning, minus the wings. "Hungry?" He wrapped his arm around me.

"Yes. Very." I scanned the meadow until I found the table where Zoey and Skylar were sitting.

Cathal followed my gaze. "Good. There's a hearty nut bread, sweet potato bread, fresh fruit, and quiche." He strode toward their table. Dad, Cha Cha, and I followed him.

Skylar jumped up to give me a hug. "Madison! Isn't this amazing? Look at all these *Sidhe*!" She pulled me onto the bench. "The mushroom and spinach quiche is delicious."

Zoey moved from the other side of the table so she could sit beside me. "Do you like your clothes?"

I nodded. "They're really soft. The bracers feel weird, though." I glanced at Dad. He was sandwiched between Diarmuid and Cathal on the opposite side of the table. "They remind me of the clothes we used to see at the renaissance festival."

His eyes brightened. "Now that you mention it..."

One of the *Sidhe* I had yet to meet handed me a cup of juice. "Orange juice," she whispered. "I squeezed the oranges myself."

"Thank you." I returned her smile.

Dad spoke before I could ask her name. "I promised we would talk..."

Another *Sidhe* with bright orange hair set a plate filled with quiche, melons, and bread in front of me. "Welcome to *Tír na nÓg*."

"Thanks." I smiled.

Dad cleared his throat. "As I mentioned last night, I wasn't aware all this existed." His hand swept toward the waterfall and the treehouses. "I thought I was going to be working on Ireland's border with Northern Ireland, airport, and seaport security."

I nodded while sampling the quiche. Skylar was right. The eggs were delicious.

"*Tír na nÓg* came as a bit of a shock. I never would have believed this place existed if I hadn't seen it for myself." He shifted uncomfortably. "That's not the only thing that proved difficult to grasp. I learned something about my past."

I stopped eating. I'd never seen him look so nervous.

"If Cathal hadn't enlisted my help..." He shook his head. "The odds of ever learning..." He released a frustrated breath. "I would have gone my entire life without knowing." His hand raked over his head. "There is no sane explanation, so I'm just going to come out and say it. Madison, I'd like you to meet my father, Diarmuid."

My jaw fell slack. My gaze slid to the warrior on his right. I couldn't help but compare the two when they were sitting side by side. Aside from their broad shoulders and their height, they looked nothing alike. "But... you said you never knew your father. You didn't even know his name."

"I didn't." He released another breath. "Your grandmother couldn't remember. Whenever I pressed for more information, she'd get upset. Her lack of memory on this frustrated her to no end."

"That's my fault," Diarmuid confessed. "I had to scrub her memories when she left *Tír na nÓg*. I didn't know she was carrying my child." He sighed. "I didn't realize I had a child until your father arrived with Cathal. I sensed the connection the moment he arrived."

My eyes widened. "Grandma traveled here... to *Tír na nÓg*?" That didn't sound like my grandmother... at all.

He nodded. "We fell in love. I brought her to *Tír na nÓg* so I could reveal who I was. She was happy, or so I thought. She missed her family. I begged her to stay, but she missed her sisters too much."

Now, that sounded like Grandma. She and her sisters were very close. They lived in the same small community, within walking distance of one another. She'd never married another.

Dad captured and held my gaze. "I didn't believe Diarmuid at first. Still, something nagged at me, deep down inside... a part of me that sensed he was right. So, I went to

Ogham and ate the berries from my birth tree. The knowledge I gained through that fruit confirmed every claim he made about *Tír na nÓg,* my purpose, and my identity."

Tears pooled in my eyes. My father finally had his dad, the father he had longed for his entire life. "Dad…"

Skylar peeked at me from beneath her lashes while Zoey squeezed my hand.

"I am a *Sidhe* warrior." His skin frosted like glass. The clothing he wore faded, revealing that same beautiful armor worn by Diarmuid and Cathal. Huge, powerful wings sprung from his back.

I jerked violently, flailing as I fell back.

Cha Cha caught me before I hit the grass. "I got you." She eased me back onto my feet.

Dad stood, as did Diarmuid and Cathal.

They fell from my periphery when Cha Cha turned me. "I swear, Madison, I didn't know. It is difficult to sense *Sidhe* in the human realm, nearly impossible when their powers are dormant. I sensed this change in your father last night. When I reached out to him telepathically, he asked me to remain silent. He wanted to tell you, but he knew you needed rest."

Dad touched my arm. "Are you okay?"

"I don't know." I frowned. "My entire world has been turned upside down."

"Mine too." He pulled me into his arms. He waited until I relaxed and then kissed the top of my head. "Will you walk with me?"

I peered up at him. He was still my father, only stronger, and a bit more angelic looking. "Sure." We walked toward the trees.

He waited until we were out of earshot before he spoke again. "My purpose wasn't the only purpose revealed when I visited my birth tree."

I closed my eyes, took a deep breath, and slowly released it. "So, you know about the *Far Darrig*, the NICU, and the prophecy?"

He stopped walking. "What have you learned?"

I turned away. I couldn't bear to see the anguish on his face. "Cha Cha told me your daughter was very ill, that the *Far Darrig* switched us at birth. I'm sorry, Daddy." Tears streamed down my face. "I'm sorry you lost your little girl."

He walked around me, so we were standing face to face.

Did he see me or the daughter he had lost? I stood there, head bowed, while my tears spilled onto the ground.

He stepped closer, folding me in his arms. "Shh. Come now." He pressed my cheek to his chest and waited for me to calm.

My tears slowed, and the trembling stopped.

He stepped back, tipping my chin, so I could see the truth reflected in his eyes. "While a part of me grieves for the child I lost, I am so grateful for you, Madison. You were a gift that grew more precious with each passing day. I want you to know this revelation changes nothing for me. You are still my child, my daughter, in every sense of the word."

I nodded, sniffling softly. "Thank you, Daddy." I hadn't realized just how sick I'd felt, worrying he wouldn't feel the same way.

He tipped my chin a little higher. "Anything else?"

I nodded, unable to divert my gaze. "I'm worried about the prophecy. Cha Cha wouldn't tell me what it was. She said I had to visit my birth tree before we could discuss it."

He released my chin and the breath he'd been holding. "You should visit *Ogham* tomorrow. You cannot comprehend this until you do." He muttered then, under his breath. "I can barely comprehend it myself."

"What about Lexie and Mom?" Surely, that was more important than a trip to *Ogham*.

He resumed walking. "We have warriors scouring the entire country. Cathal and I will join them, just as soon as you return from *Ogham*."

I grabbed his arm. "I want to go with you. Please, Dad, I want to help look for them."

He scrubbed his face with his hand. "I don't want to be separated from you again, but you must remain here with Channa. You must train with the druids so you can help eliminate these threats."

Tears welled in my eyes. "Do you think they're still alive?"

He nodded.

I blinked, trying to clear my eyes. "Do you think their disappearance is connected to the prophecy?"

"I do." He smiled sadly. "I want you to know something." He stopped walking. "Regardless of what transpires with this prophecy, with your mom, or Lexie; you are still my daughter. Nothing will ever change that. Nothing will change my love for you."

My tears came rushing back.

He grasped my hands. "Families face their demons together. They fight for one another, and they love one another... no matter what." His arms swallowed me in a hug. "Now," His voice turned gruff, "no more talk of prophecies. You need to eat and regain some strength."

I brushed the tears from my cheeks.

Cathal held up his hand when we joined the other *Sidhe*. "Grania still needs to eat."

A collective groan sounded through the meadow.

Dad chuckled. "You may want to eat slow... or fast... depending on how anxious you are to meet everyone."

Diarmuid stood as we approached the table. "May I say something?" He wasn't looking at Dad, he was looking at me.

I tugged on my bracer nervously. "Yes, of course."

He knelt in front of me, like some angelic knight. "I fear that I have failed you, Grania. Please forgive me. I should have been there for you while you were growing up."

I answered with a hug. "You are in my life now, grandfather. For me, that is enough."

He stood with tears glistening in his eyes. "We have found one another, like two missing pieces from a broken heart. Now, we must find your sister and mom."

* * *

I stared at the massive oak tree. Bright orange and gold leaves formed a perfect half-circle that mirrored the rising sun. The trunk was wide, spanning six people at least. We walked a full circle around the tree. Dark brown acorns crunched beneath our feet. "This is the entrance?"

Diarmuid gazed reverently at the tree. "Yes. This sessile oak is the *daur*, or door, to *Ogham*." He tore his gaze from the tree. "You must treat the trees in *Ogham* with respect. These are our elders, the ancient guardians of the *Tuatha Dé Danann*."

Dad squeezed my hand. "Because each *Sidhe* is granted access only once, this is as far as your guardians, the other warriors, and I can go. You girls must journey into *Ogham* without us."

I pulled away, startled by the news. "You want us to enter this forest, in an entirely different realm, by ourselves?"

"You will be safe in *Ogham*," Cathal promised. "No harm can come to you while you are there. You will return to *Tír na nÓg* through this very same tree. We will wait here until you return."

"How do we know which tree to visit?" Zoey fidgeted with the copper ribbon adorning her waist. Our guardians had insisted we wear formal gowns and capes. Apparently, formal attire was required when visiting one's elders in *Ogham*.

"Your birth tree will beckon you." Ciara adjusted the hood on Zoey's cape so it covered her hair.

Cha Cha lifted my hood. She tucked a few wayward curls in before stepping back to admire her work. "Do not decline the fruit. You will learn our history and your purpose when you eat the fruit. The insight you gain will feel overwhelming, but the transfer of knowledge doesn't hurt."

Skylar looked as worried as I felt. "Do we need to say anything special... memorize any words?"

Brigitte fixed her cape. "You will be granted access when you touch the *daur* and say *'foras feasa.'* This announces your desire to seek knowledge. When you return, you will exit through this same *daur.* Repeat the phrase we spoke when we entered *Tír na nÓg* through the human realm. Do you remember those words?"

Skylar, Zoey, and I nodded. Those words had proven impossible to forget, just as Cha Cha had predicted.

Brigitte beamed at us. "Good. This won't take long, but you will feel tired afterwards. Return to this sessile oak when the transfer of knowledge is complete."

Zoey stepped forward and touched the tree. "*Foras feasa.*"

The center of the tree grew hazy. Zoey's hand disappeared, then her arm, her shoulder, waist, and legs.

I rushed forward, not wanting her to be alone in the other realm. My hand scraped against the bark. I'd forgotten to speak the words. "*Foras feasa.*" Suddenly, my hand slipped beyond the tree. The trunk was no longer there, just the image of a tree. I stepped forward and collided with Zoey.

Skylar entered right behind me. We hugged one another before studying our surroundings. *Tír na nÓg* was no longer visible. Our guardians, Cathal, Diarmuid, and Dad were gone. The air was still. Silence hung heavy, like the entire world was waiting for something. Despite my anxieties, I didn't feel afraid. I felt oddly at peace.

"Where's the sun?" Skylar whispered. While it had been early morning in *Tír na nÓg*, it appeared to be gloaming, or dusk, in *Ogham*.

I followed her gaze. There was no moon or sun. Fireflies hovered in the mist that swirled beneath our knees. They appeared to be the only source of light. Ten massive trees formed a circle around us; along with ivy, a thick patch of reeds, and a cluster of vines. The oak tree stood directly behind us.

The fireflies gathered in the center, forming a living, breathing globe that brightened the grove. They unfurled in a glittering stream that wrapped around Skylar's legs, her stomach, chest, and head. They repeated this same circular dance around Zoey before swirling around me. They didn't touch me, but it seemed they were getting to know me. They raced around my ankles, my knees, hips, shoulders, and head before unraveling. They danced among the reeds, along the vines, and each tendril of ivy before circling the ancient trees.

We stood and watched, breathlessly.

The fireflies settled in a tree with a thin trunk and fern-like leaves. "Maolisa, Grania, and Niamh; kindred spirits forged from the Rowan Tree."

I wasn't sure if those words were spoken aloud or if they were spoken inside me. I felt more than heard them. I longed to sit beneath that glittering tree. I peeked at Skylar and Zoey. Silently, we agreed. We walked across the clearing and stood before the tree.

"What is it you seek?" the Rowan Tree queried.

"Knowledge," Zoey answered.

"An understanding of *Ogham, Tír na nÓg,* and the *Sidhe,*" Skylar added.

"My family, the prophecy, and my purpose," I whispered.

"Sit beside me."

I sank to my knees. Skylar and Zoey sat beside me. The ground was neither soft nor hard. In fact, it felt as if there were no ground at all. I wondered what, if anything, lie beneath the mist blanketing the trees.

"I will grant your request, but you must promise something in return," the ancient tree warned.

Skylar stilled. "What sort of promise?"

The fireflies doused their lights so that only a few twinkled within the tree's branches. "You must promise to fulfill your purpose."

"I can only fulfill this purpose if it is consistent with my faith," Zoey stated.

I nodded. I felt the same way.

"I do not establish your purpose. I merely reveal it." The leaves in the tree rustled softly. "Our Father established your purpose and mine long before we were born."

Zoey looked visibly relieved. "I promise to fulfill the purpose God intended for me."

I fixed my eyes on the tree. "I promise to fulfill my purpose."

"As do I," Skylar added. "I will try my best. I promise."

"That is all I ask." Three dark red berries appeared in our

hands. "This fruit will further your knowledge and reveal the purpose for which you were born."

I stared at the fruit. The berries should weigh nothing, and yet... I felt the weight of the entire world in my hand... every person, every animal, and plant. I looked at Skylar and Zoey.

Slowly, Zoey nodded.

Together we slid the firm berries inside our mouths and bit down. The bitter taste puckered my face. I could feel it in my jaw.

The fireflies began to glow. They flew around the branches and leaves... down the trunk... around Zoey, Skylar, and me. They flew faster and faster. My vision blurred. I could no longer sense anything around me. They surged with a sudden burst of energy. We fell forward, our hands colliding with the tree. Thin strands of green, gold, and blue light traveled beneath us, through the mist, along the roots of the ancient tree. Three strands twisted around the trunk of the tree. The blue strand claimed Skylar, the green strand claimed Zoey, and the gold strand claimed me. Our hands remained cemented to the tree.

Images flashed before me; spanning past, present, and future. I knew where the *Sidhe* originated from, the power they possessed, how connected they... no... *we* were to one another, to *Ogham*, *Tír na nÓg*, and God. I started crying. I could see Lexie and Mom. I knew who had them. I knew *why* they had them. I knew my purpose. I knew what God intended for me. The knowledge imbedded within that light raced through my blood, settling deep inside of me.

* * *

The fireflies scattered beneath the mist. The three strands of light disappeared inside of us. *Ogham* returned to its original state, so it appeared to be dusk. Our tears and ragged breathing sounded against the trees. Absorbing centuries of knowledge wasn't painful, but it wasn't easy either. I couldn't possibly comprehend it all. Still, the knowledge hummed inside me, waiting to be called upon.

That knowledge changed us. I could see now that Skylar was Niamh, an air spirit with sky-blue eyes and iridescent wings. Her skin shone bright, which seemed only fitting for a *Sidhe* who would replace darkness and despair with hope and light.

I studied Zoey, who was quite obviously Maolisa, a water spirit with dewy skin and shimmering wings. Her bright green eyes glowed like the water in a baptismal font, destined to build faith.

"Grania, your eyes," Maolisa marveled in a hushed tone. "They're like liquid gold."

I peered over my shoulder. The thin filigree wings the Rowan Tree had gifted me glittered like gold dust. I was a wood spirit, like Fianna. *How could I call her Cha Cha? That name was merely a cloak, concealing who she really was.* My purpose was equally clear. I would quell violence with kindness and love.

Niamh's chin quivered. "How… how can we possibly succeed? We're only twelve, and they… they're grown men." She was referring to Dain, Dother, and Dub.

Maolisa frowned. "Men filled with hate."

"All that violence and war." I shuddered. The human realm was imploding. Everyone was so angry. Dain, Dother, and Dub were preying on humans, fueling this anger, encouraging violence so they could reign. The human realm was a dark and dangerous place. *Tír na nÓg* was safe for now, but not for long. The border was crumbling, weakened by the Goddess Carman's sons.

"Heed your promise," the Rowan Tree said. "The fate of all the realms lies in the balance."

Niamh nodded. "Thankfully, we will not face these men alone."

She was building hope. Something inside of me clicked. Suddenly, I understood. Hope required effort; it was something you worked on, just like faith and love.

Maolisa stood and offered me her hand. "We're going to save your sister and your mom."

We knew where they were now. This was one of many nuggets of knowledge imparted by the Rowan Tree. They were suspended above Devil's Punch Bowl in a deep, trance-like sleep. The Goddess Carman's sons were using them as bait. They were trying to lure us there so they could destroy us. If they succeeded, the border would fall, they'd enslave the *Sidhe*, and evil would reign in all the realms.

I gladly accepted her hand. I wasn't sure how to proceed, so I dropped into a deep curtsy in front of the Rowan Tree. "Thank you."

"*Go n-éirí an bóthar leat,*" he replied.

The words shifted into English inside my mind. "May the road succeed with you." I smiled. "And also with you."

The fireflies blinked their farewell while we walked through the mist to the Sessile Oak Tree. I turned so I could admire *Ogham* one last time. If the *Sidhe* were permitted to enter only once, I wanted to commit this place to memory so I could return, at least inside my mind.

Niamh's fingers brushed against the old oak tree. "*Tír na nÓg, Draíocht Dúchas, Taisce Baile.*" She glanced at Maolisa and me before stepping wearily through the tree.

Maolisa squeezed my hand before touching the tree. "*Tír na nÓg, Draíocht Dúchas, Taisce Baile.*" She stepped forward and disappeared completely.

My hand pressed against the tree.

"Grania." The concern in the Rowan Tree's tone fell like a heavy weight in the silent grove.

"Yes?" I turned and leaned against the Sessile Oak Tree.

The silence yawned between us.

"Would you sacrifice your life for those you love?"

My heart skipped a couple of beats. "If I must."

He bowed ever so slightly. "Then you will succeed."

Tears slid silently down my cheeks. I turned on trembling knees to face the Sessile Oak Tree. "*Tír na nÓg, Draíocht Dúchas, Taisce Baile.*" I stepped forward. Darkness descended as the weight of the world came crashing down on me.

CHAPTER 5 - THE DRUIDS AND THE GODDESS

"**C**heep!"

I smiled. My eyes fluttered open and then widened. I gaped at the violet-backed starling. His feathers were so much brighter than I remembered, and his face looked more defined. I blinked a couple of times. Everything in the room seemed brighter and sharper, like I'd been peering through dirty glasses my entire life. "How long have I been asleep?"

Fianna handed me a glass of water. "Three days. Are you hungry?"

"Very." I sat up in the hammock. I was still marveling at how crisp and clear everything appeared. Fianna had the most beautiful lashes. There were so many colors in her hair, and her skin glowed. I thought it only glowed when she was speaking to the Goddess Danu. Speaking of which, my skin was glowing too. I should have toppled to the floor, but I didn't. The Rowan Tree had strengthened my vision and my coordination. The old me would have fallen flat on her face by now.

Fianna sat beside me. "Your father left with a fresh contingent of warriors. They're on their way to Mangerton Mountain. The Goddess Danu won't allow them to confront Dain, Dother, and Dub. According to the prophecy, the *Chosen Ones* are the only *Sidhe* who can triumph over them."

I guzzled the water, suddenly parched. "Why did they go, then?" I felt the loss of my father deeply. We'd finally found him, and now he was gone. Again.

She walked into the kitchen. "They're gathering information. They'll follow discreetly if they move your family, but they won't intervene unless their lives are threatened."

I stood and fell to my knees. So much for that improved coordination. "Why am I so weak?"

She set a savory smelling stew, a basket full of bread, and a bowl filled with berries on the table. "Three days without eating will do that to you." She helped me to my feet.

I sank into the chair she pulled out for me. "I can't believe I slept that long."

She sat beside me. "Our bodies absorb the knowledge we gain from *Ogham* more efficiently when we're asleep. It's difficult to absorb that knowledge when we're awake, and the transfer of such an immense amount of knowledge can be exhausting."

I dipped my bread into the stew. "I remember collapsing outside the Sessile Oak Tree." I'd felt so fatigued my legs refused to work. My father carried me back to Fianna's house. I resisted at first. I hadn't realized a warrior's wings were strong enough to support two people. I revealed what I learned about Mom and Lexie before succumbing to sleep. I sensed that's what he'd been waiting for all along. "Are Maolisa and Niamh awake?"

"Maolisa woke this morning. Niamh is still asleep." She retrieved the pitcher from the counter but stopped abruptly. She chuckled softly. "Scratch that. Niamh is awake."

I stared, thoroughly fascinated. "How do you do that?"

She refilled my glass. "Communicate telepathically?"

I nodded while shoveling food inside my mouth.

Fianna smiled. "You can do that now. You just need to open your mind."

I swallowed. Hard. "Really? How?"

She set the pitcher on the table. "Close your eyes and picture a wall inside your head." She slipped quietly onto her chair.

I closed my eyes. Gradually, a stone wall appeared.

"Now, search for the door."

My fingers trailed along the rough stone until I found a heavy wooden door. "Okay."

"Slide the bolt and open the door."

Metal scraped against metal as the bolt escaped the lock. The door creaked open. Hundreds of voices sounded at once. I scrambled out of my chair. "Make it stop!"

Fianna snagged my hand. "Give it a minute. Those conversations will sort themselves out."

Some of the voices faded. "What are the brightly colored threads for?" They swirled in the back of my mind.

"Each thread leads to another *Sidhe*. When you brush against them, you will sense who each thread belongs to. Find Brigitte's thread," she encouraged.

I called back the hand I'd pictured inside my head so I could sift through the threads. I narrowed in on a thread when I felt Brigitte's presence. "Brigitte's thread is blue."

She nodded. "That's because she's an air spirit. Ask Brigitte how Niamh is doing, silently, inside your head."

I touched the blue thread. "Hi, Brigitte. How is Niamh?" I thought more than spoke the words.

I could feel Brigitte's smile. "Hi, Grania. Niamh is well. I'm fixing her something to eat." She sounded happy and relieved.

My eyes flew to Fianna's. "That's so cool!" I dropped back into my chair and resumed eating with one ear tuned to the conversations inside my head. "Can you speak to more than one person?"

"Yes." She pulled a mug and a tin filled with tea from the cupboard. "When you want to speak with specific individuals, you pull on their threads. If you want to share information or pose a question to all the *Sidhe*, then you simply make that announcement so it travels down every thread."

I nodded, tucking that information away for later. "Brigitte and Ciara used their real names in the human realm. Why did you choose a different name?"

Fianna filled the mug with water. "Brigitte and Ciara's names are fairly common in the human realm. My name is more unique. I was concerned someone might find you by searching for me, so I chose a different name." Her hand hovered over the mug. Steam slipped between her fingers. The water inside the mug churned. She filled a mesh ball with tea leaves and dropped it into the mug.

My eyes lit with excitement. "Can I do that?"

"Yes, of course." She grabbed another mug and filled it with water. "Place your hand two or three inches above the water." She waited for me to comply. "Feel the wood beneath your feet. Can you feel where that wood connects to the tree?"

I nodded.

"Good. Now, follow the tree down through the roots and into the ground. Do you feel the heat?"

"Yes," I answered breathlessly.

"Draw on the Earth's heat, pull it back through the roots, through the tree, the wood floor, your feet, legs, and arm. Now, push it out, into the water."

I pulled the heat inside of me and shoved it out through the palm of my hand. The water bubbled over, drenching the table. "Woah!" I jumped back.

She leapt to her feet. "Not all at once!"

"Fianna," a voice chided from the doorway. "You are a guardian, not a druidess."

My godmother froze.

I turned so I could see the newcomer.

His amethyst eyes danced with humor. Two long braids fell just behind his ears, framing a glossy sheet of pale blond hair. His shoulders and wings were broad, not as broad as the warriors' wings, but power rolled off him nonetheless. "Are you ready to begin training?"

"She just woke up." Fianna huffed out a breath when she turned to face him. "Kane is one of the druids you'll be training with."

"Oh. Hi." I wasn't sure what the protocol was, so I stepped closer and extended my hand.

He appeared somewhat amused when he shook my hand. "I look forward to working with you." He dipped his head politely, stepped past me, and pressed a kiss to Fianna's cheek. "Training will commence in thirty minutes."

Something unspoken passed between them. I studied Kane with renewed interest. Fianna was blushing. Was she smitten with him?

He winked at me before he left. "There is a training arena at the far end of the meadow. I'll meet you there in thirty minutes."

My godmother busied herself with the dishes.

I stared at the empty doorway. Slowly, my gaze shifted to Fianna. "You like him."

Her eyes narrowed as she turned to face me. "How old are you?"

I tried not to laugh. "I'm twelve."

She snorted softly. "More like a hundred and twelve."

* * *

I sprinted across the meadow. "Maolisa! Niamh!" We collided in a hug, forming a knot of elbows and arms.

Maolisa grasped my hands. "Did you talk to your dad? Have they arrived at Devil's Punch Bowl yet?"

116

I glanced at Diarmuid. He and a handful of other warriors were serving as our security detail. "They're on their way to Mangerton Mountain. They're not flying, they're walking so they can sneak in undetected. They're going to monitor the situation, gather some information, and make sure my family isn't moved before we get there."

"You spoke telepathically?" Niamh linked her arm in mine as we strolled across the meadow.

I nodded, secretly pleased. "Sure beats cell phones."

Maolisa giggled. "And we don't have to worry about poor reception, dropped calls, or cell phone bills that eat up our entire allowance."

Diarmuid smiled. Niamh and I laughed.

Kane was supposed to meet us at the far end of the meadow. We were nearly there, but I had yet to spot anything that even remotely resembled a training arena. The only objects I could see were flowers, rocks, and trees.

Long, tender blades of grass brushed against my ankles. I glanced at the ground. By the time my head lifted, everything had changed. "Woah!" I backed up, looked around, and waved my hand through the air. I felt nothing. Once again, the only objects I could see were flowers and trees. The view in front of me changed the second I stepped forward.

Niamh turned slowly while studying our surroundings. "It's like we've crossed over into another world."

Kane strode across the dark, spongey soil. "We cast an illusion concealing this part of the meadow to ensure our privacy while we train." The flowers and trees had been re-

placed with an expanse of soil and four large boulders positioned directly across from one another.

Maolisa peered at the *Sidhe* conversing by the lake. "So,
we can see them, but they can't see us?"

"Precisely." Kane motioned toward the *Sidhe* who were
training in the center of the arena. "Are you ready to spar?"

"Sp... spar?" I stammered. There were several *Sidhe* hurling blue, green, and gold masses of energy at one another.
One screamed in frustration when she was struck in the
chest. She fell back onto her bottom. I looked to my grandfather for some guidance, but he was already strolling toward
the spectator seats, along with the other warriors.

Another *Sidhe* joined us. He looked like Kane, only
younger. He had long blond hair, which he wore straight
with a single braid framing either side of his face. His eyes
were that same unearthly shade of purple, and he exuded
the same air of confidence that surrounded Kane. "Hi, I'm
Cian. We're strengthening our self-defense skills." His head
tilted while he studied our faces. "Do you know how to coax
your power?"

"No." Maolisa shook her head.

"Sort of," I admitted nervously.

Niamh gaped at me.

Cian nodded. "Explain."

"Well," I began warily. "You draw on the Earth's energy,
pulling it through the soil and trees until your hands warm."

"*You* pull through the soil and trees," Kane corrected.
"You are a wood spirit, so your power is tied to the trees.
Because Niamh is an air spirit, she'll draw her power from

wind and air. Maolisa is a water spirit, so she draws power from water." He locked eyes with her. "It doesn't have to be a large body of water. You can draw power from rivers and springs, snow, fog, dew drops, and even condensation that has formed on a drinking glass."

Cian's eyes snagged on a *Sidhe* whose swirling mass of energy had grown substantially. "Pull it back inside you! You'll pass out if you expel all that energy at once!"

The wiry boy shook as he pulled the green light back through his fingertips. The swirling mass shrunk, but only a little.

"Excuse me." Cian hurried toward him.

Kane cleared his throat. "Okay, let's practice. Niamh, feel the air around you; draw it in through your mouth, nose, and skin. Maolisa, feel the moisture in the air and in the soil beneath you. There are rivers and springs hidden beneath us. Feel the mist from the waterfall and the lake behind you. Breathe that moisture in; feel it on your skin."

The air around Niamh rippled, sort of like a heat wave.

Dew drops shimmered on Maolisa's skin.

Kane turned, focusing on me. "Grania, draw the Earth's energy from the soil and trees. Gather that energy inside your chest, force it down through your arms, and release it through your fingertips. Shape it into a ball, cupping your hands like this." He positioned his hands so it appeared as if he were holding an invisible ball.

I closed my eyes so I could focus.

Kane's voice traveled while he walked between us. "Will the energy to appear right between your hands. You've drawn this energy inside of you. Now that it's a part of you, you can control it. You can tell it what to do with a simple thought. You don't have to speak any words. Good! Now, try to balance that energy between your hands."

I opened my eyes, anxious to see what he was excited about. Maolisa and Niamh were cradling green and blue masses of energy in the palm of their hands.

"Nice." I smiled, feeling happy for them. I closed my eyes and tried again. I could feel the energy pulsing beneath my feet, shimmering in the soil and trees, but I couldn't pull it inside of me. I released a frustrated breath.

"Grania," Kane whispered inside my head. "I know you're concerned about what happened with the tea. You're worried you might release too much energy and hurt your friends. I want you to focus on how this might help them… how mastering this skill will help the *Sidhe* and your family."

I took a deep breath, focused on how I wanted to help them, and searched for the energy again. The hair on my arms and scalp lifted. Suddenly, a gold light burst between my fingertips. I squealed excitedly. The energy felt warm and tingly, like static electricity.

Kane nodded his approval. "Okay, move the energy between your hands, like this." A purple light burst between his fingertips. He tossed it around like a ball.

I rolled the energy in my hands, trying to get a feel for it. "Why is your energy purple?" The other *Sidhe* wielded green, gold, or blue energy.

He smiled as if he got that question a lot. "Druids are air, water, and wood spirits all rolled into one. We draw energy from all three sources. Add a little extra magick and voila! Purple energy."

Niamh tossed her ball a little higher. "Do all druids have purple energy?"

He nodded.

Maolisa studied the energy swirling in her hands. "What about the Goddess Danu?"

Admiration shone in his eyes. "Her energy is white."

We played with the energy for a while; tossing it around, coaxing different amounts, and pulling it back inside of us.

Cian returned. "It looks like you are read to spar. I'm going to ask the other students to practice their concealing spells so you'll have the arena to yourselves. You'll join the rest of the class tomorrow."

We followed Kane into the center of the arena, juggling swirling balls of energy while the other students filed out. I looked around. "Why is my skin tingling?"

Kane nodded, acknowledging the observation. "That's the magick, or energy signature, left behind by the other *Sidhe*. I want you to remember how that feels. When your skin tingles like that, it's a sign that someone around you is using light or white magick. White magick is used selflessly and exclusively for good. Dark or black magick will make your skin crawl. You may feel nauseous, depending on the amount of magick being expelled. You won't always see the person using magick, but you will feel him."

We were listening so intently, we stopped juggling our energy.

Kane paced in front of us. He didn't appear worried, just immersed in his thoughts. "When you spar inside this arena, you won't feel pain. You will grow increasingly tired due to the energy you expend. When an energy mass strikes you, it will wear you down even more. If you are hit enough times, you'll become temporarily disabled." He nodded toward the boulders. "Those stones mark the perimeter of our arena. Outside this arena, you will feel pain when another *Sidhe's* energy strikes you. If struck enough times, you could die, so you should avoid being struck at all costs."

Niamh's face sheeted white.

"When your energy collides with another mass of energy, it disintegrates without causing any harm. I'll teach you how to use your energy as a shield, shaping it in a way that protects you. We'll practice forming shields, throwing, and intercepting energy over the next few days." He studied the expressions on our faces. "Ready?"

A wary nod was all I could muster.

He smiled, as if sensing how tempted we were to hide behind those rocks. "Let's begin. Grania, you stay there." He walked a short distance away. "Maolisa, here... and Niamh over here." He walked several feet from Niamh's spot before stopping. "Maolisa can spar with Niamh. I'll spar with Grania. We'll switch partners in a few minutes so each of you has an opportunity to spar with the other."

I forced myself to meet his expectant gaze. I swallowed nervously.

"You can't hurt me." He stood there, waiting for me to throw the first punch... or energy mass. A smile tugged at his cheeks. "If it makes you feel better, you can aim at my feet."

I lobbed the ball... and missed.

He chuckled softly. "You can do better than that."

In my defense, I was trying to miss.

Diarmuid's voice sounded inside my head. "You must lead by example."

Maolisa and Niamh were watching me. Neither had lobbed any energy.

I knew then, that intentional miss didn't help me, my family, or friends. "Did my father tell you to say that?" He'd offered that same instruction countless times.

Diarmuid smiled.

Kane's gaze slid between the two of us.

I was pretty sure we hadn't spoken aloud. I sucked in a breath and committed myself to the task. I drew more energy and pushed it out into my hands.

"Picture someone you don't like," Kane suggested.

I tried to picture the Goddess Carman's sons, but I didn't know what they looked like.

"Is there no one you dislike?" He looked surprised.

There were very few people I disliked. I settled, finally, on visualizing a bully from school. I looked at Kane, pictured the bully's face, and threw. Hard.

He stumbled back. I'd struck him right smack in the center of his face. Suddenly, he laughed. "That was perfect."

Maolisa and Niamh burst out laughing.

I grinned at them. "It helps if you picture a bully inside your head."

Kane struck me while I was talking to them. "Your enemy won't wait while you compare notes with your friends."

The impact left me feeling dazed. He was right, though. I didn't feel any pain. "Oh. That's it. Game on." I drew energy and threw it rapid fire.

Kane intercepted most of my energy. Still, I managed to sneak in a few solid hits. Intercepting his energy proved difficult, but it was far more rewarding. I weighed the level of difficulty and created a point system inside my head. One point for striking Kane. Five points for disintegrating energy balls. And, yes, that part of me that likes to win was definitely keeping score.

Our sparring session quickly devolved into a free for all where Kane was the primary target. Fighting alongside Maolisa and Niamh felt natural. We learned early on to strategize inside our heads, instead of announcing our moves aloud. Communicating telepathically was my new favorite superpower.

"That's enough," Kane finally announced. "I want you to save some energy for tomorrow."

"Thank God." Maolisa rubbed her shoulders and arms.

I took a couple of deep breaths, trying to slow my breathing enough so I could talk. "Thank you for working with us."

"Of course. It was my pleasure." He strode toward us. "You girls work well together."

"They do," Cian agreed. "Like three halves of a whole." He joined us in the center of the arena.

I fought the urge to correct his math and lost. "Three halves would make more than a whole."

"My point precisely." He winked.

"They strategize like warriors," Diarmuid boasted.

"Or druids," Kane mused.

I smiled, buoyed by the compliments.

We walked past the boulders, retracing our earlier steps. "What's on the agenda for tomorrow?"

Cian grinned. "Your first flying lesson."

"Flying?" Niamh gaped at him then tore off toward her guardian. "Brigitte! Guess What!"

Diarmuid chuckled, amused by her excitement. He nodded at one of the warriors, silently encouraging him to follow her. "You did good today."

I slipped my hand in the crook of his arm. "Thanks for the advice."

He patted my hand. "Anytime."

I smiled up at him. "You and Dad... you think a lot alike."

"I'm happy to hear that." Pride shone in his eyes.

I waved at Fianna. She was sitting across from Ciara at the table near the lake.

Diarmuid stopped walking. "Are you hungry?" The scent of warm bread wafted from the stone ovens on our right.

My stomach grumbled. "Yes," I laughed. "Starving."

He strode toward a table displaying several loaves of bread.

I followed the others, anxious to speak with Fianna.

She patted the bench. "How did it go?"

"Good, I think." I sat down beside her.

Kane chuckled. "I suspect she'll be throwing energy in her sleep."

She turned to consider her tree house before looking at me. "Maybe we should sleep outside then."

Everyone laughed.

Brigitte arrived with a pitcher of water.

Niamh trailed behind with a stack of mugs. "I'm parched." She plopped the mugs in front of us.

Brigitte filled the mugs. "I checked in with the cook. I'm sorry girls, but dinner is going to be awhile."

Diarmuid set a clay bowl heaped with bread on the table. "Maybe this will help."

"Thank you." Maolisa leaned over and admired the bread. We laughed when our hands landed on the very same piece.

I chose a different piece, tore a chunk, and shoved it in my mouth. "Oh. Wow." The bread was still warm.

Niamh guzzled her water. She grabbed a piece of bread and settled in next to Brigitte. "I can't believe we're flying tomorrow. I'm so excited. I doubt I'll be able to sleep."

"Can we get hurt?" Maolisa asked. "I mean, what if we crash into a tree?"

"You can be injured," Kane admitted, "but you'll heal quickly. Your birth tree strengthens your energy, your integrity, and health."

"No wonder my vision is so much better." Everything appeared sharper, more clearly defined. I could see every blade of grass, every dewdrop, leaf, and flower petal... and the colors... I'm pretty sure there were colors I'd never even seen before... shades of blue, purple, and green that never even registered in my brain before visiting *Ogham*. And the light... light danced on everything.

A warrior stumbled breathlessly through the trees. "The *Sidhe Sluagh*! They're invading *Tír na nÓg*!"

"What?" Diarmuid strode toward him angrily. "How can that be?"

Another warrior joined them. "Why would they even attempt such a thing?"

A brilliant flash of light burst in front of them. They stumbled back dazedly.

A woman appeared as the light receded. A dark purple gown fell in elegant folds all the way to her toes. A stunning display of copper and gold hair skimmed her narrow waist. What little skin she had exposed glowed brighter than all the other *Sidhe*. Her eyes were gold but a shade darker than mine. Her delicate face radiated so much love, compassion, and grace, tears welled in my eyes.

Despite all the noise and chaos surrounding me, I couldn't move. All I could do was sit there and stare at the Goddess Danu.

Her eyes locked on Diarmuid. "You must drive the *Sidhe Sluagh* back into the human realm. Take as many warriors as you need."

Grandpa spoke inside my head while a contingent of warriors gathered around him. "Do as the goddess says."

His command was infused with enough power to force my attention away from the Goddess Danu. My eyes sought his. "Be safe." I latched onto Fianna's hand, finally grasping the danger we were in.

Several warriors joined Diarmuid as he sprinted toward the forest. Some swept into the air while unfurling their massive wings. Those who remained drew their swords. They pushed their way through the crowd that had gathered around us, intent on forming some sort of perimeter.

The goddess looked at Kane, who was already standing before her. "Go to the border. As soon as the *Sidhe Sluagh* are through the portal, seal it. Completely."

Brigitte stood. "But the other *Sidhe* and our warriors on Mangerton Mountain, they'll be stuck inside the human realm."

Her chin lifted, regally. "You will be joining them soon enough. Those remaining, conceal everything. I don't want the *Sidhe Sluagh* reporting our location to anyone. Join me inside the palace when you're done. Grania, Maolisa, and Niamh, come with me."

Suddenly, neither druid was standing there. Two golden eagles emerged in their place, their wings straining toward the sky.

"Go," Fianna urged. "You'll be safe with the Goddess Danu. We'll meet you inside the palace as soon as we're done."

I untangled my feet from the bench, latched onto Maolisa and Niamh's arms, and hurried forward on the verge of tears. The goddess pulled us into her arms. A piercing light stole my sight. The ground fell from beneath my feet. Darkness descended. There was another flash of light, and the ground reappeared.

The goddess waited until we regained our balance and then gently released us.

I blinked a few times. My eyes wouldn't focus with all the sudden changes in light.

"Where are we?" Niamh whispered.

A soft gasp sounded.

We spun around.

A *Sidhe* with pale blond hair stood near the waterfall. He bowed.

I tried to reconcile the image against the sound. The cascading falls sounded soft and melodious, not at all like you'd expect when standing this close to a waterfall. Somehow, someone had turned the volume down.

"Bevyn," the goddess acknowledged softly. "The *Sidhe* will eat and sleep inside the palace tonight. Please ensure the staff are notified."

He nodded, straightening to his full height, and then slipped silently from the room.

The goddess walked, as if immersed in thought, toward an amethyst wall. The wall was stunning, arguably an art piece, boasting endless shades of purple... everything from the palest lavender to a purple so dark it appeared nearly black. Snow-white clouds swirled throughout the highly polished stone while stark white veins hinted at hidden images like constellations.

With wide-eyed wonder, I studied my surroundings. That same amethyst stone formed every wall, the ceiling, and floor. Jagged white crystals served as wall sconces throughout the great hall. Clear, faceted chandeliers fell from a ceiling so high I could barely see it. I counted twelve balconied floors. White-washed tree roots twined together to form a decorative but protective railing for the rooms and passageways overlooking the great hall. That same wood formed benches, tables, and chairs throughout the main floor. There were several sitting areas anchored around plush white rugs. A luminous pond glistened beneath the waterfall, and an honest to goodness throne perched on a dais by the far wall.

"We should be celebrating your arrival in *Tír na nÓg.*" The goddess's voice was tinged with regret. "Sadly, we find ourselves dangling on the edge of war with dark magick threatening the border between the realms. We must accelerate your training."

Niamh stepped closer. "How are we supposed to fight the Goddess Carman's sons? What can three twelve-year-old girls do that the warriors cannot?"

"Our warriors possess tactical skills and strength, which enables them to fight, but violence only begets more violence. You cannot extinguish evil through wit and brawn alone; and our warriors do not possess the light or the hope needed to overcome the darkness that has descended on the human realm." Her hand swept gracefully across the wall.

Several images flickered on the wall, each worse than the last, like a news feed and a horror film all rolled into one… beatings, bombings, shootings, stabbings, torture, and war… men, women, and children fleeing cities all over the world. Their desperate pleas nearly sent me to my knees.

Her hand swept across the wall. The images and the sounds faded, then disappeared completely. She turned and walked across the crystal bridge. We followed her, barely registering its beauty.

Bevyn placed a basket of bread, some apples, nuts, and cheese on an elegant stone table. "The main course will be ready shortly." He walked with great purpose toward the wood door at the far end of the room.

I eyed the food uncertainly. Those images had left me feeling queasy.

The goddess sank into the chair at the head of the table. "Please eat. You need your strength."

I perched on the chair to her right. Maolisa and Niamh sat across from me. We filled our plates while waiting for the goddess to speak. The silence stretched beyond what any of us expected. Quietly, we began to eat.

Bevyn returned, balancing a tray. He moved soundlessly, depositing a mug of tea and a bowl of stew in front of each of us.

"Thank you." The goddess blew the steam from her mug

and braved a cautious sip. The tension eased from her shoulders and the room.

Bevyn bowed politely. He took a step back and then stood there, still as could be, while quietly assessing our needs.

I dipped my bread in the hearty stew, my thoughts still tangled in the images I'd seen. With a weary sigh I acknowledged I'd led a sheltered life. My parents had done all they could to protect me from the violence and despair darkening our world. I wondered how it had gotten to be so bad. Had it always been this way or was it getting worse?

The goddess spoke while still cradling her tea. "You... Grania, Maolisa, and Niamh... are the *Chosen Ones.* You serve as a counterbalance to the Goddess Carman's sons." Her eyes met mine. "Dain is violence. Love ends all thoughts... all desire... for violence. When you love someone, you do not wish to see him harmed. Grania, you are love. Dain cannot spark violence when you inspire love."

I nodded. Her explanation made sense, although I was uncertain how I might accomplish that.

She turned to Maolisa. "Dother is evil. Evil is extinguished through faith... faith in God... faith in our people... faith in one another... and faith in oneself. Maolisa, you are faith. You must believe in yourself, lead by example, and strengthen the faith of those around you."

"Build a shield of faith with which we can extinguish all the flaming arrows of the evil one," Maolisa murmured. "That's in Ephesians."

Goddess Danu smiled. She set her tea aside, then looked

at Niamh. "Dub is darkness. Darkness cannot exist in light. Niamh, you are light. You will not fight the way they fight. You will not fight the way our warriors fight. You will eliminate darkness with light."

"Light from the energy in my hands?" Niamh asked.

The goddess laughed. "No, although I can understand why you would think that. Light is a metaphor for hope. You, my sweet child, will offer hope when there is none."

Maolisa gasped. "Faith, hope, and love."

"Faith… hope… and love," the goddess confirmed, acknowledging each of us in turn.

The door burst open at the far end of the room. Diarmuid strode forward with several warriors. They stopped a few feet away from the goddess and bowed, which made me wonder… should I be bowing too? "The *Sidhe Sluagh* have been forced back through the portal into the human realm. The druids have sealed the portal."

Her thoughts turned inward, like she was testing the veracity of that statement. "Thank you, Diarmuid. I no longer sense their restless spirits in *Tír na nÓg.* It would appear you have expelled them all."

Cian, Kane, Fianna, Brigitte, and Ciara hurried into the room. They stopped abruptly. The men bowed while the women curtseyed. "Our village has been concealed."

She nodded, thoughtfully.

Diarmuid stepped forward. "Should we remain inside the palace? The threat has been removed."

She frowned. "I would like to keep my children close for now. A dark magick still coats that portal. That magick will continue to eat away at the protective spells Cian and Kane cast on the border. We cannot be certain how long those protective spells will hold."

"We will return to the portal to assess the damage and reinforce those spells in the morning," Cian promised.

Diarmuid turned to the warriors on his right. "Relieve the warriors standing guard outside the palace at midnight. Everyone else will remain inside until Cian and Kane report back in the morning."

The goddess nodded her approval. "Please, make yourselves comfortable."

Our guardians, the druids, and several warriors joined us at the table.

"I'll bring more food." Bevyn hurried from the room.

Several *Sidhe* filed through the heavy wood doors on either side of the room. Some emerged from the pond, water spirits I presumed. They lounged near the waterfall and along the edge of the luminous pool. Some gathered in the sitting areas while others flew to the balconies overlooking the great hall.

The musicians began to play; a tin whistle, a mandolin, and uilleann pipes. My thoughts drifted to the pub where I first heard these instruments with Lexie and Mom. My eyes squeezed shut. I missed them so much.

"Grania." The goddess placed her hand on mine. The warmth from her fingertips spread through my entire body. "I'm sorry your family was dragged into this."

Tears streamed down my cheeks. "They were targeted because of me... because of my role in the prophecy."

"And why do you think that is?" she inquired softly.

I drew in a breath, trying to stem the flow of tears long enough to respond. "The Goddess Carman's sons… they're trying to draw me to them."

Her fingers curled protectively around mine. "They are trying to draw you to them for a reason, child."

My lips pressed shut. The words appeared unbidden, forever engraved on my mind. *Would you sacrifice your life for those you love?* I could hardly comprehend, let alone speak them.

"Grania," she persisted. "They want to destroy you. This is why you are here training with the druids. I know you miss your family. You long to help them, but you must strengthen your resolve, your determination to fulfill your purpose, and you must learn how to protect yourself; your mind, your body, and heart; before you face Dain, Dother, and Dub."

I nodded, numbly.

"Do not concern yourself with the passage of time," Kane advised. "Remember, time works differently here. We can train for weeks, and those who are in the human realm would barely register this same passage of time."

"Our warriors will ensure your family remains un-harmed, as will Dain, Dother, and Dub," Diarmuid prom-ised. "They know this is the only way they can draw you to them. If they wish to manipulate you, then they must keep your family alive."

I met his steadfast gaze. "With all the medications my sis-ter requires, that will be easier said than done."

CHAPTER 6 - UNICORNS AND FATED MATES

"Wow!" I pushed up off the bed. A whole lot of energy rippled beneath my skin, just itching to burst through my fingertips.

Niamh giggled. "I feel like I've got soda coursing through my veins."

Brigitte popped her head inside our doorway. "That's what happens when we all sleep under the same roof."

Ciara smiled as she stepped inside the room. "You're going to need that energy for your training today."

Fianna stopped in the hallway. "Do you prefer a cool shower or a warm bath?"

Maolisa bolted upright. "There's running water?"

Ciara stifled a laugh. Maolisa's hair was sticking out in every direction. She retrieved a hair brush from the dresser and tossed it to her.

"Some of the water from the waterfall has been diverted into private showers, and the hot springs have been sectioned off into private baths," Fianna explained.

I hopped out of bed. "I'd love a bath."

"Me too." Maolisa's head bobbed excitedly.

Niamh threw her covers off. "A warm bath sounds heavenly."

Fianna smiled. "I'll reserve the baths then."

Ciara joined her in the hallway. "I requested a change of clothes."

"There's fruit and bread on the table if you're hungry." Brigitte led the way.

We followed her out into the common area. Our suite was divided into three bedrooms and a family room with a kitchenette.

I nabbed an apple from the table. "What time are we meeting Kane?"

"In a few hours." Fianna sliced the bread. "Diarmuid is in charge of your flying lesson this morning."

Maolisa poured a glass of water. "Is everything okay?"

"Something is eating away at the protective wards on our border." Brigitte leaned against the back of the couch. "The druids have to renew their spells. They're changing them up every few hours."

Ciara frowned. "The spell Dain, Dother, and Dub cast works like a virus or a parasite. The more white magick it consumes, the more resilient it gets."

"Too bad there's not a magick antibiotic," Niamh mumbled around a mouthful of bread.

Fianna handed me a slice. "The druids have been experimenting with their spells. They've infused medicinal herbs into their magick in the hopes it might kill the virus or at least prevent it from attacking the white magick."

I tossed my apple core in the trash. "That sounds complicated."

"They'll figure it out," Niamh stated confidently.

"They will," Fianna agreed. She sipped tea while we finished eating. "The bath is free."

"Oh!" Maolisa leapt from her chair. "I'm ready."

Niamh laughed. "Those sponge baths weren't cutting it for you, were they?"

She shuddered. "Not even close."

"The sponge to water ratio was a little off," I agreed. I was looking forward to a warm bath.

We filed out into the main corridor. Ciara grabbed the clothes sitting on the hall table by our door. "Good. Looks like we've got everything we need."

I looked around uncertainly. "Should I call for Diarmuid?" The warriors had deposited us on the balcony outside our suite last night. There were no stairs inside the palace, and grandpa wasn't comfortable with us flying for the first time while inside.

He dropped down beside me. "Ready?"

Two additional warriors landed beside him.

My eyes widened. "How did you…"

Fianna laughed. "I already called him."

They swept our legs out from under us, soared above the railing, and then descended the remaining eight stories. We touched down gently.

"Thanks, Grandpa." I gave him a hug.

"Enjoy your bath." He winked and strode away.

Fianna led us through the heavy wood door. We walked past the pantry and a kitchen with stone ovens before turning down another hallway. Crystal wall sconces flared to life, one by one, just a few steps ahead of us.

Finally, I had to ask, "Are you doing that?"

"Guilty as charged." Ciara laughed.

Niamh jumped up and down excitedly. "Can I try?"

"Sure." Ciara waved her forward, encouraging her to give it a try.

"You don't have to throw energy to spark a light, just will it there," Brigitte advised.

We stopped and waited for Niamh to ignite the next light.

Her face scrunched. Light burst from the crystal sconce. "Yes!"

"You got it on the first try!" I slapped her hand in a high five.

Maolisa grinned. "I want to try!" She turned and peered down the hallway. The next light flared to life.

I smiled. Without saying a word, I lit the next light. After the first few tries, we didn't really have to think about it. We took turns igniting the lights until suddenly we were racing down the hallway. We lit the wall sconces faster than we could run.

"Girls!" Brigitte called. "Are you forgetting something?"

We stopped and spun around.

Fianna stood holding the door for us about halfway back.

Everyone laughed. We kept laughing all the way back.

"In you go." Ciara divvied up the clothes as we walked through the door.

The air inside the changing room was heavy and warm. Two walls of cubbies separated three benches, allowing for some privacy. Fianna steered me toward the bench on the right. "There's a towel, washcloth, bathrobe, laundry bag, and soap in every cubby. Put your pajamas in the laundry bag. Pinch your energy signature into this disc here," she wiggled the silver disk attached to the drawstring, "and the *Sidhe* in charge of laundry will return them to our suite. The hot spring is on the other side of this door." She strode to the far end of the bench and tugged on the wood door. The wall sconces in the adjoining room flared to life. Steam rolled over the water in the floor. The water glowed, like the pond in the great hall. "We'll be waiting right outside this door."

Ciara and Brigitte offered the same instructions to their charges before following Fianna out into the hallway. "Enjoy."

"I've never been so excited to take a bath in my life." Niamh giggled happily.

"The water feels warm," Maolisa confirmed over the top of her cubby. "I dipped my toes in when I saw the bath."

"I can't wait to try it." I stuffed my pajamas inside the laundry bag, pinched the disk, and zapped it with a tiny pulse of energy. I grabbed the bath supplies from the cubby and stepped into the other room. I closed the door behind me.

I sank onto the bench beneath the warm water with a contented sigh. "This feels heavenly." I leaned my head back and waited for my muscles to relax. My thoughts drifted toward my family. I was so afraid they might be suffering. I buried my face in my hands and released the tears that had been building inside of me.

Eventually, I realized those tears weren't helping anyone but me. I washed with the soap I found inside the cubby. The lavender scent soothed me. I didn't see any shampoo, so I used the lather from the soap to clean my hair. Some things were simpler here.

I left the bath feeling a little more relaxed. I could still feel the energy pulsing beneath my skin, but it felt more centered, like it had finally settled in. I changed into the leggings, tunic, boots, and bracers, quickly lacing everything up. I finger combed my hair as best I could. After what felt like an eternity, I joined my friends in the hallway. "What's next?"

Niamh's face brightened. "Flying lessons."

Brigitte pushed off the wall she'd been leaning against. "We're meeting Diarmuid and the other warriors in the meadow."

We started back down the hall.

Fianna draped her arm over my shoulders. She spoke through our telepathic connection while our friends chatted about the impending flying lesson. "Are you okay?"

I grimaced. "What gave it away?"

She rolled her eyes. "Now what kind of guardian would I be if I didn't notice these things?"

"Things like puffy eyes?" My chuckle turned into a sigh. "I just needed to cry."

"I'd be worried if you didn't cry." She squeezed me tight. "Did it help?"

"Yes." I took a deep breath, savoring how it felt. "I feel like I can think and breathe again."

"Good," she replied. "Holding back tears only binds our hearts and our minds."

Maolisa turned around. "Weren't we supposed to turn left, down that hallway?"

"No," Ciara answered. "We're not going back to the great hall."

Just when I thought we'd reached a dead end, Fianna placed her hand over a symbol carved into the stone wall. The symbol looked like a "t" with three additional lines crossing through it. The wall disappeared without a sound.

"Woah," Niamh breathed.

"Amazing," I agreed. We stepped outside, basking in the sunshine. Birds chirped while a soft breeze played in the leaves. Grass, rock, and soil replaced the passageway behind us.

A warrior stood guard just outside the exit. "*Maidin Mhaith.*"

Our eyes met. "*Maidin Mhaith.*" I looked around, trying to make sense of our surroundings. A few steps to our left, and it all made sense. We were nearing the opposite bank of the lake, directly across from the meadow where the *Sidhe* spent most of their time.

We continued walking alongside the lake.

"Look! A swing!" Niamh pointed to a tree near the edge of the lake. Braided vines held a wood bench that promised to send its occupant soaring over the water.

I smiled. "That looks fun."

The sun glinted off the water. The stone bridge emerged so we could walk across.

Maolisa peered over the edge when we were halfway across. "I love how this bridge arches. Have you noticed how it forms a circle, half in and half out of the water?"

My fingers trailed over the mossy rocks. "It's the prettiest bridge I've ever seen." The bridge wasn't always present, though. It appeared only when you needed it. I wasn't sure if that was due to a concealing spell or if it truly ceased to exist when it wasn't needed.

Diarmuid met us in the meadow, in the clearing between the training arena and the tables. "Ready for those flying lessons?"

Five additional warriors dropped down beside us.

"Absolutely." I squeaked my surprise when grandpa grabbed ahold of my waist and skyrocketed into the air. "What are you doing?"

"Don't worry," he answered calmly. "Ainle will catch you."

"What?" I grasped his arm.

He chuckled softly. "Trust me, this is the best way to learn how to fly."

I looked down. Another warrior was circling about ten feet off the ground. "Wh... wha... what am I supposed to do?"

Another chuckle rumbled through his chest. "Do you want to fly?" He adjusted me in his arms so I was facing him.

"Yes, but..." I grabbed his shoulders, terrified he might drop me.

"Where are your wings then?" He examined the space behind me, seemingly amused by the fact my wings weren't out yet.

I peered over my shoulder worriedly. "I... I don't know."

He laughed even louder this time. "Call them. Your wings won't appear unless you call them."

I frowned. We were gifted wings in *Ogham*, but I hadn't seen them since. "Call them, how? Wait. Won't they get stuck under this shirt?" I wasn't sure how the whole wing thing worked. They just seemed to magically appear, and aside from the warriors, they didn't look like they were attached to the *Sidhe's* shoulders. They seemed to just hover an inch or two away from their clothes. Of course, I hadn't really examined them up close.

Amusement danced in his eyes. "You didn't see the slits in the back of your tunic when you dressed?"

I glanced distractedly at the ground. *I hope the warrior who's supposed to catch me is patient.* "Well, yes, but I thought that was for something else, like a bow quiver, a knife, or some other weapon."

He laughed again.

If he hadn't been holding me thirty feet off the ground, and I wasn't maintaining a death grip on his shoulders, I would have punched him in the arm. "Grandpa!"

In one effortless movement, he lifted me above his head. When my hands slipped away from his shoulders, he dropped me.

"*Wings!*" I thought desperately, with arms and legs flailing. The air rushed past me. I felt a pinch in my shoulders. My wings! They were there! My brow furrowed. "Up!" I grunted. Before my wings could comply, I landed in Ainle's arms.

"Hi, Grania. Nice wings." He winked.

All the air had rushed from my lungs. Before I could question whether the young warrior was flirting with me, he shot into the air and dropped me. I was plummeting toward Diarmuid, who had switched positions with Ainle and was already hovering beneath me.

"Argh!" I willed my wings to move before Grandpa could catch me. Shockingly, they did. I caught a glimpse of Ainle's stunned face as I shot past him.

With two full strokes of his wings, he joined me. "Wow. That was fast. I've never seen anyone get it on the second try. They had to drop me four times before I figured out how to get these monstrous beasts to work." He turned so I could see his wings.

I fell. Again. Clearly, I wasn't ready to fly and talk at the same time. "Up," I growled. I smiled when my wings complied.

Ainle grinned as I flew past him. "After a while you won't have to think about it!" His voice carried up to me. He tapped me on the shoulder when he caught up with me. "Tag! You're it!"

I fell a couple of feet, but somehow managed to apply the equivalent of wing brakes. "What?"

He flew a tight circle around me before speeding toward the trees. "Bet you can't catch me."

"Oh," I growled. "I am so catching you." I surged forward without even thinking. My wings had simply followed my thoughts while my eyes locked on the target.

"Wheeeeee!" Niamh catapulted past me, spinning in a tight corkscrew with her arms tucked close.

"Air spirits," I grumbled. My gaze shifted back toward Ainle. *What? Where did he go?* I'd stopped to watch Niamh, and now... he was nowhere to be seen. I hovered there uncertainly, but I smiled when I realized I was hovering. Hovering required very little thought it seemed. I jumped at the sharp tap on my shoulder.

"Did you lose something?"

I spun around... again, without thinking.

Ainle smirked. He dropped below me and shot past my feet.

I dove, pursuing without thinking, and nearly collided with Maolisa.

"Grania!" Linking her arm in mine, she twirled us around in a little dance.

Ainle rocketed toward the sky and promptly performed a swan dive.

Maolisa's eyes grew wide. "How did he do that?"

"He's an air spirit," I growled. "Help me get him." When Niamh noticed our little game of cat and mouse, she joined in.

The remaining warriors stood on the ground laughing at us. When we were good and tired, Ainle joined them.

I started to follow him, but then I realized I didn't know how to land. "Hey! That's not fair. You didn't teach us how to land!"

He slapped his thigh and fell over laughing.

Maolisa and Niamh joined me. We hovered there uncertainly, about ten feet off the ground.

"Just slow your wings and allow yourself to drop little by little," Diarmuid called up to us.

I looked at Maolisa. She shrugged, so we gave it a try.

"Wow!" Niamh jumped up and down the second her feet touched the ground. "Who knew flying would be so easy?"

I released the breath I'd been holding. "Actually, that was kind of easy."

Maolisa peered at her wings. "How do we get rid of these things?"

Ainle ruffled his wings, clearly preening. "If you think you're done with them, they'll retract automatically."

I was trying really hard not to admire his wings. It wasn't easy. The warriors scored the biggest, baddest wings. "Warriors don't retract their wings like the other *Sidhe*. Why is that?"

Diarmuid studied Ainle and then me. "It saves time, so we can act quickly."

"Are we done flying?" Niamh inquired breathlessly.

Grandpa noted our flushed faces and heavy breathing. "We are unless you want to practice taking off and landing in trees."

Maolisa shook her head before anyone else could respond. "I think we should save that for tomorrow. I'm afraid Ainle wore me out."

I wasn't about to admit that, not when he was standing there looking so smug. "I'm starving."

Diarmuid chuckled. "Let's eat. The druids will be here soon. They're going to teach you how to shapeshift this afternoon."

Niamh roped her arms around Maolisa and me when we started walking. "These lessons are incredible, way better than my studies back home."

I glanced back at Ainle when I realized he wasn't joining us. There was something familiar about him, but I couldn't quite put my finger on what it was.

Maolisa snorted, then laughed. "I'd choose flying lessons over keyboarding any day."

"Keyboarding," I groaned. "Don't remind me." All those speed and accuracy lessons were piling up at home.

Our guardians met us in the picnic area. They'd already secured soup, salad, and bread.

I climbed onto the bench next to Fianna. "Thanks."

She handed me a spoon and a fork. "Did you enjoy flying?"

"Yes." I dug into the salad. "I can see where that skill would come in handy."

"I love flying," Niamh gushed. "Imagine all the places we can travel when we get back home."

Maolisa's spoon stalled right in front of her mouth. "We can't fly in the human realm. Remember?"

I looked up from my salad when no one answered.

Our guardians exchanged glances. They appeared to be hashing out some sort of response inside their heads.

Maolisa gaped at them. "Can we?"

"Yes and no," Brigitte hedged. "We can fly in remote areas when there aren't any humans around, but we've got to be careful. There could be people nearby we aren't even aware of. If they filmed us flying, we'd be in grave danger."

Ciara leaned forward, a somber expression on her face. "Cell phones, security cameras, and satellites make it a lot more difficult than you might think."

Niamh pushed the salad around on her plate, her excitement squashed. "But Naois flew in the human realm."

"The *Ellen Trechend* aren't visible to most humans," Fianna explained. "They can expand and contract their scales so they reflect different colors and patterns. This allows them to blend into their environment. Besides, we were in a remote area, it was cloudy and dark."

"So, Naois can camouflage himself like a chameleon?" I shook my head. "That's amazing."

"The *Sidhe* can fly short distances with a concealing spell," Brigitte conceded, "but we expend a lot of energy when we fly like that. I use a concealing cloak, but not every *Sidhe* is gifted one of those."

"You can shapeshift into a bird," Diarmuid suggested. "That's how warriors travel inside the human realm."

"That's true," Brigitte agreed. "Shapeshifting requires a great deal of energy, but you can fly undetected in bird form."

Niamh smiled, visibly relieved. "I don't care what shape I'm in, just as long as I can fly."

I sopped up the last remaining dredges of soup with my bread. "Does shapeshifting hurt?"

"Not at all." Diarmuid stood, noting my empty bowl. "Are you ready to give it a try?"

I turned to my friends. "You do realize we're talking about shapeshifting and flying like they are perfectly sane activities?"

Maolisa gasped. "I was just thinking that exact same thing!"

Grandpa frowned, seemingly confused by the observation. "They are perfectly sane activities."

Fianna chuckled. "In this world, maybe."

Brigitte stacked the plates. "We'll take care of this. You go on ahead."

"Yes!" Niamh jumped up, her excitement back at Mach 10.

I clambered off the bench.

"Have fun," Ciara called after us.

We hurried across the meadow, eager to see what the druids had in store for us. The training arena remained hidden until we walked through the concealing spell. Cian waved us over. Several students, who were close to our age, were standing in front of him, listening to Kane.

Diarmuid nodded politely before walking away.

Kane paused briefly to acknowledge us. "Shapeshifting is easier when you're limber, so we're stretching out."

We formed our own row in the back of the class and followed his lead.

Cian's duster swirled around his ankles while he repositioned the *Sidhe* standing in front of me. "Don't forget to breathe."

"Is that even possible?" Niamh queried through our connection. Her blond hair pooled on the ground while her fingers grazed her toes.

I tried not to laugh and ended up choking instead.

Maolisa grinned. "Apparently it is."

Kane walked us through several more stretches. Finally, he began. "You know how this works, right? Water spirits can shapeshift into anything that lives in or near water. Air spirits can shapeshift into anything that flies, and wood spirits can shapeshift into anything that lives in the woods. This includes animals, insects, and plants." He nodded toward Cian. "Cian will take the water spirits over to the lake. You'll find it easier to shapeshift there. Everyone else, follow me."

Maolisa joined Cian's group. She peered over her shoulder, waving nervously as they walked away. A warrior, who'd been sitting in the spectator area with grandpa, followed them. Diarmuid remained in the spectator area, his eyes fixed on me.

I followed Kane to the edge of the forest.

He patted one of the trees. "You must form an image inside your mind, an image of the shape you wish to assume, before you shift. You cannot shift into something you have never seen before. You will expend less energy if you shift into something you are touching or something within eyesight. In those instances, you are sharing space, molecules, and energy with that living thing. You should ask first. They'll answer, telepathically, of course. This is a courtesy, a gift, the fact that they are sharing their space with you. Don't take any action that might cause them harm, or you may lose this privilege. Trust me, word gets around. Others will hear what you've done."

The *Sidhe* next to me raised his hand. "Do you have to be touching or looking at the thing you want to shift into?"

He shook his head. "No. You can shift into plants, animals, and insects you simply picture inside your head, even when they aren't anywhere near you. That uses a bit more energy because you are creating something from scratch, an illusion if you will. So, if you're trying to conserve energy, what should you do?"

Several of us raised our hands.

Kane's eyes met mine. "Grania?"

"You should shapeshift into something that already exists, something in your immediate environment that you can see or touch."

"Precisely." He tilted his head questioningly. "Do you think you'll shapeshift by merely picturing it inside your mind?"

I answered, since he was still looking at me. "Well, no. If that were true then we'd constantly be changing into other things, things we didn't necessarily intend."

He smiled. "So, what else do you need to do?"

I thought about the energy we were working with yesterday. "You have to will it?"

"If you're working from a picture inside your head, then yes. You would will it into existence. But in those instances when you're trying to share space with something that already exists, then you must *need* it. You must truly need this protection in order to shapeshift into something that already exists."

Niamh's eyes widened. "That's good to know."

"You won't change back into your original shape until you paint a picture of yourself inside your head. Now, why might that be a good thing?" He looked at Niamh.

Her cheeks flushed pink. "That would allow you to maintain your new shape while you sleep, if you are startled, lose focus, or need to think."

"Exactly." He leaned against the tree.

Another *Sidhe* raised his hand. "Can we shapeshift in the human realm?"

He folded his arms against his chest. "Yes, but you must ensure there are no humans around to witness this."

"Why?" several students blurted. "Why do we have to hide who we are?"

Kane's jaw clenched. "Humans fear things they don't understand. They would probably kill you, use you for their own gain, or torture you with painful experiments. You risk your life and our very existence if you shapeshift in front of them. You should avoid using your powers in front of them at all costs."

Niamh raised her hand again. "Can we shift into non-living things, like cars, furniture, or rocks?"

"No. You are a living thing. If you shapeshift into something that isn't living, then *you* would no longer be living."

She squeaked, surprised by the frank response.

Another student raised her hand. "What if that animal or plant dies while we are sharing space with him?"

Kane sighed. "Then you will die. You must revert back to your original shape before he dies."

I raised my hand again. "So, if this animal is injured while I'm sharing space with him, then I'll be injured too?"

"Yes, so choose wisely." He pushed off from the tree. "Would you like to give it a try?"

My heart skipped a beat. "Me?"

He nodded.

Niamh tugged on our connection. "Don't worry. You got this!"

My gaze slid toward her and then Kane. "Okay."

He nodded toward the tree he'd been leaning against. "You can start with this guy."

I stepped in front of the tree. I didn't question whether he could talk. My perception of trees had changed a lot since *Ogham*. I flattened my hand against his trunk. "Would you mind sharing space with me?"

"Not at all." His voice sounded rough, although not in an irritable sort of way, just scratchy like his bark. "I'm happy to help."

I stepped back and studied the tree... the roots peeking up through the soil, his trunk, branches, and leaves. The "needs" requirement was a little tricky. There was no threat, no need to hide, not at this moment in time. Finally, it dawned on me… *I need to learn this skill so I can protect myself and help others, like Lexie and Mom.* There was a gentle tug and a whisper of sound when I acknowledged that need, and just like that… I was standing inside the tree.

The space inside the tree was more accommodating than I expected, or maybe I'd become more flexible, because when I sat, my legs folded up perfectly without popping out of the tree. The air inside the tree felt richer, it smelled sweeter, and it was easier to breathe. I could feel the sun and gentle bursts of energy, which I suspected was photosynthesis.

I peered out at my classmates, not at all interested in leaving. They had their faces pressed up against the trunk like they were trying to see me inside the tree. That made me laugh, but they didn't appear to hear me. The outside world was tinted brown, like an antique photograph, but my vision wasn't blurry. Eventually, I grasped that my classmates might like a turn, so I pictured myself inside my head and shifted back, landing just outside the tree.

Everyone jumped back. Cheers sounded all around.

I searched for Niamh in the crowd. "That was awesome!"

We practiced shifting into trees, grass, butterflies, and bunnies. The bunny was a little unsettling, especially when she hopped. I discovered that you have to negotiate more with animals. They maintain control over their bodies, so they decide where they're going. Still, in an emergency situation, I figured their instincts were better than mine. I could always shift back to myself if I didn't like where they were going.

"That's it for today," Kane announced.

Everyone groaned.

Chuckling softly, he pursued a slightly different approach. "Dinner's ready."

Cheers erupted. Several students sprinted across the meadow.

I was famished, but not famished enough to run. I walked toward Diarmuid instead. "Hi, Grandpa."

He smiled. "Did you enjoy yourself?"

"I did." We turned and waited for Niamh to catch up.

"Hi, Diarmuid." She linked her arm in mine. "Maolisa just finished up."

"I can't wait to hear which animals she shifted into." Visions of wiggly fish and slimy frogs hopped inside my head.

The sun fell behind us while the first of *Tír na nÓg's* three blue moons crept over the goddess's palace. The sun and the moon competed mightily, painting the landscape in a fiery orange and neon blue palette. With a sharp intake of breath, I turned so I could admire the art piece unfolding before me.

"This is your first sunset in *Tír na nÓg*," Grandpa noted with some surprise.

I nodded, far too entranced to speak. We'd arrived late the first night, retired early the second night, slept for three days after visiting *Ogham*, and were whisked inside the palace before the sun fell last night.

"I wish my parents could see this," Niamh admitted brokenly.

I tore my eyes from the landscape, startled by the sadness in her voice. My heart clenched when I saw the tears glistening in her eyes. Her pain burrowed inside of me. Niamh was always smiling, skipping, and dancing about. Seeing her like this hurt. A lot. I pulled her close, trying to ease her pain as much as mine. "I'm so sorry, Niamh. I've been so caught up with my own family, I haven't stopped to think how painful this is for you. I'm sure you miss your family terribly."

"You girls are very brave, facing so much adversity without the aid of your families." Diarmuid wrapped his arms around us, anchoring us to this time and place. "I will petition the goddess so you can bring your families to *Tír na nÓg*."

She brushed the tears from her cheeks. "Thank you, Diarmuid. That is very kind of you."

He kept one arm wrapped around each of us as we resumed walking toward the tables. "I should think that is the least I can do."

"There's Maolisa." I pointed toward the table where she was sitting with our guardians.

She jumped up when she spotted us. "Guess what! I can turn into a mermaid!"

My jaw fell slack.

Niamh looked equally stunned. "I thought you had to visualize a real animal."

"You do! I was changing into a fish, but I was experimenting a little. If you just focus on shifting certain parts, like the tail, you can keep part of your original shape and turn into a mermaid."

I shook my head, thoroughly impressed. "That is so cool."

Fianna patted the bench, encouraging me to sit next to her.

Niamh joined Maolisa on the other side of the table. "So, mermaids are simply *Sidhe* who have shapeshifted half-way?"

She nodded happily.

"Can wood spirits change into mermaids?" There were lakes and ponds in the woods, so the thought seemed reasonable enough.

Ciara slid plates loaded with potatoes, apple and sage sausages, and green beans in front of us. "No, but you can transform into a unicorn."

"Unicorns are real?" Niamh's voice fell to a mere whisper, as if she didn't dare believe it.

"Like the King of Scots would put a mythical creature on his coat of arms," Diarmuid chortled, clearly amused by the idea.

"How would she know?" Brigitte scolded. "Very few unicorns remain in the human realm. They don't exist outside Celtic territories. They remain hidden during the day, only appearing at night."

My knee bounced excitedly. "I really want to see one. Can we go looking for one? Tonight?"

Our guardians exchanged glances.

I sucked in a breath. "Please say yes," I whispered inside my head.

"Yes," Fianna finally answered. "I think we could all use a night of fun."

"Yes!" Maolisa and Niamh shouted.

I grinned, deliriously happy.

"Let's camp out by the lake," Ciara suggested. "They're more likely to join us there."

Maolisa shoved a forkful of potatoes in her mouth. "Do we need to do anything special to encourage them to come?"

Niamh wiggled a green bean. "Do they like treats?"

Brigitte sipped her tea. "There's a song they like. We can teach you the words tonight."

Fianna leaned forward conspiratorially. "Maybe we can practice some concealing spells tonight."

I nodded. I was eating too fast to speak.

Kane appeared behind her, right out of thin air. His hands fell on her shoulders while a smile played on his face. "Playing druidess, again?"

She spun around on the bench. "How do you sense these things?"

I slid further down the bench so he could sit beside her.

"Perhaps your mental shields are weak." He winked and squeezed between us.

Cian appeared on the other side of the bench, holding two plates overflowing with food. He set a plate in front of Kane. "Regan made Dublin Coddle with vegan sausage."

His smile widened. "I see you scored extra helpings. Thanks."

"My mental shields are not weak," Fianna sputtered.

Cian laughed. "Shields don't block fated mates."

I leaned forward so I could see Fianna's face. "What's a mate?"

Kane grinned. "A mate is the person you are destined to marry."

"I determine who I marry," Fianna gritted.

"Oh, no," Brigitte groaned. "Here we go again."

"I don't think the girls are ready for this lesson," Ciara warned.

Cian chuckled. "So, about those concealing spells…"

I shoved my plate aside. My eyes widened when it disappeared. I felt the space and my hand vanished. I yanked it back with a muffled yelp.

Cian snickered.

My eyes flew to his. A far too innocent look masked his face. I narrowed my eyes and prodded the space. This time I didn't panic when my hand disappeared. My fingers hit the plate, but my eyes insisted it was the table… the table and a disturbingly handless arm. "That is not right."

Kane dragged his gaze from Fianna. "That's a concealing spell." He nodded toward my missing hand. "How do you think Cian accomplished that?"

Maolisa's startled eyes met mine. When she saw I wasn't panicked, she shoved her hand into the space. Niamh did the same. Her hand disappeared, then bumped against the plate. "He's projecting an image of a table in this space."

"It's no different than painting a picture inside your mind when you want to shapeshift." Cian grinned, abandoning the innocent façade. "You're just painting a different picture."

"You simply will it into existence and specify where it should appear," Kane explained. "You can draw on the energy that is stored inside of you or draw on the energy from your source; air, water, or wood."

"You also need to specify how long the image should remain. The more complex the image and the longer the duration, the more energy you will expend." Fianna offered the additional instruction in clear defiance of Kane's druidess remark, then brazenly concealed every plate on the table.

Kane frowned when he couldn't see his sausage and potatoes anymore.

Everyone busted up laughing.

The concealing spell faded, allowing Kane to reclaim his plate.

"Illusions work the same way." Brigitte stood. "You can change your outfit with a simple thought." Her brown tunic transformed into a sparkling blue gown.

"Oh! I want to do that!" Niamh scrambled off the bench.

"Draw on the air around you, think about what you would prefer to be wearing, and then picture it on your body." Brigitte stepped back, offering her some space.

Some colors shifted around Niamh. An image wavered in and out of focus, then solidified completely. She'd paired a white t-shirt displaying the French flag and the words "Vive la France" with a pair of stylish blue jeans.

Everyone cheered.

"You forgot the shoes," Ciara noted, clearly amused.

White lace up sneakers replaced her boots.

Maolisa replaced her tunic with a teal-blue skirt and a t-shirt displaying the words "Hey! Fish are people too." She stepped back and spun around. The long, flowy skirt unveiled a beta fish with a rainbow-colored tail. When Maolisa twirled, it looked like the fish was swimming circles around her. She no longer appeared to be wearing boots. Instead, she was barefoot.

Ciara burst out laughing.

Of course, I changed into a unicorn. I didn't have to establish a need or ask for permission, since I wasn't sharing space with a real unicorn. I was projecting an image from a picture I'd seen inside a book. I felt an immediate dip in energy, but it was worth it.

Maolisa and Niamh rushed toward me, ooh-ing and ahh-ing over my silver hooves and horn. Several *Sidhe* joined us, transforming into alicorns, dragons, and creatures I'd never even seen before.

The musicians began playing, the illusions changed, and suddenly... we were attending an elaborate ball. The *Sidhe* donned a more formal attire, the fog blanketed the ground, and the fireflies drew closer so it appeared we were dancing amid the stars.

I envisioned myself in a purple and blue gown. I felt a sharp tap on my shoulder, so I spun around.

Ainle bowed. "Would you like to dance?" His broad wings were tucked neatly behind his back.

My eyes widened. "I... uh... I don't know how to dance."

With a confident grin, he grasped my hand and back. "You don't have to know the steps when I'm leading." He whisked me effortlessly across the floor.

I was stunned speechless. *Had I whispered... yes?* I studied his chest plate, unable to meet his gaze. There was something about this *Sidhe*. He was the youngest warrior I'd met. Still, he had the same confident air, the same solid build, the same weapons and wings, and he wore the same armor my father and grandfather wore. My eyes traced the elaborate design stamped into his chest plate. The floral design was so beautiful and unexpected for a warrior.

Ainle smiled when our eyes finally met. "Do you like it here in *Tír na nÓg*?"

That smile and those blue topaz eyes sparkling beneath his chestnut hair threatened a one-two punch I wasn't expecting. "Yes," I admitted breathlessly.

He twirled me in his arms. "Will you stay after you rescue your family and fulfill the prophecy?"

Fear and uncertainty chilled me. "I… I'm not sure." I still couldn't bring myself to tell anyone about the sacrifice mentioned by the Rowan Tree.

He drew me a little closer. "We will rescue them." His voice exuded confidence and strength.

I risked another glance at him. "Are you going with us?"

"Of course." He frowned. "I would never allow you to face such a thing alone."

My heart stalled. "Why… why do you seem so familiar? Have we met before?" I'd been scouring my mind ever since our flying lesson this morning. He seemed familiar, and yet… I couldn't recall seeing him at the border or with Diarmuid before.

His feet ground to a stop. "You don't remember?"

"No. Why? What am I supposed to remember?" This felt important. I sensed I should know him, but the memory was dangling just outside my recollection.

"The Rowan Tree," he prodded, "in *Ogham*? You didn't see me then?"

"Yes." The memory crashed into me. He was there in one of the visions gifted by the Rowan Tree. "We were... we are..."

He breathed a huge sigh of relief. "We're fated mates."

I tried to think... and breathe. "How can that be?" The knowledge was there inside of me, but it seemed maybe our timing was off. I was too young, and he was... well... older than me. This had to be one of those pieces of knowledge that was meant for later... when I was older... if I somehow, miraculously, managed to survive this prophecy. "I'm twelve."

His eyes captured and held mine. "We won't marry until you're older, but there can be no doubt... I am the one God intends for you."

I tried to escape but he wouldn't let me. "How... how old are you?"

"I'm sixteen." The unbreakable grasp he maintained on my hand and back gentled. "Trust me. You will feel the truth of this more with each passing year until you can no longer deny it."

I took a deep breath and slowly released it. "So, someday we'll be together?" I couldn't say the word "married." "Together" was difficult enough. I hadn't even considered dating anyone. Until now.

"Yes. We will be together." He seemed to grow a little taller and more determined somehow. "It is my responsibility, *my honor*, to keep you safe, which is why I'll be joining you on Mangerton Mountain. I would fight this battle for you if I could, but the prophecy will not allow it. So, I will stand beside you. I will protect you while you fight for your family... and *Tír na nÓg*."

Fianna spoke just outside my periphery. "Grania, are you okay?"

"Yes." My voice was breathless and weak. I wanted to look at her, but I couldn't tear my eyes from Ainle. That promise... his tone... those deeply determined eyes did something to me.

"He told you? You understand who he is... what you are fated to be?"

"Yes." My heart beat so wildly, that was the only response I could manage.

"I know it's a lot to digest, especially when you're young." She chuckled, then muttered under her breath, "I can barely comprehend it myself."

Ainle brought my hand to his lips. "Thank you for this dance. I think, perhaps, your guardian can help you better understand." He bowed, then strode confidently through the crowd.

I looked at my hand, which was now tingling. "Is it true? With each passing year, he will prove more difficult to resist?" I felt a sense of loss. I wasn't sure I liked him walking away just now.

She guided me toward the lake. "Yes. I'm afraid so."

I frowned. He was difficult to resist even now. "But you and Kane..."

"I don't care for things that are outside my control. I thought I could avoid these feelings... this pull... but there is no denying this fate. There is no amount of distance... or time... or living in different realms that will change it." She sighed. "Now that I am back in *Tír na nÓg*, that pull is a million times worse."

"Why do you resist?"

A soft growl escaped her lips. "He's just so confident and smug, and he's more powerful than me. That's just... a difficult pill to swallow."

I understood. Completely. "Kane enjoys teasing you, but he also admires you. Besides, I think you enjoy a good challenge. I think he will make you happy."

She rolled her eyes. "Of course, you do. Everyone does."

Brigitte looked up as we neared the lake. "I don't know that we'll find any unicorns adventurous enough to join us tonight. Perhaps we should sing for them tomorrow night when it's quieter." As elegant as the festivities were, the party was in full swing and didn't appear to be ending anytime soon. Maolisa, Ciara, and Niamh were among those partygoers. Diarmuid stood along the outskirts, watching us.

I tore my eyes from the festivities. "I think I've had enough excitement for one day." My mind was all tied up in the warrior who had just walked away.

"We're going to call it a night then." Fianna hugged her friend. We walked to her house arm in arm. "Do you want to fly up by yourself? Trees can be a little tricky to maneuver around."

Diarmuid caught up with us. "I got her." Within seconds he'd whisked me up onto her deck. "Ainle will stand guard tonight." He pulled me in for a hug. "Sleep well, Grania. Know that you are loved."

* * *

I scooped a large dollop of yogurt into my bowl and tossed in a handful of berries. "Can I ask you a question?" I passed a blueberry to the violet-backed starling who for some insane reason had decided he was my own personal alarm clock.

"Of course." Fianna lowered her cup of tea.

I stirred the berries. The yogurt turned a pretty shade of purple. "When we were traveling to *Tír na nÓg*, you mentioned that *Sidhe* guardians can plant ideas."

She nodded. "That's true. We can compel people to do things they wouldn't normally do."

I licked the spoon. The yogurt was creamy and sweet. "Do you think I might have that same ability?"

"I don't know." She looked thoughtful. "Guardians are gifted that ability because they may need to exert some influence while protecting others. How would manipulating others further your purpose when you're ending violence through kindness and love?"

I passed the starling another berry. "I'd like to compel Dain to release Lexie and Mom. That would be an act of kindness or love. And, if I compel him to love humans and the *Sidhe*, then he would no longer want to do us harm."

Her eyes filled with regret. "Humans are the only ones we can manipulate in this way. We cannot plant ideas, erase memories, or compel any other creature or magical being. Their shields are too strong."

"Do you know what sort of power Dain, Dother, and Dub have? Can they force me to do something I don't want to do?" I scraped the last little bit of yogurt from my bowl and washed it down with juice.

She warmed her hands on the tea. "They can force humans to do evil things, but I don't know if they can force the *Sidhe* or any other creatures to do the same. We should ask Kane."

"Ask me what?" He was leaning inside the entryway with arms and ankles crossed.

Fianna nearly fell from her chair. "Kane! Quit sneaking up on me."

He fought a smile and lost. "Would you prefer that I ignore you when you call my name?"

"I wasn't *calling* your name, I was *speaking* your name. There's a difference." She gathered our dishes and stalked into the kitchen.

"You said, and I quote, 'We should ask Kane.' Clearly, you needed me." He pushed off the door frame. "I'm just making sure I'm available when you need me."

She grumbled something under her breath.

He threw a wink in my direction before joining her in the kitchen. "I'm sorry, love. What was that?"

"Nothing." Her expression softened when she turned to face him.

I decided to duck out before they kissed. "I'll be in the meadow." I stepped out onto the deck. The violet-backed starling followed me.

"*Maidin Mhaith.*" Ainle rose in front of the deck with a lazy sweep of his wings.

My mouth opened and shut a few times. I'd forgotten he was the one standing guard last night. "How did you know I was standing here?"

He laughed. "I heard you say you were going to the meadow. Would you like some help getting down?"

I pictured him carrying me in his arms. I shook my head, determined to avoid all the confusing emotions that would likely accompany that experience. "I'd like to fly down by myself." I called my wings and shook them out.

"Instead of flying directly down, it's easier if you fly out and then down. Here, I'll show you." He dropped down beside me. "On the count of three?" He extended his hand.

I stared at him for a couple of heartbeats; then placed my hand in his.

He smiled. "Center of the meadow?"

I nodded. My heart beat wildly against my chest.

His fingers closed securely around mine. "Three... two... one."

We leapt from the deck. Ainle flew a few inches above me so he wouldn't hit my wings. His wings extended far beyond my reach. We touched down in the center of the meadow, a safe distance from the tables and trees.

"Thanks." I smiled, pleased I'd nailed the landing.

"Anytime." His hand remained firmly entwined with mine.

"*Bonjour.*" Niamh dropped down beside us. The warrior who'd escorted her continued on toward the training arena. When he hit the edge of the concealing spell, he disappeared completely.

Maolisa strolled toward us. A young warrior, who appeared to be around Ainle's age, walked alongside her. "*Hei.*" Apparently, we were greeting one another in our native languages today.

"Good morning." I coaxed my hand back from Ainle.

"*Maidin Mhaith.*" Diarmuid squeezed me in a one-armed hug. "Treasach and Ainle will be assisting us today. We're going to practice taking off and landing in trees. Everyone ready?"

"Yes." I felt happy for the first time in days. I suspected that had something to do with the people around me. As scary and uncertain as my future was, I was surrounded by kind people who wanted to help. I felt cherished, empowered, safe, and loved, and that… well, that strengthened my resolve as well as my desire to help others. I wondered how different our world would be if everyone felt like this.

Grandpa's arm remained draped around me. We walked toward the trees. "You won't see many warriors taking off or landing in trees. Our wingspan is too long for that. Your wingspan is much smaller than ours, which makes it easier for you to fly through tight spaces. In other words, this is something that you can do, that we cannot."

Niamh peered up at the branches. "Can we injure our wings?"

He nodded. "Unfortunately, yes… and while you may be able to squeeze into tight spaces, your wings are more fragile than ours. You should fly above the trees when you can, but you may need to land or take off from the forest in emergency situations. That's why we practice."

We entered through the side of the forest where fall reigns eternal. I looked up, admiring the patchwork canopy of red, gold, and orange leaves. Not a single leaf was dead, dying, or brown. It was like fall was frozen in time, before any leaves had a chance to fall.

Finally, Diarmuid stopped in front of an old oak tree. "This is a good place to start."

Our eyes followed the trunk all the way to the top.

"Choose a thick branch about midway up that you can access. Think about the route you will take. Plot it out inside your mind, lock your eyes on the target, and then give it a try. We'll catch you if you fall." Diarmuid's hand clasped my shoulder. "Do not fully extend your wings. Use rapid but shortened wing strokes as best you can."

That was a lot to remember. "Anyone else want to go first?"

Maolisa studied the tree. "I think you're better equipped for this than I am."

Niamh smiled. "Don't worry, Grania. You got this!"

I took a deep, steadying breath, picked a branch, and pushed up off the ground. I overshot a little and thumped my head on a neighboring branch. "Ow!"

"Grab the branch," Ainle shouted worriedly.

I grasped the branch I'd hit while my feet scrambled for the limb below. "I got it!"

A sigh of relief sounded below me.

"Nicely done," Diarmuid called. "I'd like you to stay put until the other girls join you."

Ainle paced directly below me while everyone else moved a little further around the tree. "See anything interesting?"

I'd been so busy watching them, I hadn't really looked. "Well, there is a nest and some acorns," I answered sarcastically. Honestly, what did he expect me to see in the middle of a tree?

His feet ground to a stop. He looked stunned, but then laughed heartily. He shook his head and peered up at me. "What about further out?"

I peered through the branches and shrugged. "Just a bunch of leaves." I studied the branch above me, thinking it might offer a better view.

Maolisa landed in the tree on the other side of me. "I did it." She whispered the words, like she could hardly believe them.

I grinned. "Of course, you did."

She looked down. "Come on, Niamh. You can do it."

She zipped around two large branches, then landed a few feet above us. "Woah! Okay, that was a little tricky."

"Are you kidding? That was awesome." I looked past her, toward the top of the tree. "Should we climb up and take off from the top?" That looked easier than flying down.

"Sure," Diarmuid agreed. "Be careful. Those branches get thinner at the top."

"Wait." My gaze slid between Maolisa and Niamh. "All three of us can transform into birds. Why don't we just do that?"

"Yes," Ainle exclaimed. "I knew she'd figure it out."

My eyes shot toward his. "What did you say?"

Diarmuid chuckled. "We asked you to fly in and out of the tree so we could test your problem-solving skills. Why fly in and out of a tree in *Sidhe* form and risk damage to your wings when you can shift into a bird?"

"You figured out a way to accomplish the task in both *Sidhe* and bird form." Treasach, the other young warrior, grinned up at us. "Very impressive."

My thoughts were racing too fast to acknowledge the compliment. "Can I shapeshift while flying?"

Silence.

I looked down again. They were all staring at one another, dumbfounded.

Finally, Diarmuid spoke. "All this time, and none of us have ever thought to try?"

Treasach eyed me questioningly. "Why would you want to do that?"

Seriously? They had never anticipated a need for that? "Well, for one, I might want to change back into myself after clearing the trees as a bird; and there's always the chance I might need to shift into a bird so I can land in a tree while flying overhead."

"She's right," Ainle boasted proudly.

"If you've never attempted to shapeshift while flying, then what do you do when you're flying over a forest and need to land?" Niamh asked.

"We look for a clearing," Diarmuid answered, "but I can see a tactical advantage to your approach. Do you want to give it a try?"

I glanced at Maolisa, then Niamh. "We'd get to be the first *Sidhe* to try it."

Niamh's eyes glittered with excitement. "I'm in."

"Me too." Maolisa grinned. "Let's do this!"

Ainle elbowed Treasach in the arm. "See? They are courageous and smart."

"Shift into birds while you have a firm grasp on the tree," Diarmuid advised. "We'll be waiting for you when you fly out through the top. Wait until we've maneuvered beneath you before you try shifting. That way we can catch you if you lose altitude."

"Sounds good." I turned to Maolisa and Niamh. "Ready?"

Maolisa nodded. "On the count of three?"

"Sounds good," Niamh agreed. "One... Two... Three." She shrank into a painted bunting. Maolisa transformed into a wood duck while I changed into a violet-backed starling. Niamh led the way out of the trees.

We soared above the warriors and shifted back into ourselves. There was a sudden drop in altitude, just as Diarmuid had predicted. Niamh and I regained altitude before anyone could catch us, but Maolisa forgot to envision wings when she shifted back into *Sidhe* form.

"Woah." Treasach captured her in his arms. "I got you."

Her cheeks turned a brilliant shade of pink. "How could I forget my wings?" They appeared instantly.

"There you go." He released her so she could fly on her own.

Cian and Kane flagged us down.

We joined them in the center of the meadow.

Cian shook his head. He looked thoroughly impressed. "That was amazing. I can't believe you shifted mid-air."

Ainle clapped Treasach on the back. "I think we should give it a try."

I winked at my friends on the sly. "I'll fly beneath you so I can catch you if you lose altitude."

The color drained from his face. "Grania, you can't..."

I burst out laughing.

Niamh shook her head. "You do not want to tell that girl she can't do something. She'll prove you wrong every time."

Treasach looked genuinely intrigued. "How would you go about catching Ainle? He is considerably larger than you."

The math nerd in me calculated Ainle's height, weight, and approximate wingspan. A smile spread slowly but smugly when the perfect solution formed inside my head. "I would tie two hammocks together to form a net and recruit Fianna, Niamh, and Maolisa to hold the other three ends while we flew beneath him."

His jaw dropped.

Ainle thumped his shoulder. "I told you. Her problem-solving skills are solid."

"Well, she is my granddaughter." Diarmuid chuckled.

"As intriguing as that experiment sounds," Kane indulged in an eye roll as he shook his head, "Cian and I need to work with the girls."

Grandpa folded me in his arms. "I'm proud of you." He nodded at Maolisa and Niamh as he backed away. "You girls did great."

Ainle's eyes snagged mine. "Good luck. I'll see you tonight."

I nodded, although I wasn't entirely sure what he was talking about. We hadn't made any plans to see one another tonight.

We followed Cian and Kane into the training area. My skin tingled. We were the only *Sidhe* in the arena, but I could feel the energy signatures the others had left behind.

Kane motioned for us to join him as he sat in the center of the arena. The boulders stood like sentinels along the perimeter. His expression turned serious. "Grania raised some important questions this morning relevant to the dangers you are facing. I'd like to answer those questions telepathically."

"We will only speak telepathically during our training today," Cian said. "We must strengthen this skill so you can keep your strategies and your intentions hidden from those who would do you harm. When you speak, make sure you are using the threads for everyone here. That way, everyone can learn from the discussion."

Kane's voice sounded inside my head. "Please summarize the discussion you had with Fianna this morning."

I gathered everyone's thread inside my head. "I was questioning whether we could compel Dain, Dother, and Dub to do things they wouldn't otherwise do... things like ending violence or releasing my family. Fianna clarified that *Sidhe* guardians cannot force other creatures or magical beings to do things against their will. They can only compel humans. I started wondering if the reverse was true. We use white magick, but the Goddess Carman's sons use black magick. So, I was wondering if this same limitation applies to them. I asked Fianna if Dain, Dother, or Dub can force us to do things against our will."

Kane's sigh traveled through our connection. "Unfortunately, we don't know if the Goddess Carman's sons wield power over magical beings. We know they're working with the *Sidhe Sluagh* and with the *Fomorians*, but we don't know if those creatures are working with them willingly or if they're being compelled to do their bidding. We've never ventured close enough to see what they can do to us. We could ask some of the warriors on Mangerton Mountain to test them, but that would compromise their position."

I shook my head. My father was among those warriors. "I don't want to put them in harm's way."

"I agree." Cian eyed us thoughtfully. "The universe instinctively seeks balance. You three serve as the counterbalance for the Goddess Carman's sons. So, on the remote chance that they can influence you, then you should wield that same power over them. The universe would not allow them an advantage over you."

"What about the *Fomorians?*" Niamh prodded. "What sort of threat do they pose?"

"The *Fomorians* are sea demons," Kane explained. "They manipulate the harsher elements, the more destructive side of nature, to achieve their objectives. Their power lies in violent storms. We cannot fly or wield our energy with any sort of accuracy during these storms, which makes it easier for them to capture us. They conquered Ireland, captured, and enslaved us once before, but we rebelled. We won our freedom during the *Second Battle of Magh Tuireadh* and forced them back into the sea where they belong."

I frowned, recalling our conversation with Naois. "The *Fomorians* are back in Ireland, near the portal."

Cian nodded. "They've found a way to adapt so they can live in fresh water now. They are no longer confined to the ocean or the coastline. They're relocating disturbingly close to us. That's a pretty good indication they're working with the Goddess Carman's sons. They prefer violence and chaos over peace, so I'm sure their interests align in more ways than one."

Niamh chewed her lip. "And the *Sidhe Sluagh?*"

"The *Sidhe Sluagh* are rogue spirits that cannot be killed. They aren't welcome in Heaven or Hell, so they are stuck inside the human realm. They seek out the souls of the dying, although you may draw them to you if you're feeling hopeless." Kane leaned forward, his expression earnest. "We have another epic battle ahead of us, one that would appear to include the demons who tortured, slaughtered, and enslaved us once before." His eyes searched Niamh's. "The darkest hour in our history may very well be repeating itself. This is why you are so important. You must ensure the *Sidhe* maintain hope, otherwise, they can steal our souls."

Niamh paled.

Maolisa's hand slid soothingly down her back. "What do they do with the souls they steal?"

Kane shrugged. "Nobody knows."

Cian reached over and turned Niamh's chin, gently forcing her to look at him. "As long as we have hope, we don't have to worry about the *Sidhe Sluagh*. They're a distraction and a nuisance, but they cannot hurt us unless we lose hope."

She released the breath she'd been holding. "Okay."

"That brings me to my next point." Kane waited until we were all looking at him. "The Goddess Carman's sons may try to communicate with you telepathically. There is only one reason why they would attempt to do so. They want to manipulate you. You must guard your thoughts and protect your minds from them, so we're going to work on this today. I want you to block Cian and me from speaking inside your heads. We're going to say some terrible things, things that are hurtful and untrue, but we want you to know what this sort of attack feels like."

Cian sighed. "I cannot stress this enough. They will say things that may cause you to lose hope... to question yourself and those you trust... things that taint your innate goodness with darkness, anger, or violent thoughts. The best way to protect yourself from this sort of attack is by erecting a strong barrier inside your head. You decide who is allowed in and who is forced outside that shield. If you feel that protective barrier crack, then apply some energy to reinforce it."

Kane rubbed his forehead. "Okay. Close your eyes and envision that shield all the way around your mind. Put your hands out in front of you when you are ready. Keep your hands raised while you hear us. Drop your hands when our voices disappear." He looked up, an apology written all over his face. "Are you ready?"

I closed my eyes. I was already starting to feel panicked, so I waited until I was breathing evenly. I formed a shield using the energy inside of me and sealed it around my mind. I locked my arms straight in front of me and nodded.

"You are stupid."

"You are worthless."

"You will fail."

My heart raced. My shield wasn't working. I scrambled to find the reason why.

"There is no hope."

"I will destroy everyone you love."

"Your family will die a painful death."

I cried out at the images that provoked. "No!" I drew energy through the soil so I could strengthen my shield. I sucked in a breath, my brain seizing on the step I'd missed. Cian and Kane's threads were still inside. I lifted the shield and forced them out.

"You... no one... survive..."

I slammed the shield back into place, fused it with energy, and then...

Silence.

I held my breath. When that sweet, blissful silence remained, I lowered my hands. I could hear Niamh crying and Maolisa praying under her breath, but I couldn't hear Cian or Kane. Finally, everything quieted. I released the breath I was holding.

Kane spoke aloud this time. "Very good. You may open your eyes."

I dove into my friends' arms so I could give them a hug. I wiped Niamh's tears with my sleeve. "Are you okay?"

"Yes," she sniffed. "I'm glad we're practicing. I don't want to hear their voices inside my head."

Maolisa frowned. "Even if we build shields, they can still say those things aloud."

"That's true," Kane agreed, "but you can drown them out with your voices, with the wind, or rain."

Niamh brightened. "Can you teach me how to use wind?"

"And rain?" A smile tugged at Maolisa's face.

"Yes," Kane chuckled, "after we strengthen your mental shields. We still need to prepare you for the illusions Dain, Dother, and Dub will create."

"Illusions?" Dread settled like a heavy weight in my stomach. I'd mistakenly believed the verbal attacks were the worst thing we'd experience today.

The smile slid from Maolisa's face. "What sort of images will they project?"

"Imagine your worst nightmare magnified a thousand times over." Cian pushed up from the ground, his expression grim.

I thought about the images the goddess had revealed. There were some horrific things happening in the human realm that rivaled even my worst nightmare… and I'd had some terrifying dreams in my short life. Tears pricked my eyes.

"How will we know what's real?" Niamh breathed.

Cian offered her his hand. "We will teach you how to see through those illusions. There are some inconsistencies and some blurring around the edges." He pulled her up onto her feet. "You will also feel the negative energy they expend."

Kane stood and reached for my hand. "This really is my least favorite part of the training."

We worked for hours. First, we practiced blocking Cian and Kane while conversing with one another telepathically. Then, we spread out inside the arena so we could spar while still blocking their telepathic attacks. Gradually, they added the illusions. We deflected purple bursts of energy while blocking their voices and trying to see through the disturbing images.

The snake pit illusion was so convincing I could feel the snakes slithering up my legs. No matter how hard I tried to prove the illusion wasn't real, my body and my brain were convinced. Those snakes were on my legs. I clawed at my leggings to get them off. When they latched onto my arms, a frantic scream escaped my lungs. I collapsed in a flinching, swatting, sobbing heap on the ground.

Kane gathered me in his arms. "Grania, there are no snakes."

I blinked back tears so I could search my arms. I trembled

violently. The snakes were gone.

"I was manipulating the moisture in the air. That's why you thought they were real. I tricked your senses into believing those snakes were crawling up your arms." He brushed the tears from my face. "Okay," he announced, "that's enough negative experiences for one day."

"Thank, God!" Maolisa collapsed onto the ground. "I've had enough spiders and snakes to last a lifetime. I know they're God's creatures and all, but they need to exist somewhere else far, far away." She scrubbed at her arms and legs.

Niamh's shell-shocked eyes met mine. She sank to her knees and started crying.

Cian knelt beside her. "Are you okay?"

Kane turned away, regret etched on his face.

I reached for his hand. "Please don't feel bad. We understand you're trying to prepare us for Dain, Dother, and Dub."

He turned his hand palm side up, stood, and pulled me to my feet. "I don't want to prepare you for them. I want to protect you. I want to shield you from them completely." He released a frustrated breath. "I cannot believe this prophecy has pit you against them."

Niamh's hands fell from her face.

Cian stared at him, the same emotions reflected on his face.

Maolisa pulled her knees to her chest. She held them like a shield while battling the fears Kane's outburst had provoked. This was the first crack we'd seen in the druids' calm, confident façade.

"You know..." I took a deep breath, acutely aware of their emotions. "I think we need to do something positive before we leave this arena... something that will restore the balance in this place."

Kane turned toward me, a strange expression on his face. "You can feel that?"

I nodded. I tried not to laugh because, seriously, how could you not? "There are a lot of negative emotions swirling around."

Cian stood, his eyes on Kane. "She's an empath."

Maolisa pushed back up onto her feet. "What's an empath?"

"A *Sidhe* who can sense how others are feeling." Cian studied me. "Not everyone can read emotions. This ability is rare."

"And useful." Kane rubbed his jaw while sifting through his thoughts. "If you can sense emotions, then you can determine what others need to feel loved. In other words, you can change how they're feeling."

Niamh was the only one still sitting on the ground, so I walked over and helped her to her feet. I wasn't sure what to make of the others eying me like I was some endangered species.

"Thanks." She wiped her tear-stained cheeks with her sleeve. "What emotions do you sense?"

The silence that followed was unsettling. Everyone was watching me, waiting to see if I could pinpoint how they were feeling. I closed my eyes so I could assess their emotions without being distracted by their facial expressions. I was worried that might prove misleading, especially when they knew they were being assessed. "I sense..." I took a deep breath, "Kane's regret, Cian's concern, Niamh's doubt, and Maolisa's fears." My brow furrowed. There was one other emotion, but it wasn't very strong. "There is a small glimmer of hope, but it's buried beneath these other emotions." I braved a peek, curious to see how they'd respond.

Cian, Maolisa, and Niamh stared at me, their mouths and eyes wide with disbelief.

I turned around.

Kane was standing behind me. He drew my back to his chest so we were facing everyone else. "Good, now show us what we need." Inside my head, he whispered, "You can draw on my energy if you need help."

My arms tensed beneath his hands. "You can draw on another *Sidhe*'s energy?"

"Yes, but only if he agrees. This requires a great deal of trust, because once that permission has been granted, that *Sidhe* can drain you completely, right down to your final heartbeat." His power pulsed beneath his hands. "I trust you, Grania. Take what you need."

His energy was depleted, likely due to the illusions he'd created, so I drew on the energy pulsing beneath my feet, in the soil that was feeding the plants and trees. I drew that energy inside me, raised my hand, and painted over the arena, transforming it into something we all needed.

Orange, lemon, and kumquat trees emerged in a perfect circle around the arena, sprouting branches, leaves, white flowers, and then fruit. Giant magnolia trees unfurled behind them, perfuming the air with the largest flowers I'd ever seen. Flowering rose bushes pushed up through the spongey soil, spiraling out from the center of the arena. The rose bushes formed a Celtic maze within the circle of trees. Hundreds of butterflies danced among their leaves. Still, it wasn't enough. I coaxed fallen logs from the forest so I could build a gazebo in the center of the arena. I added vines and climbing roses around the wood railing. And, for the finishing touch, I carved a Celtic symbol into each of the four rocks; a Celtic cross, a Celtic love knot, a Celtic spiral, and a Celtic shield. "There." My legs buckled.

Kane caught me. We were standing just outside the gazebo. The steps leading up onto the raised platform emptied out onto the four trails that formed the maze.

"Grania?" Cian turned a small circle while soaking it all in. "This isn't an illusion." He plucked a flower from one of the rose bushes, brought it to his nose, then handed it to me. "This is real."

Kane lowered me onto the ground. "How did you do this?" He sat beside me. One arm remained like a steel brace behind my back.

I brought the flower to my nose, savoring the soft, soapy smell. "I wanted to create a place that would bring you peace. I didn't want to create an illusion of peace. I wanted you to feel true joy and peace."

"I've never seen anything like it," Cian marveled. "This is amazing."

Niamh extended her hand, offering one of the butterflies a safe place to land. "You restored my hope."

Maolisa's face lifted toward the sun. "I don't feel afraid anymore."

"How did you do this?" Kane repeated. He tore his eyes from the magnolia trees so he could look at me.

"I drew some energy from the trees, thought about what you needed, and willed it into existence. I hope it's okay. Did I do something wrong?" I fought a yawn and lost.

Cian studied me. "Your energy is depleted. We should get you fed so you can rest."

A collective gasp sounded outside the arena.

Niamh turned toward the sound. "What's wrong?" We couldn't tell with all the trees surrounding us.

"I removed the concealing spell." Kane leaned back, utterly relaxed. "Everyone should get to enjoy this."

"There will be no changing it back now." Cian chuckled. "We're going to have to build another training arena."

"I can see that." Kane winked at me. "It'll be worth it, though."

Ainle landed next to me, a worried expression on his face. "Are you okay?"

My hand rose a few inches, then flopped back on the ground. "I'm fine." I wasn't really. I felt tired and dizzy.

He glanced pointedly at Kane's arm, which was still supporting my back. A growl percolated in his chest, issuing a warning I was too tired to comprehend.

Kane eased his arm out from behind my back. "She's fine. She just used a little too much energy."

Ainle caught me as I fell back. "A little?" He glared at Kane. "She's completely drained."

My eyes slid closed. Ainle smelled like warm trees and rain drenched soil. "How did you know?"

"It's a mate thing." He knit his fingers with mine. "Please, take some of my energy."

"Why?" My brow furrowed, "I..."

Kane stood abruptly. "I offered her my energy, but she refused."

Ainle tensed. "I'm the only *Sidhe* she'll be taking energy from."

I tugged my fingers from his hand. I wasn't siphoning energy from either of them. "I'll just ask the trees." I pressed my palms against the soil and drew a small portion of what I needed. I'd already drawn a staggering amount of energy from the forest when I created the garden, and I didn't want to risk damaging those precious trees by taking too much.

Ainle helped me to my feet. "Are you hungry?"

I pressed my hand to my stomach, afraid it might start growling. "Yes. I'm..."

His arm swept behind my knees.

I yelped as he swooped me up into his arms. He shot above the maze, flew across the meadow, and plunked me down at an empty table. I opened my mouth to object, but he was already gone.

He returned with a basket of bread, a pitcher of water, and two ceramic mugs. "Salad, soup, or both?" He filled the mugs and slid one in front of me.

My eyes traveled from the mug, up his arm, across the elaborate chest plate, all the way up to his breathtaking face. I wasn't sure what to make of this warrior fussing over me. I sensed he wanted, no, *needed* to take care of me. I wondered if there was any way I could talk him down from that. I felt fine, certainly well enough to dish up my own food.

He folded his arms against his chest.

Well, that certainly answers that question. I tried not to laugh. "Both?"

The tension eased from his shoulders. He nodded, then strode to the serving table.

I turned back around. When my eyes landed on the mug, I drained it completely.

Ainle set a handful of silverware and two plates heaped with heirloom tomatoes and mixed greens on the table. He walked back to the serving table and returned with two steaming bowls of potato soup. He slid onto the bench, settling in beside me. "How are you feeling?"

"Better." I shoved a forkful of salad into my mouth, worried he might try to feed me.

"I've never seen anyone grow so many things all at once." He took a bite of salad while contemplating the garden.

I followed his gaze. Several *Sidhe* hovered above the maze. Cian, Kane, and the girls were walking toward us. They looked happy, which made me happy. "I didn't stop to think I should pace myself or start small. That's what I wanted to create for them, so I did."

"That maze is beautiful." He turned. A pensive expression lingered on his face. "I wonder… maybe you don't have the same limitations the rest of us do."

"Or maybe those limits don't really exist." I nudged his shoulder playfully. "Maybe you just think they do."

Kane sat on the bench directly across from us. He nodded, acknowledging Ainle, before turning his attention to me. "I'm going to teach Maolisa how to make it rain while Cian teaches Niamh how to use the wind. You've clearly mastered how to move, build, and grow things, so I'd prefer you rest this afternoon."

"Okay." I didn't want Ainle to think I was weak, but I still felt exhausted. The energy I'd drawn from the trees wasn't enough. That reminded me, "Why would you offer your energy when I can just draw it from the trees?"

Kane's gaze slid to Ainle. Some unspoken thought passed between them before he answered. "The energy you obtain from the *Sidhe*, any *Sidhe*, is faster acting, longer lasting, and more potent. This energy will increase your power ten-fold or more, depending on the *Sidhe* you pulled energy from. It is the purest form of energy you can receive. You also gain that *Sidhe's* abilities, temporarily of course."

"Unless you drain him completely." Ainle looked at me. "If you drain a *Sidhe* completely, then his abilities are transferred to you. Permanently."

Goose bumps pricked my arms. I didn't like the sound of that at all. "So, we draw from these other sources so we don't hurt one another."

"There's more air, water, and trees than there are *Sidhe*," Ainle murmured.

"Most of the *Sidhe* who survived *Fomorian* rule died during the *Second Battle of Magh Tuireadh*," Kane explained.

"We've resisted drawing energy from one another ever since. We don't want to risk weakening or depleting any one *Sidhe's* energy reserve, especially now, when the Goddess Carman's sons are gaining in power and strength."

"Then why offer your energy to me?" I repeated incredulously.

"Because you should learn how to draw energy from another *Sidhe* before you face Dain, Dother, and Dub," Kane answered softly. "There are places in the human realm where you won't have access to trees. As one of the *Chosen Ones*, your life and your ability to fulfill this prophecy will outweigh the need to keep any other *Sidhe* alive."

Tears quickly flooded my eyes. "I won't do it. I will not risk another *Sidhe's* life."

He drew in a breath. "Then we'll lose everything. Every *Sidhe* will die."

I stood abruptly. Kane didn't know I was the one who was supposed to sacrifice my life. Not him. Not Ainle. Not any other *Sidhe*. Me. That's what the Rowan Tree said. My jaw clenched. I couldn't tell him. I knew he'd try to talk me out of it. "I'm sorry. I need to rest."

Ainle stood. "I'll walk you to Fianna' house."

"Thanks." I met Kane's gaze. "Thank you for offering your energy and for being so honest with me. I promise I will think about it. I just... I'm questioning whether this is what I'm meant to do."

The concern in his eyes deepened. "I understand."

Ainle twined his fingers with mine. He waited until we'd gained some distance from Kane before speaking telepathically. "I'm worried you may not have all the information you need to make an informed decision on this."

I nodded, reluctantly agreeing to hear him out.

"Kane's right. The *Sidhe* have resisted borrowing energy from one another since the *Second Battle of Magh Tuireadh*, but there are two exceptions. The first exception is made for life-threatening injuries. We heal quickly, and most injuries are easily treated by our healer, so that exception seldom comes into play. The second exception is far more common." Ainle paused. He appeared to be choosing his words carefully. "Fated mates frequently exchange energy so they can strengthen and combine their abilities. They don't exchange a lot of energy, just a little on a regular basis."

I stopped walking. "So that's why you were mad at Kane... because this is something special, shared by fated mates?"

Ainle nodded. He looked embarrassed, but he forced himself to meet my gaze. "That energy connects you in a very special way. It brings you closer. That's why it's allowed for fated mates."

I didn't know what to say. Clearly, he was hoping we might exchange energy like this someday. I wasn't even remotely ready for this conversation, so I resumed walking.

"You know that extra boost of energy we get when we sleep inside the palace?" He eyed me in a sidelong glance.

I nodded, wishing against all odds this might be a change in conversation. "Yes."

"We radiate energy, not to the extent the Goddess Danu does, but enough so that others feel it. That's why humans and animals are drawn to us."

My feet slowed. "Really?"

He nodded. "We also absorb energy from one another when we're together, especially inside the palace." His gaze shifted toward the waterfall and the palace hidden within the mountain. "That palace was carved in amethyst for a reason. Amethyst magnifies our energy and promotes healing."

I followed his gaze. "That's… intriguing."

He clasped both my hands, drawing me to a stop beneath Fianna's deck. "What I'm trying to say is we already exchange energy… maybe not in the same quantity we would if injured or sharing energy as mates, but it is still an energy exchange."

I couldn't resist the smile tempting my lips. That sneaky *Sidhe* had brought our conversation right back to where we'd started. "That's different. Everyone inside the palace benefits from that energy exchange. No one is at risk of being depleted. No one can get hurt."

Those blue topaz eyes sparked with a determination that stole my breath. "Mates are hardwired to protect one another. It is physically impossible for them to hurt one another, to take so much energy they risk depleting the other."

I chewed my bottom lip. Ainle made a pretty compelling case. He drew me closer, so close we were nearly touching. I could feel the energy radiating from him, inviting me to inch even closer. That warm tree and rain drenched soil smell was back too. I couldn't resist breathing it in. "I should go."

He tipped my chin up so I was forced to look at him. "Please. I just… I want you to keep an open mind."

I nodded, completely entranced by those sparkling blue eyes.

He pressed a kiss to my cheek. "I heard you're going to sing for the unicorns tonight."

"Yes. Well, I don't know if I'll be singing, but I definitely plan to be there." I stepped back so I could fly up onto the deck. I'd already caught Fianna peeking over the edge.

His smile widened. "Good. I'll see you then."

* * *

Fianna and I flew across the lake with our blankets secured beneath our arms. Brigitte, Maolisa, Ciara, and Niamh were camped out on the far side, waiting for us. Diarmuid, Treasach, and Ainle were sitting a few feet away beneath a large oak tree. I waved when we touched down.

Diarmuid grinned. Treasach and Ainle waved back at me. They were playing a board game with a grid like chess. "What game is that?"

Fianna glanced in their direction. "*Fidchell.* Ainle is defending the king."

"Won't the unicorns be afraid if the warriors are with us?" Maolisa looked up from where she was sitting. "They are kind of intimidating."

Ciara's gaze slid between the warriors and the tree line. "No. If anything, they'll feel safer."

Niamh stretched out on her blanket. She propped her chin in her hands while staring dreamily toward the sky. "Please, tell us about the song."

A smile teased at Brigitte's lips. "It's a love song, typically reserved for fated mates. There are very few words. I'm sure you'll have it memorized in no time." She glanced at the other guardians. "What do you think?"

Fianna shrugged. "It's quiet." She stretched her blanket next to mine. "Most everyone has settled in for the night."

Ciara peered up at the sky. "All three moons are full, and the weather is perfect. Let's give it a try."

Brigitte began. "*You are the light in my moon, the water in my fall, and the soil beneath my feet. Will you dance... will you dance... will you dance with me? You hold my heart, my life, my dreams. Will you dance... will you dance with me? You are mine as I am yours. My love, will you dance with me?*"

My heart fluttered when she sang the words. I risked a peek at Ainle.

His hand hovered above the board. He'd stopped mid-play to listen to the words. His eyes slid toward me. He grinned when he caught me staring at him, then winked.

My cheeks heated. I pretended to smooth the blanket before turning toward Brigitte.

Ciara joined her when she repeated the song. Fianna sang with them the third time around. Their voices sounded pure and sweet. Gradually, Maolisa, Niamh, and I joined in. I thought the warriors might sing with us, but they didn't. They listened with contented smiles on their faces, their game long forgotten.

The moons in *Tír na nÓg* bathed everything in a soft blue light, ensuring the stark white unicorn looked even more magical when she approached the lake. Her horn and hooves weren't silver or gold as I'd anticipated. She was entirely white except for her nose and eyes, which were black as night. Her horn was longer than I expected. Her mane and tail looked wild and full of tangles.

One by one, our voices trailed off.

"Hi," Brigitte acknowledged softly. "Would you like to join us?"

There was a barely perceptible nod as she approached our blankets.

Ciara smiled. "Can we comb your hair?"

She flicked her tail and nodded.

Fianna pulled three wide brushes from her bag and set them on the blanket. "There you go."

Maolisa, Niamh, and I each claimed a brush. I stood, moving slowly so I wouldn't scare her away. "What's your name?"

"Davina." She eyed the warriors curiously.

Brigitte and Ciara resumed singing.

Fianna fed Davina an apple while we removed the twigs and leaves from her mane. We brushed the silky soft strands.

Ciara gathered some flowers and wove them into her hair. I combed her tail while Maolisa and Niamh ran their brushes over her back.

Davina leaned into the brushes, savoring every stroke. We set the brushes on the blanket when we were through.

She peered into the lake to admire our work.

Our eyes met in the reflection. "You look beautiful."

Her head lifted. "Thank you. Would you like to play?"

I could barely contain my excitement. "We would love to! What do you want to play?"

Her eyes sparked with amusement. "Do you have any ribbon?"

I turned to ask Fianna.

She laughed. Three long ribbons in green, gold, and blue dangled from her hand. Clearly, she'd been expecting this. "Davina loves to play keep away. Tie them loosely to her mane. She'll dodge your efforts to capture them. The first girl to claim her ribbon wins."

"How fun!" Niamh swept the ribbons from Fianna's hand. She dropped the green ribbon in Maolisa's hand and gave the gold ribbon to me. We tied the ribbons loosely.

Davina backed away. "Ready?"

"Yes!" We jumped up and down excitedly.

Davina pranced back and forth, clearly teasing. "I'm waiting!"

We lunged for the ribbons. Our guardians cheered us on while Davina evaded us. Two more unicorns ran from the forest. They danced between us, which made it even more difficult to capture the ribbons. Eventually, we collapsed onto the grass without a single ribbon in our hands.

Brigitte laughed. "Davina gets to keep the ribbons. Here, I'll help you weave them into her mane."

We secured the ribbons and brushed the newcomers' hair before joining our guardians on the blankets. The unicorns bedded down beside us.

Softly, our guardians began to sing.

The warriors kept watch as we drifted off to sleep.

Chapter 7 – Celtic Knots

Kane led us into the new training arena, which was sandwiched between the mounds that housed the warriors and our new meditation garden. "We're going to try deflecting energy without any protective spells today. You should be prepared for what it feels like when you're struck with energy outside this arena. Our healer will be joining us shortly."

Healer? My heart skipped a beat.

Cian peered up at the darkening sky. "We'll practice throwing and deflecting energy while we fly. Drop back down onto the ground if it begins to rain. Flying is extremely dangerous in the rain." He turned toward Maolisa. "If you'd like, you can try to divert the rain."

She nodded, her eyes filled with excitement.

Kane stopped in the center of the arena. "We're going to throw some weapons into the mix... throwing knives, spears, arrows, and rocks. You should learn how to deflect those objects. The warriors will shield you as best they can, but they may have their hands full with the *Fomorians* when you're on Mangerton Mountain. Your energy shield is your first line of defense. Make sure that shield surrounds your body the entire time. If you need more energy, then you know where to find it. If you cannot obtain it from your respective sources, then you can ask another *Sidhe* to feed you energy."

I folded my arms across my chest. I couldn't believe he was bringing this up again.

"Don't seek energy from the warriors on Mangerton Mountain," Cian warned. "We want our warriors functioning at full strength so they can protect us. Your guardians and I will be there, creating diversions, controlling the elements, and deflecting dark magick while you confront Dain, Dother, and Dub. You can draw energy from us, but you must be careful. When you draw energy from another *Sidhe*, you will weaken him. If you take too much, he may not survive. Just be aware, there is more than one life on the line."

I nodded, although my decision remained unchanged. I wasn't going to request energy, not if it meant risking another *Sidhe's* life.

Maolisa shook her head vehemently. "I don't want to draw energy from anyone."

"I still don't understand how we're going to fight them." Niamh's bottom lip quivered. "Do we have to kill them? I don't want to kill anyone, not even Dain, Dother, or Dub."

That same fear had been plaguing me for days. I didn't want to kill the Goddess Carman's sons, but if it meant saving my sister and mom... A tear slid down my cheek.

Silence fell like a lead weight while the druids communicated telepathically. Finally, Kane spoke. "There is nothing in the prophecy that says you have to kill Dain, Dother, or Dub. In fact, I think that would be contrary to your purpose."

Maolisa grabbed my arm. "Thank God."

Niamh nodded.

"The prophecy states, '*Violence, evil, and darkness are threatening the balance between the realms. If they reign, they will destroy the realms. Love, faith, and light can restore the balance,*'" Cian reminded us. "If you end their reign in the human realm, that should be enough. End their control over the *Fomorians* and their attacks on humans. Inspire faith, hope, and love. That should weaken them enough to end their reign and restore the balance between the realms."

I brushed the tear from my cheek. We just had to focus on the positive, the good things we could do to end their reign. That sounded so much better than what I'd been envisioning.

Diarmuid, Treasach, and Ainle strode toward us. They had several weapons strapped onto their backs, waists, and legs. "We're ready when you are."

"The warriors are throwing the weapons?" Niamh blurted incredulously.

Cian chuckled. "Their aim is better than ours. They'll ensure no vital organs or arteries are struck."

"And this is Dian, our healer." Kane directed our attention to the man in a long, hooded robe, who had just entered the arena. "He'll ensure any injuries are healed."

Dian's eyes were intense, and he didn't look like he laughed or smiled very much. I was thinking I should avoid him at all costs.

He smiled then, as if reading my thoughts.

A reminder that I should love everyone and treat them with kindness even if they frighten me. I extended my hand politely. "Thank you for coming."

His warm hand grasped mine. "I'm happy to help, especially if it means putting an end to Dain, Dother, and Dub's attacks."

Kane clapped his hands, making us all jump. "Okay, ladies! Shields up!"

I drew energy from the trees, coaxed it to the surface of my skin, and then pushed it out a short distance. A warm, tingly sensation danced along my skin, evidence that my shield was protecting everything it should. I glanced at Maolisa and Niamh. "Ready?"

Niamh shrugged. "As I'll ever be."

We called our wings, pushed up into the air, and positioned ourselves over the center of the arena. We turned our backs to one another so we could see the entire arena and warn each other when energy and objects started flying.

The druids pelted us with purple masses of energy while the warriors stood there and watched. We deflected most of the energy. What little we missed fizzled out when it struck our shields. We had to reinforce our shields every time we took a hit like that.

Diarmuid threw the first spear. Treasach shot several arrows while Ainle flung knives. Cian and Kane alternated between hurling rocks and energy.

We ducked and bobbed, trying to avoid the objects. "How do we deflect these things?" Maolisa yelled.

I threw a handful of energy at one of the rocks. The stone burst into tiny pieces, which rained down on the arena. "I guess that answers that question." I laughed.

Maolisa obliterated several arrows. "Now this is fun."

A knife nicked Niamh in the leg. "Ow!" She scowled.

I glanced at her calf. "Are you okay?" Her leggings were torn. Blood seeped through the material.

"Yes," she gritted. "I need a thicker shield."

A small whirlwind formed near the edge of the arena.

Maolisa ducked. "Hey that was close!" An arrow soared past her shoulder.

I glanced at Niamh. "Is that your dust devil?"

She huffed out a breath. "Yes, but there's hardly any dust. The soil is too moist."

"Here, let me help." I coaxed broken twigs and pebbles from the forest and dumped them into her wind tunnel. "Take that!"

Maolisa laughed. Suddenly, it was raining but only over the top of our opponents.

Niamh sent her wind tunnel spiraling toward them.

Cian ran while Kane tried to stop all the different elements from attacking them. The warriors flew up out of the way.

Dian was laughing.

While Cian and Kane were distracted, the warriors had risen above the fray. They were at eye level now, throwing silver stars and flinging knives at us. One of Ainle's stars nicked my arm.

"Hey! That is *not* okay!" I strengthened my shield before throwing energy at him.

They were closing in.

"They're going to get us!" Maolisa screamed.

I grabbed her arm before she could flee. "We need a big burst of light. Try to blind them with your light," I urged Niamh.

Her face scrunched.

My eyes slammed shut.

Light burst from her hands, warming the air around us.

"I can't see!" Treasach tumbled toward the ground.

Dian ran to him.

The druids fired energy in rapid succession.

Niamh looked panicked. Still, she deflected energy.

I couldn't shake the feeling that we were missing something. Suddenly, the goddess's words replayed inside my head… *There are three of you for a reason.* "I know! Let's combine our energy into one solid stream. I'll weave it into a Celtic love knot when we release it. Draw on your faith, Maolisa. Niamh, give us some hope. Send the energy out and then down. On the count of three!"

We linked hands.

Diarmuid and Ainle prepared to strike.

We lifted our arms and quickly counted, "One, two, three!"

We brought our hands down while shooting the energy between our fingers. I willed it into a Celtic love knot and prayed it wouldn't hurt anyone. A sonic boom sounded as green, gold, and blue light swirled into interlocking hearts that stretched past the arena and hurtled toward the ground.

The silence was deafening.

My heart raced. "Are they okay?"

A purple shield covered Cian and Kane. They were crouched protectively over Dian and Treasach. Diarmuid and Ainle were sprawled out on the ground, looking stunned but blissfully happy.

We dropped our shields and joined them. "Are you okay?"

The druids released their shields. "What was that?"

I glanced at Treasach, concerned about his eyesight. "We combined our energy; infused it with faith, hope, and love; tied it into a Celtic love knot; and threw it so it would hit the warriors and everyone on the ground."

Cian's jaw fell slack.

"You should have felt it," Ainle crooned. "It felt like a warm blanket, the highest compliment, and a thousand hugs all rolled into one."

Diarmuid shook his head. "I've lost all desire to fight. I couldn't throw another weapon if I tried."

"Why'd you shield us?" Treasach grumbled. "I would have liked to feel that."

"Me too." Dian studied us, unabashedly curious.

The druids were too busy speaking telepathically to respond.

I knelt in front of Treasach. "Can you see?"

He flashed a charmingly crooked smile. "I'm fine. Dian healed me."

Niamh released the breath she'd been holding. "Thank goodness."

"May I?" Dian nodded toward her leg.

"Sure." She rolled her leggings up. Her hair tumbled over her shoulders while she watched him work. "That's amazing."

He reached for my arm. "Please, allow me."

I watched in amazement as the wound sealed, faded to pink, and then disappeared completely. "That's quite the superpower."

Dian grinned.

My heart tripped. "Do you..." Memories threatened to overwhelm me... Lexie in a hospital bed, hooked up to machines, taking medicine, and vomiting. "Do you think you could heal my sister, Lexie? She's been sick since she was a baby."

The smile slid from his face. "I can try."

I tried not to panic. I reached for his thread inside my head so we could speak more privately. "If I don't survive, will you still try?"

Worry darkened his eyes. "I will do everything in my power to help you and your sister regardless of what transpires with this prophecy."

"Thank you." I should have felt relieved, but I didn't. I rested my forehead on my knees as I squeezed them to my chest. I missed my family terribly.

Dian remained by my side, his shoulder subtly touching mine.

"How much energy did that require?" Kane asked. "Do you feel okay?"

I met his worried gaze. "I feel drained, no worse than yesterday, though." I flattened my hands against the soil so I could pull some energy from the forest. Maolisa and Niamh restored their energy through their respective sources.

I could almost see the thoughts churning inside Kane's head. "Do you think you can do that again?"

I glanced at my friends. They nodded, so I answered, "Yes."

Cian's eyes glittered with excitement. "So, now we know. This is how you're going to fight Dain, Dother, and Dub."

* * *

I grabbed a glass of orange juice and a blueberry muffin from the serving table before climbing onto the bench across from Maolisa and Niamh. Fianna sat down beside me.

Niamh lowered her glass. "Did you talk to your dad?"

I nodded. I'd been crying. My puffy eyes had probably given me away. "Yes. Mom and Lexie are okay. They're still being held in some sort of coma above Devil's Punch Bowl."

Niamh reached for my hand. "They aren't hurting them?"

I shook my head. "Dad said they're just watching and waiting for us to arrive."

Her eyes softened. "They know you'll come for them."

I nodded. I knew I needed to eat, but I felt nauseous. "They're keeping them alive so they can manipulate me."

Her hand tightened around mine. "We're going to make sure they lose all interest in hurting your family and every other living thing."

I smiled, grateful for the hope she was offering.

Maolisa tore a bite-size piece from the bread she was eating. "What is this Devil's Punch Bowl?"

Kane claimed a spot on the other side of Fianna. "Devil's Punch Bowl is a glacial lake that has been around since the Ice Age."

She leaned forward, anticipating some additional explanation.

He stirred marmalade into his oatmeal instead.

"Any idea why they would choose that location?" She drummed her fingers against the table when he didn't respond.

He looked up from his bowl.

Everyone stared at him.

"There's some speculation surrounding the lake." He waved it away dismissively.

Fianna nearly choked on her tea. "I don't think that's going to cut it, Kane."

"Honestly, it's just speculation." He shoved a spoonful of oatmeal in his mouth.

"You're a druid, not a guardian," Fianna chided. "Besides, they deserve to know what they're up against."

"Fine," he relented. "The water in the Devil's Punch Bowl is frigid but never freezes, even when the temperature is well below freezing. The water churns, and it is pitch black, so it looks and feels ominous. Some claim it has been touched by the devil's hand."

I swallowed. Hard. Lexie and Mom were being suspended above a giant cauldron, and my dad was one mishap away from joining them.

"What do you believe?" Maolisa finally asked.

"I believe the Goddess Carman cast a spell on the lake before she was imprisoned. I don't know why. I haven't spent enough time there to figure it out. We generally try to avoid that area." Kane curled his arm protectively around his bowl before he tucked back into his food.

Diarmuid joined us. *"Maidin Mhaith."* A steaming bowl of oatmeal plunked down in front of him.

I figured this was as good a time as any to share some of my father's observations. "Dad saw some *Fomorians* near Torc Mountain. There were more *Fomorians* than their small contingent of warriors could handle, so they didn't engage."

He didn't look even remotely surprised. "Cathal requested additional warriors. They're already en route."

Cian sat next to Niamh. "The *Fomorians* can't survive long outside of water, which is why they're gathering around the rivers and lakes."

"We should send scouts to Muckross Lake and *Lough Leane,*" Kane suggested. "The *Fomorians* will seize those lakes if they haven't already."

"Do you really think they'll venture that close to civilization?" Diarmuid frowned.

"I still don't get why they've ventured so far from the ocean," Cian grumbled.

Kane sipped his tea. "I'm telling you, it's Dain, Dother, and Dub. The *Fomorians* are gathering near them for a reason. They're working together, but why?"

Grandpa folded his arms against the table. "I'm guessing they've promised them something, but what?"

"With Dain, Dother, and Dub destroying the border, the *Fomorians* may be preparing to invade *Tír na nÓg*. They've enslaved us once before. I'm sure they'd love to do it again," Cian speculated.

Niamh shuddered. "What do the *Fomorians* look like?"

"I was contemplating that as well." I'd been picking at my muffin while following the conversation.

Cian shared an image telepathically.

"Oh, God!" Maolisa tried shaking the picture from her mind.

The *Fomorians* were deformed giants with demonic faces and eyes.

Kane set his tea aside. "The *Fomorians* are extremely violent. Some have claimed to be in excruciating pain. I think that's what causes them to go insane."

I frowned. I knew what pain did to people. It changed them. A lot. "Maybe Triple D has found a way to ease their pain."

"Triple D?" Cian chuckled. "Is that what they're calling Dain, Dother, and Dub these days?"

I cracked a much needed smile. "I'm tired of saying all three names."

Kane shook his head. "Why would Dain, Dother, or Dub ease their pain? They enjoy seeing people suffer. They like causing pain."

Cian's eyes widened. "Wait. I think she's onto something."

I nodded, certain he was on the same page as me. "Every painful experience offers an opportunity." I glanced at Kane. "If Triple D isn't helping them, then maybe we should." My gaze slid toward Maolisa and Niamh. "What do you think?"

"If we can ease their pain, they may not want to hurt us anymore," Niamh offered thoughtfully. "They may want to protect us instead."

"I'm certain we can do it." Maolisa looked downright giddy. "Think about how we made Diarmuid and Ainle feel yesterday."

"I know someone who is quite skilled in this area." Cian winked at Dian, who had just settled in at the table. "Maybe Dian should join us."

Dian pulled back the hood covering his head. "You assume I'd let the *Chosen Ones* face those monsters alone. I was already planning on joining them."

"Good." Kane smiled. "That's settled then. I'm anxious to see how the *Fomorians* behave when they're pain free. We'll stop at Upper Lake along the way. It would be nice if we could end the threat posed by the *Fomorians* before we confront Dain, Dother, and Dub."

"What sort of training are we going to do today?" Maolisa was concealing different objects on the table. It was funny watching Kane drink from an invisible mug.

Kane frowned at the missing mug. "I want you to spend some time in the meditation garden, reflecting on how your own unique powers can be used to restore the balance between the realms. How can you apply faith, light, and love to end violence, darkness, and evil throughout the human realm? Then, I'd like you to work with Dian. We need a concrete plan, a strategy we know will prove effective, before we meet with the *Fomorians*."

Cian stood. "I'd like to strengthen your defense skills after lunch. I want to see faster response times and a more intuitive response. You shouldn't have to think about this. Your response should be instinctive when your life is being threatened."

Kane gathered his bowl and mug. "We're going to see how the border is holding up." He acknowledged Diarmuid with a polite nod. "We'll join you after lunch."

We cleared our dishes. Two additional warriors joined us on our way to the meditation garden. I didn't recognize either of them. "Where's Ainle?"

"Why? Do you miss him?" Diarmuid swung his arm over my shoulders affectionately.

I tried to escape his hug, but the massive warrior wouldn't budge. "I was just curious."

Grandpa smiled like he didn't quite believe me. "Ainle is resting so he can spar with you this afternoon. You know, you knocked the fight out of us. That's not good for a warrior."

A chuckle sounded behind us.

I glanced at the warriors before meeting Grandpa's gaze. "But you seem fine."

He shrugged. "I'm a seasoned warrior. Ainle hasn't even experienced his first battle."

"How's Treasach?" Maolisa slowed so she was walking beside us. Niamh did as well.

"He's fine." Diarmuid turned when the warriors snickered a second time. "He wants to spar with you this afternoon."

We paused in front of the maze. Grandpa remained with us while the other warriors flew over the garden to confirm it was safe. They weren't taking any chances, especially with the *Sidhe Sluagh* slipping through the portal the other day. Finally, Diarmuid nodded his approval. "Whenever you're ready."

I wasn't sure how to proceed. "Should we go in together, stagger our entry, or wait for each person to finish?"

Niamh looked up from the magnolia blossom she was sniffing. "If we staggered our entry, it would allow us some time to think through our options. We can meet at the gazebo, strategize for a while, and enjoy the garden on our way out."

"Sounds good," Maolisa agreed.

Niamh was standing closest to the entrance, so I asked her, "Would you like to go first?"

"Sure." She smiled as she glanced back at us. Her fingers danced in a little wave before she disappeared between the trees.

I sat at the base of a tree. "I really admire her strength." I knew she missed her family, and she was just as scared as me, but she still managed to stay positive and upbeat.

"Me too." Maolisa reached between the trees.

Diarmuid settled in beside me. "You know, I've heard her say the same thing about the two of you."

A smile tugged at Maolisa's lips. "How long should we give her?" She tossed an orange in the air.

I shrugged. "Five maybe ten minutes? I'll just hang out here with Grandpa if you want to go next."

"Sure." She peeled the orange while pacing in front of us. She slipped a wedge between her teeth and bit down with an appreciative hum. "I love oranges."

I smiled at the juice glistening on her chin. "I noticed. You know, the one thing I couldn't add was a water feature." Maolisa was the water spirit, not me. "If you'd like to add one..."

Her eyes brightened. "Really? You wouldn't mind?"

"Of course not." I liked the idea of it being a group project. "Let me know if you need help with rocks or anything."

She swiped the juice from her chin. "Thanks!" She popped another orange wedge inside her mouth and disappeared inside the garden.

Diarmuid stood. He held his hand out and pulled me to my feet. "You're a good friend, Grania." He plucked a flower from the tree and tucked it in my hair.

"Thanks, Grandpa." I wrapped my arms around his waist. "Thank you for being here for me."

His chin settled on top of my head. "There's no place else I'd rather be."

I closed my eyes and savored the hug. With a grateful smile, I stepped back and ventured into the trees. The trail branched into three different directions. I chose the path on my right. The roses smelled amazing. The air was filled with happy chirps, birds chattering, and singing.

I thought back on the conversation I had with my dad this morning. I could tell he was worried about Lexie and Mom but was hesitant to expose me to Dain, Dother, and Dub. He understood my purpose and was trying to be supportive, but he was still my dad. He was doing his best to protect all three of us while still safeguarding *Tír na nÓg*, something all warriors were called to do.

My fingers trailed along the roses perched atop the bushes. I knew we could eliminate the threat posed by the *Fomorians*. With Dian's help, we'd find a way to ease their pain. I was certain their alliances would change after that. Cian didn't think we should concern ourselves with the *Sidhe Sluagh*. They couldn't hurt us as long as we maintained hope. Niamh wouldn't allow us to lose hope. That left Triple D. With the *Sidhe* warriors supporting us, I believed we could rescue Lexie and Mom. The more pressing question was how to restore the balance between the realms. If we combined our energy like we did yesterday, we might be able to remove Dain, Dother, and Dub's desire to hurt others, but would that be enough to restore the balance? What about all the violent crimes and wars that were already being waged all across the planet? How could three twelve-year-old girls end that? I was still struggling with that question when the trail emptied in front of my friends.

I shared my concerns when I joined them on the steps. "We're supposed to restore the balance between the realms. So, what are your thoughts? Is it enough that we stop Triple D? What about all the other violence they've incited? There are wars being waged all over the planet."

Niamh studied the butterfly perched on her knee. "There must be some way we can expand our reach."

Maolisa appeared deep in thought. "Why don't we use the five-fold Celtic knot? It's a directional knot. The four outer circles represent North, South, East, and West while the center circle unites all the elements and seeks to achieve balance."

"That would allow us to expand our reach," Niamh agreed. "I think we should apply the Celtic love knot first. If Triple D are at the center of all this violence and darkness, then we need to remove their desire to hurt others before we apply the directional knot."

I turned the idea in my head. "Do you think we'd have enough energy to do that, to tie our energy twice, applying the love knot first and then the directional knot?"

Maolisa stood and walked around the gazebo. "Yes, as long as we have access to our energy sources."

Niamh smiled. "I like it… it's sort of like a one-two punch."

I pushed up off the steps. "Okay. I think we've got a solid plan."

Maolisa returned from her stroll around the gazebo. "Do you want to build a fountain?"

The excitement dancing in her eyes made me smile. "Sure."

"Absolutely." Niamh leapt from the steps.

She led us to the perfect spot. "Okay, Niamh's going to do her wind thingy to keep the water moving. If you can gather some rocks and maybe hollow out a large boulder, I can fill it with water."

I was getting ready to coax some rocks from the forest when her words caught up with me. "You want me to hollow out a boulder?"

She nodded. "Well, yes. I need something to put the water in."

"I can hollow it out with the wind," Niamh suggested.

I eyed her with some surprise. "Niamh, that's a fantastic idea. I hadn't a clue how I was going to cut through that rock." I coaxed two boulders, several odd shaped rocks, and smooth pebbles from the forest.

The warriors looked a little alarmed when they saw the rocks flying toward us. Maolisa reached out to them telepathically. She assured them we had requested the rocks for a project we were working on. They seemed to relax after that.

I lowered the boulders and rocks gently onto the ground. "I thought one boulder could serve as the base. If you cut the second boulder in half and hollow out each end, the top half could sit on the base, and the water could trickle down into the bottom half."

Maolisa smiled. "Sounds like a plan."

The violet-backed starling, who regularly mooched berries from me, landed on the hedge. He watched while we built the fountain.

Niamh cut the boulder and hollowed each end with a tiny wind cyclone. We positioned the boulders as planned. I added several pebbles and rocks. Maolisa made it rain directly over the basins. The violet-backed starling hopped in and splashed us before Niamh could add the wind. Before long, the water was gurgling in our stone fountain. The birds loved it.

We walked through the maze, feeling lighter, more confident, and at peace. Diarmuid was waiting for us when we stepped from the trees. "How'd you do?"

I slid my hand in the crook of his arm. "Good. We've got a plan."

"I look forward to hearing about it." We walked toward the training arena. "I heard you built a fountain."

"We did." Maolisa grinned. "You should see what Niamh can do with wind."

Niamh's cheeks turned pink. "It was nothing, really."

One of the warriors who had been circling overhead dropped down beside us. "Nice work."

"Thanks." We burst out laughing when we answered at the exact same time.

Diarmuid smiled. "It's nice hearing you laugh." We walked past the training arena, toward the *Sidhe* mounds. "This is Dian's place."

We stopped in front of the mound sandwiched between the training arena and the warriors' quarters. The mound itself was deceptive. From the outside, it looked like a small, grassy hill with a stone entrance. The entrance didn't look big enough to accommodate Diarmuid's wings, but it did. Stone steps dropped us further beneath the ground. The inside was a lot bigger than the outside suggested. While the ceiling was wood, the floor was stone. The two elements met about midway up the wall. There were two separate rooms with cots, herbs, and medical supplies near the bottom of the steps, an eat-in kitchen, a library, and a bedroom near the back. There were several lanterns lit throughout the home.

Diarmuid walked straight through to the kitchen with nary a knock while our security detail remained outside. "I see you snagged some cookies."

Dian set the plateful of cookies on the table. "Yes. They are remarkably easy to obtain once the cook learns you're entertaining these three." He winked at me. "Would you like some tea?"

"Sure." Mugs and tea infusers of varying shapes and sizes were scattered on the table. We chose our mugs and infusers before settling into the chairs.

Niamh dangled one of the tea balls from its delicate chain. "Where did you find these?"

"Our artisans make them. They make all our dishes, furniture, jewelry, weapons, and clothes." Dian set three tins filled with crushed tea leaves on the table. "I have black tea, blackberry tea, and mint." He retrieved a teapot, a bowl full of sugar, and a small pot of honey from the counter and set them on the table.

"Thank you." I filled one of the infusers with blackberry tea and plopped it in my mug.

Dian poured the water for everyone. "There you go. Enjoy." He grabbed a cookie before claiming his chair.

Niamh watched the infuser bob up and down in her mug while she tugged on the chain. "How does that work exactly? I mean, we have all these beautiful clothes, this handmade pottery, and all these wonderful meals prepared for us, but I haven't seen anyone exchange any money."

Dian polished off the last little bite of his cookie. "Our artisans make things because they enjoy making things. This holds true for the artisans who cook. I heal people because it is something I've been called to do. Our guardians and warriors keep us safe. Everyone is doing what he loves to do, and that is reward enough."

Diarmuid removed the infuser from his mug. "We enjoy sharing our talents and helping one another, so we don't need money. Money just complicates things, especially when you already have everything you need."

I thought about the bills my parents had to sift through at home. "I wish the human realm worked like that."

"Me too." Maolisa swirled honey in her tea.

The room fell silent. I suspected we were all contemplating why that wouldn't work.

Dian blew steam from his mug. "So, you want to heal the *Fomorians*..."

Niamh looked up from her tea. "Is it true that they're in pain?"

"The few I've spoken with have been in excruciating pain." His voice remained even. Still, I could sense his empathy for their plight.

"Do you know why?" Blackberry scented steam curled above my mug. I took a cautious sip. The tea tasted just like blackberries, only sweeter. The hint of lemon rind surprised me.

Dian studied us over the top of his mug. "I believe they suffer from musculoskeletal pain, which is linked to their deformities. Some have lost limbs in battle. I'm sure that has led to some pain as well."

"Do you have any medicine that might ease their suffering?" Niamh inquired hopefully.

"I could mix some minerals in an ointment, but any pain relief they would gain from this would be temporary. They would have to reapply the ointment multiple times throughout the day, and I'm not sure I have enough for all the *Fomorians*. I could try to heal each one individually, applying some of my own energy, but that would take some time. I couldn't heal them all in a single day, a week, or even a month given the energy that would require. Changing one's bone structure is not a simple task. It's never been attempted, so I don't know what the impact would be to their muscles or their function. I am not aware of any *Fomorians* who would allow me to experiment on them in this way."

I tried one of the chocolate chip cookies. They were crunchy on the outside, soft in the center, with just the right amount of chocolate and vanilla. "You mention minerals. Is there a mineral hot spring where they can soak to ease their pain?"

"Most hot springs contain these same minerals," Dian confirmed, "but the only hot spring I'm aware of near the Tomies Wood is the one that marks the portal between *Tír na nÓg* and the human realm. We cannot reveal that location to the *Fomorians*."

Maolisa leaned forward, eager to share her idea. "The *Fomorians* have already gathered at Upper Lake. What if we draw some of these same minerals up through the soil beneath Upper Lake and warm the water for them?"

He turned the idea in his head. "That could work, but it would draw even more *Fomorians* to this area. I don't know that we want the *Fomorians* living so close to us, given all their warmongering and other violent tendencies."

Niamh plucked a cookie from the plate. "The violence and warmongering may end if they're not in pain."

My mind kept circling back to our strategy in the training arena, when we tied our energy into the Celtic love knot. I couldn't see how that would relieve pain, but a similar approach was worth considering. "Is there a Celtic knot that promotes healing?"

His brow furrowed. "There isn't a knot per se, but there is a symbol that could prove useful. Ailm is the Celtic symbol for good health. It is most often associated with the fir tree, resilience, longevity, and healing."

"Ailm is also a letter in the *Ogham* alphabet," Diarmuid mused. "It looks like a perfectly square cross." He shared the image with us telepathically.

"Maybe we can combine our energy and channel it into that symbol to ease their pain." I wasn't sure a Celtic symbol would work the same way as a Celtic knot, but I figured it was worth a try.

"That Ailm should prove far simpler than the Celtic love knot you created yesterday," Maolisa said, quickly weighing in.

Niamh grinned. "That love knot was something else."

Dian turned to Diarmuid. "Do you have any warriors who have been too stubborn or proud to seek relief for their pain?"

He brushed the cookie crumbs from his chest plate. "I can think of a few."

"A few?" Dian rolled his eyes. "Why don't you gather them in the training arena so we can see how this works? Don't tell them what we're doing. I want an unbiased assessment of how they feel after being exposed to the girls' power. Just tell them the girls are testing out a new skill."

Grandpa nodded. "They're on their way."

I was still trying to envision how this was going to work. An important piece seemed to be missing, and I was pretty sure he was sitting right in front of me. I met Dian's gaze. "You're our healer. Maybe we should feed you our energy so you can form the Ailm."

That intense gaze of his softened. He looked honored, but he shook his head. "You three are the only *Sidhe* who can merge their power in this way. If anything, I should feed you my energy." He began clearing the table.

Niamh jumped up to help him. "I know the symbol itself has healing power, but it couldn't hurt to have our healer involved."

"I agree." I gathered the few remaining mugs on the table. "I think we need Dian."

"I will gladly contribute my energy if it helps end this conflict with the *Fomorians*." He waved us out of the kitchen. "I am anxious to see how the warriors respond."

"They should be in the arena by now." Diarmuid led us past the infirmary, up the stone steps, and out into the sun-drenched meadow. He strode toward the arena.

I draped my arm around Maolisa's shoulders. "I think you should create the symbol and direct the energy this time. The Ailm represents healing, but it's also a cross, a symbol of faith."

She nodded, a thoughtful look in her eyes. "Faith, hope, and love all aid in healing, but I'd be happy to give it a try."

We joined the warriors when we entered the arena. Diarmuid stood, arms crossed, posture strong and wide. "The *Chosen Ones* have acquired a unique skill from *Ogham*, an ability to combine their energy for a variety of purposes. They need to perfect this skill. I don't want you to raise your shields or resist in anyway. I'd just like you to stand here and then tell us how you feel afterwards."

Kane landed a few feet away. "I got your message."

Diarmuid nodded. "How's the border holding up?"

"Cian's still working on it." Concern rolled off him in

waves, but he was doing a decent job hiding it. No one else seemed to notice. His eyes locked on mine. "I heard you want to change things up a bit. I'm anxious to see how this works." He turned to the warriors. "I'm going to remove the protective spells."

All but one shifted uncomfortably.

Ainle winked, exuding confidence.

I hadn't heard he was hurt, although he did seem to be the sort of person whose pride might prevent him from admitting he was in pain. I frowned. Come to think of it, there were an awful lot of warriors standing in front of us. Maybe they were all hard wired that way. I lowered my mental shields and opened my senses. *Yep. Uncertainty and a hefty dose of pain. Except for Ainle... Ainle was in pain, but he wasn't feeling uncertain. He was feeling admiration and a far mushier emotion I wasn't about to acknowledge.* I tugged my mental shields back into place.

Dian's wings popped out, reminding us to call our own. "Ready?"

"Sure." Maolisa, Niamh and I joined him about thirty feet off the ground.

He eyed the warriors below. "I don't think we should get any closer than this. The *Fomorians* may not even allow us this close. It's not like we're seeking their approval. They wouldn't trust us, even if we told them we're trying to help. They'll view us as a threat, and they'll use the elements against us. We'll have to ask the other *Sidhe* to keep the storms at bay so we can focus our energy on this."

"Okay." I glanced at my friends. "Let's do this back to back and clasping hands but sending our energy to Maolisa this time. Up, out, and down. Maolisa, you got that Ailm symbol down?"

She laughed. "Oh, yeah. That symbol is firmly engraved in my mind."

We pulled our wings in tight and clasped hands as we turned our backs to one another. Dian was sandwiched between Niamh and me. We drew our energy with a deep intake of breath and forced it down to our fingertips before raising our arms up over our heads. Green, gold, and blue light sparked between our hands, just itching to burst free. "Healing through faith, hope, and love on the count of three!"

Together we counted, "One... two... three!"

We brought our clasped hands down, shooting the energy between our entwined fingers. Maolisa coaxed it into a perfectly symmetrical cross. A sonic boom sounded. The green, gold, and blue cross blazed across the warriors' wary faces.

Our breath caught. We hovered there uncertainly, waiting for their reactions.

I lowered my shield, anxious to see how they were feeling. *Confusion and relief.* They shifted, rolled their shoulders, and glanced at one another, gradually sensing the changes within. *Gratitude... jubilation... and an even deeper sense of relief.* I released my friends' hands so I could face them. "They can feel it."

Dian began questioning them the second we touched down. "How do you feel?"

One of the older warriors, Phelan, approached Diarmuid. "They weren't trying to hurt us, they were trying to heal us?"

Grandpa nodded.

The warriors gazed at us in wonder.

"Thank you," Phelan said. "I'm very grateful. I feel at least a hundred years younger, but why? What sort of fighting is this?"

"The *Chosen Ones* are not meant to fight the way you fight," Kane answered loud enough so everyone could hear. "They're going to heal the *Fomorians* so they will align with us instead of aiding Dain, Dother, and Dub."

Understanding dawned in Phelan's eyes.

"That's right." Kane's chest puffed out with pride. "These ladies just made your jobs a whole lot easier. Now, all you've got to do is keep them safe while they heal the *Fomorians* and confront Dain, Dother, and Dub."

Phelan laughed a warm, boisterous laugh. "With how I feel? Piece of cake."

* * *

I settled onto the wood swing, clenched the braided vines, and gazed out over the sparkling lake.

"Ready?" Ainle pulled me back against his chest and gently released the swing.

My toes skimmed the water before the swing swept over the lake. "Thanks, Ainle."

His hands greeted my back with another gentle shove. "No problem. I'll remain quiet so you can talk to your dad."

My gaze caught on the mossy bridge, which had just emerged from the lake. I waited until it formed a complete circle with the reflection in the water before reaching out to my dad. We were speaking telepathically, of course. "Dad?"

A few seconds ticked by and then… "Hi, Madi-moo."

I smiled. That was my dad's favorite nickname for me back in the human realm. My smile wavered, then fell. That life seemed like a distant memory now. "I miss you guys. I miss…" I frowned, trying to find the right words. "I miss how easy our lives used to be."

"I know, honey. Me too. How's your training coming along?"

Another gentle shove.

My toes skimmed the lake again. "Good. If all goes well with our training today, we will leave tomorrow morning."

"I can't wait to see you," he said. "I wish it were under better circumstances."

I soared out over the water again. "Me too."

"How are you feeling?"

"Scared." I wouldn't have admitted this to anyone but Dad. "What if we fail? People could die. Mom and Lexie…"

"We won't fail." His tone allowed no room for argument. "Ending violence… that's your purpose. You have a prophecy to fulfill, and *Ogham* has given you everything you need to overcome Dain, Dother, and Dub."

I bit back a sob. I wanted to save my family and *Tír na nÓg*, but I couldn't stop thinking about that sacrifice mentioned by the Rowan Tree. I closed my mind against the thought. If Dad knew, he might not let me confront them, and if that happened, we'd lose everything including Lexie and Mom. I forced my thoughts back to Dain, Dother, and Dub. "What do they look like? Do they look as scary as the *Fomorians* or the *Sidhe Sluagh*?" The *Sidhe Sluagh* reminded me of the dementors from Harry Potter. They weren't so bad when they were ravens, but when they shifted into those lost spirits… I shuddered. "Will you send me an image of them so I'll be prepared?"

"Dain, Dother, and Dub look a lot like us. They don't look scary like the *Fomorians* or the *Sidhe Sluagh*. I think that's why it's so easy for them to deceive humans. They don't look threatening unless they want to. They can shift into just about anything, although they prefer darker images."

I frowned. In some ways, that was even more concerning. "How will I know who they are if they can shapeshift? Can they make themselves look like you or the other *Sidhe*?"

"Yes. I suppose they could. You will sense the evil in them. You will feel physically ill and deeply depressed when they are near. That's why we monitor them in shifts, so we can limit our exposure to them." Concern crept through our connection. "I heard you have a plan for healing the *Fomorians*. Please be careful, Grania. They killed two of our warriors yesterday."

My heart stalled. "Please don't tell me how they did it. I don't want to know. What about Mom and Lexie? Are... are they okay?"

"For now. I don't know how much longer they can remain like this. They haven't had any food or water, and Lexie hasn't had her meds. The *Sidhe Sluagh* have been circling around them. They're still breathing, thankfully, and it doesn't appear they've been harmed."

Another gentle push. Ainle had kept his promise. He hadn't spoken a single word since I first climbed onto the swing.

I did the math in my head. Mom and Lexie were taken by the *Sidhe Sluagh* fourteen days ago. Panic clawed at my chest. "They've been without food and water for two weeks. How are they still alive?"

"It hasn't been two weeks, not in the human realm. Remember, time works differently in *Tír na nÓg*. The gravitational pull from those three blue moons will either speed or slow the rotation of our realm, so some days are shorter, others longer, depending on the proximity of our moons."

The human realm only had one moon to contend with, so this made sense in some weird scientific way. Our days did seem to fly by in *Tír na nÓg*. I'd just assumed that was because of all the training we were cramming in. "How long has it been in the human realm, then?"

Dad sighed. "Four days."

A tiny bit of tension eased from my arms. I leaned back, stretching my legs toward the lake again. Four days was better than fourteen, but that was still an awfully long time to go without food and water. I wondered if Triple D were keeping them alive somehow. "Will you send me a picture of Lexie and Mom so I know what to expect?"

"Yes. I'll send an image when we draw closer. Please let me know how the training goes and whether you still plan to leave in the morning. It may be a few days before we see one another, especially if you have to heal the *Fomorians* along the way."

Tears welled in my eyes. "I love you, Daddy. Please be safe."

"You too, Madi-moo. I love you. Be safe."

My vision blurred. While my friends back home were worrying about their exams, I was preparing to battle some of the cruelest beings on the planet. How did my life turn into this?

Ainle gentled the swing as I began to cry. "Grania…"

I buried my face in my hands. "I don't want this. I never asked to be chosen. Why does my family have to be involved in this?"

He pulled me into his arms. "I don't know, Grania, but you and your family were chosen for a reason. You were meant to fulfill this prophecy. Please trust in that."

Diarmuid pushed off the tree. "Come here, little one."

Ainle transferred me into my grandfather's arms.

"I can't believe she's held it together this long," Fianna admitted softly. "Any other person, human or *Sidhe*, would have fallen apart by now."

Diarmuid's arms tightened around me. "You will not face this alone, Grania. Your father, Fianna, and I will be right there beside you, every step of the way."

"We all will." Brigitte, Ciara, Maolisa, and Niamh landed beside us.

Fianna brushed my tears away, her face mere inches from mine. "Just think, by this time next week your family will be together again. They'll be here in *Tír na nÓg.* Your sister is going to freak when she sees you fly." She pried Diarmuid's arms loose so she could give me a hug.

Cian, Dian, and Kane strode toward us. "Everything okay?"

"Yes." I smiled shakily.

Niamh captured my hand when Fianna released me. She squeezed it gently. "What sort of training do you have in store for us today?"

Kane smiled. A challenge sparked in his eyes. "We're going to see if you can repeat what you did yesterday but with a different knot."

"Really?" Maolisa claimed my other hand. "Which knot?" She offered a reassuring squeeze, a smile, and a wink.

Cian grinned. "You tell us. Which knot would you recommend for securing the border?"

"Wait." My heart leapt. "We're securing the border?"

They nodded, without hesitation, completely confident in our ability to do so.

I really wanted to prove we could. I sifted through the knowledge provided by the Rowan Tree before sending an image to Maolisa and Niamh. "The shield knot?"

"That's the one we use on battlefields to ward off danger." Clearly, Diarmuid liked the idea.

Dian's eyes met mine. "It's also used to keep evil spirits away from people who are ill."

"That sounds perfect." Niamh peered past me at Maolisa. She nodded. "I agree."

Kane smiled, obviously pleased. "Well, then, let's get this portal secured so Cian and I can join you tomorrow."

We followed him through the trees. I loved this part of the forest, where two different seasons ruled each side of the trail. Only twelve days had passed since I first walked this path. In many ways, these trees and the *Sidhe* surrounding me felt like home. I wondered whether my father would want to live here or return to our home in Virginia when our family was reunited. I wished it were possible to live in both places, to have a home and a home away from home.

Kane stopped when we reached the tree line. He eyed the clearing. "The spell that has been eating away at the border and all our protective wards was cast in the human realm. We should begin there. I'm going to unseal the portal so we can cross over."

Several warriors appeared along the tree line. They didn't step inside the clearing. Their toes remained flush with the trees.

"The warriors will cross through the portal first," Cian explained. "They'll confirm it's safe and secure the area on the other side."

Kane nodded. "Please, remain behind the tree line." His eyes locked on the meadow as he began to chant.

The wind stirred. I could feel the energy around us shift. It didn't feel unpleasant, just… different… like the first few seconds of a storm, when the world falls silent and the wind whispers a warning.

The chant ended. Kane reached down, snatched a twig from the ground, and tossed it in the meadow. He smiled when it struck the ground. "When the portal is sealed, the air locks everything in place. Nothing can move until the seal itself is removed."

The warriors added two additional words to the phrase we used to enter *Otherworld*. "*Slán agaibh, Tír na nÓg, Draíocht Dúchas, Taisce Baile.*" They disappeared among bright flashes of light.

"What does *Slán agaibh* mean?" Niamh inquired in a hushed tone.

"Farewell. Be safe." Brigitte turned so she was facing the three of us. "Be sure to add those words when you leave."

"Should we take our boots off?" I noticed the warriors hadn't removed their boots.

Fianna shook her head. "You don't have to remove your boots if you don't mind them being wet."

A single point of light flashed in the center of the meadow a few minutes later. Phelan emerged. He offered a curt nod. "Everything is clear."

We joined the warriors in the human realm, transporting amid sharp bursts of light. Ainle caught me as I stumbled blindly through the hot springs.

My vision returned after several hard blinks. "Why is the air so heavy?" My entire body felt weighted down.

He guided me onto a large, mossy rock. "You've grown accustomed to the air and the gravity in *Tír na nÓg*." He grasped my foot between his hands. A mini-wind tunnel formed between his palms, completely drying my boot. He switched to the other foot.

Maolisa joined us. "I miss *Tír na nÓg* already."

"I know what you mean." After being in *Tír na nÓg*, this realm felt darker, more threatening, and depressing. I couldn't believe I'd never noticed that before.

Niamh plunked down beside me. "An automatic dryer? That's brilliant." She watched Ainle spin the air around my boot, before trying the same technique with her shoes. "Maolisa, can I dry your boots?"

She backed out of reach. "I'm a water spirit. I like being wet."

My gaze shifted to Cian and Kane. They were chanting something while facing the hot spring. A vortex appeared in the center of the hot spring. A purple web glittered all around it, but there were some pockmarks... dark, inky spots that were eating away at the web.

"What is that?" The oily blobs made my skin crawl.

Kane turned as the chant ended. The vortex loomed behind him. "That's Dain, Dother, and Dub's spell."

"How do you know all three brothers were involved?" I stood, fighting against the gravitational pull.

His eyes held mine. "Let your shields down."

Keeping those mental shields up had become instinctive for me. I didn't like feeling what everyone else was feeling all the time. I didn't like hearing all those telepathic chats either. I only lowered my shields when I felt a sharp tug, which signaled when someone wanted to speak with me; when I wanted to speak telepathically with someone; or when I wanted to see how people were feeling. Warily, I complied.

Cian turned so he could see me. "What do you feel?"

A shudder rolled through me. "Evil... darkness... hatred and violence... but there's also a twisted sense of glee, like they enjoy threatening us." I yanked my shields back up.

"I want you to see what you'll be replacing." Kane studied the vortex. He glanced at me when I joined him. "Don't try to repair our work... that's the purple web. Cian and I will destroy that completely. When our wards fall, their spells should fall with them. This will leave the portal completely unprotected, so the second that web collapses, you must place your shield over the vortex."

"I understand." My heart pounded hard and fast. This would leave *Tír na nÓg* vulnerable to an attack, so we must act quickly. I turned toward Maolisa and Niamh. "I think we should face one another this time. That way we can stretch the shield and attach it more securely." I didn't think we should drop this knot haphazardly.

Niamh nodded while contemplating our surroundings. "We want this knot to be as strong as possible. Let's pull some energy from our energy sources so we can strengthen what we've got in reserve."

Maolisa pulled energy from the mist hovering above the hot spring. Niamh pulled from the air, stirring a subtle breeze. I called to the trees guarding the hot spring. "Please, lend me your strength." A warmth spread through me when they agreed. My skin started tingling. I pulled the extra energy close to my heart. "Okay. I'm good."

We called our wings, flew a few feet above the vortex, and turned so we were facing one another.

Cian and Kane stood on opposite sides of the vortex half in and half out of the water with their palms stretched toward the swirling mass of energy. "We'll destroy our wards on two, you secure the shield on three."

"Please, don't start counting until our arms are raised." Maolisa's eyes locked on mine. "Faith, hope, and love, but the greatest of these is love. Grania, it's got to be you. You're the one who should tie the knot."

Her faith in me soothed every nervous bone in my body. "Okay. Let's coax our energy." I shifted the energy stored inside me down through my arms until it dripped from my fingertips. "Ready?"

Maolisa and Niamh's energy arced toward mine. "Ready." We clasped hands and lifted our arms up over our heads.

Kane started counting. "One... two..."

I glanced down briefly. The purple wards and all those dark, inky spots had fallen. The vortex was spinning at a dizzying speed.

"...three!"

My gaze shot back toward our fingertips. Green and blue energy surged, mixing with the gold streaming through my hands. I tied the shield knot as quickly as I could, then checked with my friends.

They nodded, anticipating my question.

We dropped closer to the vortex, each holding an end. We flew further apart, pulling the shield over the top like a blanket. We pulled it taut over the water so we could secure the knot.

With one final burst of energy, I fused the knot. The excess energy rebounded, throwing me back onto the bank.

Fianna, Diarmuid, and Ainle sprinted toward me. "Are you okay?"

"I... I..." My head slammed against the cold, hard ground. Darkness descended, stealing my response.

* * *

My eyes fluttered open. I frowned, confused by the downy soft bed. Slowly, I connected the dots. I was sleeping inside the palace again. "What happened?"

Fianna looked up from the book she was reading. "Finally! I was beginning to think you might sleep the entire day." She came and sat on the edge of the bed. "How are you feeling?"

I pushed up against the bed. "Okay. Good, actually."

She fluffed the pillows behind my back. "You were knocked unconscious by that blast. Your energy was so depleted, we panicked when you wouldn't wake. I tried to infuse you with some of my energy. Diarmuid attempted to share his energy as well, but Ainle wouldn't allow it. He insisted it was his responsibility as your fated mate."

I gasped when her memory played inside my head. My heart raced. I could feel their panic... their fear... and pain.

She grasped my hand. "Please understand, he was really upset. We couldn't even get close enough to attempt it. The grief and anguish fated mates suffer when they lose one another..." She shook her head. "There's no reasoning through that. He thought he was losing you. That's why he transferred his energy into you."

All the air rushed from my lungs. I pressed my hands to my chest. Panic clawed at my heart. "Is... is he okay?"

Her eyes widened. "Yes. Oh, God, yes. Ainle's fine. He's better than fine. He's insanely proud of the fact he saved your life."

My eyes closed, heavy with relief. I tried to even out my breathing.

She smoothed the blankets on the bed. "Thankfully, with the previous wards gone and this new shield in place, we were able to transport you back through the portal without speaking the required phrase. Kane added some additional wards after we crossed over, but I think they'll allow more than one *Sidhe* to cross through at a time... something we didn't realize we needed until now."

My eyes popped open. "Is everyone else okay?"

She nodded. "Everyone is fine."

I sank back against the pillows. "Does the shield knot work? Did we destroy Triple D's spell?"

"Yes." A smile played on her lips. "They must have sensed some change in the portal, because the *Sidhe Sluagh* came rushing back. The shield knot works like some sort of invisible force field that repels evil spirits. The *Sidhe Sluagh* couldn't even get close. They kept getting thrown back, like they were being electrocuted. Kane was thrilled. He thinks the shield knot will repel any additional attempts to cast corrosive spells, and that's assuming Dain, Dother, or Dub could get close enough to cast such a spell."

I breathed a huge sigh of relief. "It worked."

Her smile widened. "Of course, it did."

I flung the covers off. Fianna stood so I could swing my legs over the side of the bed. I could feel the energy humming beneath my skin. *Ainle's energy*, I reminded myself. "Are we still leaving tomorrow?"

"Yes, but the goddess has requested we sleep inside the palace tonight. This will strengthen us for the journey ahead." She grabbed her book from the nightstand. "Would you like to see your friends?"

I hopped from the bed. "Yes. Please."

She grabbed a pile of clothes from her room while I waited in the hallway. "Let's shower and change first. We're celebrating your success in securing the border, and our friends would like to wish us well before we leave." She handed me a dark purple dress, some undergarments, and ballerina style flats with wide satin laces.

"Thanks." I hugged the clothes to my chest.

We flew down to the far end of the great hall and slipped through the heavy wood door. Fianna lit the wall sconces. We walked past the kitchen and the pantry. The showers were a few doors down from the private baths. We stepped inside the locker room, collected our towels and soap, and stripped out of our clothes. I tugged the bathrobe on, worried someone might walk in on us. "There aren't any boys allowed in here are there?"

Fianna laughed. "No. They have their own showers." She shoved our clothes inside one of the laundry bags and gave the disk a little squeeze so the *Sidhe* who were in charge of laundry would know where to return the clothes.

I set my dress and shoes inside the cubby. "Who makes these clothes?" I had yet to meet a *Sidhe* who sewed.

"Wood spirits make them, naturally." She steered me toward the stone showers, whisked a soft fabric curtain aside, and shooed me inside. "There's a hook right outside the shower for your bathrobe and towel. Just turn that center stone to control the flow of water. There's no need to adjust the temperature. Trust me, this water is the perfect temperature." She disappeared inside the shower next to mine.

I hung my towel and bathrobe on the hook and slid the curtain closed. "I'm a wood spirit. Can I make clothes?"

"That's not really your purpose, but as long as you stay true to who you are, then you can do anything you set your mind to. You know, they're not just sewing things together. They're making the fabric and thread too. The trees in *Ogham* gave them the knowledge and skills they need to complete those tasks."

I washed with the lavender soap from the cubby. Then, I just stood there and enjoyed the water massaging my back. "Will I still have a purpose after we confront Dain, Dother, and Dub?"

"Yes, of course. Confronting them is just one of many ways you inspire kindness and love. The kindness you show others… offering the *Fear Gorta* food, befriending the *Kelpie* and the *Ellen Trechend.* building the meditation garden, taking time to play with the unicorns, and your efforts to keep us safe by securing the portal… all those actions reflect love, Grania."

I released the breath I'd been holding. Deep down inside, I'd been afraid my purpose would be fulfilled and my life over once I confronted the Goddess Carman's sons, but Fianna was right. Our realms would still need faith, hope, and love. I turned the water off, snagged the towel from the hook, and dried off. I wrapped the towel around my hair, cinched the bathrobe around my waist, and walked back to the cubby where my clothes were stashed. I admired the pretty purple dress after tugging it over my head. The off-the-shoulder sleeves fit snug near the top, especially with the laces crisscrossing around my biceps. The laces anchored bell sleeves that floated down around my fingertips. The dress ended above my knees in the front but tapered so it was longer in the back. I watched it swirl around my legs while I twirled in a circle. "Wow! I love this dress."

"Good. Our dressmaker will be thrilled to hear that." Fianna fastened her dress. She was wearing purple, like me, but her dress had gold leaves embroidered on it. "Can I braid your hair?"

"Sure." I sat on the bench.

She retrieved a comb and several gold ribbons from a basket in the end cubby. "I want you to enjoy yourself tonight. You've had a rough couple of weeks, and we have some challenging tasks ahead. I'm sure we could all use some more positive experiences to draw on when we face Dain, Dother, and Dub."

My knees bounced. I was already feeling the spike in energy that comes when sharing the same roof with several *Sidhe*. It felt exhilarating especially when combined with Ainle's energy. "I will."

Several tugs ensued while she braided the ribbon into my hair. "There! I need a minute to braid mine, then we'll go."

Her fingers worked quickly, twisting and tugging several strands into a work of art. "Ready."

I jumped up and gave her a hug. "Thank you for being my godmother… and my guardian."

She held me a little longer than I'd been expecting. "It's been an honor, Grania." She grasped my arms when she stepped back. "Now, let's go have some fun."

We walked arm in arm toward the festivities. My breath caught when we stepped through the heavy wood door. Thousands of fireflies twinkled inside the great hall. They shone so brightly there was no need for any other lighting. The musicians played a festive tune. Hundreds of *Sidhe* were dancing, singing, eating, and laughing. "Everyone looks so happy."

"Grania!" Diarmuid swept me up in a hug. "I was so worried." He lowered me gently. "How are you feeling?"

"I'm fine." I captured his hands in mine. "Thank you for helping me. I heard the portal is secure. I'm so relieved."

"That shield knot is working beautifully." Kane planted a kiss on Fianna's cheek. He squeezed in front of Diarmuid so he could hug me. "We have much to celebrate. Come, let's get something to eat."

"Grania," Ainle called, "may I have a minute?"

Our eyes met. My heart fluttered nervously.

Grandpa patted my back. "Join us when you can."

Ainle stepped closer.

His energy, the energy he had transferred inside of me, wrapped around my heart, then tugged me closer. I couldn't think or breathe. That energy seemed to be working wholly separate from me... it pulled us closer so it could feel complete.

He pressed a kiss to my cheek. "Do you mind if we talk first?"

"No. Um... talking is good." I wanted to thank him, but I was struggling with the feelings sparked by his energy. There was no denying we belonged to one another. Ainle's energy ensured I felt the same exact way he did. Our emotions were aligned for the very first time.

Ainle tucked my hand in the crook of his arm. He led me across the crystal bridge and veered right, toward the waterfall. "I want to apologize for my behavior this morning. I know you didn't exactly have a say in the matter, and you were hesitant to receive energy from me before, when you made the meditation garden."

My feet stalled. "You're apologizing... for saving me?"

"No. I mean… well… I wanted to help, but I know how you feel about drawing energy from the *Sidhe*." He pulled me onto a bench near the waterfall.

I met his worried gaze. "I don't mind receiving energy when it's necessary. I just… I don't want to weaken anyone for my own gain. Besides, Cian advised us not to accept energy from the warriors. You need to be functioning at full strength so you can protect us and keep us safe."

He searched the great hall, presumably for Cian. "That may be true in the heat of battle, but warriors hold more energy than most *Sidhe*. It helps with our endurance and strength, but mates are different, Grania. Mates are supposed to strengthen one another in this way. Besides, you were helping me and all the other *Sidhe* when you secured the border. I was just returning the favor."

A smile tugged at my cheeks. "Then why are you apologizing?"

He sighed. "After I calmed down, I realized you may have preferred your grandfather or your guardian, and I didn't allow them to help. I went a little crazy when you were unconscious. I didn't like seeing you like that. My desire to help you was so strong, I wasn't really capable of thought."

I reached for his hand. "I don't mind. Honestly. Besides, I kind of like having a little extra fight in me. That might come in handy when I confront Triple D."

He twined our fingers together. "So, you aren't mad at me?"

I laughed. "No, Ainle. I'm grateful. Thank you for helping me."

He stood and pulled me onto my feet. "Will you dance with me after we eat?" He kept a firm grasp on my hand as we walked toward the bridge.

"Sure." Memories of our first dance played inside my head. Ainle was the only boy I'd ever danced with, the first boy to kiss my cheek, and the only boy to hold my hand. I peeked at him from beneath my lashes. I wondered how he'd managed to finagle all that in only two weeks' time.

Ainle handed me a plate when we reached the buffet table. "After you."

"Thanks." I started making a list inside my head while piling food on my plate. *Smart... supportive... confident... respectful... protective... courageous... and kind.*

Diarmuid waved when we turned around. He'd saved us seats at the head table.

I recognized some of the *Sidhe* at the other tables, but the ones I felt closest to were all seated with the Goddess Danu. I wondered if there was some sort of hierarchy among the *Sidhe* that dictated where everyone sat or if she simply requested certain people join her at various times.

The goddess stood when we neared. "Grania, I'm pleased to see you are feeling well."

Kane stood and took our plates.

Ainle bowed.

I dropped into a curtsy. "Yes, ma'am. Thank you for inviting us to stay with you again."

Kane set our plates in front of the two remaining chairs.

Ainle stood there patiently, waiting to pull my chair out for me.

The goddess clasped my hands. Warmth spread from my fingertips all the way down to my toes. "My brave girl, you secured the portal. *Ogham, Tír na nÓg,* every living thing in *Otherworld* is safe once more."

"*We,*" I corrected. I smiled at Maolisa, Niamh, Cian, Kane, Ainle and the other warriors gathered around the table. "We secured the portal together. No one could have done it alone."

Her eyes softened. "Indeed. We accomplish far more when we work together." She released my hands so I could take my seat.

Ainle pulled the chair out for me.

"Thank you." I added *chivalrous* to my list.

He smiled while claiming the chair next to mine.

Kane relaxed against the back of his chair. "Now that the portal is secure, Cian and I can both go tomorrow." He tugged Fianna's chair a little closer before dropping his arm around her shoulders. She shot him a look that would have leveled most men, but Kane just grinned.

"Good. We could use another druid." Diarmuid leaned forward, his arms braced against the table. "Several warriors will be joining us as well."

The goddess nodded. Her eyes searched mine. "I know you are anxious to free your family, but you must pace yourself. I don't want you draining your energy reserve like you did today. I want you to rest a day or two after healing the *Fomorians*. We must ensure your energy has been completely restored, that all three of you are functioning at full strength, before you confront the Goddess Carman's sons."

"Yes, ma'am." After today's events, I could easily grasp the importance of that.

She glanced at Kane. "How will you travel?"

He exchanged some unspoken thought with Diarmuid before answering. "On foot."

"We're walking?" Niamh's gaze bounced between the two of them. "I thought we were going to fly."

Kane's eyes met hers. "I'd prefer to fly, but we would have to shift into birds to avoid being seen. Holding that shape while traveling across Black Valley to Upper Lake would require a great deal of energy. You would need to restore your energy and rest before approaching the *Fomorians*, so the journey would take longer in the end."

The goddess followed their exchange, interest and concern etched on her face. "And once you heal the *Fomorians*?"

"We will establish a camp at the base of Torc Mountain," Kane answered. "We can rest there, cross over the mountain and stay the second night behind Torc Waterfall. Ruarc and the other warriors have established a camp there. We'll climb Mangerton Mountain together and ensure everyone is in position at Devil's Punch Bowl before the girls confront Dain, Dother, and Dub. If all goes well, we will return in five days' time."

"Some of our warriors will be traveling ahead to scout the terrain," Diarmuid clarified. "We don't want any surprises."

"Speaking of surprises…" The goddess beckoned to Bevyn, who was standing attentively nearby.

He stepped forward. With a slight bow, he offered Maolisa, Niamh, and me white fabric pouches cinched with red string.

Energy hummed along the string. I wasn't sure how I knew, but I sensed the string had been dyed with berries from the Rowan Tree.

The goddess nodded as if reading my thoughts. "Each pouch contains a handful of berries and a cross made from the Rowan Tree. As your birth tree, the Rowan offers you protection while strengthening your energy and intuition. Please, carry these objects with you at all times."

I peeked inside the bag. There were fresh berries and a square cross. The same red string that cinched the pouch held two twigs together so they formed a perfect cross. The cross looked just like the Ailm, the symbol that strengthens healing and faith.

I wasn't sure if it was appropriate, but I stood and gave her a hug. "Thank you."

Her arms tightened around me. "It is I who should be thanking you, Grania."

"Thank you, Goddess." Maolisa stepped forward and gave her a hug.

Niamh did the same. "Will you be traveling with us?"

Her eyes softened. "I'm afraid I must remain in *Tír na nÓg*. My presence in *Otherworld* ensures the Goddess Carman remains imprisoned in *Tech Duinn*."

Ainle held my chair when we returned to our seats. "Would you like some carrageen moss pudding?"

"Sure." I smiled up at him.

Fianna's head ducked close to mine. "I have something for you as well." She opened her hand.

My fingers slid admiringly over the harp and the word *Éire* before turning the coin. A horse stood proudly on the other side. "This is the coin from the *Fear Gorta*."

She clasped the chain around my neck. "I hope you don't mind that I had it made into a necklace. The *Fear Gorta* gave this to you for a reason. I don't know why, but I suspect you're going to need this. Like the Goddess Danu's gift, I think you should wear this at all times."

Tears welled in my eyes. "Thank you for bringing me here, for introducing me to all these wonderful people, for helping me understand my purpose, and for standing by me through all this."

She gathered me in her arms. "Oh, Grania, that's what guardians and fairy godmothers are for."

"Fairy godmother?" I leaned back so I could read her face.

"Godmother plus *Sidhe* equals…"

Everyone laughed. The mood suddenly lightened as everyone relaxed.

Ainle returned with the pudding. "I added some raspberry compote. I hope you like it."

"Thank you." I sampled the creamy dessert. The tart berries complimented the sweet treat perfectly. "It's delicious." I added *thoughtful* to my list.

Treasach rose from his chair. I thought he might be leaving, but he approached Maolisa instead. "Would you like to dance?" He extended his hand.

Her cheeks turned a pretty shade of pink. "Um." She glanced at her guardian.

Brigitte's eyes sparked with amusement. "Treasach can dance. Trust me, you don't want to miss out on that."

Maolisa's fingers disappeared inside the warrior's hand. "I would love to. Thank you for asking."

Cian approached Niamh before anyone could comment on that juicy little development. "I was hoping you might honor me with a dance."

My jaw dropped. Cian and Treasach were close to Ainle's age. I wondered…

"Fated mates," Ainle confirmed telepathically. He stood as they began to leave. "Shall we?"

"Sure." I stood. My heart skipped a couple of beats.

Ainle tucked my hand in the crook of his arm. "You have a question?" He steered me toward the dance floor.

My eyes snapped toward his. "How do you know what I'm thinking?"

He laughed. "You are very easy to read. Your question…" He took the long way around the pond instead of walking across the crystal bridge.

My gaze drifted toward Cian and Niamh. "How do you know they're fated to be together?"

He smiled. "Both Cian and Treasach asked how you handled the news when I revealed we were fated mates. It wasn't difficult to connect the dots when I saw how they were looking at Maolisa and Niamh."

I eyed him curiously. "You are really good at reading people."

"All warriors are." He placed my hand on his chest and pulled me in his arms as we stepped onto the dance floor.

The harp, violins, and flute slowed, easing us into a romantic dance. The fireflies dipped between each couple in an enchanting dance of their own. The crystal bridge, the luminous pond, the twinkling fireflies, the amethyst walls, and Ainle... everything exuded beauty and strength.

I soaked it all in, savoring the memory, engraving it on my very soul. A memory to draw on... something more to fight for.

Ainle twirled me around, chasing away my thoughts.

I drew in a grateful breath.

His eyes warmed.

This was the calm before the storm.

CHAPTER 8 – THE FOMORIANS AND THE AILM

Cian steadied Niamh. As graceful as she was, she kept tripping over the jagged rocks. Far less treacherous terrain beckoned from the valley below. Sadly, that route was not an option. The warriors who were scouting the area ahead of us had spotted some *Fomorians* near the river slaughtering sheep. Ainle had been singing to me ever since we first heard those sheep scream. The valley was eerily quiet now, but he was still singing telepathically. I didn't mind. He had a beautiful voice.

We remained inside the tree line, where the uneven ground sprouted boulders and rocks. Purple heather, wild fuchsia, and bright yellow gorse grew just outside the tree line. We'd crossed over several rocky streams and drank from the sparkling cascades. What few glimpses I'd caught of the valley were breathtaking.

We were vibrating with energy when we began the hike. Sleeping in the palace had strengthened us all, but we'd been hiking for eight hours now. I was well past the point of needing a break, but Diarmuid and the other warriors showed no signs of stopping.

Maolisa peered through the gold and green leaves. "It's going to rain." She'd twisted her ankle earlier, but Dian healed it.

We stopped just inside the tree line. The clouds were heavy and gray. Fog poured like molasses into the valley.

Ainle stopped singing.

Diarmuid studied the terrain. "We won't find any more trees tall enough to conceal us until we draw closer to Upper Lake. This fog is a blessing. I wonder how Manannán knew we would need this. He unraveled thin silver fabric from a metal ring cinched at his waist. "The Cloak of Mists will allow us to proceed undetected without expending any more energy than is necessary."

"Is that the *Faeth Fiadha*?" Ciara blurted incredulously.

"Yes." Grandpa's chest puffed out proudly. "It is."

Niamh crept closer. She studied the odd material, which shifted from silver to gray, back to silver, and then white. "Is that... alive?"

"Somewhat." Diarmuid shook the wrinkles from the fabric. He flung the cloak over his shoulders and snapped the clasp against his chest plate.

I stared, thoroughly entranced by the cape. The texture and the colors were subtly changing. A thin white cloud formed near the bottom of the cloak. "How can one single piece of material conceal thirteen people?"

"The Cloak of Mists will generate enough fog to conceal us all." Kane's boots disappeared when he stepped into the fog.

Maolisa stepped back, avoiding the fog. "What about the warriors who have been scouting the forest?"

"They will shapeshift into white-tailed eagles so they can alert us to any danger," Diarmuid explained. The fog snaked around our legs, hips, and waists. "I want a warrior and a guardian walking on either side of the girls. Whatever you do, do not release their hands. Dian and I will walk in front, Cian and Kane in the back. There will be no talking, except telepathically, from this point forward. Understand?"

"Yes." I wrapped my arms around his waist, needing one last hug before the fog enveloped him completely.

His hand smoothed my hair. "I love you, Grania."

"I love you too, Grandpa." I stepped back so he could lead us through the fog.

Fianna and Ainle grasped my hands. We followed Dian and Diarmuid into the barren valley. A soft, gentle rain escaped the clouds, coaxing that wet soil smell from the ground.

My ears tried to overcome the vision loss, but it was surprisingly quiet. The rain generated a bit of white noise. The fog muffled the remaining sounds. "How do you keep your armor from making any noise?" I asked Ainle telepathically.

He squeezed my hand encouragingly. "The armor is magick. That's why it feels soft and light, despite the fact it is stronger than any metal known to man. It's no different than your boots. Haven't you noticed? They don't make any noise."

I stared down at my feet, even though I couldn't see them. "How did I miss that?"

Ainle chuckled through our connection. "I believe that's the point. Your footsteps are supposed to go unnoticed."

I smiled. I liked hearing him inside my head.

Diarmuid spoke to our entire group. "We'll stop in one hour so we can restore our energy before proceeding to Upper Lake. If all goes smoothly, we will heal the *Fomorians* and proceed to Torc Mountain by five o'clock."

"I don't anticipate needing much time with them," Kane said, "but we should speak with them afterwards so we can determine whether they remain a threat."

"I'd like to know what Dain, Dother, and Dub promised them," Cian admitted.

"As would I," Phelan agreed.

"Torc Mountain is a three-hour hike from Upper Lake," Diarmuid warned. "We should try to reach that mountain before nightfall."

Three hours? I nearly groaned aloud.

"What's wrong?" Fianna inquired. "Do you sense something?" The fact that we couldn't see anything beyond the dense white fog was unnerving.

"No," I admitted. "It's just... healing the *Fomorians* will deplete our energy. I can't imagine another three hours of hiking after that."

"We can stop and restore our energy afterwards," Kane assured me.

"This fog is really something. I can't even see my hand when I hold it in front of me," Niamh marveled.

"Where did you obtain this cloak?" Maolisa asked Diarmuid.

"Manannán mac Lir leant it to me. Manannán is a sea deity, a powerful guardian who transports both *Sidhe* and *Fomorian* souls to the afterlife. He rules *Tir Fo Thuinn*, the underwater *Otherworld* in the Celtic Sea."

A chill trickled down my spine. If I had to sacrifice my life, would this deity escort me to the afterlife? Should I fear him, or should I be grateful I didn't have to make that journey alone? Maybe he was nice. He did loan Grandpa the cloak.

"There are two *Fomorians* heading this way," Diarmuid warned. "They cannot see us. No matter what happens, don't say anything, keep walking, and maintain a firm grip on Maolisa, Grania, and Niamh."

The ground vibrated beneath my feet. Two lumbering figures stomped through the fog, giant hunchbacked beasts with thickly corded muscles, spiked bracers, and clubs that were almost as big as me. Flaming red eyes pierced the fog. They were heading straight for me. I tried to break free from Fianna and Ainle so I could duck out of their way, but they wouldn't release me. I cried out telepathically. "They're going to plow into me!"

I braced myself for impact, but the *Fomorians* walked right through me. They were so big, they walked through Fianna, Ainle, *and me*.

I fought for my next breath. I could feel their pain... pain so excruciating my knees wobbled, threatening to give out. How could they remain standing? I turned, but I couldn't see them behind me. The fog had swallowed them... or me.

"Keep walking," Fianna urged.

"But they walked straight through us. How... how did they do that?"

Ainle gently squeezed my hand. "The cloak transforms us into fog. We remain solid only in our thoughts."

"But I can feel you. I can feel your hand! How can I feel your hand, but I couldn't feel them?" I paused. That didn't make sense. "Well, I could *feel* them. They were in excruciating pain, but they walked straight through me."

"The fog works like shapeshifting," Kane explained. "We can feel one another because we are sharing this space, the molecules that form this fog. I'm sorry you felt their pain."

I tried to calm myself, but it was disturbing, this thought that someone could walk through me. It made me feel like a ghost, like I didn't really exist anymore.

"They felt cold," Niamh complained. I could feel her shudder even though she wasn't touching me.

"Their eyes were glowing," Maolisa whispered. "They smelled like an electrical storm."

"They're heading the opposite direction," Treasach noted. "I wonder why?"

"Hard telling," Phelan answered. "Hunting maybe."

"We can heal some, but not all the *Fomorians* if they're all spread out. How are we going to do this?" Niamh inquired worriedly.

"Once we heal the *Fomorians* at Upper Lake, they'll spread the word," Dian surmised. "The others will come looking for us."

"We could set a date and heal the remaining *Fomorians* on our way back," Kane suggested.

"As long as the girls have sufficient time to recover in between," Diarmuid agreed.

The rain tapered off.

We walked a little further. Finally, Diarmuid stopped. "The scouts circling overhead have confirmed this area is clear. We can rest and replenish our energy here. They'll keep watch." He removed the cloak, folded the material, and threaded it through the metal ring attached to his belt.

The fog lifted, revealing a river lined with rocks. "It looks a little dryer over there." Phelan pointed. A smattering of trees stood on the opposite bank.

Kane lifted the knotted walking stick he'd conjured up at some point during our hike. The long, knobby stick turned into a wooden bridge when he tipped it toward the ground.

"Wow." I rapped my knuckles against the nearest plank. "That's amazing." The bridge was anchored into the ground, solid as could be.

Cian joined Niamh as she crossed the bridge.

Ainle and I fell in behind them.

Kane was the last to cross. He flicked his wrist, and the bridge morphed back into a walking stick. A second later, the walking stick shrank into a wand. He secured the wand beneath his bracer.

I tugged on Fianna's arm. "That's going on my Christmas list."

A chuckle escaped her lips. "Mine, too."

We cupped our hands in the icy river, drank several handfuls of water, and settled in to eat. We were carrying bread, cheese, fruit, and nuts in pouches tied to our waists. We conversed, but only telepathically. I pulled energy through the trees when I finished eating and promptly fell asleep.

I woke unexpectedly. Something felt off. "Why is the ground vibrating?"

Diarmuid, Phelan, Treasach, and Ainle leapt to their feet.

I flattened my hand against the ground. "I know that rhythm." Horse hooves pounded against the ground.

"It's the *Dullahan*." Diarmuid drew his sword.

My eyes widened. "What's a *Dullahan*?"

Ainle dragged me to my feet.

A man stormed toward us atop a pitch-black horse. An inky robe whipped the air around him. Bright blue flames curled around the horse's nostrils and his hooves. The Earth was scorched behind them.

Maolisa stumbled back. "Where's his head?"

My gaze slid reluctantly toward his chest. My stomach lurched. "He's holding it in his hand." A putrid green aura trailed behind the head. His neck was torn and ragged, his face pale and taut. He thundered closer.

Fianna eased in front of me. "If he speaks our names, we're dead."

Dian, our guardians, and the druids formed a tight circle around us. Energy sparked from their hands. Diarmuid, Treasach, Phelan, and Ainle formed a wall in front of them.

Warriors rained from the sky, shapeshifting midflight until we were protected on all sides.

The *Dullahan* pulled sharply on his reins. The horse reared back on his hind legs before landing in front of us.

The silence was deafening.

The mouth on the severed head opened, then snapped shut. The man lifted his head and shoved it toward us.

Niamh sucked in a breath.

The *Dullahan's* dark, soulless eyes roamed separately, searching for something. One eye twitched. The other flicked nervously toward my chest. "What is that?"

My fingers crept instinctively toward the necklace. "A coin from the *Fear Gorta.*"

He shrank back. He looked like he wanted to say something. His frustration grew. An angry roar ripped through his chest. The flames inside the horse surged, licking at them both until they dissolved into a wisp of smoke.

I sank against Maolisa, too relieved to speak.

Several warriors turned and inventoried our group. "No one died."

"He didn't speak a name," Phelan explained. "You don't perish until the *Dullahan* speaks your name."

"The coin stopped him." Diarmuid lowered his sword.

Treasach did the same. "The rumors... they must be true."

Niamh forced her gaze from the scorched grass. "What rumors?"

"The *Dullahan* can only speak once each time his horse stops." Cian glanced at my necklace. "He asked about the coin, so he couldn't speak a name."

Kane's gaze slid between Cian and the scorched grass. "I've heard his fear of gold is so great that he will leave without speaking a name."

"I knew that coin would come in handy." Fianna wrapped me in a hug.

Phelan peered out over the valley. He studied the ridges jutting up on either side of us. "We shouldn't linger."

Ainle stepped closer. "Are you okay? Can you walk?"

I nodded. "My legs feel a little shaky, but I'm okay."

Several warriors leapt into the air. They transformed into white-tailed eagles before circling overhead.

Diarmuid unraveled the Cloak of Mists. "We should arrive at Upper Lake within the hour. We may see more *Fomorians* as we draw closer, so no speaking aloud." He shook the fabric gently.

The fog coiled around our legs. Maolisa, Niamh and I fell in behind Dian and Diarmuid with a guardian and a warrior walking on either side of us. Cian and Kane took their positions in the back.

"Diarmuid," Brigitte said over our shared connection, "I've never seen *Moralltach* before. That's some sword."

"Wait," Niamh begged. "Your sword has a name?"

"Yes," Grandpa confirmed. "*Moralltach* was forged by the gods, it has been passed down through the centuries, and I assure you, it has more than earned its name."

A weapon forged by the gods? My interest piqued. "What does *Moralltach* mean?"

Diarmuid's hand closed around the hilt of the sheathed sword before the fog obscured him completely. "Great fury."

Ainle chuckled. "Not to be confused with his short sword, *Beagalltach*, which means 'small fury.'" He shortened his stride so it matched mine as we climbed the mountainside.

"There aren't many warriors who can wield *Moralltach*," Treasach stated admiringly. "That sword is really heavy. I swear it grows in size and strength every time Diarmuid wields it."

"*Beagalltach* is less bulky," Diarmuid agreed, "but I doubt either of those swords would have stopped the *Dullahan*. He doesn't require a weapon. He can steal your soul simply by speaking your name."

"I bet the *Fragarach* would have stopped him," Phelan boasted. "'The Answerer' can cut through anything."

"The Answerer? Is that another sword?" Maolisa sounded winded, even inside my head. The mountain we were climbing was steeper than anything we had hiked earlier. I suspected we were nearing Upper Lake.

"Yes. 'The Answerer' can penetrate any object," Phelan claimed. "Even if only minimally injured, the enemy cannot survive, and when held to a person's throat, that person cannot tell a lie."

The fog thinned, revealing a glimpse of my grandfather hiking up ahead. He shook his head. "Nonsense. No sword, not even King Lugh's mighty *Fragarach,* can cut through death."

So, the Dullahan was death? I shuddered, recalling how close he'd been. "Death should be gentle and sweet, not some raggedly looking guy carrying a putrid head."

Phelan laughed. "I agree."

"King Lugh?" Maolisa murmured. "Why does that name sound so familiar?"

"King Lugh led us in the *Second Battle of Magh Tuireadh,*" Kane answered. "He killed King Balor, the King of the *Fomorians,* effectively freeing us from *Fomorian* rule."

"Most of King Balor's warriors were killed during that battle," Cian added. "Those who remained were driven into the sea."

"King Lugh was half-*Sidhe,* half-*Fomorian,* and the subject of another prophecy," Diarmuid revealed. "This prophecy claimed King Balor would die at the hands of his grandson. King Balor, in an attempt to thwart the prophecy, killed every grandson but Lugh, although that wasn't from lack of trying. After one of many failed attempts, Lugh sought refuge with Manannán mac Lir, the sea deity who loaned me the Cloak of Mists. Eventually, Lugh came to live with Nuada, the High King of the *Tuatha Dé Danann.* When King Balor killed King Nuada in the *Second Battle of Magh Tuireadh,* Lugh retaliated, killing his grandfather and thus fulfilling the prophecy."

"So, the *Sidhe* made Lugh their king," Niamh surmised.

"Yes," Phelan confirmed. "Lugh possessed every quality you could possibly desire in a king. He was courageous, fair-minded, loyal, and kind."

"There wasn't a single skill he couldn't master," Ainle chimed in. "He was extremely talented, one of few people skilled in all the arts. He created *fidchell*, that board game we were playing the other day. He loved games, not just intellectual games but physical games too. He brought people together through sport, inspiring the *Tailteann Games*, which is our version of the Olympics."

I smiled. King Lugh enjoyed competing, just like me.

"What do you think the *Fomorians* will do when they see us?" Maolisa asked, drawing our attention back to the task at hand.

"They just killed two of our warriors the other day, so they'll assume we're there to retaliate," Diarmuid predicted. "I'm tempted to do just that, but this conflict with Dain, Dother, and Dub is our priority, not retaliating."

"I agree," Kane said. "Besides, our efforts to heal them may generate enough gratitude to end this age-old conflict between the *Fomorians* and the *Sidhe* once and for all."

Grandpa stopped and turned around. "I'll try to assure them we mean no harm, but I want you girls to remain thirty feet above their camp. Cast that Ailm symbol as wide as you can. The *Fomorians* cannot fly like we can. This frustrates them to no end. They will conjure a violent storm so they can force us down onto the ground where they can gain the upper hand. Please work as quickly as you can."

The fog lifted as we gathered around. Thunder rolled through the valley, although it wasn't like any thunder I'd ever heard before. My eyes widened when I realized why. This thunder was filled with emotion. I must have allowed my mental shields to drop because I could feel the anger and frustration riding those grumbling sounds. I forced my mental shields back into place so I could focus on what Grandpa was saying.

He peered at the darkening sky. "Upper Lake is on the other side of this ridge. According to the scouts flying overhead, the *Fomorians* are camped alongside the lake. We're going to hold here until those scouts are in position. When I give the all clear, we'll secure our shields and take to the air."

The wind picked up. We looked around nervously, worried we might have been spotted. The temperature dropped.

"We'll form three layers of protection around Dian and the girls," Grandpa continued. He glanced pointedly at our guardians. "You will remain closest to them as the third and final layer of protection. Intercept any objects that escape the warriors and keep them dry so they can remain in the air long enough to cast the Ailm."

Fianna, Brigitte, and Ciara nodded, their bodies tense.

His hand fell instinctively to his sword. "Phelan, Treasach, Ainle, and I will form a layer of protection around the guardians. We will intercept any weapons, bursts of energy, or debris caused by the storm. The scouts will assist, but they'll be working more discretely from the ground. With the *Fomorians'* eyes trained on us, we're going to need their help." He turned to Cian and Kane. "You will extend the first layer of protection. Insulate us from the elements as best you can."

Cian glanced at Kane. "I'll work from the adjacent ridge-line so we can expand our coverage a bit."

Kane nodded. "I'll remain on this ridge then."

Cian pressed a kiss to Niamh's forehead. "Be safe." He shifted into a white-tailed eagle. We watched him fly away.

Maolisa chewed her bottom lip. "Will we be using the Cloak of Mists?" The fog had disappeared with the wind.

"No. I want the *Fomorians* to see who is healing them. If they don't, there will be doubt, and they will have no reason to align with us." Diarmuid grew quiet while he communicated with the scouts. He checked to make sure Cian had arrived on the adjacent ridge. "It is time."

Ainle wrapped me in a hug. "Just focus on the Ailm. I promise we will keep you safe."

Treasach hugged Maolisa. "Keep the faith."

My eyes widened when Fianna allowed Kane to do the same. I suddenly realized just how grave a threat we faced. I swallowed hard against the fears percolating inside of me. I forced my thoughts toward the Ailm, just as Ainle had encouraged.

Dian's robe whipped around him in the wind. "Don't forget your shields."

I forced energy through my pores until a gold shield shimmered all around me. Collectively, those green, gold, purple, and blue shields formed a rainbow of sorts. If we weren't preparing for battle, the sight of all those luminous shields would have been stunning.

Diarmuid nodded his approval. His wings unfurled as he swept into the sky.

I took a deep breath, called my wings, and followed him. Maolisa, Dian, and Niamh flew beside me while our guardians and the remaining warriors secured their positions. I searched for the *Fomorians* when we crested the ridge. I could sense their pain even with my shields in place.

Hunched figures lurched angrily to their feet with their faces turned toward the sky.

My heart skipped a couple of beats. The *Fomorians* were huge, they'd clearly seen us, and boy did they look furious.

Diarmuid dropped dangerously close to them.

Lightening snapped to my right while soot colored clouds churned all around us. The temperature fell until it was shockingly cold. I reached out to Dian, Maolisa, and Niamh telepathically. "Is this a good spot?" My breath formed tiny clouds in front of me.

"There are several *Fomorians* in the lake," Dian replied. "We need to make sure the Ailm covers their camp and the lake."

"I can't get close enough to speak with them," Diarmuid gritted. He backed away.

We angled closer to the lake.

Niamh stopped and turned around. "As long as we aim out toward the ridge and the far edge of the lake, we should be able to cover this entire area."

"Watch out!" Maolisa cried. A mini cyclone formed beneath us. The snarling winds snatched water from the lake, broken twigs, and rocks and then thrust them toward us.

I curled into a ball with my wings tucked close. My eyes shut instinctively. One of our three layers of protection must have intercepted the objects because nothing struck me. I peeked at my friends. "Are you okay?"

"Hurry," Diarmuid urged. "The longer you wait, the more power they gain."

I tried to force my thoughts away from the storm raging around me. It wasn't easy. The wind shrieked like a banshee while icicles formed on my wings. Dian grabbed my hand before linking hands with Niamh. We pulled our wings in tight, turning back to back. I grasped Maolisa's hand.

"When you pull energy from your life source, try to avoid the storm," Dian warned. "That energy doesn't feel right."

"There are too many negative emotions tied to that storm." I drew energy from the plants and trees dotting the ridges around the lake. While sparse, that energy felt more positive, less tainted by anger and resentment. "Ready?" Sand from the storm pelted my skin, forcing my eyes closed.

The storm surged, whipping our hair and clothes into a frenzy. "I don't know how much longer we can hold them," Phelan warned.

We coaxed the energy down to our fingertips and lifted our arms above our heads. Green, gold, and blue light crackled between our hands.

The storm grew deafening.

"On the count of three," Maolisa encouraged.

Together we counted, "One… two…"

The cyclone gripped my ankle, tearing us apart.

Niamh screamed.

Like a rag doll, I plummeted toward the ground. A spear pierced my wing. All the air rushed from my lungs. Frigid, murky water enveloped me. *If only I were a water spirit,* I thought. Darkness descended with a finality that stole my breath.

* * *

Floating.

I was floating for what seemed like an eternity… unable to see… to think… to breathe. I found comfort in the white silken strands that caressed my face and hands. There was something vaguely familiar about the velvety soft nose that nudged me higher and higher… something so inexplicably comforting that I wasn't sure I wanted to go wherever it was we were going. I wanted to stay here forever.

Something… a memory… tugged at me.

Kelpie.

I smiled. My arms folded gratefully around Elgin's neck. "I feared I'd never see you again." I spoke the words telepathically. Murky water still surrounded me, so I couldn't speak or breathe.

Still, he answered. "You are safe with me."

I rolled onto his back. My skin tingled, alerting me to the magick surrounding us. Elgin was keeping me alive. No air filled my lungs.

He slowed our ascent. "I am not certain I should return you to the surface. It doesn't feel safe."

I buried my face in his mane. "My friends need me." I wanted to stay here in the lake. Elgin felt safe.

"Don't let go." His long, graceful legs moved in a gentle trot as we swam toward the surface. "If the situation is unsafe, we will return to the bottom of the lake."

My head and hands remained buried in the silken strands floating around his neck. "Thank you."

Our heads breached the surface. I marveled at how still the water remained. Not a single ripple betrayed our presence. No sound escaped our lips. I didn't even suck in a breath. There was no need to breathe as long as Elgin was touching me. We remained in the center of the lake. The scene before us unfolded like a hazy dream.

Niamh's cry echoed through the valley, drawing my attention to the shoreline. "Stop! You're hurting me!"

My arms tightened around Elgin's neck.

"Release them," Diarmuid growled. "They mean you no harm." Every *Sidhe* who had accompanied me was being forced onto his knees or was already sprawled brokenly on the ground.

"Elgin," I whimpered. Tears slid silently down my cheeks.

"Wait," he encouraged telepathically. "Do not make a sound."

The *Fomorian* who was tying my grandfather's hands behind his back struck him against the head. He fell face forward onto the rocky ground.

"Stop! How dare you injure him!" Phelan, Treasach, and Ainle struggled against their restraints.

"Why aren't they using their magick?" I frowned.

"Are there no others you can call?" Elgin prodded.

My thoughts spun chaotically. "My father and the other warriors are meeting us at Torc Mountain."

He shook his head. "That is too far."

Something niggled at the back of my head. "Naois, the *Ellen Trechend*."

The *Fomorian* who was pacing behind Grandpa unsheathed a sword that glinted in the fading light.

My heart pounded. A scream fizzled in my chest.

"Speak his name," Elgin encouraged. "Call him now. Quietly. You do not have to speak loudly. He will feel it the minute his name touches the wind."

Whatever magick Elgin had used to suppress my scream lifted so I could speak his name. "Naois," I pleaded. "We need you at Upper Lake."

Elgin tensed. "That sword. I know that sword, Grania. Don't look."

The *Fomorian* raged unintelligibly. The water in the lake shook as he lurched and waved his sword about. A silver aura trailed after the sword, like it had an energy all its own.

My breath caught. "Does that sword have a name?"

"Yes," Elgin whispered. "The *Fragarach*."

"The *Fragarach*," I repeated. "Phelan spoke of this sword. It belonged to King Lugh."

His ears twitched. "No mortal or immortal can survive even the smallest scratch."

There was a disturbance in the air behind us.

Elgin turned.

"Naois!" I cried.

One of his three heads nodded briefly. The other two remained fixed on the scene unfolding up ahead. His dark scales glinted orange instead of blue, mimicking the setting sun. His eyes glowed, two pools of liquid gold. His mouths stretched in a ferocious yawn. Vibrant streams of fire shot toward the *Fomorians*.

"Look," Elgin whispered.

Six *Ellen Trechend* barreled down the ridge.

My body sagged with relief.

The *Ellen Trechend* forced the *Fomorians* to back away from the *Sidhe*. I marveled at how precisely they wielded fire. Not a single *Sidhe* was harmed.

I clung to Elgin's neck as I began to weep.

Cautiously, he swam toward the shore. "Your friends need you now."

Naois met us at the water's edge. "Climb aboard." He lowered his head.

"Thank you." I kissed Elgin on the cheek, reached up, and hooked my arms around Naois's neck. My legs followed as I hoisted myself up. Little rivulets of water trickled from my wet clothes, down Naois's chest.

He straightened to his full height. "You are injured."

"Yes." My left wing hung brokenly against my back. "I don't think I can fly."

"We can gather your friends and leave," he offered kindly.

I eyed the *Fomorians* nervously. "Can I try to speak with them first?"

He nodded, gently.

"The one with the sword," I told him.

Naois turned and approached the *Fomorian*, his movements strong and graceful. The *Fomorians* quieted as we approached.

"Grania, keep back," Ainle pleaded. He inched closer, sword drawn.

Dian was healing the fallen *Sidhe*. Some of our friends were helping him, others joined Ainle.

My gaze returned to the *Fomorian*. This was the same *Fomorian* who'd struck my grandfather. "Your name?"

He growled and spit at the ground.

Naois emitted a quiet but steady flame toward his feet.

"Cromm," he grumbled.

"I'm Grania… one of the *Chosen Ones*. Honestly, we mean you no harm. We only wish to heal you."

His jaw fell slack.

The *Fomorians* exchanged nervous glances. One grasped his arm. They spoke in hushed tones.

A single word reached me.

Prophecy.

His shoulders fell. "You have come to heal us?"

"Why should we believe you?" a Fomorian blurted, loud enough to be heard from the edge of the crowd. "You were trying to kill us."

"I speak the truth." My eyes met Cromm's. "You hold the *Fragarach*."

He nodded. His hand clenched the hilt.

I took a deep breath. "When held to a person's throat, that person cannot tell a lie."

Again, he nodded.

"If you promise not to hurt me, Naois will lower me so you can hold the sword to my throat. I will prove I speak the truth."

"No!" Fianna stumbled forward.

"Fianna!" Kane's arms locked around her waist.

"Grania," Naois growled. "I do not wish to endanger you."

My hand slid soothingly down his neck. "You can keep me safe." My eyes collided with Cromm's. "Naois will burn you to a crisp before your blade can pierce my skin."

He swallowed. Hard. Slowly, he nodded.

Naois steeled himself before lowering me. His remaining heads drew closer. His eyes fixed on Cromm, his mouths open, ready to breathe fire.

Cromm's hand shook as he raised the sword. He steadied the unwieldy object with both hands before lifting it to my neck. "Why…" He glanced nervously between Naois's three scowling heads. "Why have you come?"

"Maolisa, Niamh and I are the *Chosen Ones*, the counter-weights to the Goddess Carman's sons. We have found a way to combine our energy so we can heal you. We do not want to harm you. We wish only to heal you so we can restore the balance between the realms."

His eyes slid toward the *Sidhe* standing behind Naois. "And what of the others?"

I met his wary gaze. "They are here to protect us."

He lowered his sword. "The prophecy. It's... true."

A rumble sounded among the *Fomorians* as they grappled with this news. "The *Chosen Ones*. They're here. They're here to fulfill the prophecy."

Naois backed away.

Cromm sheathed his sword. He lifted his hand, issuing some unspoken command.

Everyone quieted.

He searched for Diarmuid.

Grandpa had pushed to the front of the *Sidhe* as soon as he regained consciousness. He was standing next to Ainle, his hand on *Moralltach*.

Cromm straightened to his full height. He stood at least twelve inches taller than Diarmuid, with shoulders wider than any two of our warriors put together. "We were not aware the *Chosen Ones* had been born, let alone would arrive on this day to heal us. We thought you were coming to retaliate for the *Sidhe* warriors my soldiers killed the other day."

"As well we should," Phelan muttered over our connection.

Diarmuid's jaw clenched.

Cromm's gaze lingered on his people before returning to us. "Our druids foresaw this event decades ago, but we questioned this prophecy. This thought that three young *Sidhe* would one day heal us was difficult to believe, given the history between our people."

Hope surged within me. I glanced at Niamh.

She smiled and winked.

Cromm's voice thundered so that all the *Fomorians* could hear him, including those cowering near the lake. "This *Sidhe* speaks the truth. They have come to heal us."

His announcement was met with silence. No cheers erupted from the *Fomorians*. No collective release of breath. If anything, they looked dejected.

I lowered my mental shields a tiny bit. "They fear we have changed our minds," I shared telepathically. "Dian, do you have any energy left?" He'd healed so many *Sidhe*. I wasn't sure he could even participate at this point.

"I just need a few minutes to restore my energy," he admitted wearily.

"Can we still proceed then?" I directed this question at Diarmuid.

He nodded. "Yes. I think we should."

I met Cromm's disheartened gaze. "If you can give us a few minutes to recover and restore our strength, then we will heal you."

His eyes closed briefly, his face softening with relief. "Thank you."

I acknowledged his response with a curt nod. "If you could gather your people in one spot, it would make things easier. We'll join you in thirty minutes." Naois and I turned to go.

"Wait," Cromm begged.

Naois turned ever so slightly. So did I.

"I don't understand." Cromm's knobby fingers raked through his disheveled hair. He released a frustrated breath. "We've done nothing to deserve this... this... kindness."

"That may be true, but Cromm..." I waited until he was looking directly at me, "no one deserves to be in pain." Naois snorted his agreement as we turned away.

"Let's gather back behind the ridge so we can have some privacy. I do not wish for the *Fomorians* to see how we restore our energy," Diarmuid stated telepathically.

My hand smoothed over Naois's neck. "Would you be willing to fly me to the other side of that ridge?" I pointed in the direction we had come.

He nodded all three heads. "Hold tight." He crouched low to the ground, then leapt up into the air. After a few brief strokes of his wings, he landed gently on the other side of the ridge.

I slid from his neck. Naois's wingspan was so wide, we'd beat everyone there.

He steadied me when my knees collapsed. "We will stand guard while you regain your strength."

I followed his gaze. The *Ellen Trechend* circled overhead, their scales reflecting the orange and purple sunset.

He nudged my broken wing with his nose. "Do you need help with this?"

I trembled, more exhausted than I'd ever been. "You can heal me?"

He smiled. "A little-known secret about the *Ellen Tre-chend*."

I turned, resting my cheek against his chest. "Yes, please."

His tongue swept over the thin filigree in my wing.

I peered over my shoulder, trying to see. My wing perked up immediately.

He grinned. "Give it a try."

I fluttered my wings cautiously and smiled. "Good as new. Thank you, Naois."

Fianna dropped down beside me. "Are you okay?"

I was relieved to see she wasn't injured. "Yes. Just tired."

Ainle pulled me into his arms the second he touched down. "How did you survive that fall?"

Maolisa wrenched me from Ainle. Niamh threw her arms around us, rounding out our group hug. "Elgin saved you."

"Elgin and Naois," I corrected. "What happened? Why were you on the ground?"

"We were trying to get to you." Fianna's eyes welled with tears. "When you struck that water…"

Diarmuid peeled every finger and arm off me. "Grania," he rasped. "I thought I'd lost you." He swept me up in a massive hug.

"Grandpa." My arms tightened around his neck. The tears I'd been holding back suddenly burst free.

"I'm so proud of you," he finally whispered. "You were very brave."

Dian's hand reached tentatively for my arm. "Do you need my help?"

I swiped the tears from my cheeks. "No. You should save your energy."

"You're soaked," Ainle said. "Let me help."

I was shivering too hard to argue. I hadn't realized the extent to which Naois had been keeping me warm.

Ainle spun warm air all around me. "There, that's better."

My eyes closed as I began to yawn. "Yes, but now I'm even sleepier."

"I think you should eat one of the berries the goddess gave you," Fianna encouraged softly.

Naois walked in a tight circle before flopping on the ground.

I settled in next to him.

His tail curled protectively around me.

I leaned back, savoring his warmth. The rise and fall of his chest reassured me I was not alone. With shaking fingers, I removed a rowan berry from the pouch and slipped it in my mouth. The bitter taste puckered my face while nipping at the back of my jaw. *Like lemons,* I thought. I slid the rowan cross from the pouch and turned it in my hand. My other hand fell to the ground. I dug my fingers into the soil and drew energy from the trees. My body began to hum.

Naois purred.

My leaden eyes shut.

"Grania."

A rumble rolled through Naois's chest.

"Easy, Naois. We need to wake Grania."

My eyes fluttered open. "It's been thirty minutes already?"

Fianna sighed. "I'm afraid so."

Naois unfurled his tail.

I slid the rowan cross back inside the pouch. "I just closed my eyes two seconds ago."

"I'm sure it feels that way, but I swear, it's been thirty minutes." Fianna helped me off the ground. "I'm sorry, honey. The sun has fallen, and the *Fomorians* are getting restless."

Ainle offered me his canteen. "Would you like some water?"

I nodded, suddenly parched. The cool liquid spilled down my throat. I wiped my lips with the back of my hand and passed the canteen back to Ainle. "Thanks."

Energy hummed through me once more. I didn't feel a hundred percent, but close enough. I glanced at the moon, surprised to find the sun had already gone. At least we didn't have to battle any storms while casting the Ailm. I turned to Naois. "Can you help us fly to the base of Torc Mountain when we're done? My dad," I paused as I tried to recall his *Sidhe* name, "Ruarc, Cathal, and some other warriors are meeting us there."

"I met your father, Ruarc, a few weeks ago." Naois eased onto his feet. "I know where their camp is by the waterfall. I can deliver you there in thirty minutes."

I smiled, thoroughly relieved. "Dragons rock." Thanks to Naois, we wouldn't have to hike all those miles in the dark.

He grinned, proudly displaying his razor-sharp teeth.

Diarmuid joined us. "We'll stand guard along the ridge while the *Ellen Trechend* keep watch overhead."

"Don't worry, Grandpa." I kissed his cheek. "We got this." I joined Dian, Maolisa, and Niamh.

"Ready?" Dian smiled encouragingly.

"As I'll ever be." With one last look at Naois and a fluttering of my wings, I pushed up off the ground. My injured wing felt strong, like it had never been punctured at all.

Niamh crested the mountain first. "Look! The *Fomorians*, they've dropped to their knees."

There were a lot more *Fomorians* than we'd encountered previously. "How did their numbers increase so quickly?"

Maolisa scoured the terrain. "Maybe they were in the lake."

I glanced at the lake. "I didn't see any *Fomorians* in the lake when I was with Elgin."

"Elgin may have scared them away," Dian said. "They looked scared when he climbed out of the lake." He chose a spot about twenty feet above their camp.

"Ready?" Maolisa grasped my hand.

I peered down at the camp. The *Fomorians* were kneeling, their faces raised, eyes filled with hope. I tucked my wings in tight as we positioned ourselves back to back. "Does anyone need to pull more energy?"

"I'm good," Dian answered.

"Me too," Niamh agreed.

Maolisa drew in a breath. "The Ailm, on the count of three, then."

We pushed energy down toward our fingers and lifted our arms above our heads. Green, gold, and blue light pulsed between our hands. "One... two... three!"

A stream of energy shot through our fingertips. Maolisa coaxed it into a perfectly symmetrical cross. A sonic boom sounded as we forced the Ailm down. The shimmering cross hurtled toward the ground. The *Fomorians'* upturned faces glowed in the sudden wash of light.

We hovered breathlessly.

I lowered my shield. "I can feel their relief."

They stood slowly. They were asking one another something, bending elbows and knees. The tension eased from their shoulders. Instead of walking hunched, they stood taller and walked without lumbering.

A low rumble sounded among them, building until...

"Is that..." Maolisa looked at me.

A smile tugged at my cheeks. "They're laughing."

"They're not in pain anymore," Dian marveled.

"We did it!" Niamh spun me around.

Maolisa peered at the ground. "They don't look as scary when they aren't in pain."

I followed her gaze. We'd healed whatever ailments had plagued the *Fomorians*, so they didn't look deformed anymore. They looked... well... normal... just larger than the average person.

Diarmuid joined us. "I'm going to speak with Cromm. I want to see if they will help us when we confront Dain, Dother, and Dub."

Dian nodded.

My fingers brushed against Grandpa's arm. "I would like to join you."

He nodded. "I'm sure Cromm would like to speak with you as well."

Our guardians and the warriors drew closer as we lowered onto the ground. Naois and his friends remained circling overhead.

A hush fell over the *Fomorians*.

Cromm's eyes welled with tears. "I can hardly comprehend this." With a deep, shuddering breath, he sank to his knees, his head bowed humbly. "Thank you for freeing us from this crippling disease."

I reached for his hand, coaxing him to his feet. "I hope that we can live peacefully... maybe even be friends."

His hands engulfed mine. "I would like that."

I sensed no anger, malice, or pain. "Me too." I smiled warmly.

Cromm studied his people. "There are others... the *Fomorians* who reside in the ocean... will you heal them too?"

I glanced questioningly at Diarmuid.

He nodded. "We will return in three or four days' time."

Niamh twined her fingers with mine. "The Goddess Carman's sons are holding Grania's family hostage. We must secure their release."

Cromm shook his head. Fear warred with concern, disappointment, and regret. "The Goddess Carman's sons promised us *Tír na nÓg* if we eliminated your warriors. That is why we have gathered here at Upper Lake. That is why we attacked your warriors the other day."

Grandpa fought to keep his emotions in check. "Why would you want to serve the Goddess Carman's sons? They're using you, manipulating you for their own gain."

Cromm looked ashamed. "Because we knew they would retaliate if we didn't cooperate." His chest fell with a weighted sigh. "We will no longer do as they asked. We will not harm your warriors unless it is in self-defense."

Diarmuid grew pensive. "Will you fight alongside us, join us in protecting the *Chosen Ones*?"

He shifted uncomfortably. "I will not force my people to fight. They have already suffered enough."

Diarmuid's jaw clenched. Cromm wanted us to heal the remaining *Fomorians*, but he wasn't willing to protect us so we could follow through on that.

I shared Diarmuid's frustration, but I didn't want Grandpa to say anything he might regret. I shared my thoughts telepathically. "He's afraid Triple D will punish them for disobeying their orders. He's worried they will find a way to restore their pain."

Maolisa drew closer to me. "They are fearful. Fear is a powerful thing."

Grandpa looked at us. With a barely perceptible nod, his gaze returned to Cromm. "We will confront the Goddess Carman's sons at Devil's Punch Bowl in two days' time."

"I can make no promises," he replied.

There was nothing more we could say. I called for Naois as we walked away.

Maolisa turned. Her eyes snagged on Cromm's sword, then rose to his face. "Where is your shield?"

"I have no shield." He shrugged, seemingly uncon-cerned. "Why do you ask?"

"Well," she confessed, "there is a shield stronger than any weapon, a shield that can withstand any attack, that would enable you to conquer any fear. I thought you might possess it."

His eyes lit with interest. "This shield... does it have a name?"

"Yes," she said, "it is the Shield of Faith."

CHAPTER 9 – DAIN, DOTHER, AND DUB

"Daddy!" I slid from Naois's neck and ran full force, barreling into my father's chest. "I've missed you so much."

"How's my brave girl? Here. Let me look at you." His eyes scoured my hands, my wind ravaged clothes, and face.

Maolisa and Niamh slid from Naois's back. Our guardians, Cian, Kane, and Dian leapt from the remaining *Ellen Trechend*. The warriors landed beside them while shifting into their *Sidhe* form. They'd been flying as white-tailed eagles, which I learned was their preferred means of transportation in the human realm.

I tried to hold still while my father searched for injuries, but I wanted to thank Naois. I turned in Dad's arms. "Thank you, Naois. You are a true friend."

He bowed all three heads. "It was an honor, Grania. Remember, you need only speak my name. I will be there when you need me." With a deep intake of breath and a sweep of his wings, he leapt straight into the air.

We watched the *Ellen Trechend* until their silhouettes faded in the moonlit sky. "Are you hungry?" Cathal finally asked.

"Starving," Dian admitted. We hadn't stopped to replenish our energy or eat since healing the *Fomorians*.

"Our camp is behind the falls, about midway up. Be careful on the rocks. They're slick." Cathal turned to lead the way.

The trees thickened, forming a canopy over the frothy water. We picked our way single file through the mossy boulders and rocks. Dad walked directly in front of me while Ainle hiked close behind. I lowered my mental shields so I could get a read on my dad. I picked up on Ainle's emotions instead. He was worried I might fall.

"Through here." Cathal ducked beneath some low-lying branches. He disappeared behind a stone wall.

Dad held the branches for me. "Watch your step."

I followed Cathal through a stone passageway. My eyes widened when it opened into an enormous cavern. "Wow." A river swirled like liquid silver through the center of the room. Moon drenched water spilled from the gaps in the rocks above, filling the river and bathing us in a soft, luminous light. Trees stretched against the cavern walls, their thick roots forming benches and beds while their limbs curled protectively overhead. Vines draped the ceiling while moss carpeted the ground.

Maolisa sucked in a breath. "It's beautiful."

Kane nodded his approval. "There's something for everyone… air, water, and wood."

Niamh stood in a moonbeam. "The air feels warm."

"This mountain puts out a fair amount of heat." Dad strode toward the camp-style kitchen. "Roasted vegetables anyone?" He handed me a bowl heaped with potatoes, green beans, carrots, and squash.

I carried my bowl to the long, rough-hewn table where several warriors were already eating. "May I join you?"

"Of course." They scooted further down the bench, ensuring there was plenty of room for the newcomers.

I sat down beside them. Fianna, Dad, and Diarmuid joined me.

Thin tendrils of steam curled around Dad's mug. "Diarmuid briefed me on the *Fomorians*."

I frowned, reflecting on the day's events. "We shouldn't have forced our solution on them. They responded violently out of fear. They could have killed Diarmuid, Niamh... everyone, really. If only we'd spoken with them first. They were cooperative once they learned why we were there."

"We didn't know about their prophecy, and nothing in our previous encounters suggested they might cooperate with us." Dad eyed me a little more closely. "I heard you injured your wing when you fell into the lake. Are you okay?"

Ainle climbed onto the bench opposite me. "Grania is very brave. You should have seen the way she stood up to Cromm. She told him to hold the *Fragarach* to her throat."

Dad shot Diarmuid a scathing look before his gaze returned to me. "Your grandfather left that part out."

"I was trying to deliver the negative news in small doses," Grandpa grumbled. I was surprised he spoke at all given the speed at which he was devouring his food.

I dug into the warm vegetables. "I'll be fine once I get some sleep."

Fianna nodded. "I think we could all use some sleep."

I recalled the boost of energy I felt when we slept under the same roof as the other *Sidhe.* I was certain I would need that and more for the confrontation with Triple D. "How are Mom and Lexie doing?"

"I don't want you worrying about them," Dad answered dismissively. "I want you to eat and get some sleep. I promise, you will receive a full update in the morning."

I could tell he was holding something back, something he thought would sabotage any chance of sleep. I didn't push, although I suspected the not knowing would make it even harder to sleep. My mind would fill in the missing pieces until I knew for sure what we were facing. What awful images would my mind conjure? How would those images compare to what we were really facing?

Ainle must have sensed my frustration. "Would you like to play a game of *fidchell* when we're done eating?"

I stared at him for a couple of heartbeats. "Sure." A distraction was exactly what I needed.

He grinned, obviously pleased.

I ate while Diarmuid groused about the *Fomorians'* unwillingness to help. Honestly? If the Goddess Carman's sons weren't holding my family hostage, I would try to avoid them too.

Ainle cleared our dishes from the table. He returned with the *fidchell* board. "Would you like to capture or defend the king?" He sat directly across from me.

I thought about Mom and Lexie. "I'll defend the king." I studied the markings on the board while he removed the game pieces from the pouch. The board was set up like a grid, similar to chess. A trinity knot appeared faintly in the center, like a watermark. Quaternary knots flanked the trinity knot on all four sides. I chuckled, quickly grasping the message imbedded in those knots. "So, there are infinite possibilities."

"Precisely." He set a deep emerald green stone in the center of the trinity knot. "The king sits in the center, on the throne. He is the only one who can sit on the throne."

I fought a giggle and lost. "Makes sense since he's the king."

Maolisa squeezed in beside me. "Ah, *fidchell*. Can I watch?"

"I want to learn, too." Niamh plunked down on the other side of me.

I smiled at my friends. "We're defending the king."

Ainle stilled. "That's three against one."

Laughter bubbled up from Maolisa's lungs. "We're the *Chosen Ones*... a package deal... three for the price of one."

Treasach patted Ainle on the back. "Yeah, good luck with that." He clambered onto the bench so he could watch.

Cian sat across from Niamh. "This I've got to see."

Ainle grumbled something under his breath. He set two light green stones above, below, and on either side of the king, essentially forming the Ailm. "Your pieces are green since you're protecting the king. Your goal is to help the king escape safely to the edge of the board." He arranged topaz stones around the outer edges of the board.

I counted, recounted, then frowned. "Why do you have more pieces than me?"

A smile tugged at his cheeks. "Because I'm attacking the king."

Niamh counted the pieces. "Sixteen to eight? That's a pretty big advantage."

"Yes, but his task is more difficult," Cian explained. "Ainle has to surround the king on all four sides in order to seize him. Grania really only has to shield the king while he moves to the edge of the board."

Maolisa studied the board. "Do they move along these lines?" Her finger traced an unobstructed line.

I'd been wondering that very same thing. Ainle was positioning our stones on the lines, not inside the squares.

"Yes," Ainle answered. "You can stop on any of these dots." A small black dot marked each spot where the lines intersected on the grid.

"All these pieces move in a straight line, like the rook in chess." Treasach demonstrated. "You eliminate your opponent's pieces by flanking them on either side." He flanked one of my defenders with two of Ainle's attackers. "Now, if Grania moved her defender in between the two attackers, her defender would remain safe. You only lose your piece when your opponent makes the move that flanks your stone."

"Attackers move first. We take turns, moving one piece at a time." Ainle grinned at me from across the board. "Are you ready to give it a try?"

"Sure." I smiled. "Why not?"

Ainle moved one of the topaz pieces next to a green, immediately putting me on the defensive.

Dad leaned over my shoulder and whispered, "Think three moves ahead, like you do with chess."

I moved the piece Ainle was flanking to the left.

He moved another piece on the opposite side of the board, and thus began our dance.

* * *

"No!" I clawed at my throat.

"Grania."

I shook my head, still struggling for breath.

"Grania, wake up."

I bolted upright with a gasp.

Fianna knelt beside me. "Are you okay?"

Slowly, I registered my surroundings. We were inside the cavern. I'd fallen asleep while listening to the warriors strategize in hushed tones. "Yes. It was just…"

"A bad dream?" Ainle dropped down beside me.

My cheeks heated when I realized everyone had probably heard me. "I was drowning. Elgin wasn't there to save me."

He leaned back against the tree. "I'd hoped our *fidchell* game would give you something else to think about." He'd beaten me quite soundly.

Fianna rubbed my arm. "I'll make you some tea."

I scooted closer to Ainle so we could talk without waking Maolisa and Niamh. "You did give me something to think about," I nudged his shoulder with mine, "like how I'm going to beat you the next time we play."

He chuckled softly. "I suppose you could beat me. Eventually."

I crooked an eyebrow. "I'm going to beat you tomorrow."

His body shook with barely suppressed laughter. "That's doubtful."

I bit back a smile. "Challenge accepted, warrior."

Fianna handed me a steaming mug filled with tea. "Don't stay up too late."

"I won't. I just need to distance myself from that dream." I sipped the peppermint tea. The sweet, woodsy scent soothed me.

Ainle's expression grew serious. "What did you learn?"

My brow furrowed. "From the game?"

He nodded.

I stopped to think about it. "I learned that it helps when you outnumber your opponents and that you might need to sacrifice some of your defenders in the end."

His eyes held mine. "That holds true for real battles too. Did you know our warriors are required to master *fidchell* before they go into battle?"

"No." I feigned a frown. "Funny how you didn't mention that when you invited me to play the game with you."

He shrugged. "I didn't want to scare you off."

I rolled my eyes. "You know I don't scare easy."

The smile slid from his face. "I know. You are one of the bravest *Sidhe* I know."

That brought my thoughts full circle. I set the tea aside.

Ainle's hand blanketed mine. "You are not alone in this, Grania. Your guardians, the druids, the other warriors, and I will fight beside you. We will protect you and your family as best we can."

Tears welled in my eyes. "I don't want to lose any of my defenders. I don't want anyone to die."

His hand tightened around mine. "We outnumber our opponents. We have air, water, and wood to draw on, so the Earth itself supports us. Your strategy is sound. I am certain you will restore the balance between the realms."

"Yes, but at what cost?" I was so worried that Mom or Lexie wouldn't survive. And... I couldn't stop thinking about that question posed by the Rowan Tree.

Ainle lifted my chin so I was forced to look at him. "What is it? What do you know that I don't?"

I shook my head. I didn't want to burden him with this. If I was supposed to sacrifice myself, he might try to intervene. He could end up dead.

"Please, Grania," he implored. "I must know. We can work through this together. Remember, two heads are better than one."

Tears spilled down my cheeks. "The Rowan Tree," I finally relented, "in *Ogham*, the Rowan Tree asked if I would be willing to sacrifice my life for those I love. He... he assured me if I am willing to sacrifice my life, then I will succeed."

Ainle shook his head. "Surely you misunderstood." He looked desperate to unhear this news.

I brushed the tears from my cheeks. "I didn't."

"I..." his voice broke as tears welled in his eyes. "I will not allow it."

"We have no choice," I whispered. "Regardless of what transpires with Dain, Dother, or Dub, I must sacrifice my life to save the ones I love."

He drew my head to his chest. "There are an infinite amount of possibilities, more choices than any one person can possibly comprehend. Of all the lessons I've learned from *fidchell*, that is the most critical one. We're going to find another way to solve this problem... one that won't cost you your life."

Sacrificing my life was the only option mentioned by the Rowan Tree. Still, I prayed he was right.

Ainle rubbed my back until my shoulders relaxed, until my tumultuous thoughts subsided, and I finally succumbed to sleep.

* * *

"Talk about a team meeting." Maolisa fidgeted nervously. Every *Sidhe* inside the cavern gathered around the table while a handful of warriors stood guard outside.

I wasn't surprised. Ainle had already confessed he'd mentioned my conversation with the Rowan Tree to Cathal.

Cathal had been immersed in conversation with Diarmuid, Phelan, and Dad ever since. Maolisa, Niamh, our guardians, Dian, and the druids sat at the table with me. The warriors drew closer. Cathal spoke. "Tomorrow may very well be one of the most critical days in *Sidhe* history. You know what we are facing on Mangerton Mountain... three of the most powerful beings to wield dark magick. Unfortunately, we don't know the extent of their capabilities. What we do know may barely scratch the surface of their power. We must prepare for the worst, think at least three steps ahead, and weigh each course of action, their potential response, and countermoves for every possible scenario."

There were murmurs of agreement, especially among the warriors.

Cathal continued. "This is what we do know." He sent some images that unraveled like a movie inside my head.

I gasped. The images were from his last reconnaissance mission on Mangerton Mountain. The grass had shriveled in on itself. The soil was parched and cracked. There were no trees. Even the rocks looked black.

"As you can see, the evil seeping from Dother has impacted the entire mountain. He is choking the life out of everything, the water, the air, and ground." He glanced at Niamh. "We have been monitoring their activities through short rotations. Even with our mental shields in place, Dub's darkness permeates our minds. Even our strongest warriors report feeling hopeless. The despair that follows is completely overwhelming. Dub's darkness isn't just about the absence of light, it is the absence of everything that is good and right."

Several warriors nodded.

Niamh shuddered. "That's awful."

He looked at me. "Because we've masked our presence, we have not yet seen what Dain is capable of. There is an undercurrent of violence that feels like a tangible thing... sort of like a sleeping giant or the calm before a storm. As best I can tell, Dain is the one in charge. Physically, he remains closest to your sister and mom. He's the one who is keeping them suspended in a coma above Devil's Punch Bowl. It appears he is drawing on their pain, harvesting it in some way, although we aren't entirely sure why." Cathal paused as if weighing his next statement. "I'm sorry, Grania, but they do not look well." He shared an image of their emaciated bodies lying suspended above a crater filled with tar.

A strangled moan escaped my chest. "No."

Dian reached for my hand. "Grania, I can heal them."

Dad eased onto the bench. "I'm sorry, honey. I wish you didn't have to see that." He brushed my tears away with his thumbs and pulled me in his arms. "Cathal is trying to prepare you so you can act quickly. There can be no hesitation once we get there."

I sniffed, still feeling miserable and small. "I know."

"Okay." His eyes met Cathal's. "What do we do?"

He paced across the cavern floor. "This will be unlike any battle we have waged before. Drawing energy from wood, water, and air will not be feasible given how tainted everything is on Mangerton Mountain. We will draw energy from our respective sources before approaching Devil's Punch Bowl, but this energy may not be sufficient to last the entire battle. If your energy is depleted, the only safe source of energy will be the energy you obtain from one another."

Diarmuid squeezed my shoulder. "Do you still have the berries the goddess gave you?"

I turned to look at him. "Yes, all but one."

"Try to save them for the very end," he said. "They will boost your energy when we have nothing left to give."

I swallowed. Hard. I didn't want to deplete anyone's energy, especially when battling amid such dire conditions.

"This sounds like a battle of wills, a mental war more so than a physical one." Kane's eyes softened when he caught me looking at him. "We should all seek to strengthen our mental shields before we go."

"The onslaught of negative emotions may prove disabling," Cian agreed. "We should maintain an open link so we can help keep one another sane if they do penetrate our shields."

"You should expect to feel pain," Cathal warned. "Dain can inflict pain every bit as excruciating as a knife wound with a simple flick of his wrist. He doesn't need to be near you to cause this pain."

"I think a diversion would help," Phelan said, eager to hammer out a plan, "a mock attack that would allow the *Chosen Ones* an opportunity to cast their knots."

Diarmuid nodded. "We could separate into two groups, with one contingent creating a diversion and the other protecting the *Chosen Ones*."

Maolisa raised her hand. "Are we flying or hiking in?"

Cathal shook his head, his expression grim. "I'm afraid hiking won't be feasible under these conditions."

"We've been scouting the area in small groups comprised of two or three eagles in order to avoid detection and to minimize our exposure to the toxic conditions," Dad explained.

"So, we're flying in as birds and shifting back to our *Sidhe* form once we arrive at Devil's Punch Bowl," Maolisa guessed.

"I don't see the point of flying in as birds," Phelan admitted. "There are fifty of us now. A flock of fifty birds or a convocation of eagles is bound to raise some suspicion. We may as well fly in *Sidhe* form."

Fianna frowned. I knew what she was thinking. We weren't supposed to fly in front of humans in *Sidhe* form. "Have you seen any other signs of life on the mountain?"

"Aside from a conspiracy of ravens, there have been no other signs of life, mortal or immortal on Mangerton Mountain," Cathal assured her.

"Oh!" Niamh's hand shot up. "I know how we can fly in undetected. We can shapeshift into ravens."

"Wood and air spirits can shapeshift into ravens," Phelan rebutted. "Water spirits cannot."

"But water spirits can shapeshift into storm petrels," Cian countered. "Storm petrels would blend in with a conspiracy of ravens."

Cathal's feet ground to a stop. "That could work." He waited to see if there were any objections. There were a few nods, reluctant grunts, and shrugs, but no one objected. "Ravens and storm petrels it is then. Now, about that diversion. Ruarc has suggested he attempt to save his family."

"Dad." Panic clawed at my chest.

He stood, intent on making his case. "The Goddess Carman's sons kidnapped my family so they could draw us to them. They're not likely to see this as a diversion but as a genuine attempt to save my wife and child."

Cathal's eyes skimmed the rest of us. "Thoughts?"

Dad's voice slipped quietly inside my head. "Please understand. I could never forgive myself. I need to save them."

I squeezed my eyes tight. A single tear escaped along with a defeated sigh. I was worried my father might be injured or killed, but I knew he was right. The Goddess Carman's sons wouldn't see this as a diversion. They would expect a *Sidhe* warrior to fight for his wife and child.

We contemplated Triple D's response, plotted countermoves, and fine-tuned our strategy over the next several minutes. In the end, we agreed that Cathal and Dad would lead the diversion, flying up to Devil's Punch Bowl in *Sidhe* form. Diarmuid and Phelan would lead the team protecting us. We were flying in as ravens and storm petrels, shapeshifting, and casting the knots as soon as we were in position.

Despite the extensive planning session, Cathal wasn't finished with us. "There is one last thing…"

My knee stopped bouncing.

His eyes locked on mine. "Grania, please reveal the question your birth tree asked when you were in *Ogham*."

My face sheeted white.

He stepped closer, unmoved by the panic raging inside of me. "Don't summarize, repeat it exactly as it was framed by the Rowan Tree."

I searched for my dad, but Cathal was standing between us, limiting my sight. I took a deep breath and slowly released it.

The room quieted.

My eyes slid closed while I conjured an image of *Ogham* inside my mind… the rough bark from the Sessile Oak supporting my back… the heavy silence… the absence of moon and sun… and the fireflies glowing beneath the mist. It was then the Rowan Tree spoke. "Would you sacrifice your life for those you love?" Slowly, I opened my eyes.

"And your answer?" Phelan inquired.

"If I must," I drew in another breath, "to which the Rowan Tree replied, 'Then you will succeed.'"

Ainle spoke before anyone else could. "I believe the Rowan Tree was using this word 'sacrifice' figuratively or in the broadest sense of the word, essentially encouraging Grania to help others instead of pursuing her own interests."

"She has already met this requirement," Dad interjected.

Cathal turned so I could see him.

His shoulders tensed. "Grania has already demonstrated a willingness to sacrifice her life. She did precisely that when she encouraged Cromm to hold the *Fragarach* to her throat. As far as I'm concerned, that condition has been met."

"I disagree." Phelan eyed me apologetically. "The trees in *Ogham* are ancient... and in ancient times, when you sacrificed a life, that life ended."

Maolisa sucked in a breath.

Ainle growled deep inside his chest. "My birth tree, the Alder, offered glimpses of our future together. This is how I know Grania is my fated mate. Why would the Alder Tree share those images if she is not meant to survive this confrontation tomorrow?"

"Our destiny is not fixed," Kane answered gently. "Something may have happened to change Grania's fate between the time you visited *Ogham* and the time she spoke with the Rowan Tree."

Ainle stood in front of me, his arms folded across his chest. "If that is true, then we can change her fate again."

* * *

"Come with me." Maolisa tugged me toward the entrance to the cave.

I peered over my shoulder at Dad. "Where are we going?"

"We're going to shower in the waterfall. The warriors who are standing guard have promised not to watch." She giggled. "Actually, Ainle, Treasach, and Cian have threatened to kill them if they do."

Niamh met us at the entrance. "I've got soap." She dangled the creamy white bar in front of us.

I gaped at the bar of soap. "Where on Earth did you find that?"

She leaned forward conspiratorially. "Brigitte had it. You should see her travel kit."

Maolisa laughed. "Ciara's emergency kit is impressive too. She should have been a healer. I think she envies Dian's skills."

"Have you seen the way he looks at her?" Niamh led us out through the trees. "I think there's more than envy between them."

I just shook my head. We inched out onto the rocks, called our wings, and flew to the bottom of the falls. After studying the warriors to make sure they were standing with their backs to us, we stripped out of our leggings, tunics, boots, and bracers. Getting undressed in front of my friends wasn't all that different from P.E. class. Showering outside was an entirely different story. I felt uncomfortable, but my desire to feel clean won out in the end. My nervousness faded once I was immersed shoulder deep inside the frothy water. The water felt refreshing and surprisingly warm. "We should wash our clothes." I crept out onto the rocks and grabbed the garments.

"Good idea." Niamh passed me the soap before retrieving her clothes.

Maolisa giggled. "If only we had a washboard. I remember reading something about this in my history book... people scrubbing clothes in rivers and lakes."

I lathered the soap against my clothes. "Do you miss all the modern amenities, the technologies back home?"

Maolisa used the soap while I rubbed my clothes together. She poked her arms and legs out of the water while she washed up. "I miss my family and friends, but no, I don't miss cars, computers, or television."

Niamh returned with her clothes.

Maolisa handed her the bar of soap.

"In some ways *Otherworld* seems more advanced." Niamh scrubbed her clothes. "Who needs a computer when infused with all that knowledge from *Ogham*? We don't need cell phones either. Communicating telepathically is more efficient and fun. And television?" Her eyes sparked with amusement. "People are infinitely more entertaining than television."

"Who needs cars when we can fly… or a stove when we can warm food with our hands?" Maolisa shook her head. "I'd choose these abilities over modern amenities any day."

I spread my clothes out on the rocks so they could dry. "I don't want to return to Virginia. I want my dog, but that's about it." I hoped my parents would choose to remain in *Tír na nÓg*… assuming everyone survived.

Maolisa frowned as if reading my thoughts. "There is something that has been worrying me about our strategy for tomorrow."

Niamh drifted closer. "What?"

She glanced briefly at the warriors who remained standing with their backs turned to us. "What if our warriors are impacted by the knot, and they have no desire to fight?"

The thought had crossed my mind. "The warriors aren't trying to destroy anything, and they're not acting out of hate. They're not fighting to secure land, wealth, or other material objects. They only want to protect the people and places they love. As long as their actions are motivated by love, I think they'll be fine."

"I agree. I think the warriors will be fine, but..." Niamh eyed us uncertainly.

"What?" I whispered.

She sighed as if disappointed to be harboring any doubts. "What if Dain, Dother, and Dub aren't close enough to cast the knots over all three at once? The *Fomorians* couldn't fly, but they can. We're already casting two knots, the love knot and the five-fold Celtic knot that expands the area of impact. What if one of the brothers flies above us, and we have to cast those knots a second time? All the trees, the water, and the air on Mangerton Mountain have been destroyed. Where will we find the energy?"

Maolisa forced her eyes from the frothy water. "Aside from the berries?"

She nodded. "Three berries may not be enough."

I released a shaky breath, knowing what needed to be said. "Ainle told me that mates are supposed to strengthen one another in this way. I wouldn't accept energy from all the warriors, but drawing energy from Ainle and Treasach shouldn't compromise their capabilities too much. Of course, you would be drawing energy from Cian, since he's your fated mate. The druids wield massive amounts of energy. I'm sure they'd offer it up in a heartbeat. As a healer, Dian is used to expending enormous amounts of energy. I know he's anxious to help. We could draw energy from him and my grandpa if we need more."

"We should get their permission before we leave, just to be on the safe side." Maolisa sighed. "Now, about that question from our birth tree…"

* * *

I frowned at Fianna. "You could have told me the tea was drugged."

She spared a sidelong glance while we trudged through the dimly lit forest. "The tea wasn't drugged. Not really. Dian just added some herbs to help you sleep."

"My head crashed against the *fidchell* board," I stomped my foot indignantly, "in the middle of the game. Look! I even have a bruise from where my forehead hit the king."

"That was a really lame strategy by the way." Ainle chuckled. "You still haven't beat me."

Dian grimaced beneath his hooded cape. "I may have added a little too much valerian to your tea."

My eyes widened. "You think?" I scowled at Ainle. "Protecting the king with my forehead wasn't my strategy. I fell asleep."

"No more sleep supplements," Niamh agreed. Mine wasn't the only tea that had been spiked. Maolisa and Niamh had fallen headlong into sleep just like me.

"I don't know if I would have been able to sleep without the tea," Maolisa admitted, "although it would have been nice if you'd offered us a warning so we could avoid having our faces smashed against the table."

"I tried to catch you, but it happened so fast." Treasach shook his head, his eyes widening with disbelief. "I've never seen anyone fall asleep that fast."

"This is the meadow I was telling you about." We held our position while the scouts cleared the area. Cathal waved us forward when they gave the all clear.

Nervous energy bounced through the meadow. My heart began to race. This was it. Within minutes, we'd confront three of the most dangerous creatures ever born. I prayed we'd be strong enough to survive their wrath, to save my family and *Tír na nÓg*.

Dad folded me in his arms. "I'm so proud of you. No matter what happens on that mountain… to me, to Lexie, or your mom… I want you to know I love you. I will always love you, no matter what."

"I love you too, Daddy." Tears threatened to fall. "If anything happens to me, please tell Lexie and Mom…"

He shook his head. "Our warriors won't allow any harm to come to you."

I choked back a sob. "Tell them I love them. Please, Daddy, it's important to me."

He nodded solemnly. "I will if I must, but I want you to tell them yourself." His arms loosened. He stepped back so he could look at me. "Stay strong, stay smart, focus on fulfilling the prophecy, and everything will work itself out."

I flung my arms around his waist. "Please be safe."

"I will," he promised.

Our friends were forming a circle in the center of the meadow. Fianna gave me a hug when we joined them. "Who wants to solve the case of the missing mom?" She smiled when I chuckled. So much had changed since she'd posed that question about my dad. But, my godmother? She remained the same. She grasped both my hands. "You are not alone in this battle. We will fight beside you every step of the way."

My smile was tremulous at best. "Thank you."

"No crying," she lectured sternly. "Crying is not a good look for me. You know, snot streaming down my face? I can't do that in front of Kane." A look of mock horror shone on her face.

I nearly choked. The tears that had been threatening collided with the laughter in my throat. My eyes flew toward Kane. He was studying us, intently. "You know he loves you?"

"Yeah." She huffed out a breath. "I suppose I'll have to do something about that."

Cathal began. "While our roles and our tasks vary, our objectives remain the same... retrieve Ruarc's family and restore the balance between the realms. There is no room for fear, for worry, or doubt. We must abandon those toxic thoughts. Acknowledge and release them now."

I took a deep breath and quietly assessed my thoughts. I discarded all the negative ones on an exhale. My emotions proved a little trickier. I had to pry them from my heart.

Cathal nodded his approval. "Now, let's forge our connection."

We linked hands. I was standing between Fianna and Dad. I gathered the threads for each *Sidhe* present. I felt better, less alone, after that. We shared some encouraging words and prayed together while testing the connection.

"Seek energy from your respective sources. When your reserve is full, raise your shields." His eyes traversed every *Sidhe*. "We will depart shortly."

I drew energy from the trees. My skin tingled, my reserve filled to bursting. I tugged my mental shield into place, ensuring our communication threads were tucked safely behind the wall. Gradually, I coaxed energy out through my pores. A soft gold light emanated from my skin when the protective shield formed.

"Grania," Cathal called softly. Our eyes met. "Follow your instincts and your heart. They will guide you when the time comes." With a final nod, he stepped back.

Dad released my hand. All the warriors who were tasked with the diversion stepped back. With a strong sweep of their wings, they departed. I felt the loss the second Dad's fingers slipped from mine. Diarmuid closed the gap between us. Our circle shrank, but our hands remained clasped.

The minutes ticked away.

I fought the anxieties rising inside of me.

Cian shared an image of the meditation garden in *Tír na nÓg*. The image was so vivid, oranges, roses, and magnolia blossoms scented the air.

I took a deep, steadying breath.

Cathal televised their progress. He sent some images from the decaying mountain.

Phelan acknowledged the information.

Niamh painted vibrant trees, a crystal blue lake, purple heather, and bright yellow gorse over Cathal's image. The mountain was completely restored, at least inside our minds.

Fear and uncertainty slammed into me. The warriors' emotions hurtled across the open line, broadcasting just as strong as if they'd been standing right in front of me.

We rallied against their emotions. I conjured an image of Lexie and Mom inside the Goddess Danu's palace. Fianna added a few more details. A celebration.

A sudden spike of fear surged through our connection.

"It is time." Diarmuid announced. "They have engaged with the Goddess Carman's sons."

My heart stuttered.

He gave me a hug. Fianna did the same.

Ainle strode through the center of the circle. Tension rolled off him in waves. He captured my hands when Fianna released me. "Be safe." He kissed the top of my head.

My heart stuttered when our eyes met. "You too." I conjured an image of a raven inside my mind. We shifted and took flight as the sun began to rise. The remaining *Sidhe* joined us. Even though Fianna, Diarmuid, and the other *Sidhe* had transformed into ravens and storm petrels, I recognized each instinctively. *Sidhe* energy was like a signature, distinctively unique.

The lush green grass morphed into dry, shriveled blades as we approached Mangerton Mountain. The soil was dry and cracked. My eyes snagged on the inky black rocks. There was something wrong, something unnatural about those rocks. Dark, desperate emotions clung to those boulders, although I sensed no life, no souls, as with other living things.

"What happened to the sun?" Niamh wondered aloud.

The mountain became a mere shadow of itself, a granite rock cast in shades of gray and black. I searched for the sun. Dark, ominous clouds rolled over us, forcing us closer to the ground. "I hope it doesn't rain."

"Brace yourselves," Treasach gritted.

An unbearable pressure built inside my head. I heard something like ice breaking inside my mind. Tiny cracks crept through my mental shield. Violent images slithered through... men, women, and children stumbling over discarded bodies, slipping through rivers of blood. Fear then dread pierced my heart. "Oh, no."

"It isn't real," Fianna assured me. "It's just Dain. Strengthen your shield." She shared images from *Tír na nÓg*... the emerald green lake that swallowed the sun... the magical bridge that dripped moss... the meadow, the meditation garden, and her tree house.

I clung to those images while strengthening my shield. When I heard a whimper escape Maolisa, I played my memory of her dancing in that "fish are people too" shirt. A beta fish with a long rainbow-colored tail swirled around her legs. I immersed myself and everyone around me in the memory.

"Do you feel that?" Brigitte gasped.

"Yes," Diarmuid confirmed. "From what the other warriors have reported, it will only get worse."

Pain laced with sorrow and despair.

"Where are all these emotions coming from?" My chest ached. My wings felt too heavy to move. My stomach felt nauseous... so nauseous. "I need to land. I'm going to be sick."

"Keep flying." Ainle maneuvered closer to me. He shared his memories from that magical ball... images of me, prettier than I ever imagined I could be, adorned in a purple and blue gown. My cheeks flushed pink as we danced against a backdrop of sparkling trees.

When I closed my eyes, I could feel Ainle's arms around me. I could smell the meadow, hear the flutes and the uilleann pipes. Of course, I couldn't really fly with my eyes closed. I forced them open. The last thing we needed was a mid-air collision.

We drew closer to Devil's Punch Bowl despite every fiber of my being demanding I flee. By the time we caught sight of the crater that used to hold a lake, the air felt so heavy I could barely breathe. There was no wind or breeze to speak of. The water inside the crater churned, thick and black like sludge. Black hands clawed through the bubbling tar. Oblong heads pushed through the sludge, mouths open with soundless screams as they reached for us. "It's not real," I whispered over and over again.

So many dark emotions clung to me. I trembled violently, more fearful than I'd ever been. I'd been plagued with nightmares my entire life. You could have rolled all those frightening dreams into one terrifying experience with no end, and it still would have paled when compared to this. I choked back a sob. "There they are."

My heart sank. I couldn't even begin to comprehend my mother's skeletal frame. My sister was so emaciated she looked like death. "No." I stopped abruptly to clutch my head, but I couldn't. I didn't have any hands, only these long-feathered wings.

A lone *Sidhe* with long black hair and dark warrior-size wings lingered above them. He was dressed entirely in black... black boots, black pants, a black shirt, and a black sleeveless duster that swirled like smoke beneath his wings. Three strands of black beads draped across his chest, flanked by bronze medallions clutching blood red stones. Black bracers with bronze buckles protected his arms. A twisted, claw-like torc encircled his neck. A matching ring cradled the blood red stone on his hand. He looked beautiful but frightening at the same time, with black, soulless eyes glinting against a pale canvas of skin.

I knew. With the violent aura emanating from this dark winged *Sidhe*, there was no mistaking him. "Dain."

His gaze slid from my family's lifeless forms. He frowned at our little conspiracy, his eyes locking on mine. "Grania."

I sucked in a breath. I could feel him inside my mind.

A dark chuckle chilled my blood. "But of course. You belong to me."

He could read my mind? My wings and beak disintegrated. Dain was inside my head, willing me to shift into my *Sidhe* form. "He knows it's us." My eyes squeezed shut in a vain attempt to block him out.

"Come, Grania. You've kept me waiting far too long."

I cried out in frustration as he forced me back into my *Sidhe* form. "No!"

Everyone around me shifted.

Light flashed in the corner of my eye.

Pain sliced through me when I tore my eyes from Dain. He was punishing me for looking away.

"Dad," I gasped. I'd been so distracted by Dain, I hadn't seen the warriors fighting Dother and Dub. Their swords lie strewn across the ground.

Dother, who looked far more frightening than Dain, hurled a disc of flames toward Dad.

I dove toward them when it crashed into his chest.

"No." Diarmuid blocked me. His sudden appearance sent me reeling back. "Grania, focus. Join Maolisa and Niamh so you can form the knot."

Tears streamed down my cheeks. Confusion warred with disbelief as my father's body plummeted toward the ground. A warrior caught him before touching down. My father slumped weakly in his arms.

A fiery mass of black energy sailed past us.

Diarmuid drew his sword. "I'm going to help Cathal." He sped toward Dub.

Ainle appeared out of nowhere, forcing me behind his back. "Grania, watch out!" With a vibrant pulse of light, he obliterated the spear hurtling toward us.

Dain growled.

Ainle cried out, suddenly collapsing in on himself.

I grabbed him before he could lose any altitude, although he was seriously weighing me down. My eyes flew toward Dain. He looked pleased. He'd stabbed Ainle with some invisible twist of pain.

Treasach helped me with Ainle. He was trying his best to straighten and fight the pain.

Fianna pointed toward the ground. "The *Fir Bolgs* have arrived, and they're not fighting on our side."

Fir Bolgs? I scoured my mind for some discussion that might have involved them, but I drew a blank. I looked around, stunned by the violence surrounding me. Every *Sidhe* was dodging the deadly energy lobbed by Dother and Dub, as well as the spears, rocks, and axes launched from the ground. With wide eyes I gaped at the ground. "Those are *Fir Bolgs?*" The primitive looking men sprinted toward Phelan and another warrior, who was lifting Dad from the ground.

My eyes narrowed. That scene triggered a memory. *The Far Darrig! He'd lumped them in with the Fomorians and the Goddess Carman's sons.* His warning sounded in my head, *"They are your enemies, not I."*

"The nightmare in Dublin!" That long reddish blond hair and those beards twisted into braids looked exactly the same. Claw necklaces jostled against bare shoulders and chests. Animal skulls spun wildly from the leather belts cinched around their waists. Bones clunked against axes and picks. Brown leather pants and boots covered them from the waist down. They weren't massive, like the *Fomorians*, but they looked muscular and strong. They threw spears, axes, picks, and rocks while racing toward the *Sidhe*, who were struggling to get off the ground.

"Dad!" I dove toward him again.

Fianna lunged for my arm. "No. You must form the knot. The sooner you do that, the sooner this will be over."

I tore my eyes from Dad... glanced frantically at Lexie and Mom. Treasach was protecting Ainle, who appeared to be recovering. I searched for Maolisa and Niamh... and groaned. With all the weapons hurtling toward us, we were being driven further and further apart. I fought to ignore the *Fir Bolgs* who were trying to kill my dad and flew toward Cian and Niamh instead.

"He's already dead," Dain whispered inside my head. "The Cauldron of Bran the Blessed is in my possession. I will bring him back if you join me. I can resurrect your entire family."

I stopped suddenly. "They're not dead." My eyes flew wildly to each of my family members. I could still feel their energy and their emotions. Their signals were weak, but they were still there.

Gold energy sparked from Fianna's hands. "What's wrong? Is Dain speaking with you... inside your head?"

Phelan intercepted a spear before it could hit Dad. He broke it in half.

Their lives could end any second. I dragged my gaze back to Dain. "What do you mean by 'join you?'"

Fianna grasped my shoulders. "Grania! Why is Dain looking at you? Is he speaking to you telepathically?"

I nodded. My eyes remained locked with Dain's. He looked so beautiful. *Frighteningly beautiful.* Was that real or another illusion? I shook my head. I wasn't even sure those were my thoughts. I reinforced my mental shields again.

"Hurry." Fianna's hands were on my back, urging me closer to Niamh.

Maolisa was drifting perilously close to Dother.

"Maolisa, stop!" Treasach sped toward her.

Ainle rushed toward me. "Grania, quickly."

Dain breached my shields again. "You were made for me. We were meant to be together, to rule the realms together, according to the prophecy."

I thought about the *Fomorians'* prophecy, which was different but consistent with our own. Did the Goddess Carman's sons have their own prophecy?

A fiery mass of energy sent Fianna and Ainle careening toward the ground. Suddenly, Dain appeared in front of me. He caressed my cheek. "You belong with me."

A single word appeared inside my mind.

Sacrifice.

He stabbed his fingers in my hair and tugged sharply. "Come with me."

I fought the urge to flee. "Free my family."

He laughed harshly. "I'll free your family when you free mine."

I blinked. Twice. "I don't have your family."

Anger flashed in his eyes. "My mother is imprisoned in *Tech Duinn.*"

"Grania!" Ainle screamed. "What are you doing? Fight back!"

His desperation washed over me, then his grief. My gaze shifted, despite the pain I knew it would cause me. Sure enough, some invisible knife twisted in my heart. I sucked in a breath. I could hardly breathe. I fought against the pain so I could soothe Ainle. Softly, I began to sing, "*You are the light in my moon, the water in my fall, and the soil beneath my feet. Will you dance... will you dance... will you dance with me? You hold my heart, my life, my dreams. Will you dance... will you dance with me? You are mine as I am yours. My love, will you dance with me?*" Like an ocean wave, the pain receded.

Dain drew me closer. "You are so beautiful... more beautiful than I could have ever dreamed." A spark of longing, of love, shone in his eyes. He gazed at me.

My brow furrowed. Was my energy affecting him? Was he drawn to me because I offered something good? Did he long to feel loved too?

He stumbled back. Diarmuid, Ainle, and Fianna had launched a coordinated attack, striking him at the exact same time. A massive amount of energy for any *Sidhe* to absorb, black-winged or otherwise.

My thoughts scattered. The fury emanating from Dain was terrifying.

He unsheathed his sword. The hilt unfurled in an artistic melding of dark steel with sharp claws protecting a blood-red stone. His voice literally roared, "Grania is mine!" He attacked Diarmuid and Ainle so violently I had to close my eyes.

"Grania," Niamh whimpered.

My eyes darted frantically, trying to catalog everything going on around me. Finally, I caught sight of her.

She pointed with trembling fingers. "The stones."

My eyes slid toward the ground. "The *Sidhe Sluagh*." Those dark, desperate emotions I'd sensed clinging to the boulders and lake were peeling themselves from the ground. Thousands of soulless spirits circled us, seeking our energy, sensing our hopelessness.

I twisted frantically, unable to comprehend what we were facing. "Our opponents outnumber us."

"Faith, hope, and love," Kane forced between clenched teeth. He was fighting desperately to protect Fianna from the *Sidhe Sluagh*.

Dother's laughter felt like spiders crawling up my arms. "We've promised the *Sidhe Sluagh* your friends' souls." Maolisa squirmed in his arms.

Ciara and Treasach fought to free her.

Dain battled Diarmuid, Fianna, and Ainle.

Dub struck Cian, forcing him away from Niamh.

Brigitte darted in front of Niamh. A burst of energy shot from her fingertips, but Dub swiftly extinguished it.

Maolisa spoke. She was still struggling against Dother. "One may be overpowered, two can defend themselves, but three... a cord of three strands is not easily broken."

An axe nicked my shoulder and wing, but Dian caught me. His strong hands clamped over my shoulder and the injured wing. His energy warmed my blood while he healed me.

Dain roared, inflicting Dian with shards of pain until he released me. He flew toward me but Ainle intercepted him again.

I grasped Dian's hand. "Heal yourself… then please, heal my dad."

He was in so much pain, he couldn't respond.

The *Sidhe Sluagh* swarmed around Lexie and Mom.

Energy surged into my hands. "They're harvesting their souls!" My right hand cradled the energy, then wound back toward my shoulder.

Niamh grabbed my arm. "Stop! They're stealing souls because they think that will get them into Heaven."

I pulled the energy back into my hands. "They can't steal their way into Heaven. They need…" My eyes flew to hers. "They need forgiveness."

Warriors surrounded us on all sides. They fought to protect us against the *Sidhe Sluagh*, the *Fir Bolgs*, Dain, Dother, and Dub. The sky was nearly black with all the *Sidhe Sluagh* flying around.

I tugged on Maolisa's thread. "We've got to fly above the *Sidhe Sluagh* so we can form the Celtic Cross."

"The Celtic Cross?" She twisted away from Dother, but he grabbed her arm. "Why are we changing knots?"

"The *Sidhe Sluagh* are seeking a way into Heaven." I ducked as bits of rock exploded all around us.

Her eyes widened. "The Celtic Cross forms a bridge between Heaven and Earth."

Ciara broke Dother's hold on Maolisa arm while Treasach distracted him.

Maolisa surged skyward.

Niamh and I sped toward her. We turned, so our backs were protected, and quickly grasped hands.

"They've got to ask for forgiveness," Maolisa panted.

"They will." I closed my eyes so I could focus. The noise and chaos surrounding us quieted as my thoughts turned inward. I thought about the *Sidhe Sluagh*. Their souls were lost. They longed for peace, but they hadn't thought to ask for forgiveness. Still, as damaged as those rogue spirits were, they'd held fast to hope... hope that if they attached themselves to our souls, they would gain entrance into Heaven. They didn't know. They didn't need our souls. What they needed was forgiveness. "I forgive you," I whispered.

Collectively, they stilled. The *Sidhe Sluagh* turned as one, drawing closer to us. A low hum sounded.

I listened closely. Within that hum I heard voices roughened from disuse, an anguished lament, and then, "They're praying! The *Sidhe Sluagh* are seeking forgiveness!" I forced energy down into my hands.

"I forgive you," Niamh repeated.

Sparks dripped from our fingertips. We raised our hands toward the sky.

"I forgive you," Maolisa cried.

Our energy merged seamlessly through our entwined hands. Maolisa coaxed the green, gold, and blue strands into a brilliant cross. Our arms swept toward the ground. A sonic boom sounded. The air rippled all around us.

Light pierced the ominous clouds, stretching toward the ground. A truly divine ray of light joined Heaven and Earth despite the evil surrounding us.

Every face turned up, including Dain, Dother, and Dub's.

The *Sidhe Sluagh* shifted back into ravens. They flew toward the light, changing mid-flight into gray mourning doves. When they entered the light, they transformed once more... into snow-white doves.

Joy collided with relief. "We did it." I flung my arms around Maolisa and Niamh.

The light vanished.

Not a single *Sidhe Sluagh* remained.

My emotions swung wildly. As darkness descended, I grieved the loss of that light.

"We're not done." Niamh swiped the tears from her cheeks.

A rumble sounded beneath us.

"Look!" Maolisa pointed. "The *Fomorians* have come to help!"

Cromm led the charge toward Phelan, Dian, and Dad.

I burst into tears. "Thank God." Finally, things were turning around.

Niamh untied the pouch from my waist and shoved it in my hands. "Hurry! We should eat the berries before they retaliate."

"No," Dain screamed.

With anguished cries, the *Fomorians* collapsed onto their knees.

Dother's eyes darkened maliciously. With a twist of his wrist, he forced our hands open.

We watched, horrified, as every last berry fell toward the ground.

"No!" Niamh dove for them.

Dub intercepted her. They struggled briefly. She was forced to retract her wings when he pulled her back against his chest. His arms locked around her waist. "Enough!"

The sky darkened as did the ground.

"Grania," Dain growled. He was hovering over Lexie and Mom. "Come or they die."

"The sacrifice." How could I think things were turning around?

Maolisa struggled against Dother. "No, Grania. The moment he possesses you, they've won. They'll destroy everything... everything good in all the realms."

"What choice do I have?" I cried.

Ainle blocked me. His hands clamped around my arms. "Please, Grania. I'm begging you. If you comply, everything we've worked so hard to achieve will be lost."

"Now," Dain gritted. Mom and Lexie writhed in pain.

Diarmuid, Phelan, and Dad sped toward them.

Dain's sword... that dark, beautiful sword... arced expertly toward Ainle.

"No!" I broke Ainle's grasp, and with a strength I never knew I possessed, I forced him behind me. The air rushed from my lungs as the sword pierced my stomach. Tears streamed down my cheeks. My wings receded. My fingers brushed against the smooth stone embedded in the hilt. I bit back a sob as I fell toward the ground. This wasn't how it was supposed to end... with so much pain and nothing resolved.

"No!" Dain disappeared, then reappeared beneath me, catching me in his arms.

I clung to him without thinking. Blood dripped from my waist.

Ainle and the other warriors surged toward us.

Dian pushed past them. "Let me heal her!"

"No!" Dain deflected the warriors with a short sword while holding me close. He sought to reassure me, speaking inside my mind. "I can save you. I possess the cauldron, but I need your energy, your strength. Without it, I cannot restore any life."

My eyes fluttered closed. More than anything I wanted to end this. Maybe if I gave him my energy, he would lose his will to fight.

"That's right. It's the only way," Dain pleaded. He could feel the life, the energy, bleeding out of me.

A deep sense of despair settled like a weight inside of me. None of this felt right.

"Surely, you sense our connection." Dain ducked. Metal sparked against metal. He turned and thrust.

"The sword," I groaned. "Please, take it out." All those jerky movements made it hurt even more.

His grief slammed into me. "Love me. Choose me, Grania. You are my counterweight, the missing piece of my soul."

Our connection... was that the key? With what little energy I possessed, I tugged on Maolisa and Niamh's threads. I prayed Dain wouldn't hear me. "Use your connection to Dother and Dub."

I sensed their confusion before they spoke. "What?"

With a strangled cry, Dain removed the sword.

"Oh, God! It hurts so much." Blood bubbled up through the gaping wound, drenching my tunic. *How could Dain possibly comprehend love? He knew how to incite violence, how to inflict pain. Maybe he needed to be on the receiving end for a change... feel some of the pain and suffering his violence caused before he could truly comprehend love.*

While Dain, Dother, and Dub were opening themselves up to us, they weren't expecting to feel the deep, dark despair they were inflicting on everyone else. I tugged on Maolisa and Niamh's threads again. "Draw on the darkness, the evil, and pain they've caused and send it back to them over the connection. Only then will they comprehend faith, hope, and love."

I didn't wait for their response. I could feel the last remnants of life draining from me. While the battle raged around me, I opened my mental shields fully. I drew on the pain Mom, Dad, and Lexie were feeling. I pulled pain from the injured warriors... Cathal, Diarmuid, Treasach, Phelan, and Ainle. Every single warrior had been injured. I harvested the pain radiating from the *Fomorians* below. I siphoned all their pain and pulled it deep inside of me. I was already in excruciating pain. What harm could come from more?

With a hard mental shove, I forced the pain back through my connection with Dain.

As if scalded, he released me.

I fell, weightless and free.

Strong arms caught me, jarring me, causing me pain. *Ainle.*

I pushed past the pain so I could speak. "You and the remaining *Sidhe* must form the knot."

He shook his head. "No, Grania. The *Chosen Ones* are the only *Sidhe* who can combine their energy to form knots."

My hand brushed his cheek then fell away. So little strength.

Ainle chocked back a sob. "Take my energy. Please."

"No." I squeezed my eyes tight, clearing the tears before I peered up at him. "Remember our conversation in the meadow... after I created the garden?"

Slowly, he nodded.

"Those limits you have been applying to yourself don't really exist." My teeth clenched against another wave of pain when he ducked away from Dain. "Do you understand? Those limits don't exist. Like in *fidchell*, there are an infinite amount of possibilities... more options than any one person can comprehend. You can achieve anything you set your mind to... you and the remaining *Sidhe*."

Pain radiated from his eyes. In order to form the knot, he had to release me... and I was too weak to fly.

"You have to sacrifice some of your defenders." I smiled shakily. "Have faith. Naois will catch me."

"I love you, Grania, with all my heart." Ainle pressed his lips to mine.

Dain screamed.

Ainle's arms loosened. Grudgingly, he released me.

I held fast to faith.

Faith in Ainle and the other *Sidhe*.

I knew they could form the knot.

Faith in Naois.

I knew he would catch me.

Faith in myself.

I knew this would fulfill the prophecy.

I forced all the fear and pain from my mind so I could speak to Maolisa and Niamh one last time. "Each of us was meant to reflect all three... faith, hope, and love. Use your connection with all three brothers. Don't limit yourself to one."

My hair whipped around my face as the air rushed past me. I was seconds from death, but I wasn't scared. I reflected on every hope filled moment... drew on the love that others had poured into me... gathered my faith and sent it all out to Dain, Dother, and Dub.

"I love you," I whispered to every life I'd ever touched.

CHAPTER 10 – THE CLADDAGH RINGS

"Grania."

"I'm still sleeping." The down-filled mattress felt soft and warm. I burrowed beneath the blankets.

A soft chuckle sounded. "You're not. If you were sleeping, you wouldn't be talking to me."

I forced one eye open. "Dad?" Fragmented memories rearranged themselves like puzzle pieces inside my head.

He brushed a stray curl from my forehead. "There's my brave girl. How are you feeling?"

There was no mistaking the energy thrumming inside me or the room framing my father's shoulders and wings. We were back inside the palace. My hand slid cautiously toward my stomach. "Where's the wound?"

A smile tugged at his lips. "Dian worked his magick."

"That's some magick. It's completely gone." I flung the covers off. "I want to see Lexie and Mom."

"Coming," Mom called.

My breath caught. I wasn't really expecting her to be there. She sounded so excited. Energetic. *Alive.*

They hurried into the room.

"Lexie. Mom!" I sprinted from the bed, and then fought my momentum so I wouldn't crash into them. My hands flew anxiously over their limbs. "Thank God you're safe. You're truly safe." They'd seen better days, but there wasn't a scratch on them. "You're so skinny. Can I get you something? Would you like some bread? Maybe we can find some soup."

Mom half laughed and half sobbed as she pulled me in her arms.

Lexie's hands fisted on her hips. "No… and just because you grew wings doesn't mean you're the boss of me."

I jerked her forward and gave her a hug. "I missed you so much."

"You did?" She looked stunned.

I steered her toward the bed. "Yes, of course. Have you seen *Tír na nÓg?* I can't wait to show you around."

Dad smoothed the covers while making room for us. "Let's take it slow, maybe ease into things."

My heart stalled. "Is everyone okay?"

"Yes," he assured me, "everyone is fine."

"Wait." I sat beside him on the bed. "Why are we here? I thought we were going to Upper Lake."

"Naois brought you back to the portal after Dian healed you. He was worried about you, and after everything that happened, we thought you should rest." He glanced at

Mom. "We're meeting with the *Fomorians* at the end of the week."

I was pleased to hear we were following through on that promise, especially since they came to our aid on Mangerton Mountain. "But Fianna, Diarmuid, and Ainle… they're okay? What about Maolisa and Niamh? Can I see them?"

"Dian is the only *Sidhe* who is still recovering." His gaze slid toward Lexie. "He healed a lot of physical and mental injuries."

My eyes flew to hers. "Do you remember anything?"

"Not really." She picked at a string on the edge of the comforter. "I remember being surrounded by these inky shadows on our way back to the bed and breakfast, but that's about it. I felt scared, but something made me fall asleep. When I woke, I was in Dad's arms."

I breathed a small sigh of relief. "That's good."

Mom sat next to Dad. It felt so good seeing them together again.

I reached for her hand. "What about you? Do you remember anything?"

"There was a huge conspiracy of ravens, more ravens than I've ever seen before, but then they morphed into something else." A shadow passed through her eyes. "I held Lexie's face against my coat so she wouldn't see. They lifted us up off the sidewalk. I couldn't speak. I couldn't even scream. I was praying, but then I lost consciousness. When I woke, Diarmuid was holding me. I thought he was an angel. I mean… he has wings. Then, I thought I was dreaming because I saw your father and his wings. I was so relieved he had Lexie, but I was worried about you. Diarmuid assured me you were safe. He said there was a three-headed dragon taking care of you, which is kind of cool. I still questioned whether I was dreaming because it sounded so far-fetched. Your dad assured me I wasn't crazy. He insisted it was all true."

"You think a dragon taking care of me is cool?" I stared at her, deadpan, for a couple of heartbeats. "Who are you and what have you done with my mother?"

Everyone burst out laughing.

A question struck so fast it wiped the smile from my face. "What happened to Dain, Dother, and Dub?"

Dad shrugged. "I don't know. Nobody does."

My stomach plummeted. "What?"

"Well," he said carefully, "they just sort of disappeared. They didn't fly away. They just evaporated right in front of us."

A soft light filled the room. "Hi, Grania. I'm so pleased you are awake."

Lexie gaped at the Goddess Danu. The bright white energy that typically shone all around her was softened so Lexie and Mom could look at her.

I dropped into a curtsy. My cheeks heated when I realized I was still in my pajamas.

"Do not worry, sweet child. You look fine." With an elegant sweep of her hand, the goddess transformed her ivory and gold gown into lavender pajamas, complete with bunny slippers. "There. Now we're both wearing pajamas."

Mom giggled behind her hand.

The goddess laughed. Suddenly, everyone was wearing pajamas, including Dad. "How are you feeling?"

I met her gaze. "I'm feeling well. Thank you for asking."

She clasped my hands gently. "You were very brave."

The warmth radiating from her fingers spread from my fingertips all the way down to my toes. "Everyone was brave. Truly, this was a group effort."

She nodded. "I've heard. Still, you demonstrated profound courage and strength while your family was being threatened. I am very proud of you."

My eyes teared. "Thank you."

She stepped forward and acknowledged Dad. "Now that your entire family is here, there is something we must discuss."

He acknowledged her statement with a subtle nod. His arm wrapped protectively around Mom.

Goddess Danu noted the expression on his face before drifting a few feet away. "You are aware of our policy and the protective wards we have in place?"

He nodded. "Very few humans are allowed to enter *Otherworld*." His eyes met Mom's. "Before we return to the human realm, you will be required to choose one of two options. Your memories of *Otherworld* can be erased, or you can be rendered completely incapable of discussing *Tír na nÓg* with other humans."

The goddess turned so she was facing them. "I want you to know that policy doesn't apply to you."

Dad stilled. Mom looked thoroughly confused.

"Ruarc was half-*Sidhe* when you conceived." She smiled at Lexie. "That makes you part-*Sidhe* too."

Lexie sucked in a breath. "Can I grow wings, like Madison?"

She nodded. "You will become fully *Sidhe* and gain wings when you visit *Ogham*, just like your dad."

"So, Lexie can keep her memories of *Tír na nÓg*?" Mom asked.

"As can you," the goddess said.

Mom shook her head. "But I'm still human... I mean fully human. I'm as human as they come."

She shook her head. "That is no longer true. Your body changed on a molecular level when you conceived Lexie. You became *Sidhe*. It is the only way you can carry a *Sidhe* child to term. Like any *Sidhe*, your powers remain dormant until you visit *Ogham*."

Her eyes widened.

"Mom," I gasped. "You're *Sidhe*. We're all *Sidhe*. Do you know what that means?"

She laughed, nervously. "Honestly? I haven't a clue."

Dad twined his fingers with hers. "We can stay... and if we stay, we won't get sick, and we won't age."

Mom stilled. Her eyes slid toward Lexie, then back toward Dad. Her voice fell to a mere whisper, like she didn't dare hope, let alone speak. "You mean..."

He nodded. This was an answer to nearly every prayer we'd ever breathed.

Lexie's breath caught on a sob. Tears streamed down her cheeks.

I grasped her hands. "No more hospitals, sissy." I knelt at her feet. "No more doctors, IVs, medicine, or rejection. Your birth tree will restore your health completely. You'll never be sick again."

Our father swept us into a hug. Our tears merged with joy and relief.

Goddess Danu smiled, obviously pleased. "I hope you will choose to live here. Is there anything I can do to make that decision easier for you?"

I swiped at my cheeks. I glanced at Dad briefly before answering the goddess. "Please, can we bring our dog, Miko?"

Her brow arched questioningly. "Do you think he will get along with the other animals?"

"Yes," I promised. "He's a very good dog."

She nodded her consent. "Anything else?"

I knew I was pushing my luck on this one. "I know this is asking a lot, but Elgin and Naois saved my life, and the *Ellen Trechend* protected us when we met with the *Fomorians*. I think we should invite them to live in *Tír na nÓg*."

She turned the idea in her head. "You may extend the invitation. I draw the line at the *Fomorians* and the *Fir Bolgs*, however."

"I understand." I looked at Mom and Dad. "Can we? Please, can we live in *Tír na nÓg*?"

They exchanged glances.

Lexie held her breath.

Together, my parents nodded. "Yes."

"Thank you!" I dove into their arms. "I can't believe we get to live here!"

The goddess restored her shimmering gown.

I slipped from my parents' arms. "Thank you." I dropped into another curtsy, then gave her a hug.

She smoothed my hair. "Thank you for saving *Tír na nÓg*."

Had we? I wasn't so sure given what Dad had revealed. I stepped back. "Do you know what happened to Dain, Dother, and Dub?"

"No, I'm afraid not." Her eyes turned pensive. "I sense the balance has been restored. Evil, violence, and darkness will always exist in the human realm, but it is less prevalent now. *Tír na nÓg* is safe once more."

With all the questions clogging my head, I'd forgotten to ask Dad, "So Ainle and the other *Sidhe* cast the knots?"

"Yes. You have taught us to question what we perceive as our limits. That lesson has served us well." The smile she offered was breathtaking. "Please, try to get some rest. We will celebrate tomorrow." She disappeared amid a soft pulse of light.

I shook my head. "Wow. I wish I could do that."

A soft, musical laugh, and then... "Those limits don't exist. They never have."

* * *

"I could really use your help," Diarmuid gritted inside my head.

"Um... okay." I continued blotting the moisture from my hair. "What's going on?"

He didn't answer.

"Grandpa?"

"Do you feel well enough to fly over here?" He fell silent, and then, "We're in the training arena."

"Sure." I dropped the towel on the bench and ran the comb through my hair.

"Now," he urged.

The hair rose on my arms. Grandpa sounded anxious. I couldn't imagine what was going on. "Should I send for Maolisa and Niamh?"

"No." He grunted. It sounded like he'd been struck.

I shot to my feet. The comb clattered against the floor. "Are you okay?"

"I will be." Silence, and then, "Please hurry."

My wide eyes met Mom's. "Diarmuid needs my help."

"Now?" She frowned. "But you just woke up."

"I'm fine... more than fine," I corrected. "I've eaten. I've taken a shower. I feel great." I hadn't seen anyone outside my family aside from Phelan, but that was about to change.

Her eyes slid grudgingly toward the door leading into the bath. "Lexie is still in the tub."

"Please, let her enjoy her bath." I shoved the towel inside the linen bag and pinched my energy signature onto the disc. "I know the way, and I got the impression I shouldn't wait." I didn't tell her how anxious Diarmuid sounded. She was already worried enough. "I'll tell Dad." I hurried toward the door. "I won't be long. I promise."

"Okay," she answered uncertainly. "Please don't get into any trouble."

I stopped mid-step and turned around. "Me? In trouble? Mom, I'm the only member of this family who hasn't gotten into trouble."

She blinked in surprise. Her hand flew to her mouth as laughter bubbled up from her lungs.

I grinned, thrilled to hear the sound. "If I haven't returned by the time Lexie is done, then ask Dad to bring you over to the training arena. I want to show you around."

"Sounds good." She smiled.

I tugged on the door.

Dad pushed off the wall across the hall. "That was fast."

Phelan turned and offered a polite nod. He'd flown Lexie from the balcony to the ground floor while Dad carried Mom. Apparently, he was keeping my father company while we finished up.

"Grandpa called." I chuckled, thinking how funny that sounded. "He needs my help in the training arena."

"Yeah, I heard." Worry warred with amusement. "Phelan is going to escort you over there."

"Okay." I hurried toward the exit. My thoughts were so tangled in what Diarmuid might need that I barely registered the fact Phelan was walking beside me.

He pressed his hand against the etched symbol when we reached the end of the hall. The wall disappeared without a sound. "After you." He nodded, acknowledging the warrior standing guard outside the mountain.

"Thanks." I stepped outside, called my wings, and took flight.

"We should land before crossing into the training arena," Phelan warned. "You never know what sort of weapons are being tossed around in there."

"Good idea." We touched down softly onto the ground.

He grasped my arm before I could cross through the concealment spell. "Careful now."

I took a single step forward, just beyond the illusion, then stilled. The scene inside the arena unraveled before me. My heart refused to beat.

Diarmuid's eyes met mine.

Ainle saw his opening. He hurled a mass of energy at Grandpa. The impact knocked him off his feet.

Phelan winced. "Oof. That had to hurt."

Ainle was throwing energy like a madman. Several warriors surrounded him. They were deflecting his energy, but they weren't returning fire. Instead, it appeared they were trying to console him.

"He's a mess," Phelan warned under his breath. "Diarmuid thought this sparring session would help him work through his fears and frustration while you slept, but the situation spiraled out of control. His mental shields are up. He's blocked everyone out, and he refuses to hear a word anyone says. We've tried telling him you are awake and feeling well, but he bombards us with energy every time we try to speak. We finally realized he needs to see you with his own eyes. The sight of you should free him from the fear and the grief that is ravaging his mind."

Ainle stilled. He turned uncertainly, following Diarmuid's gaze.

Tears welled in my eyes.

His hands fell to his sides.

One by one the warriors stepped back. Silence descended as everyone watched and waited to see how he would react.

The pain etched on his face pinned me in place. My heart thundered. I could barely breathe.

"I don't think he's capable of taking a single step," Phelan said.

I realized then, I would have to go to him. I walked toward him as calmly and confidently as I could.

His eyes were wide and wild, his chest heaving with every breath... but the closer I got, the more his demeanor softened. His relief slammed into me, then his exhaustion. He swayed unsteadily, then fell to his knees. All the while, his eyes remained on me, like he was afraid to blink.

I stood before him, painfully aware of what it had cost him, what he'd suffered when he released me so he could cast the knot. My hand smoothed over his handsome face, trying to erase the pain.

Tears fell like rain.

With a muffled sob, I fell into his arms.

He rocked me gently, mumbling broken words filled with gratitude and relief.

The warriors drew closer. One by one, they fell on bended knee. With heads bowed, they pressed their hands to their hearts in silent acknowledgement of the sacrifices we had made.

* * *

Ainle scrutinized the forest. He looked every bit the warrior, standing guard over the portal. Wispy clouds drifted lazily over the water. "So, how does this work?"

I smiled. Clearly, he'd never called a dragon before. "Like this." I danced a little jig and performed a back flip while a barely audible whisper passed through my lips. "Naois." I was tricking Ainle of course.

"You can't be serious." He frowned.

"As a heart attack." I grinned.

Naois barreled through the trees.

Ainle stepped back, stumbled over a rock, and fell with a loud kerplop into the water.

Naois ignored him. He nuzzled me with all three heads. "Grania."

My hand slid lovingly over his colorful scales. A purr rumbled through his chest, tickling my bones. I leaned close. "How would you like to live in *Tír na nÓg*?"

His eyes glowed like liquid gold. "But the portal…"

"The enchanted waters will allow you to enter as long as you don't harbor any ill will toward the *Sidhe* or the Goddess Danu," I assured him. "You just step inside the water and speak the words, '*Tír na nÓg, Draíocht Dúchas, Taisce Baile.*'"

He deciphered the words. "Land of the young, magick birthright, treasured home."

Ainle joined us. A tiny cyclone spun all around him as he dried himself off. "You may share these words with the *Ellen Trechend*, but no one else."

One set of eyes remained on Ainle while the others looked at me. "My family, they are welcome too?"

My smile widened. "Yes. This is our gift to the *Ellen Tre-chend*, a reward for helping the *Sidhe*."

Naois's smile revealed razor-sharp teeth. "Thank you. I promise, we will cherish this gift. Always."

I knew he would. "There's a celebration tonight. The Goddess Danu has requested your presence so your courage and aid may be properly acknowledged. Will you attend?"

"Yes, of course." Tears filled his molten eyes. "Thank you."

I palmed his cheek and kissed his nose. "Thank you, Naois. You saved my life."

"That was my birthright." He straightened to his full height. "We will be there tonight."

Ainle and I watched as Naois eagerly took flight. My eyes scoured the forest when he faded from sight. "Elgin? Are you there?"

He stepped warily from the tree line. "Yes."

My heart broke a little. I wondered how long he'd been shunned and left to wander alone. "Ainle won't hurt you."

Ainle lowered his head, a sign of respect. "I am in your debt."

Elgin stilled. "There is no debt."

Ainle met his gaze. "I owe you everything. You saved my fated mate."

Elgin shook his head. "Grania is my friend. When friends help one another, they accrue no debt."

Tears welled in my eyes. Slowly, I extended my hand.

He stepped closer. "It is good to see you again." His velvety soft nose nuzzled my fingertips.

Ainle watched, enthralled by the unlikely friendship.

My fingers sifted through his silky mane. "Can I give you a hug?"

He nodded.

I stepped close and pressed my cheek to his. "Please join us in *Tír na nÓg*."

His hoof pawed uncertainly at the ground. "For the celebration?"

"Forever, if you'd like." I stepped back so I could see his eyes.

"The *Tuatha Dé Danann* would welcome me?"

I nodded. "With open arms."

He glanced longingly at the hot spring. "Are there lakes in *Tír na nÓg*?"

I held his face while painting an image inside his mind. "There is an emerald green lake that glows like it swallowed the sun. Fall reigns eternal on one side of the forest while spring reigns on the other. There are three blue moons, a sparkling waterfall, and unicorns who like to play keep away with the ribbons we tie in their manes."

His eyes sparked with interest. "I've never seen a unicorn before."

Ainle smiled. "Then you'll join us?"

His head dipped in a graceful bow. "I would consider it an honor to live among you in *Tír na nÓg*."

* * *

"The fireflies have come out to play." Fianna's voice rang from the balcony. She'd woven a delicate chain through my braid and was now offering me some privacy so I could change.

I stepped through the door. Fireflies hung like soft twinkling lights across the deck. "Do you think the unicorns will join us?"

She admired the lightening bug perched on the back of her hand. "Absolutely. I've heard Davina is excited to meet the *Kelpie*."

"Elgin will be thrilled." I joined her at the edge of the deck. "Oh, Fianna, look!" Snow-white columns framed a crystal floor in the center of the meadow. Fireflies glistened in the low-lying clouds. The moons cast everything in a soft blue light, making it look even more magical.

Her breath caught, but she wasn't looking at the meadow. She was looking at my dress. The silver sequined gown fell in elegant waves toward the floor like a waterfall. Tears filled her eyes. She dragged them up to mine. "You look beautiful."

"Thank you." My gaze shifted skyward when the firefly perched on her hand suddenly took flight. I stared, completely enthralled. Soft white flowers dripped from the branches above. "When did your tree start flowering?"

"While we were inside." She turned so she could see the meadow. "Oh, my."

The harpist plucked a few soft notes. Gradually, the violins began to play. I smiled when the flute joined in. I couldn't wait for Mom and Lexie to see this.

Fianna forced her eyes from the enchanting sight. "I better get dressed."

I barely registered her absence. Several warriors had garnered my attention when they strode from their mound. I giggled when their stony expressions transformed into looks of awe.

"Grania, come join us."

I turned around. Maolisa had spoken inside my head. She wasn't in the meadow, so I searched by the lake instead. I smiled when I caught sight of her.

"I'm going to say 'hi' to Maolisa and Niamh," I called into the treehouse. "They're on the swing by the lake."

"Okay. I'll meet you down there," Fianna sang.

I called my wings and leapt from the deck.

"Hi, Grania." Niamh's fingers danced in a little wave. The rhinestones on her pale blue gown shimmered when she pushed the swing. Her hair fell in soft waves, skimming her shoulders and waist.

"Hi!" I landed softly beside her. My toes curled in the soft grass. I'd learned while dressing earlier that the *Sidhe* don't wear shoes with formal gowns. Instead, they wear jewelry on their feet.

"How are you feeling?" Maolisa leaned back in the swing. She'd tucked her dress around her knees so it wouldn't get wet. The dark green fabric looked like it had been sprinkled with pixie dust.

"Better… a little conflicted about going home." We were leaving in the morning, healing the *Fomorians* at Upper Lake, driving back to Dublin, and then flying home. I was anxious to see Miko, but I knew saying goodbye to my old life would be difficult. I loved my family and friends in *Tír na nÓg*, but I was going to miss the people I'd grown up with.

"Me too." Niamh pushed gently on the swing.

Maolisa's legs unfurled. "Me three."

"What do you think your parents will say?" I didn't envy them that conversation, although I wouldn't mind seeing the looks on their parents' faces.

Maolisa's toes dipped in the water. "I don't know. Ciara is going to project images from *Tír na nÓg* and the battle at Devil's Punch Bowl inside their minds. They may ground me for a year or two, but at least they'll believe us." The swing slowed. "I don't want to have any secrets between us."

"The goddess is allowing us to reveal our true selves, wings and all. My parents are going to freak out." Niamh held the swing while Maolisa hopped off.

I'd been so startled when Dad revealed his wings, I'd fallen off the bench. The memory elicited a soft chuckle. "Do you think they'll want to move here?"

"Absolutely." Maolisa brushed the wrinkles from her dress.

Niamh grinned. "Mom will be packing our bags the second she learns we can't get sick and they won't age."

I was thrilled the goddess was allowing their families to live here. "*Tír na nÓg* wouldn't be the same without you. Even if you must wait until your eighteenth birthday, you must promise you'll return."

Niamh linked her arms in ours as we ambled toward the meadow. "Don't worry. We'll be back."

"No matter the distance or the realm, we've still got this." Maolisa tapped on the side of her head.

"That's right." I hadn't stopped to think we could still use that telepathic connection regardless of the miles that separated us.

Niamh slowed. "Where did all these *Sidhe* come from?"

I looked around. There were several *Sidhe* milling about, some I was certain we'd never seen before.

"Treasach said there would be *Sidhe* traveling from some of the other realms in *Otherworld*," Maolisa said.

I searched for my parents and frowned. "Is that..."

Niamh followed my gaze. "What? Who do you see?"

"Nothing." I shook my head. "My mind is playing tricks on me."

We wandered through the crowd, searching for someone... *anyone*... we knew. Finally, I spotted Ainle. He was standing with his back to me. I pointed him out to my friends, pressed a finger to my lips, and snuck closer. I barely suppressed a giggle before tapping his shoulder. "I thought we were playing *fidchell*."

His lips parted as he turned. He'd been planning some sort of retort, but then his jaw fell all the way open. "Grania. You look..." his eyes catalogued everything from my head to my toes, "breathtaking."

Maolisa giggled.

His cheeks flushed pink. "All three of you do, really."

Treasach offered his arm to Maolisa after a polite nod acknowledging Niamh and me. "Would you like to dance?"

Her blush shone even brighter than Ainle's. "Uh... sure."

Cian's amethyst eyes glittered when he stepped behind Niamh. He whispered a kiss against her cheek. "Will you dance with me?"

A smile spread like wildfire across her cheeks.

Ainle watched them leave. He smiled as he turned toward me. "And then there were two..."

I gasped. "There he is again!"

He peered over his shoulder before making a complete turn. "Who?"

I plowed through the crowd, dragging him behind me. "The *Far Darrig*. I'm pretty sure it's the same one I met in Dublin. He's about three feet tall... he's wearing a red hat... and a matching coat."

We scoured the crowd. He moved quickly, and those low-lying clouds weren't helping any.

"There!" Ainle surged forward.

I nearly plowed into Kane. "Oh! Sorry. I just..." Kane and I dodged right then left at the same time, so it looked like we were dancing. I caught another glimpse of red. "Hey! Mr. *Far Darrig*, I just want to say 'thanks!'"

He peeked out from behind Fianna, slowly, until half of his face was showing. He looked worried until he saw it was me. "Hi, Grania." He smiled.

Fianna stepped aside so he was no longer hiding behind her champagne gown. "Perth." She frowned, just a little, as she peered down at him.

He swiped the hat off his head and twisted it in his hands. His eyes flitted toward me again. "I heard what happened at Devil's Punch Bowl. You were very brave."

Ainle, Kane, Fianna, and I formed a half circle around him. I extended my hand. "I want to thank you."

He glanced at my hand. He looked like he was uncertain about what to do with it. He dipped down, like he was attempting a curtsy and a bow, then quickly kissed my hand.

My eyes widened. I'd been trying to shake his hand. "Uh… thank you?"

"You're thanking me… for what?" He looked genuinely at a loss.

I fought a laugh and lost. "I wanted to thank you for that dream, the one in Dublin, when you warned me about the *Fir Bolgs*." My head tilted with another thought. "Did you place me in the NICU?"

He nodded. Worry lines marred his face once more.

"Then I would like to thank you for that too," I added hurriedly, anxious to end his worrying. "You picked the perfect family for me."

"I'm glad you like them." He stood there proudly tugging the wrinkles from his coat.

My smile widened. "I admire the way you help others." I leaned forward and gently kissed his cheek. "I hope we can be friends."

His cheeks flamed bright red.

"I see you've met Perth."

We turned toward the familiar voice.

The crowd parted, revealing the Goddess Danu. She was

wearing a snow-white gown, covered in part by a gray hooded cloak. Embroidered snowflakes glittered along the edge of the cloak. A silver wolf walked beside her. His ice blue eyes looked so intelligent, I questioned whether that was his true form.

Fianna and I curtseyed.

Ainle, Kane, and Perth bowed.

When I rose from the curtsy, I noticed Elgin, Davina, and several unicorns had gathered along the edge of the crowd. The violet-backed starling fluttered around them before landing on my shoulder. I pet the top of his head. "Where have you been?"

He crooked his head.

"I've got berries with your name on them back at Fianna's," I whispered for his ears only.

He chirped, ruffled his feathers, and settled in.

With nearly silent wing strokes, Naois and the *Ellen Trechend* landed in the meadow. Their tails swished as they meandered closer.

Brigitte and Ciara hurried toward us, Brigitte in a blush colored gown and Ciara in a dress that looked like watercolor art with shades of teal, green, and brown swirled throughout. They bobbed in polite curtseys when they stopped.

Cathal, Dian, Diarmuid, my parents, and Lexie appeared with deep bows and curtseys all around. Dian was wearing a navy-blue vest and a matching jacket with silver embroidery on the sleeves. The warriors were dressed in their standard attire, their platinum armor polished to a sheen that shimmered in the moonlight. Mom's pale blond hair was piled atop her head in an elegant upsweep adorned with a silver barrette. She wore a silky gray gown. Lexie was wearing a coral chiffon dress with sequins on the bodice. Her gold and brown hair tumbled around her shoulders in loose, spiraling curls.

"Hey, sissy." I linked my arm in hers. "You look beautiful."

"Thanks." She did a double-take when she noticed the bird perched on my shoulder, then giggled. "So do you."

Cian, Niamh, Treasach, and Maolisa squeezed in next to Ainle and me, rounding out our little crowd.

Everyone quieted in anticipation of the goddess's speech.

Her gaze traversed the crowd. "We have so much to be thankful for this evening. The *Chosen Ones* are finally home. They have fulfilled the prophecy and restored the balance between the realms. *Tír na nÓg* is safe once more."

Cheers rippled through the meadow.

"This was a collaborative effort between the druids, our healer, the warriors, the *Chosen Ones*, and their guardians." She turned toward Elgin and Naois. "The *Kelpie* and the *Ellen Trechend* exhibited immense heroism, aiding us at every turn." Her head dipped in a regal nod as she acknowledged them. "You are family now."

A thunderous applause reverberated all around us.

The *Ellen Trechend* flashed their razor-sharp teeth in proud smiles.

Elgin bowed his head politely in acknowledgement of the compliment.

Her eyes landed on Perth. "The same holds true for you, old friend. Thank you for helping us."

Tears filled his eyes as he bowed. "I am happy to help."

Her hand slid soothingly through the wolf's silver tipped fur. "Enjoy the festivities, everyone."

When the *Sidhe* resumed dancing and eating, the goddess spoke a little more quietly to our group. "I understand you will be returning to the human realm so you can gather your families and perhaps a few keepsakes."

Maolisa, Niamh, and I nodded. "Yes, Goddess. We will return as quickly as we can."

A stunning smile brightened her face. "I have a gift that will expedite your travels. May I see your hands?"

We exchanged glances but held our hands out, palm sides up.

She placed a silver ring with two hands clutching an amethyst heart in each of our hands. A silver crown sat atop the heart. "The hands represent friendship, the heart love, and the crown loyalty. I want you to remember our friendship, the love awaiting you in *Tír na nÓg*, and our unwavering loyalty."

She waited while we slid the rings on our fingers. "The amethyst stones are enchanted. They are in essence a part of the palace. They will enable you to travel more quickly while in the human realm. If you twist the band around your finger three times to the right, the Claddagh ring will teleport you directly to the border between the realms. You must still prove your good intentions before being transported

through the portal, so you must step into the hot springs before crossing over."

I stared slack-jawed at the ring. "That's amazing."

"There's more." She winked conspiratorially. "If you
twist your rings three turns to the left, they will transport
you anywhere you wish to go inside the human realm."

"Woah." Maolisa held her hand out while admiring the
stone. "So, we can visit Disney World before we return?"

The goddess laughed. "You can travel anywhere your
heart desires."

My parents exchanged worried glances.

Goddess Danu glanced pointedly at Dad. "You can establish any rules you deem necessary… and your entire family
can travel with her. If you touch Grania, you will teleport
right alongside her."

Mom released the breath she'd been holding. "Thank
you."

The goddess eyed her curiously. "Will you visit *Ogham*
when you return?"

"Yes," Mom answered. "Lexie and I will visit *Ogham* just
as soon as we're settled in."

"We will have even more cause for celebration then." She
exchanged a long look with the wolf, then glanced at us
again. "We're going to mingle. Please enjoy the festivities."

There was a collective release of breath when she left.
Standing in her presence was always pleasant but intense.

Mom's eyes snapped toward mine. "No twisting that
ring without obtaining our permission first."

I laughed because *that* was the mom I knew and loved. "I won't use it without your permission unless it is an absolute emergency."

She looked shocked at the unexpected caveat.

"She makes a valid point. We wouldn't want to restrict her from using it during an emergency, and we can't always anticipate what dangers she might face in the human realm." Dad folded Mom in his arms. "Our little girl is growing up."

Dazedly, she nodded.

The violet-backed starling took flight.

"We're going to get a bite to eat," Lexie said. "Would you like to join us?"

I locked eyes with Ainle. "I would love to, just as soon as I dance with Ainle."

His eyes widened. "Did you just ask me to dance?"

My brow inched up my forehead. "Do you require a more formal invitation?"

Hurriedly, he hooked his arm in mine. "No. Absolutely not."

Our friends' laughter followed us out onto the dance floor.

Ainle twirled me in his arms. "I can't believe you asked me to dance." He pulled me close.

My chin inched up proudly. "I won't always choose defense, you know."

He frowned. "What?"

"There will be days I seek to capture the king instead." I smirked. I rather enjoyed throwing the warrior off his game, and I wasn't just referring to *fidchell*.

Ainle chuckled. He'd quickly connected the dots. "I'm sure going to miss you."

"We'll be back soon." I surrendered a smile when he twirled me again. "Okay. Okay! I'll miss you too."

He laughed. "I'll keep the *fidchell* board warm for you."

"You better." Silently, I committed this moment to memory… the warm but wintry wonderland, the fireflies twinkling in the fog, the flowering trees, the three blue moons of *Tír na nÓg*, Ainle, Elgin, and Naois.

Ainle spun me around.

My eyes snagged on the Claddagh ring, which adorned the hand Ainle now cradled in his own.

Of all the places that ring would take me… *this* was the place I desired most.

EPILOGUE

 set the box filled with childhood pictures and all my favorite books next to the door. Dad was allowing us to bring one box of keepsakes each. I stepped back and contemplated the box. Limiting myself to a single box proved easier than I'd thought. Few things were truly needed in *Tír na nÓg*.

Miko dropped his ball next to the box.

I chuckled softly. "Should I pack your ball?"

He barked.

"Is there someone at the door?" Fianna called from the garage. She was marking items for the yard sale. We were donating the proceeds to the children's hospital. Mom was at the pharmacy ordering the last prescriptions Lexie would ever need while Dad wrapped things up at work.

I threw Miko's ball down the hallway leading to the garage. "No. Miko just wants to play ball."

The doorbell rang.

"Oh. Somebody is here." I flipped the lock and tugged on the door. My eyes snagged on the realtor's sign piercing the front lawn. A brown box was sitting on the porch. The delivery truck was already gone.

Fianna wiped her hands on her jeans. "I thought I heard the doorbell ring. What's that?"

I scooped the box off the porch and leaned against the door until it clicked shut. "A package. It's addressed to me."

She turned the box in my hands. "Is there a return address?"

I peered at the label. "Not that I can see."

"That's odd." She frowned.

I shook the box gently. "Can I open it?" I could hear paper rustling inside. The package was really light.

She eyed the box. "Who would send a package without a return address?"

I generated a quick mental list of people who might want to surprise me. "Maybe Perth delivered it for Ainle," I suggested hopefully.

She stepped around me, opened the door, and poked her head outside. "Maybe."

I could picture Ainle doing that. I loosened the tape and lifted the cardboard flaps.

Fianna closed the door. "I don't know, Grania. This doesn't feel right."

I picked through the crinkly paper.

My pulse thundered.

My heart stalled.

The box tumbled to the floor.

There, lying perilously close, was a bronze ring with a blood red stone.

GLOSSARY AND PRONUNCIATION GUIDE

Ailm (al-im) - the Celtic symbol for good health. It is most often associated with the fir tree, resilience, longevity, and healing in *Ogham*. *Ailm* is also a letter in the *Ogham* alphabet. It looks like a perfectly symmetrical, square cross.

Ainle (ein-lee) – a young *Sidhe* warrior. Grania's fated mate.

Beagalltach (bay-go-tasch) – a sword Diarmuid carries. The name means "small fury."

Bonjour (bone jor) – good morning in French

Brigitte (bree-ghit)– a *Sidhe* guardian. Niamh's godmother. She is an air spirit.

Cathal (ca-hull)– a Sidhe warrior. He is an air spirit and the chosen leader of the *Sidhe* warriors.

Cauldron of Bran the Blessed (cul-dren of bran the blessed)– a cauldron that is purported to bring slain *Sidhe* warriors back from the dead. Also known as the Cauldron of Rejuvenation or rebirth.

Changeling (change-ling) - a human baby the *Far Darrig* exchange with *faerie* or *Sidhe* babies. When the babies are exchanged, the human babies are called changelings.

Chosen Ones (chozen wons) – three *Sidhe* who represent faith, light (hope), and love. They serve as the counterweights to the Goddess Carman's sons.

Cian (kee-yan) – a young druid in training. He wields purple energy and has a special ability to draw energy from all things. He is Niamh's fated mate.

Ciara (kee-ra)– a *Sidhe* guardian. Maolisa's godmother. She is a water spirit.

Claddagh ring (claw-da reeng) - a traditional Irish ring depicting two hands holding a heart with a crown. The hands represent friendship, the heart represents love, and the crown represents loyalty.

Cluricaun (clear-i-con) – a small, wily faerie who behaves like a drunken old man. He loves playing practical jokes and is frequently seen riding on the backs of dogs or sheep.

Cromm (crum) – leads the *Fomorians*. Currently possesses the *Fragarach*, a powerful sword known as The Answerer, because no one can tell a lie when it is held to his throat.

Dain (day-n) – violence. A beautiful, black-winged *Sidhe*. Dother and Dub's brother. The Goddess Carman's son.

Daur (dower) – door.

Davina (dah-vee-na) – the first unicorn Grania meets.

Dian (dye-an)– a *Sidhe* healer. Not to be confused with Dain! He is a wood spirit.

Diarmuid (deer-mid) – a mighty *Sidhe* warrior. Grania's grandfather. He is an air spirit.

Dother (duh-ther)– evil. One of three black-winged *Sidhe*. Dain and Dub's brother. The Goddess Carman's son.

Draíocht Dúchas (dree-ocht doo-has) - magick birthright.

Dub (doe-vh)– darkness. One of three black-winged *Sidhe*. Dain and Dother's brother. The Goddess Carman's son.

Druid (drew-id) – a powerful teacher who masters white magick. They teach the *Tuatha Dé Danann* how to shapeshift, build protective shields, and wield their energy. They build on the knowledge gained in *Ogham* and strengthen the *Sidhe's* skills. They also serve as prophets.

Dullahan (dull-a-han) – the headless horseman. He is an omen of death, but he is afraid of gold. Nobody knows why.

Elgin (el-gen)– Grania's beloved *Kelpie*.

Ellen Trechend (ellen trekh-end) – a massive three-headed fire-breathing dragon with scales.

Erie (air-eh)– Ireland

Faerie (ferry) – essentially a fairy but not the Tinkerbell type. These are the fairies that exist in Irish mythology, otherwise known as the *Sidhe*, the *Seelie*, or the *Tuatha Dé Danann*.

Faeth Fiadha (feh fee-o-ha) – the Cloak of Mists. Generates a concealing fog. Once belonged to Manannán Mac Lir.

Far Darrig (far dareeg) - a type of faerie, small and wily like a *Leprechaun*, who is totally enamored with the color red. He often wears a red cap and coat. He causes nightmares (for good reason); steals bright, pretty babies; and leaves change-lings in their place.

Fianna (fee-an-ah)– a *Sidhe* guardian. Grania's godmother. While her *Sidhe* name is Fianna, her chosen name in the human realm is Channa. Grania grew up calling her Cha Cha. She is a wood spirit.

Fidchell (fit-chul) – an ancient Celtic board game that predates chess, where you must defend or capture a king. Allegedly created by King Lugh.

Fir Bolgs (fear bolg)– Primitive warriors known to wear braids in their beards and hair. They tend to run hot, so they seldom wear shirts. They collect and wear the bones of the animals they kill. They favor picks, axes, and spears as weapons. Most live on the western side of Ireland now, in an area known as Connaught. Some claim that *Leprechauns* descended from *Fir Bolgs*.

Fomorians (fo-more-ee-an) – deformed, demonic looking giants who were driven into the sea after the Second Battle of *Magh Tuireadh*. Limbs are twisted. Rumored to be in pain. They manipulate the harsher elements, the more destructive side of nature, to achieve their objectives.

Foras Feasa (forus fassa)– foundation of knowledge.

Fragarach (frea-gar-thach)– a sword that belonged to King Lugh. Also known as "The Answerer." This sword can penetrate any shield or object. Even if only injured, the enemy cannot survive, and when held to a person's throat, that person cannot tell a lie.

Garda (guard-a) – police force of the Republic of Ireland.

Goddess Carman (goddess car-muhn)– the Goddess of Dark Magick. She has three sons, Dain (violence), Dother (evil), and Dub (darkness).

Goddess Danu (goddess da-new)– the Great Goddess of the *Tuatha Dé Danann*, often referred to as their mother. She resides and rules over *Tír na nÓg*.

Go n-éirí an bóthar leat (guh nye-REE un BO-har lat)– An Old Irish proverb which means "may the road succeed with you."

Grania (grawn-ya)– kindness and love. The Goddess Danu's daughter who serves as a counterweight to the Goddess Carman's sons. While her *Sidhe* name is Grania, her given name in the human realm is Madison. She was hidden by the *Far Darrig* in the United States. She is a wood spirit.

Hei (hay) – hello in Finnish.

Kane (kay-n) – a powerful *Sidhe* druid. He wields purple energy and has a special ability to draw energy from all things. He is Fianna's fated mate.

Kelpie (kel-pee) – A horse with an adhesive coat. If he senses any bad intentions, he'll drag you into the water and drown you.

King Lugh (king loo) - led the *Tuatha Dé Danann* in the second battle of *Magh Tuireadh* against the *Fomorians*. He killed King Balor (his grandfather), who was the King of the *Fomorians*, effectively freeing the *Tuatha Dé* from *Fomorian* rule. He was extremely talented, one of few Sidhe skilled in all the arts. He also created the game of *fidchell*. He brought people together through sport, inspiring the Tailteann games, their version of the Olympics. King Lugh was often referred to as the sun god, the storm god, and the sky god. He was half-*Fomorian* and half-*Sidhe*.

Leprechaun (lep-ra-con) – a small, wily faerie. Reputed to be the most notorious tricksters on the planet. Most sport beards, suit jackets, buckled shoes, and hats. They are drawn to gold and focused almost exclusively on amassing treasure.

Lough Leane (loch lee-in) - Lake of Learning

Maidin Mhaith (maj-in moy) – Good morning in Irish.

Magh Tuireadh (moy tura)– A battle for Ireland waged between the *Fir Bolgs* and the *Tuatha Dé Danann*. The *Tuatha Dé Danann* won. The *Fir Bolgs* have been holding a grudge ever since.

Manannán mac Lir (mon-a-non mac leer)- a sea deity and a powerful guardian who transports both *Sidhe* and *Fomorian* souls to the afterlife.

Maolisa (mail-eesa) – faith. The Goddess Danu's daughter who serves as a counterweight to the Goddess Carman's sons. While her *Sidhe* name is Maolisa, her given name in the human realm is Zoey. She was hidden in Finland by the *Far Darrig*. She is a water spirit.

Moralltach (mural-tasch) – another one of Diarmuid's famous swords. The name means "great fury."

Naois (nay-oh-ease)– the three-headed dragon who keeps saving the day.

Niamh (nee-uhv)– hope and light. The Goddess Danu's daughter who serves as a counterweight to the Goddess Carman's sons. While her *Sidhe* name is Niamh, her given name in the human realm is Skylar. She was hidden in France by the *Far Darrig*. She is an air spirit.

Ogham (og-um) – a realm of trees that lends knowledge and wisdom to the *Sidhe*. The *Tuatha Dé Danann* visit their birth trees in *Ogham* so they can gain knowledge, discover their purpose, and awaken their powers. Their birth tree is determined by Celtic tree astrology. The *Tuatha Dé Danann* are only permitted to visit the ancient trees in *Ogham* once. *Ogham* inspired an Early Medieval alphabet, used primarily in Ireland.

Otherworld (other-world) – a magical realm where time stands still, and people don't age. *Otherworld* arguably contains multiple realms, including *Tír na nÓg* (where the *Tuatha Dé Danann* live), *Ogham* (where ancient trees lend knowledge and wisdom to the *Sidhe*), *Tech Duinn* (where the Goddess Carman is imprisoned), and *Tir Tairngire* (where the sea deity *Manannán mac Lir* transports souls to the afterlife). There is also a gateway to an underwater *Otherworld*, known as *Tir fo Thuinn* near *Tir Tairngire*.

Ruarc (roo ark) – Grania's father. A half-human, half-*Sidhe* warrior. His given name in the human realm is Tobin. He is an air spirit.

Second Battle of Magh Tuireadh (moy tura)- A battle for Ireland waged between the *Fomorians* and the *Tuatha Dé Danann*, during which King Lugh killed King Balor, the King of the *Fomorians*, effectively freeing the *Tuatha Dé Danann* from *Fomorian* rule. Most of the *Fomorians'* warriors were killed during this battle. Those who remained were driven into the sea.

Selkie (sell-key) - seals that shed their skin. They turn into beautiful men or women, and dance naked along the shore. No one really knows why.

Sidhe (shee) - fairies, children of the Goddess Danu, also known as the *Tuatha Dé Danann*. *Sidhe* are generally divided into three categories: wood spirits, air spirits, and water spirits; based on where they draw their energy.

Sidhe Sluagh (shee sloo-ah) - rogue spirits that are not welcome in either Heaven or Hell, in the human realm or in *Tír na nÓg*. They often appear as an unkindness or a conspiracy of ravens. They seek out the souls of the dying, although you may draw them to you if you feel hopeless.

Slán agaibh (slan agee): farewell, be safe.

Tailteann Games (tale-tin games): an ancient sporting competition held in Ireland, similar to the Olympics. This competition tested both mental and physical abilities. King Lugh, who excelled in all games, founded this competition in memory of his foster-mother, *Tailtiu*.

Taisce Baile (tash-ka ball-yeh) - treasured home.

Tech Duinn (tek doon) – a realm that can be accessed through *Otherworld*. The place where the Goddess Carman is imprisoned. Also known as the House of Donn. A place where the souls of the dead gather before traveling to their final destination. Allegedly located near the tip of the Beara Peninsula.

Tír na nÓg (teer-nah-nog) – a realm within *Otherworld* where most of the *Tuatha Dé Danann* live. Also known as the Land of Youth. Time works differently there, so the *Sidhe* never really age. They grow until young adulthood, but they stop aging after that. There is no illness and injuries heal fast.

Treasach (tree-sach) – a young *Sidhe* warrior. He is Maolisa's fated mate.

Tuatha Dé Danann (Tooha day Danon) - descend-ants/children of the Goddess Danu. Some live among hu-mans. Most live in *Tír na nÓg*. They heal quickly. Once they eat the fruit from their birth tree in *Ogham*, they are practi-cally immortal. Also called *faeries,* the *Sidhe,* or the *Seelie.*

ABOUT THE AUTHOR

I live in Northern Virginia with my football-crazed husband, two beautiful daughters, and two psychotic Shih Tzus. I teach courses in international relations, environmental security, and peacekeeping for the American Military University. What can I say? I still love school.

I'm fascinated by unicorns, dragons, kelpies, leprechauns, and fairies. I suspect that's the Irish in me. The Irish aren't afraid to believe in magical things. More than anything, I'd like to adopt a dragon. Unfortunately, I haven't found an animal shelter brave enough to house them. You should see the looks I get when I ask. I don't understand. It's not like this would be difficult. You just need a good sprinkler system, fire-resistant suits, and maybe an obedience class or two… for the humans, not the dragons, of course.

I love meeting new people, exploring magical places, and all the sticky predicaments that exist in books. Reading and writing are two of my favorite things. I haven't a clue what's going on around me when I'm writing. The house could be burning down, and I wouldn't even notice. I'm counting on my husband to save the children and the dogs. If we had a dragon, he could save us all.

I've written supreme court briefs, academic journal articles, legislation, government publications, a children's book entitled Brave Just Like Me, and several romantic suspense novels. Saving Tír na nÓg is my first young adult fantasy novel.

A NOTE FROM THE AUTHOR

Thanks for reading Saving Tír na nÓg. I hope you enjoyed spending time with Grania and her friends. I'm plotting some new adventures for the *Chosen Ones*. As you have likely discovered from the maps at the front of this book, *Tír na nÓg* is merely one of many realms in *Otherworld*. There are so many realms to choose from, I can't decide where to send our friends next.

They could visit *Tír fo Thuinn*, the underwater *Otherworld*. That might prove a little tricky, breathing under water and all. We could send them to *Tír Tairngire*, also known as the Land of Promise, where Manannán mac Lir, the sea deity, transports *Sidhe* and *Fomorian* souls to the afterlife. That could prove interesting. Or, maybe *Tech Duinn*, the House of the Dead, where the Goddess Carman is imprisoned. Now that would be creepy.

Perhaps you can help me decide. Peruse the maps in the front of this book and e-mail me through my author website to let me know where you'd like to see Grania and her friends venture next. Which characters would you most enjoy hanging out with? I'm still wondering who that silver wolf was... what happened to Dain... and what should we do with that mysterious ring?

If you enjoyed reading this novel, please consider posting a review on Amazon. Authors love reviews. They're like a warm blanket, the highest compliment, and a thousand hugs all rolled into one.

Finally, if you'd like to join Grania, Maolisa, and Niamh in their fight against violence, evil, and darkness, then please join our Sidhe Street Team. You'll find additional information about the Sidhe Street Team and other fun activities on my website (kimberlyruff.com).

Go n-éirí an bóthar leat.
Kimberly

Made in the USA
Middletown, DE
14 September 2018